THE LAFITTE AFFAIR

THE LAFITTE AFFAIR

A BRUNEAU ABELLARD NOVEL

NORMAN WOOLWORTH

First published by Level Best Books 2024

Copyright © 2024 by Norman Woolworth

All rights reserved. No part of this publication may be reproduced, stored or transmitted in any form or by any means, electronic, mechanical, photocopying, recording, scanning, or otherwise without written permission from the publisher. It is illegal to copy this book, post it to a website, or distribute it by any other means without permission.

This novel is entirely a work of fiction. The names, characters and incidents portrayed in it are the work of the author's imagination. Any resemblance to actual persons, living or dead, events or localities is entirely coincidental.

Norman Woolworth asserts the moral right to be identified as the author of this work.

Author Photo Credit: Tom Cogill

Map Graphic Credit: Wright Deter

First edition

ISBN: 978-1-68512-698-8

Cover art by Level Best Designs

This book was professionally typeset on Reedsy. Find out more at reedsy.com

To Lori
And Our Three Masterworks
Nathalie, Alexander, and Rachel

As you from crimes would pardoned be,
Let your indulgence set me free.

>   —William Shakespeare
>   (The Tempest)

Praise for The Lafitte Affair

"Norman Woolworth is a writer with an impeccable eye for detail, and his cleverly plotted novel is infused with the sights, sounds, smells, and tastes of New Orleans. His descriptions of food and beverages alone will leave you eager to book the next flight to the Crescent City."—Proal Heartwell, author of *In Beauty It Is Finished* and *The Boardinghouse*

"*The Lafitte Affair*, exquisitely written and full of delightful plot twists, is peopled with Southern eccentrics drawn with insight, humor, and compassion. Those who love great Southern mystery writers like Greg Isles and John Berendt will appreciate Woolworth's weaving of real-life history with a modern New Orleans flare. Don't miss the first book in this series, featuring gourmand antiques dealer Bruneau Abellard as the quirky, loveable sleuth."—Claire Holman Thompson, author of *The Ring* and *The Blue Water*

"Bruneau Abellard doesn't necessarily need a mystery on his hands, but his friends think otherwise. With colonial pirate treasure, grave-robbing, decoding secret letters, and ties to Napoleon, the New Orleans gourmet finds himself tangled in an investigation of international proportions. Wonderfully intriguing; a little gritty and a lot of fun, Woolworth's debut offers good food, great wine and an exceptional whodunit."—Chris Keefer, author of *No Comfort for the Undertaker* and *Tragedy's Twin, the Carrie Lisbon Mysteries.*

"*The Lafitte Affair* is set in contemporary New Orleans but vividly evokes the 1820s. The novel is as much about the city's colorful characters as it is about the unfolding mystery. ... A fast-paced, edge-of-your-seat read. ...Worthy of the big screen! Five Stars ✶✶✶✶✶ "—Carol Thompson, *Readers' Favorite*

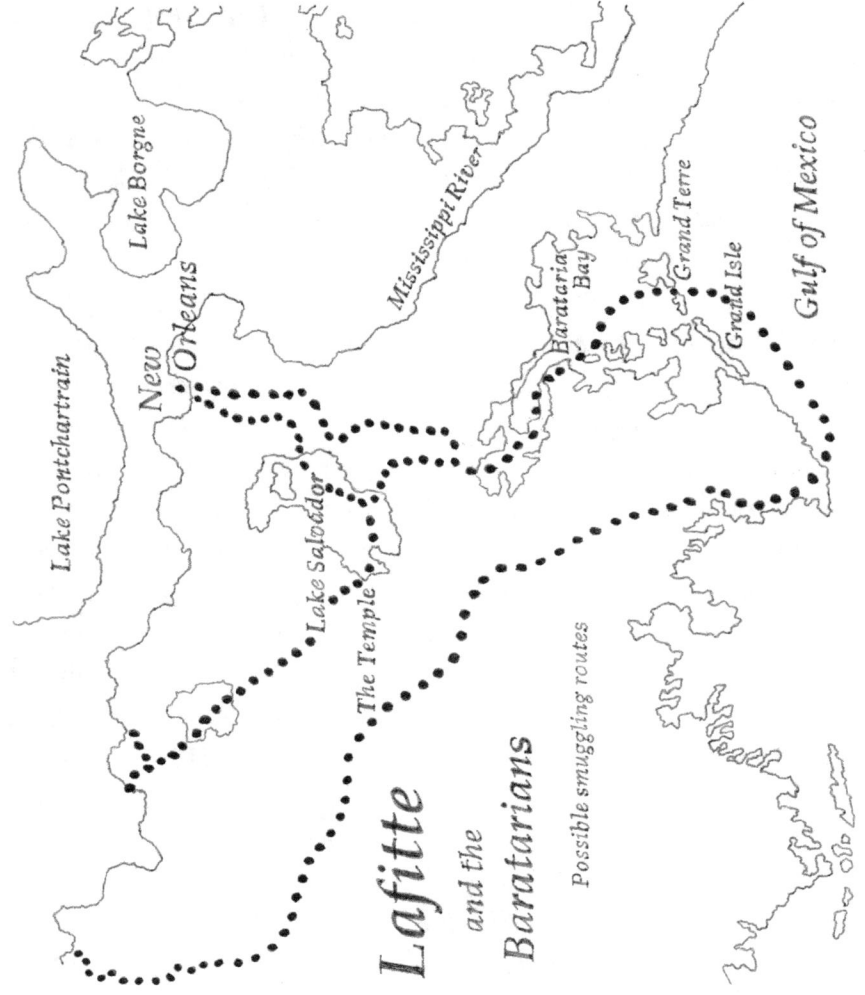

Foreword

As the turbulent 1700s careened to a close and a new century dawned, the Golden Age of Piracy had long since run its course. Having endured a half-century of losses on the high seas, the European naval powers grew more organized and determined to hunt down the seafaring marauders who vexed them. And so, one by one, they fell, the Muslim corsairs of the Barbary Coast and the Anglo-American plunderers of the Atlantic and Caribbean: Captain Kidd, Calico Jack, Anne Bonny, Blackbeard, and the rest, until the prospect of a career in pirating no longer held out the promise of long-lived prosperity.

But for a short period at the turn of the 19th Century, a new brand of pirate flourished in the waters of the Gulf of Mexico, spurred by a series of importation embargoes imposed by the fledgling American republic. They thought of themselves not as pirates but as privateers, and many did sail under letters of marque from a revolving carousel of nation-states. They were mercenaries, and their fealty was not to country, but to a way of life, and to the riches to be gained from smuggling foreign goods, and people, to a city that did not yet think of itself as American.

Preeminent among these was a tall, handsome, trilingual Frenchman with long black hair, a dark complexion, and piercing eyes. He was a pirate, a smuggler, and a slave trader, but also a leader of men, a visionary in business, and a logistical mastermind. He was, at times simultaneously, hero and thief, patriot and turncoat, statesman and spy, straight dealer and habitual liar. He could be charming or aloof, refined or crude, practical or romantic. He co-existed peacefully with the scabrous rabble of the pirating trade while rubbing elbows comfortably with the most distinguished personages of his age. He donned many guises and employed various aliases. He rose, and he fell, and rose and fell again.

The pirate's name was Jean Lafitte.

Chapter One

I had just pushed the last remnants of Hollandaise-soaked spinach toward the wedge of artichoke I'd reserved for my final bite of Eggs Sardou when my phone vibrated loudly on the tabletop. I cursed silently, noted the caller's identity, and tapped the "End Call" icon on my screen. I continued my meal in stubborn defiance, savoring its textures and flavors. A trickle of thick yellow liquid escaped to my chin. I dabbed it clean with the napkin I had tucked into my collar and chuckled to myself as I imagined the caller's reaction to having been rejected.

The phone buzzed again, this time with a text directing me to "call me asap."

I sighed, took a final slug of chicory, and signaled Jacqui, the waitress, to charge my account and include my usual 22 percent tip. Then I rose slowly, squeezed my ample frame inelegantly between the tightly spaced tables, and lumbered outside.

It was a bright August morning, and the heat was already thick and close. I squinted at my phone, cupped my right hand over my eyes to cut the glare, and stabbed at the screen.

"Bru, where are you?" the voice on the other end answered mid-ring.

"It's Sunday morning. Where the hell do you think I am?"

"Oh, right. Sorry. Atchafalaya?"

"Katie's."

"Ah! Seafood Omelet? Sausage Frittata?"

"Neither. Eggs Sardou. Is there a point to this call?"

"Yes. Listen, I just caught a strange one. Can I convince you to come take a look?"

The caller was Detective Thibodaux "Bo" Duplessis of the New Orleans Police Department, Property Crimes Section, my childhood pal and lifelong friendly antagonist. I own an antiques store on Magazine Street and from time-to-time Bo turns to me for help when a valuable object goes missing.

"Where are you, and what's so strange that you thought to call me?"

"I'm at a cemetery. There's been a break-in and possibly a grave robbery that might be up your alley. I'd really like to get your take."

"A grave robbery? In what universe would that be up my alley?"

"Let's just say there might be some historical intrigue involved. I thought maybe you could help me sort it out. I'm just a couple minutes from you. How about I swing by and pick you up?"

"Did it ever occur to you that I might have something better to do?"

"Nah, I know you better than that. I'm jumping in the cruiser now."

* * *

I stood on Iberville Street directly across from Katie's Restaurant, feigning rapt interest in a message on my phone, when Bo pulled up in his unmarked black Dodge Charger.

"Hey brother, hop on in," Bo barked, leaning across the front seat to open the passenger side door.

Betraying no haste, I slipped my phone into my pants pocket, stepped gingerly off the curb, hooked my right arm to the car's roof, and gradually lowered myself into the passenger seat. I swept the cords from Bo's police radio out of the way, grunting emphatically as I pulled the door shut and strained for my seatbelt. Yanking the handkerchief from my breast pocket, I tamped at the beads of sweat forming on my forehead. My method-acting performance may have been a bit over the top, but I was trying to make a point.

"Sorry to put you out like this," Bo said. "I know you don't have much spare time on account of your three-course brunch and the Sunday crosswords. Am I cutting into nap time?"

CHAPTER ONE

"Actually, I'm entertaining tonight, so I don't have all day," I said.

"Don't worry, we won't be long, I promise."

There was a short silence.

"So! How are you doing?" Bo asked.

"About as well as could be expected, given it looks like I'm about to pass up a relaxing afternoon for some morbid tale from the crypt."

"Aw, c'mon Bru, when're you not relaxing is what I'd like to know."

"Whenever I'm around you, for starters."

Bo chuckled. He enjoys my curmudgeonly streak, maybe because it's a useful foil for his own leap-before-looking approach to life. Beneath my sometimes-gruff exterior, he knows I value our relationship more than I like to let on. Not to mention, if you make your living investigating the theft of valuable objects, it doesn't hurt to have one of the city's more knowledgeable antiques dealers as a trusted resource.

"What've you been up to?" Bo asked. "Haven't seen you for a couple weeks."

"Usual routine. Everything good with Angie and the kids?"

"All good, other than I just found out Little Bo's going to need braces. There goes another three, four grand. Can't never seem to get ahead."

I nodded knowingly, although as a lifelong bachelor who has never had to support anyone other than myself, I am aware that my commiseration can come across as more pro forma than heartfelt.

"They grow up fast, I guess. Everybody off to a good start in school?"

"Yeah, I think so. Looks like Sophie's gonna kill it, but that's nothing new."

Sophie is Bo's middle child, in eighth grade now, and a bookworm after my own heart. Little Bo is a sophomore in high school. He's all boy, a lot like his dad at the same age, antsy and athletic. Monique, the youngest, is beginning the sixth grade. She reminds me more of her mom, fiery with a pronounced independent streak.

We turned right on Canal, crossed Carrollton, and were heading into the residential Mid-City neighborhood between Carrollton and City Park Avenue, where lollipop palm trees and crucifix-shaped trolley poles embellish the wide neutral ground. I guessed our destination must be one of the half dozen or so cemeteries a bit further up the way, probably St. Patrick's or Greenwood.

"Are you going to tell me about this grave robbery and why on earth you need me?"

"I wish it was that simple," Bo exhaled deeply. "Truth is, we're not sure what we're dealing with. Ever hear of Crypt 1083-A?"

"No. Is that a Stephen King novel?"

"No. It's from the Girod Street Cemetery."

Girod Street is the Protestant cemetery that fell into disrepair and was deconsecrated and built over back in the fifties. It was near where the Superdome is now. Back when the Saints had all those losing seasons, folks said it was on account of the site being cursed.

"You know what happened to all the remains?" Bo asked.

"No, I don't think so," I said. "I assume they contacted the families and offered the opportunity to relocate."

"Yes, and I suppose a few families did, but not many. It couldn't have been easy tracking down descendants in a lot of cases. Anyway, what ended up happening is they scooped up the remains, packed 'em in drums, and sent them to Saint John out here on Canal."

"Okay, I guess that's interesting, but what's the history lesson got to do with our little expedition?"

Bo smiled and pointed up ahead as an imposing, two-story Art Deco structure came into view along the right side of the street, running the full length of the block. If I didn't know what it was, I might have mistaken it for a military fortification of some kind.

"That's Hope Mausoleum," Bo said. "It was started back in the thirties, and they kept adding on to it until now it surrounds the cemetery. Basically, Saint John Cemetery is the courtyard of the mausoleum."

"Yeah, I know. I've been out here before," I said. "Took in a lot of water during Katrina, as I recall."

"Yes, it did."

Bo swung into a curbside space near the mausoleum's entrance, and we climbed out of the vehicle, Bo quick and catlike, me unhurriedly and with a

CHAPTER ONE

conspicuous show of effort.

Despite my love of history and old things, I detest cemeteries and, even more so, mausoleums. At least outside there is vegetation, maybe a squirrel or two scurrying around, signs of life. Inside is just the cold sterility of death.

"So, here's the deal," Bo explained as we approached the broad granite entranceway. "The Girod Street remains are in Crypt 1083-A, which is basically just a crawl space under the ground floor. Last night, somebody tore open a hole in the floor and crept around in there among all the bones and dirt."

"Sounds like a messy business."

"It gets messier. Most of the remains are unidentified and packed up in drums, but it turns out there were six caskets that hadn't been opened, and they were put in there, too. They're commemorated on a plaque I'll show you. All prominent types from the 1800s; five men and one woman. It was the woman's casket that got broken into."

I arched my eyebrows.

"So, let me get this straight. You're thinking somebody went to the trouble of breaking into this fortress of a building, busted open the crawl space, dragged themselves around in the dirt and the dust and the bones, just to peek into or maybe snatch an item from this lady's death box?"

"That's what it looks like."

"Can't be necrophilia if it's just bones, right?"

"I wouldn't think so, but who knows. Can't rule out anything at this stage. You've got a dirty mind, you know that?"

"So, I've been told. Can you tell if anything was taken?"

"We're not sure. The Crime Scenes Unit says that based on some bits of decomposing material, it looks like she had on a velvet dress. There wasn't any jewelry, so possibly that's what they were after. There were also some small pieces of brittle paper that had some writing on them we couldn't make out. They're taking them back to the lab to do their magic and see what they can come up with."

"Who was this woman?"

"Her name is Jane Placide. She was a leading actress back in her day, apparently. Died in the Yellow Fever outbreak of 1835, at age thirty-one."

"I've heard of her," I said. "She appeared on all the big stages of the antebellum south. Quite the celebrity in her day, I imagine. Why on earth would somebody be interested in her remains?"

"That's where you come in, my man," Bo grinned. "I thought maybe you could do a little research for us."

"Not really my area of expertise."

"Yeah, I know, but you've got the skill set, and once you pick up the scent, you don't give up. I like that about you."

"Please."

"No, seriously. Tell you what, I'll sweeten the pot. Dinner on Friday. You name the dish, and I'll see that Angie makes it."

"Alright, whatever," I relented. "I'll do some research, make a few calls, but no promises beyond that. And you tell Angie to make whatever she damn well pleases."

"Thanks, Bru, you da man! Before we go, let me show you the crime scene."

I followed Bo through two sets of bronze doors into an open-air corridor lined with the marble facades of crypts stacked three high in both directions. A cool breeze funneled in from the cemetery, and I recognized too well the clammy sensation beginning to creep through me as we turned right and strode silently through the grimly sanitized passageway. We proceeded maybe 20 yards to the end of the hall, then turned left down another crypt-lined corridor until we came to a wide marble staircase. Crime scene tape surrounded the area at the base of the stairs, in the middle of which was a small, jagged hole cut into the marble floor. Bo spoke with police personnel processing the scene, while I took note of a plaque on the wall opposite the stairway. It was made of a darker, almost roseate marble, and read as follows:

IN LOVING MEMORY OF THOSE ONCE
INTERRED IN THE GIROD STREET CEMETERY

CHAPTER ONE

(FOUNDED 1822) WHOSE MORTAL REMAINS
WERE REMOVED AND RE-ENTOMBED IN THIS
BUILDING BY CHRIST CHURCH CATHEDRAL
(EPISCOPAL) A. D. 1957. AND OF

REV. JAMES F. HULL D. D. 1797-1833
RECTOR OF CHRIST CHURCH 1816-1830
REV. WILLIAM T. LEACOCK D. D. 1797-1884
RECTOR OF CHRIST CHURCH 1852-1882
RICHARD RELF 1776-1857
A WARDEN OF CHRIST CHURCH FOR 52 YEARS
REV. JOHN HENRY KLEINHAGEN 1815-1885
PIONEER EVANGELICAL AND LUTHERAN PASTOR
GLENDY BURKE 1806-1879
MERCHANT BANKER LEADING CITIZEN
JANE PLACIDE 1804-1835
DISTINGUISHED ACTRESS
WHOSE REMAINS LIE IN CRYPT 1083-A

AYE, 'TIS A HOLY RITE,
REMEMBRANCE OF THE DEAD,
THAT WILL NOT LET OBLIVION'S BLIGHT
AROUND THE GRAVE BE SHED

Turning back to the crime scene, I couldn't believe how small the opening was.

"Bo, who the hell could fit in that space? Are you looking for Tom Thumb? I don't think I could get my leg through there, much less the rest of me."

"Yeah, me neither. Definitely narrows the field, doesn't it? We had to find a couple really small female officers to get in there for us."

"Can't say I envy them that job."

"No. They're still collecting evidence, but we already know a few things." According to Bo, the cops had determined there were at least two burglars, with probably a third as lookout, and they knew what they were doing. The crime scene team found footprints and scratch marks on the mausoleum's rear wall, facing Iberville, indicating that the intruders had scaled the wall using a grappling hook and then dropped down the other side into the cemetery, artfully avoiding the video surveillance cameras set up around the perimeter of the building. They pried open the heavy bronze doors facing the cemetery on the Canal Street side and then bore into the crypt. Bo said they probably used a small hydraulic breaker hammer, which is like a jackhammer but quieter.

"More than likely, we're looking at professionals," Bo said. "I'm sure they cased the place in advance. Getting inside without being seen and opening the crypt without waking the dead takes knowledge and skill. Pun intended."

I groaned.

"And then the fact that they seem to have known exactly what they were looking for," Bo continued. "It all screams contract job."

"But why? What could be buried with Jane Placide that would explain someone hiring a team of pros to do all this?"

"I know, it doesn't add up," Bo said. "C'mon, I want to show you one more thing."

"Okay, but I need to get home to get ready for tonight."

"No worries, this will be quick."

Bo took me outside to the cemetery and pointed to a series of fifteen headstones salvaged from Girod Street and affixed to the exterior wall of the mausoleum, facing in toward Saint John's. Jane Placide's was one of the older ones and badly cracked, but we could still make out the writing:

Sacred
To the memory of
JANE PLACIDE
Died May 16, 1835
Aged 31 yrs

"We talked to the mausoleum's archivist, and she said that most of the Girod

CHAPTER ONE

Street records are lost or unreadable," Bo said, "but she was able to confirm that Jane Placide had been interred in a free-standing mausoleum and it had this verse engraved on it. And before you ask, no, she never married."

Bo handed me a slip of paper:

TO THE MEMORY OF JANE PLACIDE
There's not an hour of day, or dreamy night but I am with thee;
There's not a wind but whispers o'er thy name.
And not a flower that sleeps beneath the moon,
but in its hues of fragrance tells a tale of thee.

"Sounds like she had an admirer," I said. "I'll see what I can turn up about her love life. What else do you want to know about?"

"Anything and everything," Bo said. "Life story. Friends, enemies, love life. What she owned. Who she knew, what she knew. We've got nothing to go on here, so literally, whatever you can find."

Chapter Two

Bo had stoked my curiosity, as no doubt he knew he would, having had plenty of practice. Growing up in Hammond, an hour north of New Orleans, we were improbable pals. Had there been such a category in our high school yearbook, I would have been voted least likely to play a leading role in a swashbuckling criminal investigation, and nobody would have pegged Bo for most likely to unlock a fantastical two-hundred-year-old mystery lost to the annals of history.

My full name is Bruneau Ignatius Abellard, and Bo is the only person who calls me Bru. Back in the day, he was an athlete who ran with the in crowd, and I was a pudgy, physically awkward kid with few friends but good grades. People pleasing came naturally to Bo, who was an indifferent student. I took solitary refuge in books and scholarly interests. And while I developed what some might call sophisticated tastes for a schoolboy, Bo was happiest kicked back in his Dad's recliner with a box of Popeye's, a cold Barq's, and football on TV.

Though unalike, we were the same age, attended the same schools, and lived next door to each other in a mixed-race neighborhood of modest ranch-style houses. Our fathers both worked for the railroad, and our families were friendly, if not close, in the way that hard-working whites and blacks managed to get along in the Louisiana of the 1980s and 90s. Bo would seek me out for help with schoolwork, and in a tacit exchange of schoolyard currency, he saw to it that I didn't get picked on.

I remember one time during recess, it must have been sixth or seventh grade, a couple of farm boys were having fun with me, poking and pushing,

CHAPTER TWO

mocking my unwillingness to respond physically. Bo was playing catch maybe twenty-five yards away, when he saw what was going on. He sprinted over, came up behind one of my tormentors, and sent him sprawling. The kid landed hard, scraping his chin and losing his wind. He started to cry, and his friend backed away.

"What's the matter? Can't take as good as you give?" Bo asked, chin jutting out. "I see you messing with my friend again; you're gonna be sorry. You got that?"

The kid just whimpered.

"I said you got that?"

"Yes."

"You?" Bo glared at the one still standing.

"Yes."

The unscathed boy picked his friend up warily, and they walked away, looking over their shoulders every few steps. Word got around about what had happened, and I never had a problem after that.

Bo and I were useful to each other, but also genuinely close. I quietly marveled at Bo's easy way with people and appreciated his protection. Bo seemed to respect my intelligence, and the way I didn't seem to care much what other people thought. As I grew older, I developed a caustic sense of humor as a way of showing the world that I didn't take myself, or life, too seriously, and Bo delighted in prodding me with good-natured banter to draw out sarcastic or complaining responses. Ours was an easy camaraderie.

Bo quarterbacked the Hammond High Tors as a junior and senior, which resulted in a free ride to Grambling. After graduating college, he enrolled in the NOPD Training Academy. He worked a beat for a few years, before making detective and finding his way to Property Crimes. Along the way, he met, courted, and eventually married Angeline Landry, a saucy eyeful from proud middle-class Creole stock in the Gentilly neighborhood. They bought a three-bedroom ranch in Kenner, and within a year, Little Bo came along, followed by sisters Sophie and Monique in 18-month intervals.

While Bo used football to leverage his education, I earned an academic scholarship to Loyola, where I double majored in Classics and Art History. I continued my intellectual pursuits overseas, thanks to a research fellowship at Oxford that allowed me to nurture an interest in Beaux-Arts architecture and furnishings. Eventually, I returned to New Orleans and put my skills to work as an assistant curator at the Cabildo for a few years before using my savings and a small business loan to open Abellard's Antiques.

It was slow going at first, but gradually, word got out that I was both knowledgeable and a bit of a raconteur. I did my best to charm the well-heeled ladies of Uptown and the Garden District, and in time the business caught on. I became a sought-after guest at teas and ladies' luncheons and a trusted confidant to many a doyenne of upper-crust New Orleans society. As such, I know where more than a few skeletons are buried, even if my experience with the real thing is limited to what little I can remember from a high school anatomy class.

During our college years, Bo and I would see each other and catch up when home for the holidays, but when I headed to England and he immersed himself in police work and starting a family, we fell out of touch. Unbeknownst to each other, we'd been living in the same city for a few years when Bo heard from his mother that I had settled in New Orleans and opened an antiques store. He popped in unannounced one day, dressed in a brown plaid suit and a maroon knit tie. He was older, of course, and maybe a little thicker in the mid-section than I remembered, but he still had the nimble gait of an athlete and the youthful smile of an inveterate optimist.

Bo told me later he was worried our meeting might be awkward, but within minutes I was referring to him as "Inspector Duplesseau" and he hassled me with antiques jokes.

"You know, ever since ma told me about your store, I've been wondering, what's *new* in antiques?"

"Very funny," I groaned.

"Knew you'd like that."

"Anything else you've been wondering about?"

"Actually, now that you mention it, yes. Serious question. Before I came in, I was standing outside for a while, finishing up a call, and I noticed those poles in the corner with the carvings on them. What are those things?"

CHAPTER TWO

He sounded genuinely interested, so I answered straight up.

"They're old spears, probably from the Tunica-Biloxi tribe. They're cypress, from the early 18th Century, I think. Missing their heads, obviously."

"In other words, you got shafted?"

"That is *so* weak," I said, shaking my head and laughing despite myself. "I see some things haven't changed."

"Admit it! You missed me!"

"I have, I suppose. In the way a squirrel misses his nuts, if you know what I mean."

"Hah!" Bo howled.

"You know what, Bru? You've gotta come out and meet Angie. She's a great cook, and you're a world-class eater, so it'll be a perfect match. I've told her all about you. How about dinner on Friday night?"

"I'd be delighted. To meet Angie, that is."

As Bo had expected, Angie and I bonded effortlessly. Whether that owed more to our shared culinary interests or our mutual enthusiasm for needling him, I can't say. Bo made it clear he was thrilled to have me back in his life, and in truth, the feeling was mutual, even if I was less transparent about it. Dinners at the Duplessis household became a monthly ritual, and in time, my visits were eagerly anticipated by Bo and Angie's growing brood, who knew they could rely on "Uncle Bru" to dispense a box or two of exotic sweets whenever I dropped by.

* * *

As a bachelor with few prospects for and little interest in romance, I maintain a patterned, some might say eccentric lifestyle. This reduces life's complications, I find, and keeps surprises to a minimum.

I live above the store with Hugo, my black and white French Bulldog. I rise at seven each morning, take Hugo out for his morning constitutional, then greet the day with a cup of French press chicory, a couple eggs, usually soft-boiled, and a toasted English muffin or almond croissant on the side.

After a leisurely perusal of the morning's papers, I shower and change, and then Hugo and I shuffle downstairs to my office. I catch up on emails and bookkeeping, and he curls up on his day bed. The shop opens at 10, we close for a civilized lunch from noon to two and then open back up until six. Dinner is at 7:30, more often in than out, followed by some TV or reading, Hugo's evening stroll, and bedtime at 11 sharp.

The routine varies but little, and much to Bo's amusement, extends to my dining habits. Sunday brunch rotates between Atchafalaya and Katie's. Monday dinner must be red beans and rice, usually at Mandina's, where they serve garlicky Italian sausage over the thick stew. Most Wednesdays I meet for lunch at Lilette with Charlotte Duval, grand dame of old money New Orleans and queen of the hush hush scoop. On Fridays and Saturdays, I usually accept an invitation to someone's dinner party, or host one of my own.

My routine does not usually include entertaining on Sundays, but this was the week my old college friend Annie Russell and her husband Bert Kingsley were back in town after summering at their cottage in mid-coast Maine, where I had visited them a couple months previous. They'd be leaving again in a few days for a week in Barcelona, so Sunday was our best option for getting together. I'd missed Annie, who is always the life of the party and great fun to be around. Her older husband, Bert, is a semi-retired lawyer and a very nice guy but also a colossal bore. My other guests were the banker John Roseberry and his wife Pamela; and Grace Simmons, a seventy-something widow who was one of my first champions among the old guard moneyed set. Like Grace, the Roseberrys are getting on in years, but John remains a formidable figure in the local business community, and Pamela is as up on society gossip as anyone.

By the time I got back from Hope Mausoleum, I only had about three hours before my visitors were due to arrive. Fortunately, the apartment was clean, and I'd prepped most of the food the day before, so it was mostly a matter of setting up and then adding a few last-minute touches. I took some time to lay out the table settings with a few fanciful touches and then set up my bar. There was ample time left over for a leisurely shower.

CHAPTER TWO

I've been told that entertaining brings out the showman in me. For this occasion, I dressed in my dark green velvet smoking jacket with a deep purple cravat tucked inside a gray open-necked shirt. I cued up my Joe Pass playlist and then, as is my custom, I greeted each arrival with a tray of the evening's featured cocktail, in this case, the Vieux Carre, an old standby I concoct with equal parts rye, cognac, and sweet vermouth, a drop of Benedictine, and a splash of Peychaud Bitters. Drinks in hand, I ushered my guests into the salon, where dark burgundy walls with gold trim engulf a mélange of antique furnishings, eclectic objets d'art, and ornate fixtures. Charlotte Duval calls my design sensibility "collectivist collage," but it wouldn't be bragging to say that I managed to wrest an elegant symmetry from what might otherwise seem an anarchic assemblage of elements.

Henry Wilkins, my long-time pick-up and delivery man for the store, passed around a canape assortment I had prepared. He was dressed in the white shirt, black pants, and black bow tie traditionally worn by African American servers in the Old South. I've grown more than a little uncomfortable with this nod to inglorious custom, but Henry insists.

Once seated, we began the meal with a rabbit and pistachio terrine Henry had laid out for us, which I paired with an aged Amontillado. The main course was a smoked duck and andouille gumbo, which diners could choose to wash down with a sturdy Morgon or an off-dry Riesling from the Mosel. All but John and I opted for the red. We cleansed our palates with a tangy watercress salad, and then I disappeared into the kitchen to put the finishing touches on the grand finale, a decadent bread pudding soufflé with Chantilly cream.

"Oh, my goodness, Bruneau, you have outdone yourself!" Grace exclaimed after her first taste. "I'll have to start on Weight Watchers in the morning."

"It's sublime," Annie chimed in. "We love our Maine lobsters and berry pies, Bruneau, but there's nothing up north quite like the delicacies you prepare for us."

I accepted all the compliments with as much nonchalance as I could muster, and then, once everyone had had their fill, I led the caravan back to the salon, where Henry had set out coffee, tea, and a tray of digestifs for those with the inclination, which turned out to be everyone.

Conversation at dinner began with local politics and grumbling about all the construction projects in the CBD and their effects on traffic, but as is usually the case, it eventually devolved into tittering high society gossip. We were onto lines of succession for the Rex and Bacchus krewes when, in an effort to steer us toward less trodden ground, I told them about the violation of Jane Placide's remains.

"How extraordinary!" Bert exclaimed, characteristically without elaboration.

"Indeed!" John added. "What on earth could they have been after?"

"That *is* the question," I said, affirming the obvious.

"Why were you called in, Bruneau?" Annie wanted to know. "Are you a closet expert on nineteenth-century theatre?"

"Not exactly," I said. "I guess my detective friend Bo equates a knowledge of antiques with an all-encompassing grasp of history."

"After the Grover case, it's a wonder he hasn't formally deputized you," Pamela sniffed. "As I've said before, you should be on the NOPD payroll. It's scandalous the way your friend takes advantage of you."

The Roseberrys and Kingsleys had been introduced to Bo some years ago when I tried including him and Angie in a few of my gatherings, but it was an uncomfortable fit. Bo and Angie made an effort to engage with the other guests, but by evening's end, they were hanging out in the kitchen with Henry. I got the message, and from then on, dinners with the Duplessises were casual get-togethers among just the three of us, although sometimes I included their kids.

The Grover case is a story unto itself. Initially, when Bo first asked if he could use me as a professional resource, it was just to appraise the value or research the provenance of a stolen item or two. But then I somewhat unwittingly helped him crack a big one. Over dinner, Bo had described to Angie and me a case he was working on, in which a handful of the city's wealthiest residents had come to the belated realization that some of their finest antiques had been replaced by high-quality imitations. They were mystified as to how this could have happened.

CHAPTER TWO

"We're talking about pieces by some of the best-known artisans of their day, worth upwards of fifty thousand each, if not well into six figures," Bo had said.

Intrigued, I managed to track a few of the missing pieces back to Richard Grover, a well-known Houston-based dealer, who was quietly peddling the stolen items to an exclusive listserv of high-end collectors. I knew that some years prior Charlotte Duval bought a Samuel McIntire rocker from Grover, despite my having advised her that the price was too high. I asked Charlotte if she had access to Grover's listserv and, if so, whether I could borrow her login credentials. Charlotte said she did, in fact, receive Grover's email notifications but had long since stopped clicking through to read them. She readily shared her ID and password, and I located the items while impersonating her on Grover's private marketplace platform.

Meanwhile, Bo determined that each targeted homeowner had used the same house painting crew over the previous few years. From there, the modus operandi quickly emerged. Grover's brother was a well-connected interior decorator in New Orleans. While out on the job, he would photograph the contents of his clients' dwellings, take measurements, and send the pics on to Grover, who would then instruct another accomplice, a furniture maker in Lake Charles, to make replicas of the best pieces. Once the knockoffs were completed, Grover's designer brother would send in his painters, who would swap the counterfeits for the originals.

The arrests garnered a story in the *Times-Picayune*, headlined "Property Detective Cracks Counterfeit Ring." The good press helped catapult Bo to the upper echelon of the Property Crimes food chain, and from then on, if he thought a case had the slightest hint of intrigue, he involved me. I make a point of grumbling and acting put off when Bo calls with a new case, but inevitably I come around. Secretly, as I suspect Bo well knows, I rather enjoy these amateur sleuthing adventures.

* * *

After seeing my guests out, helping Henry with the clean-up, and taking

Hugo out to do his business, I was still wide awake. I sat down to do battle with the *New York Times* crossword, which on a normal Sunday I would have long since completed, but my thoughts kept returning to Jane Placide. Clearly, this was an altogether different kind of case. A person of note from the distant past. Her resting place, disturbed by a team of professional burglars. No proof of anything having been taken, just the presumption that something must have been. Scraps of mysterious writing, as yet undeciphered. What to make of it all?

I started by hopping online and pulling up photos of Girod Street taken in the 1950s. I'd seen them before, but still, I found it hard to suppress a shudder. They depict a horrific wasteland of vine and weed-covered tombs in various states of disrepair, many of them vandalized. There are wall vaults the length of a football field with crypts stacked six high. Once ornate, individual tombs stand next to others with 100 or more vaults. Though not pictured, it was easy to imagine all manner of vermin having the run of the place.

A few simple internet searches established the basic outline of Jane Placide's life. She was born in Charleston, South Carolina, to Alexander and Charlotte Placide, French immigrants by way of Saint Domingue, or modern-day Haiti. Alexander managed the Charleston Theatre, and Charlotte was an actress and opera singer. Jane made her acting debut as Volante in *The Honey Moon* in 1820, when she was just 16. A couple years later she joined James Caldwell's American Company in New Orleans, where Caldwell's Camp Street Theatre had introduced the English language stage to the city.

Jane quickly won the admiration of playgoers for her portrayals of a wide range of heroines. But her time in New Orleans was not without scandal. In 1824, Caldwell hired a young Edwin Forrest, who would go on to earn fame as the pre-eminent Shakespearean actor of his generation. Forrest fell madly in love with Jane, now 20, with whom he co-starred in *Romeo and Juliet.* He began writing her amorous poems and pressing his case, only to come to believe that the married Caldwell also had designs on the young actress. Caldwell cast himself, rather than Forrest, opposite Jane's

CHAPTER TWO

Olivia in *Twelfth Night,* which prompted Forrest to challenge Caldwell to a duel. Caldwell declined the provocation, and Forrest quit the company soon thereafter and left the city, but not before calling out Caldwell as a "scoundrel and coward" in print.

The exact nature of Caldwell's relationship with Jane is unclear. It was at least partly paternal, though likely a good deal more. Prior to establishing himself in New Orleans, Caldwell was a player in the Charleston theater scene, where he would have known Alexander and Charlotte Placide and almost certainly encountered Jane as a young girl. Caldwell was ten years older than Jane, who would have been 13 when he left town. As the full scope of her talent became apparent, and they came to realize that she deserved a larger audience than Charleston could provide, Jane's parents may have felt comfortable entrusting her to Caldwell's oversight.

Caldwell's troupe toured the antebellum southern circuit, with engagements in Natchez, Nashville, Mobile, and the like. Jane would have been in his company almost constantly during these sojourns while his wife remained home in New Orleans. Given Forrest's accusations, it requires no great leap to imagine the relationship between Caldwell and his protégé as having evolved into something extra professional. But whether sugar daddy or paramour, Caldwell's devotion to Jane appears never to have wavered. He lavished her with gifts, made sure all her needs were tended to, managed her finances and personal affairs until her death, and ultimately paid for her funeral and contributed the epitaph on her tomb. I Googled the first few lines of that passage to find that it was from an early work by the Victorian poet Bryan Procter, who wrote under the pen name Barry Cornwall.

My interest was more than piqued by Jane's story, but nothing I learned gave me a clue as to why someone would seek out the actress' coffin. I could see no obvious next steps other than to wait and see what Bo's crime lab turned up. In the meantime, I resolved to brush up on some history.

1836

GIROD STREET CEMETERY
NEW ORLEANS, LOUISIANA
AUGUST 1836

T*he corsair stands stiffly in the shadow of his son's damp grave as the priestess limps unsteadily toward the object of their nocturnal quest. The night is dark and heavy with alluvial decay, and somewhere in the distance a lone African drum thumps a languorous beat. Around him, ornate marble structures and humbler tenements of concrete vaults stacked six high bear the names of friends and enemies and more than a few associates in commerce.*

Ghosts. He knows he himself must appear spectral, returning now after so many years. He'd seen the glimmer of recognition in the priestess' careworn eyes and the averted gaze of the liveryman who'd driven him from the wharf. The corsair had often imagined himself passing into a spirit world more familiar to him than the one in which he'd lately resided. Now, amid this dismal necropolis, he feels poised between two spheres. One ethereal and beyond his reach, yet familiar somehow. The other, terrestrial but altogether alien.

The priestess slows now, turning to her left and raising her torch for closer inspection of a headwall. She'd found it, he could see. Reaching deep into folds of billowing calico, she removes a small object the corsair cannot discern and begins waving it in a series of spasmodic motions, murmuring a deep-throated incantation that seems to emanate from the depths of the earth beneath her. This is followed by louder staccato chanting and the discordant rattling of a small percussive instrument made of what might have been bone.

1836

Minutes pass, the corsair fidgeting with his cane, poking at the wet moss and gravel, losing himself in fleeting evocations...the actress' porcelain skin against her crimson glove...her honeysuckle scent and practiced blush beneath attentive mahogany eyes...the pompous impresario with his ivory-handled cane and resplendent cravats. A charlatan, yes, but true to her to the end. Truer than he.

Ah, Cher Jane. Ever present to him, even now, though endlessly elusive. Had she taken their treasure with her to eternity, as she had said she would? Would they meet again? The corsair is not normally given to such contemplations, but more and more, he finds himself lost in these thoughts.

Her ministrations concluded; the priestess produces a small leather pouch which she presses against the headwall. She intones a few short phrases and then, stooping gingerly, places it against the base of the structure. She takes a few steps back, turns slowly to face the corsair, nods gravely, and hobbles away, her white headdress receding into the deep night like a waning moon on the ocean's horizon.

Apprehensive, the corsair lets some time pass before beginning his own halting approach. The tomb is surprisingly plain, the corsair thinks, given Caldwell's penchant for the ostentatious. Two simple columns support a granite arch with an inverted torch carved into the center of its façade. Inset between the columns, a gray marble headwall bears Caldwell's epitaph:

TO THE MEMORY OF JANE PLACIDE
There's not an hour of day, or dreamy night but I am with thee;
There's not a wind but whispers o'er thy name.
And not a flower that sleeps beneath the moon,
but in its hues of fragrance tells a tale of thee.

He'd lifted the passage, the corsair knew. The actress would have expected as much from the man she chided as "Poseur!" But whatever else Caldwell may have been, he'd provided security and stability, two things the corsair could never promise. And, after all, the actress was herself no stranger to the arts of deception. "I pray you, do not fall in love with me, for I am falser than vows made in wine..."

The corsair glances down to where the priestess' gris-gris stands sentry against *malign spirits. He hopes it will bring the actress peace, but what does he know of such things? Leaning forward, he presses his lips to the marble.*

"Au revoir, Cher Jane," *he whispers.* "Je suis desole, je n'etais pas un homme meilleur."

Yes, I should have been a better man. To you. To so many.

Pushing away from the tomb, the corsair turns, leaning on his cane, and begins to drag himself away through the darkened avenues of death, away from time and memory, toward his own final resting place.

Chapter Three

I'd baited Bruneau's line and attracted a nibble, but the hook was not yet set. He was going to need more coaxing, I could tell. For as long as I've known him, Bru has been easily bored by the ordinary. It doesn't matter if it's food or antiques, or crime for that matter; only the best or most unusual of anything holds his attention for long. A mysterious grave robbery with a historical twist held potential, but to get his full buy-in, I needed to put some meat on this skeleton of a case. All I had so far were bare bones.

Usually, I form a theory of a crime within minutes of arriving at a scene. I'm not bragging when I say my instincts rarely fail me. But like I told Angie in the kitchen after dinner, this one had me baffled and irritable.

"You said they're pros, right? If they're pros, someone has the means to pay them," Angie said. "And no one is going to go to the trouble of hiring a team of pros unless what they're looking for is either extremely valuable or really important to them for some other reason."

"Thank you, Captain Obvious."

I regretted the words as soon as they left my mouth.

"Really, Bo?"

Angie had spun toward me with her left hand on her hip and was flapping a dish sponge in front of my face with her right.

"You tell me you're stumped, and I try to help, and that's what I get?"

"I'm sorry, babe, it's been a long day," I said, hands up. "I didn't mean it like that. And you're right; that much must be true."

I came up behind my wife, who had turned back to the dishes piled in the sink and began to nibble at the side of her neck, which was moist and smelled like flowers mixed with soap and sweat. She shoved me away, but not hard, and I was pretty sure I caught a hint of a smile. I knew I couldn't force the issue, but also that I wasn't in real trouble. Not yet, anyway.

"Thing is, unless the lab turns up something, I don't even know where to start," I said, stepping to Angie's right and grabbing a pan to dry.

"We don't know what was stolen or even *if* anything was stolen. We've got three sneaker footprints, one a men's size twelve, one a men's ten and a half, and the other a women's four and a half, which explains how one of them was small enough to wriggle into the crypt.

"But that's it in terms of evidence. We're going to check out home security cameras along Iberville and North Anthony and North Bernadette streets to see if they caught anybody coming or going or maybe a getaway vehicle, but I'm not optimistic."

"What about Bruneau?" Angie asked. "Does he have any theories?"

"No, I don't think so. He's doing some research on the actress, but I can't imagine he's going to find anything that's going to make sense of this."

"He's surprised you before."

"Yeah, I guess."

* * *

Normally, I spend Monday mornings at the office catching up on paperwork, but Jane Placide's remains were on my mind, and I knew I wasn't going to get anywhere without a crime lab report, so instead of heading into the station, I turned on some of R.L. Burnside's Delta blues and opted for the 10-minute drive to the lakefront, where the NOPD Crime Lab and Evidence Division is housed. There are faster routes, but I like to hop on Lakeshore Drive by Landry's Seafood House and cruise in that way. Traffic is light, and there's usually a soft breeze coming in off the lake. I enjoy the frenzied *yeows* and *ha-ha-ha's* of the seagulls as they hover and dive. As usual, lots of joggers were out, and some Asian men were practicing their Tai Chi.

As I pulled into the parking lot, I felt more optimistic about the day ahead.

CHAPTER THREE

I'd seen that the scraps of paper from my case had been assigned to Dr. Minh Ngo. That was a good thing, so far as I was concerned.

I have colleagues who don't like working with "Doctor No," which is what we call Minh because none of us can pronounce her last name. There's no doubt that the good doctor can get a little testy, which intimidates some of the guys, but no one argues she's not as good a forensic scientist as we've got. And she is that, a legit scientist, not just a tech.

I've tried to get to know Minh these past few years. Her parents were part of the first wave of Vietnamese immigrants to escape the communist regime at the end of the war and arrive in Louisiana in the mid-1970s. They settled in Algiers first, picking up whatever work they could find, until they'd saved enough to open a small grocery and deli in Gretna in the late eighties. I drop in for a banh mi whenever I'm in the neighborhood, which isn't all that often these days.

Minh is an only child. Growing up, she spent a lot of time at her parents' store, most of it with her nose in a book. She put herself through Nicholls State and went on to earn a PhD in Chemistry from LSU. But rather than seek an academic position, Minh chose to enter a forensic science training program instead. One day I asked her why, and she said she was drawn to the variety that case work brings, and to seeing her efforts lead to speedy results. As a research scientist, she might have spent years and years on a single project.

Big surprise, but the reality of a crime lab job is less exciting than a younger Minh may have imagined. There are only so many fingerprints to run or blood tests to conduct before they all run together, and I guess it's that monotony that makes her prickly from time to time.

But as I'd figured, a historical mystery involving scraps of 200-year-old paper was just the thing to perk up Doctor No.

"Good morning, Detective Duplessis," Minh greeted me cheerfully as I knocked on the half-open sliding glass door to her lab. "This is an interesting case you've brought me to start the week."

"I'm glad you approve, Doc."

A slight smirk crossed Minh's lips. She was seated on a stool in her lab coat in front of a microscope that was almost as big as she is, which isn't very.

"What've you got for me?" I asked.

"Not as much as you're probably hoping for," Minh said, looking down at a slide and jotting a note. As I've grown to expect, Minh looked up only occasionally when talking and avoided eye contact. I don't know if that's a cultural thing or just the defense mechanism of a shy, socially awkward only child.

"In total, there were eighteen pieces of paper, some tiny and some larger, from what appear to be two different source documents," she explained. "I was able to use infrared and ultraviolet light to read the few areas where there were still traces of ink. The rest I had to send to Baton Rouge. They've got an ESDA up there at the state lab that may help us visualize more writing than we can see with the naked eye."

"ESDA?"

Minh smiled and looked down again, as if she'd been waiting for the question. One of the things I think she likes about me is that I take an interest in her work. Most of the other detectives just want answers and don't care about the methods used to get them.

"An Electrostatic Detection Apparatus or ESDA uses a combination of electrical charges and toner to visualize areas of indented writing that we can't otherwise see," Minh explained, warming to her topic. "It acts on the idea that indentations in a document carry lower negative charge than the areas that surround them. That's what causes the toner used in the ESDA to be attracted to the indented areas and fill them in. You'd be amazed at what can be recovered this way."

"I'm all for being amazed, Doc. Do you think you can recover it all?"

"Oh no, I doubt it, but hopefully, we'll get more than we have so far. The paper is badly deteriorated and extremely brittle, although honestly, I'm surprised it's in as good a condition as it is given the age and the degradation you'd expect from air and water infiltration into the tomb."

Minh went on to explain that one of the documents found in the coffin may have been a diary or journal, perhaps Jane Placide's. There were 10 different scraps from it and the writing that could be seen looked like it may have been in a female's hand. The other document looked more like a letter. There were only eight pieces found and they were smaller and in worse condition than the journal scraps. The handwriting was from a different author, and probably masculine.

"How can you tell if the handwriting came from a man or a woman?" I asked.

"You can't always," Minh cautioned, "but in general, men put more pressure on their writing implement than women, because they generate their power more from their fingers than their arms. Also, male handwriting is typically less curvy than female writing. Men tend to crowd their letters and words more, and their punctuation marks tend to be placed closer to the letters."

I made a mental note to compare Angie's writing with mine. Hers is a hell of a lot neater; I know that much.

When I asked Minh to show me what she'd been able to figure out so far, she motioned for me to join her at the microscope, explaining that while she'd sent the source documents to Baton Rouge, she had captured images of the words, or in most cases just letters, she was able to read. She slipped a slide under the scope, got up off her stool, and motioned for me to take a peek.

Settling onto Minh's stool and looking into the eyepiece, it took me several seconds to adjust to the scale of what I was seeing, which I eventually realized was the letter "J" written in a fancy, old-fashioned cursive.

"That's a J, right?"

"Yes," Minh said, replacing the first slide with another. "There's a character between the J and this next letter that I couldn't make out."

"Is that an F?" I asked, guessing a bit.

"Yes."

"Is it possible to see more than one letter at a time?"

"It's possible to see, yes," Minh said, "but you won't be able to read anything. Don't worry, though, I've prepared a draft transcription for you."

I smiled with relief at not having to move one letter at a time. Minh handed me a piece of paper, which she also displayed on the pull-down projector screen she uses to share enlarged images of crime scene evidence. She had organized the 18 pieces of paper into two groups. The eight scraps from the letter, marked Source A, came first, followed by the ten pieces from the journal, marked Source B. The order was random. She said she'd need more data before attempting a chronology.

SOURCE A
(possible letter in male hand)

1. J#F
2. no# #r#st Ca#dw### w##h #### Ta#k to L###n#s#on ### te## ##m
3. Ch## J### ## t#a#m# #ou# l#e#ern##e
4. B######te
5. # can sta# no ###### C#e# Jane ### dev## #s at my ##els To the #ea# I s#a##
6. J#F
7. ### ##easu## You mu## #### ### a#wa#s even ## ### nex#
8. G#an# T#### ##e T#m### C####c#e #ou# #on# mo##s

SOURCE B
(presumed journal or diary in female hand)

1. J k#sse# me #as# n#g## an# #o## me #e #ove# me He as### me to go awa# w### ##m bu# w#e## wou## we go# To ## f#ee to #ove
2. J ca##s #e# La V#o#e##e He sa#s ### ## #mag#qu##" If I #eep he# a#ways we w### ##nd eac# o##e# Even #n the nex# wo###
3. mus# no# ### C f#nd ou# ##easu#e ## ## the map #o
4. I w#### ## Ca####n# an# #### ##ou# J an# w#### #o ##n# ou# ###asu##

CHAPTER THREE

5. W##r# ## J# #### h# k#ow I s#a## soon d### Does he s#### ##ve# I sha## keep LV ## ## #### for e#e####y He shall f#nd me We s#a## be #oge##e# at #as#
6. Neve# have # seen suc# a man C sa#s #e ## a d##g#ac## p#rate bu# I see #ow o##e#s #espec# an# won#e# and #ea# Even L#v#####on ### G##me# make way #o# ##m
7. To#a# I me# w### L####g##on a##u# La V#o##### H# w### sa##g#### ou# tr#a#u##
8. C ## pa##e##c w### h#s comp#a###ng an# ##s w##mpe##ng and ### t##a#e# fo##owed by g######ng apo#og###
9. J came aga## #as# n#gh# ## a ####e#en# ##sgu#se #### #### I to#d ##m no# #o come aga#n T#e ##sk ## #oo g#ea# He sa## ## must go awa# pe#Ha## fo# a #ong ##me but t#at #e sha## ##turn fo# me some ### He shall #### me no ma##e# w#e#E I #al# #e
10. neve# #### ## ## pu###c I #o## he# a# n###t ### I see J as ## ## ## #e## b# ## She ## us and we a## s#e

"Not a lot to go on here," I said.

"No, perhaps not," Minh responded. "But if you look closely there are a few things worth pointing out. For example, is the J cited multiple times in Source B, the same J that appears twice as J-blank-F in Source A? Also, there is what might be the same word that appears three times, in B-three, B-four and B-seven, which if you fill in the letters we can read in one reference, with the letters we can read in the other references, may spell *treasure*. And in B-three there is a reference to *the map*. Could that be what the thieves were after, a treasure map?"

"Damn, you're good!" I said, offering Minh a high five. She gave my hand a disinterested tap.

"I could be wrong. It's just a theory for now," Minh cautioned. "But just for kicks, detective, consider this. There is a word in B-six that looks like it might be *pirate*. Combine *pirate* with *treasure* and *map*, and then think about J-blank-F. What if the blank is an L? Could this be Jean Lafitte, the famous pirate?"

"Jean Lafitte?" I whistled. "I don't know, maybe. People have been searching for his buried treasure forever. I know that. My history's not too good. Were Jean Lafitte and Jane Placide alive at the same time?"

"Yes, he was older, but their lives did overlap," Minh said. "Beyond that, I have no idea. Not my area."

"No worries, I know who to ask," I said, starting for the door. "Thanks for this, Doc. When do you think you'll have the results from the state lab?"

"Probably by tomorrow morning," Minh said.

"Excellent. In the meantime, if you wouldn't mind emailing me your transcription, I'd appreciate it."

"Certainly, detective," Minh responded, not looking up from behind her massive computer monitor. "It's on its way."

**

On the way back to the station, I made two calls. The first was to Mike Rodiger, a rookie from Lake Charles who was still a little wide-eyed but otherwise showed great promise. Rodiger was a standout at the Academy, a tech whiz kid apparently, who earned one of three spots in a management training rotation program the department was piloting. He'd already done a six-month stint in Narcotics and was now a few weeks into helping us. The captain asked me to take the kid under my wing for a bit, so I asked him to collect video from the streets surrounding the mausoleum. He reported that a couple of home security cameras on North Bernadette Street caught blurry glimpses of three individuals in baseball caps and what looked like dark sweat suits walking away from the mausoleum at a brisk pace around 2:30 a.m. One was much smaller than the other two. He couldn't say for sure if it was a woman or man, or even a juvenile possibly. I thanked him, made a mental note to see the clips for myself, and hung up. Then I called Bruneau.

"Hey, Bo," he answered after two rings.

"Hiya, Bru. What you got, my man?"

"Nothing much, just been reading some history. It may prove useful if

CHAPTER THREE

this thing develops, but I don't have any specifics of interest right now. I'm meeting a friend for lunch who might be able to fill in some gaps. How about you?"

Bru sounded interested in Jane Placide in a general way, but not yet captivated. I gave him a rundown of my lab visit and he listened quietly, but he perked up when he heard the name Jean Lafitte.

"My, my Jean Lafitte," he said. "That would be something, wouldn't it? A treasure hunt would be kind of cool. Just like old times. Remember those scavenger hunts my dad used to send us on?"

"I do," I said, smiling. "They were a blast. Hey, do me a favor and ask your friend about Jean Lafitte. And Jane Placide, for that matter. See if there's any connection there."

"Alright. Seems a little far-fetched, don't you think?"

"Yes, but it wouldn't be the first time reality turned out to be stranger than fiction."

"True," Bru said. "Can you send me the images of those transcriptions?"

"Sure."

My fish was still playing with the line, I could see, which was encouraging. But as I parked, got out of the car, and headed into the station, I had that unsettled feeling you sometimes get in this business. We'd gathered some facts and a little bit of context, but few connections. It was a little like starting on a jigsaw without knowing what the completed puzzle was supposed to look like.

Chapter Four

I parked Liesel, my 1979 red Peugeot 604 Turbodiesel sedan, on Dryades Street, across from the entrance to Manale's, where my friend Christopher Keating, a Tulane history professor, greeted me warmly.

"Good to see you, Bruneau; it's been a while."

"Yes, it's been too long. Good to see you, too."

Chris is a fair skinned, slightly built forty something man with a short beard and shoulder length blond hair he ties in a neat ponytail. His horn-rimmed glasses complete the vaguely effete professorial image, but his handshake is firm and his manner direct.

"That thing's still running, I see," Chris said, nodding at my car.

"Thing? She's no thing. She's Liesel! Only car I've ever owned and the only one I plan to. She's running as good as ever."

"Till death do us part?"

"Something like that."

"Huh. Liesel the diesel?"

"That's my girl."

I opened the door for Chris as the familiar gust of sizzling garlic beckoned us inside. The hostess escorted us through the memorabilia-laden bar to a corner table in the main dining room, beneath one of the large picture windows looking out over tree-lined Napoleon Avenue and its wide neutral ground. As Chris scanned the menu, I filled him in on what I knew of Crypt 1083-A and Jane Placide.

Chris specializes in the history of the 18th and 19th-century American South. Every other semester, he teaches a popular lecture course titled

CHAPTER FOUR

"The Making of New Orleans: From Bienville through Reconstruction." He invites experts from other disciplines, such as architecture and engineering, music, and the arts, to contribute guest lectures. The class draws a large cross-section of non-history majors interested in learning more about the singular city in which they find themselves.

Chris and I got to know each other a few years back when he wandered into the shop. A question he asked about a pair of rosewood chairs led to a lengthy discussion of antebellum interior design, a subject about which, it turned out, I was a good deal more knowledgeable than the professor. Chris ended up using me as a resource for a book he was writing on customs and cultural mores in the Old South. We became semi-regular lunch pals with a shared fondness for time-worn New Orleans institutions like Manale's. Now, I hoped he could return the favor.

"I'm vaguely familiar with Jane Placide and Caldwell and the Edwin Forrest incident," Chris said. "But as to what she might have taken to the grave, I don't think I can be much help on that front."

"I didn't figure you could," I said, "but I was hoping you might paint a picture for me of the New Orleans of the 1820s and 30s."

"Sure," Chris nodded as our waiter approached, notepad in hand. Chris ordered the turtle soup and the barbecue shrimp sandwich.

"Make that two turtle soups," I said, "and I'll have the catfish. We'd also like a bottle of the Gavi, please, with a bucket of ice."

"You got it, boss," the waiter responded.

According to Chris, the main thing to keep in mind about New Orleans during the dozen or so years of Jane Placide's residency, is that the city was finally beginning to think of itself as American. The signing of the Louisiana Purchase in 1803 may have nominally marked New Orleans as American, but its laws, language, and culture remained decidedly Francophile, though the residue of forty years of Spanish rule was also still felt. There was the additional problem of the Spanish Crown believing the purchase was illegal because Napoleon never paid Spain for the Louisiana territory before he sold it to the United States. It took nine years of working through these complications before Louisiana finally became a state.

Around the same time, a combination of demographic changes and geopolitical events influenced how New Orleans saw itself. Between May and September of 1810, thousands of refugees from the Haitian Revolution arrived in the city, more than doubling the local population. Meanwhile, statehood opened new markets and quickened what had been a trickling influx of "Kaintucks" into the local economy, rough-hewn river traders from the Mississippi Valley and Appalachia. And then, finally, there was the Battle of New Orleans in 1815, when the city's disparate populations made common cause against the invading British and helped Andrew Jackson pull off one of the more improbable upsets in military history.

"There was a swelling of local pride after the Battle," Chris said. "There were huge celebrations involving every stratum of society, and the city began to think of itself as a distinct, unified entity in a way it hadn't previously. And remember, it hadn't just defended itself. It had fought for the United States of America."

"Yeah, I can see that," I said, pausing to sample the splash of Gavi I'd been poured. Exactly perfect. I nodded to the waiter, who began filling Chris' glass.

"You know, if you think about it, there's no better symbol of the Americanization of New Orleans than James Caldwell's Camp Street Theatre," Chris reflected. "Before that, all local theatre was French."

"Got it," I said. "So, when Jane Placide arrives in town in 1822 or 23, what kind of scene does she walk into?"

Chris thought for a minute while taking a sip of wine.

"It was a New World version of La Belle Époque, a true golden age," he said. "Business was booming. Banks were opening to service the southern planter class who by now had established cotton and sugar as big money crops, not to mention the shipping interests and all the various middlemen supporting the port economy. You had fancy restaurants and shops popping up along Royal Street, and of course, theatres and burlesques and all that. It was probably the most cosmopolitan city in the country in those days."

"What about the social framework?" I asked.

"Well, the city was quite a bit whiter than it had been just a decade earlier,"

CHAPTER FOUR

Chris said.

He explained that in 1810 the population was two-thirds black, about half free and half enslaved, with many free blacks owning slaves themselves. Ten years later African Americans accounted for less than half the city's population of roughly 100,000. And of that number, only about forty percent were free.

"Don't get me wrong," Chris continued. "The free black population still wielded influence. They owned businesses, belonged to the professional classes, and, in some cases, amassed significant fortunes or held political office. But as time went on, a lot of them looked at the discrimination and restrictive laws spreading throughout the south, saw the writing on the wall, and emigrated to Mexico or France or somewhere in the Caribbean."

"Was placage still a thing?" I asked as our soup arrived. The waiter offered a splash of sherry, which I accepted, and Chris declined. I didn't hold it against him.

"Oh yes. Free women of color outnumbered men by almost two to one, and many ended up in long-term kept relationships with white men who supported them, along with the mixed-race children they sired. Modern-day historians, including myself, have cast doubt on the prevalence of formal placage contracts and the infamous quadroon balls we used to read about, but informally, at least, it was a common practice."

I nodded and took a second to appreciate the soup. A tad salty, but delicious, as always.

"Pascal's or Commander's?" I probed, pointing at my bowl.

"I don't know, they're both delicious," Chris considered with a wry grin. "Maybe Commander's by a whisker? I like the chopped egg they bring."

"I tend to vote for whichever I had last," I quipped.

I put my spoon down and leaned in toward Chris.

"Okay, I think I get the overview. What about the people? Who were the players in those days?"

"Depends on what you mean by that," Chris answered. He pushed his empty cup away and exhaled.

"I could give you a stock answer about who the politicians were at the time and the wealthy planters and whatnot, but if I understand the spirit of your question, you're more interested in the schemers and brokers and wheeler-dealers. Do I have that right?"

"Yes, probably."

"Well, it was the wild, wild west back then, so there were any number of speculators out to get rich quick. Edward Livingston is the first name that comes to mind."

"He was Secretary of State, wasn't he?" I asked.

"Yes, under Jackson. Before that he served in the House and Senate, and he was notable for drafting his own proposed criminal and civil codes of Louisiana. They were never adopted but were hugely influential in the development of modern jurisprudence in Europe and the Caribbean. Legal scholars consider him to have been way ahead of his time."

"Yeah, believe it or not," I said, "back when I worked at the Cabildo, I helped curate an exhibit on the Livingston Codes."

"I'm so sorry for you," Chris said, smiling. "Must have been a thrill a minute."

"Indeed."

Chris went on to explain that Livingston was part of a group of influential friends who had their fingers in a lot of pots, some of them conspiratorial in nature, not only in New Orleans but also in Washington and Texas and elsewhere.

"They were all hyper-connected," he explained, "and always looking to manipulate events for their personal gain. They were Freemasons, all of them. I imagine a lot of business got conducted in the lodges."

"You say 'they.' Who else?"

Chris mentioned John Randolph Grymes, like Livingston a lawyer and politician; a merchant named John West; Abner Duncan, who was Jackson's aide-de-camp during the Battle of New Orleans; and two Frenchmen, Arsène Latour and Barthelemy Lafon, who were both accomplished architects, engineers and surveyors. Then, unprompted by me, he mentioned the pirates Jean and Pierre Lafitte and their sometime confederate, Dominique Youx.

CHAPTER FOUR

"Jean Lafitte?" I registered my surprise. "Pierre was his brother, I take it?" Chris nodded.

"What would they have been doing hobnobbing with the movers and shakers?"

"The Lafittes never regarded themselves as pirates," Chris informed me. "And they were welcome in the highest rungs of New Orleans society, at least before things went south for them."

"Because they got raided, right?" I asked, dipping into my memory banks.

"Yes. They salvaged their reputations and were pardoned when they helped Jackson win the Battle of New Orleans, but they never regained their former wealth and ended up moving their operations to Texas."

"Interesting," I said. "Would they still have been around when Jane Placide arrived in town?"

"No, they were long gone by then," Chris said. "I could be mistaken, but I think Pierre died in 1820 or 21, and Jean four or five years later."

"There goes one theory down the tubes," I said, drawing a quizzical look from Chris.

"Oh, nothing," I said, "just thinking out loud. So, Livingston and his cronies?"

Chris explained that some historians refer to Livingston and his circle as The New Orleans Associates, or alternatively, just The Associates, which in his mind made them sound more formally organized than they really were. He prefers to think of them as a loose confederation of opportunists who operated in the shadows but nonetheless left their fingerprints on many of the headlines of the day.

"Interesting," I said. "Do you know if James Caldwell ran in those circles?"

"Not to my knowledge," he responded. "I'm sure he would have known some of the men I mentioned, but whether he had any formal dealings with them, I couldn't say. I tend to doubt it, though. From what I know about Caldwell, he was a show biz guy through and through, although later, he was instrumental in bringing gaslight to the city and formed a company that was basically the first utility in these parts. But from what I know, he was not a political schemer."

Just then, the busboy appeared to clear the table and place a bib before Chris as the waiter arrived with our food. He served Chris first. His sandwich, a classic hollowed-out Leidenheimer loaf stuffed with spicy shrimp, was accompanied by a bowl of dunking sauce. Chris began tying the bib behind his neck as my catfish was placed before me. It was pan-seared, still sizzling, doused with a lemon butter cream sauce, and topped with fresh baby artichoke hearts and a generous dollop of crabmeat. Perfection. I have long preferred this dish to the restaurant's signature shrimp, which are a bit messy for my liking.

"Okay, so Livingston and his Associates, or the Masons, or whatever you want to call them. Their schemes..." I reminded Chris.

"Right," Chris said, pausing as he chewed through his first bite of sandwich and washed it down with a swill of wine.

"In those days, there was constant intrigue involving both Spain and France. Spain's control of Mexico was weakening, and therefore, its claim to Texas, which was tenuous to begin with. Meantime, there were a host of Bonapartist exiles who fled France for the U.S. when Napoleon fell the second time. Many of them aspired to create a New France, perhaps in Texas or Mexico."

"Wasn't there a plot to rescue Napoleon from Saint Helena?" I asked.

"Yes, there were a few actually, including one hatched here in New Orleans that the Lafittes and some of the others I mentioned were involved with, along with the mayor at the time, Nicholas Girod, the namesake of your cemetery. He lived in what we now call Napoleon House, because the plan was for Napoleon to reside there until he could reestablish himself somewhere else. Anyway, it all came to naught because Napoleon died in 1821 before they could get the plot off the ground."

"Yeah, I knew about that," I said. "Sorry, I think I took you off-topic."

"No worries." Chris took another bite of his sandwich while I sopped up as much sauce as I could to coat my next forkful of fish.

"There were various efforts by these French expats to establish settlements in what was nominally Spanish territory. They were called filibusters back then, a distant relation to today's legislative maneuver. Some of them

CHAPTER FOUR

formed private armies with the aim of helping Mexico gain independence from Spain. They even talked of installing Joseph Bonaparte, Napoleon's brother, as Emperor of Mexico. He was living in New Jersey at that point and may have been the richest man in the country because of all the crown jewels and priceless artwork he brought with him from France. He helped fund some of the filibustering efforts.

"Anyway, I digress. Livingston and his buddies basically used their influence and sometimes their money to aid and abet some of these plots in the belief that an untethered Texas would offer a ripe environment for personal financial gain. But they also hedged their bets."

"How so?"

"By spying for Spain, obviously," Chris deadpanned before breaking into a wide grin.

"The priest at Saint Louis Cathedral at that time was a fascinating figure known as Padre Sedella, and he ran a large intelligence network on behalf of Spain. The Spanish were extremely paranoid about who was settling in their lands and with what intentions. And so, some of 'The Associates,' if we can call them that, worked both sides of the fence. They aided the filibusters with their schemes but then were paid by Spain to report on the filibusters."

"Brilliant!" I exclaimed. "What years are we talking about?"

"Probably from right after the Battle of New Orleans into the mid-1820s," Chris said. "I'd say their influence was beginning to wane by the time Jane Placide arrived in town. Individually, some of them were still major players, but as a semi-organized group, their activities lost steam because none of the filibuster efforts ended up bearing fruit."

The conversation paused as we focused on our food, punctuating the brief silence with grunts of epicurean pleasure.

"Would Jane Placide have known Livingston or any of his Associates?" I asked, pushing my empty plate away.

"Oh, I would think so, yes. Livingston and Grymes and others would have seen her perform and no doubt paid their compliments as leading citizens. They probably encountered each other at high society balls and that sort of thing."

"But no reason to believe she was in on or privy to any of their schemes?"

"No, I don't think so. Similar to Caldwell, her universe was show business and hers was likely a more cloistered version at that. It's hard to imagine her getting involved in political machinations. It was a man's world back then."

The waiter approached and enquired about dessert, which we both declined. Chris asked for green tea, and I an espresso and the check.

"I'm sorry I can't be of more help regarding your actress, Bruneau," Chris said. "She's a little outside the scope of my scholarship."

"I understand," I said, "but you've been very helpful nonetheless."

Chris and I exchanged small talk and made plans for lunch at Tartine's the following week. When we parted, I walked back to Liesel, opened the door, and stood there for a moment or two to organize my thoughts.

According to Chris, Jane Placide arrived during a prosperous but disruptive time in New Orleans, full of conspiracies and shifting alliances and an intriguing cast of characters. It's unlikely that she was involved in anything untoward, but she probably knew most of the power brokers of the day, at least socially. I couldn't rule anything out.

Chapter Five

It is hard to live in this part of the world and not be at least vaguely aware of Jean Lafitte. His brand is ubiquitous. You see it in street names, historical designations and all manner of commercial appropriations. And so, I have long known the basic tourist bureau talking points. Lafitte was the last great pirate. The Lord of Barataria. A notorious smuggler and slave trader. A hero of the Battle of New Orleans. A possible burier of untold treasure. The namesake of the town of Lafitte, Louisiana, the Jean Lafitte National Historical Park, and, of course, Lafitte's Blacksmith Shop, purveyor of Voodoo Daiquiris to French Quarter tourists for as long as anyone can remember.

I had known too that Lafitte was the subject of a large body of folklore, some of it possibly true, but until I got off the phone with Bo, took Hugo out for a walk, and started digging a little deeper, I hadn't appreciated the full extent of the Lafitte mystique. There are countless books about the man, ranging from historical fiction to serious scholarly works to pure quackery. There is even a Lafitte Society to which members pay dues to access information behind an internet paywall and argue competing theories of Lafitteology on the site's message board. To some, Lafitte was a self-aggrandizing scoundrel. To others, a misunderstood gentleman of honor. There are disagreements about where he was born, when and where he died, how he spelled his name, what he looked like, which languages he spoke, and a long list of other arcana.

I didn't have a dog in this fight. I was just looking for facts, a commodity I found to be in short supply. What can we say about Lafitte that separates the man from the legend? A quick tour of the Internet filled in the broad brushstrokes of my understanding.

Lafitte was born in 1782, probably in France but possibly in Saint Domingue. He and his older brother Pierre arrived in New Orleans around 1804 and built a large-scale smuggling operation based out of Grand Terre, the barrier island that separates Barataria Bay from the Gulf of Mexico. Both pirates and middlemen during these years, the Lafittes made a fortune selling property stolen by themselves and others. The contraband included luxury goods like linens, china, furniture, spices, coffee, wine, and whisky. It also included enslaved Africans. Congress had banned the importation of slaves, so for Mississippi Delta plantation owners who couldn't breed their own workforce fast enough to meet their production goals, the Lafittes' slave market became the principal means of acquiring new labor.

Against this backdrop, as Chris had said, the Lafittes hobnobbed comfortably with the upper crust of New Orleans society and generally lived a comfortable life. Until, that is, the U.S. Navy raided their Barataria operation in 1814 and burned it to the ground, confiscating their inventory and charging them with a laundry list of crimes. Ever resourceful, Jean Lafitte managed to escape from Barataria and made his way to New Orleans, where he obtained an audience with then-General Andrew Jackson, who had been sent to protect the city. He told Jackson about an offer he'd received from the British to assist them in their planned naval invasion of New Orleans. Knowing that Jackson was both under-manned and under-armed, he let the general know he was still in possession of thousands of gun flints the raid had missed and offered him all the resources at his disposal in exchange for pardons and the release of his men from prison. Jackson begrudgingly accepted Lafitte's offer, and historians mostly agree he could not have prevailed were it not for the Baratarians' ammunition, skilled cannon work, and intimate knowledge of the labyrinthine bayous that led from the Gulf to the city.

When the city celebrated its glorious triumph, Jackson publicly thanked the Lafitte brothers, and a full pardon from President Madison followed. But what would not be forthcoming, despite the advocacy of Edward Livingston

CHAPTER FIVE

and John Grymes on the Lafittes' behalf, was the recovery of their seized assets. The Lafittes spent the next few years petitioning the government for restitution while also making money by feeding information to the Spanish spy ring Chris Keating had mentioned. Eventually, they rebuilt their smuggling empire, relocating it to Galveston Island, Texas, which the Lafittes called Campeche. But after only a couple years, the operation was again destroyed, this time by a hurricane. From there, the history gets hazy. There is broad agreement that Pierre Lafitte died from an illness in the Yucatan in 1821. Jean may have obtained a small fleet and continued pirating, possibly under a letter of marque from Cartagena or Cuba. Some say he died at sea off the coast of Honduras, or perhaps Venezuela. Others say he succumbed to illness on Isla Mujeres, or was it Cuba? Theories abound, but there is no formal record of Lafitte's death. Most accounts have him perishing in 1825 or 1826.

I called Bo and told him his Lafitte theory was a non-starter.

"How come?" he wanted to know.

"Because by the time Jane Placide arrived here in 1822 or 23, Lafitte was long gone."

"You sure about that?"

I gave Bo the *Reader's Digest* version of the Lafitte story, stressing the timing of the Galveston hurricane in 1818 and the peripatetic existence Lafitte led between then and his death seven or eight years later.

"Just because he was moving around doesn't mean he couldn't have spent time here," Bo countered.

"I can keep looking if you want me to," I offered, without conviction, "but as far as I can tell, there are no accounts of him being in New Orleans after 1818."

"No, that's okay," Bo said. "Hold off for now. Let's see what the state lab comes up with first. I should have those results in a few hours."

* * *

"Why, what a remarkable story, darling," gushed Charlotte Duval, in the husky voice of a lifelong smoker, when I told her about Jane Placide and the possible Jean Lafitte connection.

"Such intrigue! But do be careful, dear," she said, patting my hand. "These grave robbers don't strike me as a class of people a gentleman such as yourself should be consorting with."

Like many southern women of a certain vintage and pedigree, Charlotte makes liberal use of terms of endearment and affects a veneer of omniscience no matter the subject. As it happens, Charlotte does know her way around jewelry, antiques, and the decorative arts, and she is my go-to source for any inquiry regarding the ancestral history of old-money New Orleans. But she's an unapologetic snob, particularly when it comes to the city's "newly arrived" carpetbagger class, by which I take her to mean those of us who showed up sometime after the Civil War. As off-putting as she can be, I have a soft spot for Charlotte, and I enjoy the reliably entertaining repartee of our weekly luncheons.

"What do you make of it?" I asked. "Is it plausible, do you think, that Jean Lafitte and Jane Placide knew each other?"

"Knew each other? Don't be silly, dear. They more than just knew each other."

"You're saying you think they had a thing going on?" I asked skeptically. "A forty-something wanted man and an ingénue twenty-plus years his junior?"

"Why, it's plain as day, Bruneau!" Charlotte laughed dismissively. "Lafitte was a notorious Lothario, was he not? How could the poor girl resist his charms?"

"I didn't know he was such a ladies' man," I shot back, testing. "Are you sure about that?"

"Of course, my dear. A famous womanizer. His string of conquests is legendary."

I doubted Charlotte had the slightest idea as to Lafitte's romantic predilections, but she long ago mastered the art of speaking authoritatively on topics about which she knows little. Her skill is to avoid the telling detail and artfully change the subject if the conversation begins to penetrate the surface.

CHAPTER FIVE

"How are your escargots, Bruneau?" Charlotte pivoted gracefully, sipping from her Sapphire martini, very dry with a twist.

"C'est magnifique," I replied, with a tip of my Muscadet. "The Calvados cream gets me every time."

It had been a few years since we settled on Lilette as our monthly rendezvous spot. There are sexier restaurants in town and God knows it's not cheap, but there is an honesty to the French bistro food that we both appreciate. You can have your sustainably foraged oysters served atop a bed of Rusty Fence Farm spinach, floating in Devon cream butter, and topped with a drizzle of organic elephant garlic emulsion. I'll have the Oysters Rockefeller, please.

"Bruneau dear, be a doll, will you, and order me another martini while I visit the powder room," Charlotte commanded, rising from her chair.

As she made her way to the ladies' room, I marveled at her self-assurance. Even pushing 80, Charlotte walks with a regal bearing that is in no way sexy yet draws the attention of men half her age. She stands maybe five foot nine with a sturdy build that is only now beginning to sag a bit at the shoulders and dresses in a style that favors non-fussy elegance over ephemeral chic. But it's her air of unflinching entitlement that catches you. It's not the pretentious aura of privilege conveyed by the newly rich nor the sheepishly apologetic elitism of inherited wealth. It's more like an inbred, deep-seated belief that, as a Duval, she naturally possesses sovereign license over her dominion.

Charlotte has few friends. No, that's not quite right. Charlotte has a wide circle of "friends" who respect, admire, or, more likely, fear her and who work diligently to solicit her favorable opinion. But she has few *friends* in the sense that Bo and I are friends, for example. I come closer than most to fitting the definition, I suppose, but even with me, Charlotte is never going to play true confessions, especially when it comes to her personal life. Other than the occasional reminder that the Duval family's New Orleans lineage traces back almost to Bienville and the city's founding, she holds her cards close to the vest.

Most of what I've learned about Charlotte I've picked up from others.

She was married while very young and widowed just a couple years later. Cancer, I think. In an unusual move for the time, Charlotte took back her maiden name. There were offers from various suitors over the years, but all were rebuffed without undue deliberation. She has a daughter and a couple grandkids who live in St. Louis but visit only occasionally. Whether owing to her inheritance or her husband's estate, she has enough money to live comfortably, but it is unclear how well-off she really is. She resides with Isabella, her longtime housekeeper and gal Friday, in her ancestral home, a large Greek Revival mansion with Italianate touches in the Garden District, a couple blocks off Jackson. The exterior is well kept, as are the first-floor suite of rooms fronting Phillip Street, where she entertains. But I don't know anyone who has seen the rest of the house, so one wonders whether, in keeping with Old South tradition, a well-to-do façade masks back-of-the-house decay.

"Ah, thank you for the drink, dear," Charlotte said upon her return. "Where are those entrees? I'm getting my hair done at two, and I hate to keep Omar waiting."

"You've got plenty of time, I should think," I replied. "Here they come now."

Charlotte had ordered the hearts of palm salad, and I went for the bavette, which was grilled to medium rare perfection, charred on the outside, red on the inside. I washed it down with a glass of the house Bourgogne. Charlotte nursed her martini.

"Charlotte, do you know of any Lafitte experts in town?" I asked.

"Well, dear, I don't know about experts, but I'm sure Phillip would know a thing or two," she replied.

The Phillip in question was Phillip Boyer, an exemplar of a type I encounter often in my business. Phillip is a rail-thin, white-haired dandy with an extensive bow tie collection, assiduously curated to augment his summer seersucker and winter tweed. He is seen as a highbrow by the stable of older women he cultivates as benefactors, including Charlotte, and in truth, he does know a little about a lot. But if his intellect is a mile wide, it is but a centimeter deep. His avocation, such as it is, is walker. He provides companionship and ostensibly clever conversation to lonely old ladies, and in return, he eats and drinks well and, for all I know, may receive other favors, financial or otherwise. He may be harmless, but I neither like nor trust him.

"I had in mind more of a specialist," I said.

"Go ahead and talk to your specialists if all you're looking for is academic answers," Charlotte said, sensing my disdain. "But don't underestimate people like Phillip, who sometimes know the history behind the history that your fancy academics miss."

"I'll start with the experts," I replied as politely as I could, "and then if I think I need more, I'll consider talking to Phillip."

Charlotte raised her eyebrows as if put out and emitted a "humph" to indicate she could be of no further assistance.

"At any rate, I should get the bill," I deflected, reminding her that it was my turn to treat.

"Thank you, dear," Charlotte said. "I hate to be rude, but I really should be going."

"No problem. I'll stay and settle up."

"It was divine as always," she said, gathering her purse and rising. "I thought I might stop by the store tomorrow and have a look around. It's been a while."

"That sounds great. We'd love to have you."

Leaning over to peck the top of my scalp, Charlotte paused to regard me with a cock of her head and a look of maternal concern.

"I don't like the sound of this Lafitte business, Bruneau. Do be careful, won't you? I'd hate to see you get involved in something over your head."

"I'll be careful, I promise. I'm just the brains of this operation, not the brawn."

Charlotte smiled faintly, laid an approving *there, there* on my shoulder, and sauntered off toward the door, pulling a box of Newports and her lighter out of her purse as she went.

What a dame, I thought to myself.

1825

CAMP STREET THEATRE
NEW ORLEANS, LOUISIANA
APRIL 1825

As the actress enters stage left, she feels the warmth of oil lanterns above her and the audience below. She scans the crowd for a friendly set of eyes, and homes in on the sympathetic scrutiny of a society matron with whom she is casually acquainted. But she is drawn as if by gravity to the lady's immediate left, where a man's dark orbs peer up from hooded brows and rivet her attention. He is taller than those seated around him. Dressed in black, with a furled white shirt, his flowing hair is dark like coal and his complexion dusky. The intensity of his gaze catches the actress short. She senses an impalpable danger and tries to suppress the feeling that a trespasser has breached the inner sanctum of her soul, only to realize she is late with her opening line.

> "I pray you, sir, is it your will
> To make a stale of me amongst these mates?"

For the remainder of the performance, the actress is aware of the stranger's simmering focus. During the curtain call, he does not clap or cheer, but his attention remains singularly fixed. She shivers but cannot look away when her eyes, guided as if by an invisible magnetic force, meet his.

* * *

1825

A few hours later, having changed into her evening dress, Jane Placide enters a ballroom on the arm of her benefactor, James Caldwell. She is met by the applause to which she has become accustomed at these after parties and begins working her way through the gauntlet of admirers who have lined up to congratulate her. Almost immediately, she again senses the stranger's scrutiny, though she cannot yet see him.

At the end of the greeting line, she disengages from Caldwell and smiles at the friendly face of her dear friend Thomas Shields, the disabled purser who lost his left arm in the Barbary Wars but nonetheless proved indispensable in helping Jackson prepare his navy for the British. As they greet one another, she peers over her friend's shoulder and spots the dark stranger in the corner, engaged in conversation with Arsène Latour, his eyes still upon her.

"Thomas, who is that man with Monsieur Latour?" *she asks, nodding tactfully toward the corner.*

Shields swivels nonchalantly to determine the object of the actress' curiosity and turns back to her with a bemused smile.

"Why that is Captain Lafitte, my dear," *he says.*

"The pirate?" *she asks, affecting mock incredulity.*

"One and the same, although he prefers the title privateer."

"I thought he was persona non grata in our city and either dead or a fugitive out on the seas."

The purser smiles knowingly. "It is true that Captain Lafitte's star has fallen, but he is a resourceful man, and very much alive. He still has friends in high places and there are many here who remember him fondly. Shall I introduce you?"

The actress pauses briefly and cocks her head.

"Yes, would you? I should like to make the acquaintance of the notorious Captain Lafitte."

Purser Shields offers his good arm, which the actress accepts, and escorts her to the corner where the Frenchmen remain engaged in conversation, Latour animated and gesturing, Lafitte nodding quietly with one eye still trained on the approaching actress.

"Bon soir, mes amis," *Shields interjects.* "Captain Lafitte, it is my pleasure to introduce you to our actress non-pareil, Miss Jane Placide. Monsieur Latour, I *believe you and Miss Placide are already acquainted."*

"But of course," Latour says, bowing and kissing the actress' extended hand. "It is always a pleasure to see you mademoiselle. Your performance was très extraordinaire."

"Thank you, Monsieur. Your kind words flatter me."

The actress turns toward Lafitte, who takes her hand and bows unhurriedly. Looking up, he speaks sonorously.

"Enchanté, mademoiselle."

Chapter Six

I thought about calling Bruneau but decided on an early morning visit instead. Minh had received the state lab results the day before but didn't share them with me until later in the day after she'd had a chance to add some of her own magic. Having slept on the updated information, my mind was racing, but I wanted to see Bru react in real-time.

He was sitting on his wrought iron second-floor balcony overlooking Magazine Street, wrapped in his bathrobe, eating breakfast, and reading the paper. Hugo, his French bulldog, stood on high alert at his feet. I tooted my horn and swung into a parking space across the street.

"Good morning," I shouted as I got out of the car. It wasn't hot yet, but the soapy moisture from a recent street cleaning rose as steam from the pavement. It was going to be a scorcher with wet, heavy air.

"Morning," Bruneau replied, a bit startled, over Hugo's snarling. No matter how many times I'm around that dog, it's always the same.

"Got something to share. Mind letting me in?"

"Mind? Why would I mind? It's seven thirty in the morning. Perfectly normal time for a visit."

The sarcasm continued as I crossed the street and met Bruneau and Hugo at the side door that led up to their apartment. Up close, Bru was scruffier than he'd looked from the street. He hadn't shaved, and stray wisps of his graying hair stood up at odd angles on his otherwise bald head. He might have lost a few pounds, but it was hard to tell.

"So, what is it that's so important? Due to unforeseen circumstances, I am now officially wide awake," Bru said over Hugo's barking. "Hugo, quiet!"

The dog stopped barking on cue but didn't look happy about it and sniffed hard at my pant leg.

"Ah, Bru, it's good to see you greet the day at full throttle. You should try it more often."

"Uh-huh. Coffee?"

"Sure, sounds good," I said, following him up the stairs into his kitchen and nearly tripping over Hugo in the process.

"I got the state lab results back, and it looks like it really is Lafitte. I thought we could have a look at this together."

"Really? I'll be damned. Sure, let's have a look."

Bruneau handed me a steaming mug and motioned that we should head to the dining room, where he cleared a few stacks of papers so we could sit side by side at the table and look over the transcriptions Minh had provided. I took a sip of coffee while opening my folder.

"Jesus! What is this, unfiltered crude oil?"

"Just a little something for you to start *your* day," Bru said with an evil smirk. "Let's see what you got."

I had printed two copies of Minh's transcription and handed one to Bruneau.

"Before you get started, let me explain the legend," I said. "The lab has full confidence in the accuracy of everything that appears in plain type, unless it's a pound sign, which means they have no clue. If a letter is bolded, it means they believe it is accurate, but there is at least some possibility it could be a different letter. And anything in brackets represents an educated guess or a shot in the dark. Make sense?"

"Yes, got it," Bruneau said. "Is it possible there are missing letters or words that weren't detected at all?"

"I asked the same question. The lab seems confident they've found all the indentations, although apparently, it is possible there could be a couple blended letters where you see one pound sign. Also, punctuation marks may or may not show up."

Bru nodded.

"One more thing to keep in mind," I added. "The order in the transcription represents the lab's best guess only. We don't really have any way of knowing when these lines were written. The journal entries almost surely come from different dates, but we don't know when."

"Okay, got it. Can I start reading now?"

"Yes. Just a quick reminder that Source A appears to be a letter or letters written by a man, and Source B seems to be a diary or journal, probably written by a woman, possibly Jane Placide."

"Um yeah, it does say that right here," Bru smirked, pointing to the relevant lines in the document. He really can be a pain in the ass when he puts his mind to it.

Bruneau slipped on his readers, bent over the papers, and began tracing the lines of text with his finger, letting out an occasional "huh" or "hmm" as he went.

SOURCE A

(possible letter in male hand)

1. **I** can stay no ###### [longer], Cher Jane. **The devil is** at my **he**els. To the **sea**# I sha**ll**
2. Grand T#### **the** T#m### C####ch# tou**s** sont morts

[English translation from the French "tous sont morts": all are dead.]

1. ### ##easu**re** [pleasure or treasure]. You must #### ### **always** even ## ### [in the] next [world]
2. JLF
3. **not trust Caldwell** with #### Talk to Li**vi**ngston ### **tell** ##m [him]
4. JLF
5. B#######t#
6. Cher J### [Jane], ## [Je] t'**aime pour** l'eternite

[English translated from French: Dear Jane, I love you for eternity.]

53

THE LAFITTE AFFAIR

SOURCE B
(presumed journal or diary in female hand)

1. Never have **I** seen such a man. C says he **is** a d**i**sgra**ced** p#rate but I see how others regard ### [him] **with** respect and wonder and fear. Even L**i**v**i**ngst**on** ### [and] Gr#mes make way **for him**.
2. J k**i**ssed me last n**i**ght and **to**ld me he love**d** me. He as**ked** me to go away **with hi**m but where would we go? To ## [be] free? Free to love.
3. J ca**ll**s her La Violette. He says ### [she] is "magique!" [French for magical] If I **keep** her a**l**wa**y**s we w### [will] find eac**h** other. Even **in** the next wo### [world].
4. never #### ## ## pu###c. I **hold** her at night ### [and] I see J as ## ## ## **here** by ## She **is** us and we **are** she.
5. J came again last night, **in a different d**is**guise** #### #### I told **him** not to come again. The risk **is** too **great.** He sa**id** he must go away, per**haps** for a **long time**, but that he sha**ll** ret**urn** for me some ### [day]. He shall #### [find] me no ma**tter** where I shall be.
6. I w###e #o Ca#o##ne and #o## her about J an**d where** to find our tr**e**asure
7. C ## [is] pathetic w### [with] his complain**ing** and his wh**im**peri**ng** and ### [his] t**i**rades followed by g#######ng [groveling] apologies.
8. must not **let** C find our **tre**asure. ## ## the map to
9. Today I met **with** Livingston a##u# [about] La Violette. He w### sa##g#### ou# tre**a**sure
10. Where is J? Does he know I sha**ll** soon die? Does he s#### [still] **live?** I shall keep LV ## ## #### for ete####y [eternity]. He shall find me. We shall be **to**ge**ther** at last.

Bru had finished one pass through the document and was about to start on a second when I interrupted.
"What do you think? First impressions?"
"Shhh!" he shot back. "Don't rush me."
"Okay, okay, just let me know when you're ready to talk."

CHAPTER SIX

I looked down at Hugo under the table, who I swear rolled his eyes. I wondered if our relationship had entered a new phase.

"Well, it certainly does seem to be Lafitte, even though, in theory, he wasn't alive at this point," Bru finally said, leaning back in his chair, taking off his glasses, and rubbing his forehead. "We should probably see if we can find a writing sample to be sure. I think I know where to look."

"Okay, sure. Anything else?"

"I mean, assuming J and JLF are both Lafitte, as seems likely, then it looks like he and Jane really were having an affair, as improbable as that may be. I should probably apologize to my friend Charlotte."

"What's that?" I asked, not following.

"Oh, nothing, just a conversation I had."

"Yeah, okay," I said, a bit too impatiently. I try to respect that Bru likes to take his time working toward conclusions, but sometimes I wish he'd just cut to the chase.

"I got the romance angle. What else?"

"What do you want from me, a full-blown theory?" Bru sniffed.

"No, I just want to know what else pops out at you," I said.

"How about you go first?"

"Fine," I said. "What jumps out first is exactly what Minh had thought. There was a treasure map that Jane took to the grave and that's what the burglars were after. Lafitte's visits were incognito, which accounts for why there is no record of him in New Orleans during that time. They didn't trust Caldwell and possibly turned to that Livingston guy as a custodian of some sort."

"That's excellent work, Bo. What do you need me for?"

I might not be the sharpest tool in the shed, but I do know when I'm being patronized. Then again, I've never been above taking one for the team, if it will lead to results.

"Because I know perfectly well your mind is going a hundred miles an hour, and you're seeing things I'm not," I said.

Bru snorted. Then he turned serious.

"Look, I'm going to need more time with this by myself. But before we jump to the treasure map conclusion, I think there are some questions we need to answer."

"Such as?"

"First and foremost, who or what is La Violette? Who or what is it that Jane holds at night and what does she mean by she is us and we are she? When Lafitte says all are dead, who or what does he mean? What are the first few words of item B-six having to do with where to find the treasure? Where is Lafitte while Jane is dying? Was he already dead, as the history books suggest? That's just for starters."

"See, I knew you were way ahead of me," I said. "Do you know where to look for answers?"

"Maybe, for some of them. I'm not sure."

"Okay, I get it. You need time," I said. "Take whatever time you need, but keep me posted on your progress, alright? I've got to get to work. Think maybe you'll have something by dinner tonight?"

"Oh, sure, no problem at all. It's not like I have a shop to open or anything else going on in my day that could possibly be more important than my unpaid charity work for NOPD."

"That's what I like!" I exclaimed. "A man who keeps his priorities in order!"

I had him now, I could tell. The crusty lunker was hooked.

* * *

After leaving Bruneau's, I drove to the station to check in with Rodiger, but before I could get to him, I was intercepted by Captain Hugh MacLaren, my boss in Property Crimes.

"Yo, T-Bo!" he called from his office. "A minute, please."

The captain and I started out together as rookies back in the day, not as partners but in the same precinct. He started calling me T-Bo the day we met and never stopped. He's fourth-generation Irish and looks the part, hard as iron with a barrel chest, bowling pin forearms, and an ornery expression permanently carved into his freckled face. He likes to remind you that his great-grandfather worked on the docks and that his father and grandfather before him were both cops. He usually leaves out the part about his dad getting kicked off the force for taking kickbacks.

"What do you need, Mac?" I asked as I entered his office and closed the door. He doesn't mind me calling him Mac when we're alone, but in front of others, it's always got to be captain. Basically, we get along fine, so long as I remember my place.

"The kid briefed me on your grave robbery. Said you don't know if anything was taken."

"Yeah, well, it's early," I said. "I gotta think they were after something, don't you?"

"Could be a pervert."

I could see where this was going. Like most of the brass, Mac's always got one eye on his stats. Unsolved thefts don't look good when he's reporting up. A simple breaking and entering, and nobody really cares.

"If it's a pervert, you think an accomplice is going to go to all the trouble of helping him just so he can get his rocks off?"

"You never know these days; there's all kinds of freaks out there," he said, "although the kid tells me it might've been a woman."

"Yeah, might be."

"You got any leads or theories the kid doesn't know about? Maybe one that doesn't involve a god damned pirate, for Christ's sake?"

"Not yet, Mac. Like I said, it's early."

"Sometimes it gets late early."

"I understand."

"Alright, keep working it for now, but if you're not getting anywhere soon, we'll need to talk about re-classing this one. Keep me posted."

"Damn, Mac, the paint's still wet, and you're already talking B&E? Give me some time, will you?"

"That's what I'm doing," he said, "so get on it."

After leaving Mac's office in a pissed-off mood, I found Rodiger at his desk, head toggling back and forth between two monitors, coffee and a half-eaten donut by his side. Like a lot of rookies, the kid's a walking cliché.

Within a year, he'll have gone one of two ways. Either he'll stay hooked on sugar and caffeine and spend his days bellyaching with the other fat losers in blue, or he'll quit the junk and carve out time to get in shape and take care of himself. He's a bright kid and ambitious, so I'm betting on the latter.

"Better lay off those donuts, son," I barked, walking up behind him. "They'll come back to bite you."

"Oh hi, detective," Rodiger said, turning to look over his shoulder. "Yeah, I've been thinking I need to cut back on my sugar intake."

"There's thinking, Rodiger, and then there's doing. What you got for me that you didn't already spill to the captain?"

Rodiger rolled his chair around to face me. "Sorry, sir. He pulled me into his office."

"It's alright. What you got?"

"Well, I've been working through all the databases looking for similar fact patterns. I don't have any names for you, but I found three robberies through Interpol that seem to fit the model."

"Okay, let's hear it."

"Sure. The first was in Morocco in 2004," Rodiger said. "A thief with at least two accomplices entered a historic mosque in Fez by climbing through a window that was only eighteen inches wide and used a rope to drop down thirty feet to the ground. He or she took a 12th-century Quran in a 24-carat gold encasement that weighed almost 30 pounds. They think it was attached to the rope and hoisted out. It's never been recovered."

Rodiger paused.

"Three years later, in Marseilles, thieves broke into a villa, cracked a safe, and made off with more than $10 million in jewelry. The initial entry was with a rope through a skylight. Two people this time. Footprints recovered from the scene were a men's ten and a half and a women's four and half."

"That sounds familiar," I said. "What about the third one?"

"Amsterdam, 2014, at the tightly secured private estate of Jan Van de Berg, one of the world's best-known art collectors," Rodiger replied. "Entry was through a skylight that was under repair and, therefore, not wired at the time. Two masked intruders dressed in black tied up the night guardsman

CHAPTER SIX

and made off with a small painting by the French artist Eugene Delacroix, plus a diamond necklace worth about $3 million. Two things to note here: one, they could have taken several paintings but chose only one, and not the most valuable by a long shot. And two, the guard said one of the thieves was less than five feet tall."

"Did the guard say if one of the intruders was a woman?" I asked.

"He thought they were both male, but he said he couldn't be certain."

"What was the subject of the painting?"

"It was a half-naked odalisque, or harem girl," Rodiger replied at the ready, impressing me. "She is reclining on some pillows and blankets. It's a watercolor."

"Good work, Rodiger," I said. "Does Interpol believe the same crew pulled off these jobs?"

"Yes, sir, they do. But the trail has led nowhere."

"Do they think this was contract work?"

"Most likely, yes," Rodiger explained. "The M.O. is more or less the same but the objects taken are different enough that it's unlikely that the same collector or fence would have interest in books and jewelry and art, at least in Interpol's view."

"In other words, same team working for different clients," I said.

"Yeah, exactly."

"Do you agree with Interpol's take?" I asked.

"I think so. But the one caveat I'd add is that the Delacroix doesn't fit. You've got a priceless book and some mega-expensive jewelry, so you assume money is the motive. But then they take the Delacroix when they could have had Rembrandts or a Van Gogh or God knows what else. It feels different somehow. Personal, maybe."

"I like the way you think, Rodiger," I said. "Keep on this."

Chapter Seven

I'd given Bo a hard time about police work interrupting my busy schedule, but in truth, I had the day off. My part-time helper, Victoria, was scheduled to hold down the store, which meant I had plenty of time to devote to our Jane Placide mystery. I did have some paperwork to attend to, so Hugo and I made our way downstairs to my office. Ignoring more pressing matters, I laid the NOPD's transcription out on my desk.

It was a bit overwhelming at first, but once I began focusing on one piece at a time, I found I was able to fill in a few blanks without much effort. The Grand T#### in A-2 must be Grand Terre, I figured, and the Gr#mes in B-1 had to be the lawyer John Randolph Grymes. I guessed that the missing character in sea# in A-1 was an exclamation point, in which case Lafitte was saying, "To the sea!" I looked up La Violette in my high school French-English dictionary, and unsurprisingly, it translates to The Violet, which didn't help me at all.

I'd spent most of the previous night skimming through books on Lafitte that I'd checked out from the library, and the more I read, the more improbable a romance between Jane Placide and Jean Lafitte seemed. Not only was there no evidence of Lafitte having been in New Orleans during the period in question, but there was also little in his history to suggest he was the type to form romantic attachments. I found vague references to his having had relations with slave women in Barataria and again at Campeche. And in between, there was a relationship of sorts with the sister of his brother Pierre's longtime companion, a mulatto woman in New Orleans, who bore him a son. But all in all, the historical record suggests he took a

CHAPTER SEVEN

mostly transactional approach to women.

And yet, it was hard to dispute Bo's conclusion that the writer of Source A, as well as the J in Source B, was indeed Lafitte. There was, as the lawyers like to say, a preponderance of evidence to substantiate the claim. The French phrases, the initials J-L-F, references to the sea and known associates Livingston and Grymes, not to mention the words *pirate* and *treasure* and *map*. All buttressed the case. Still, what if Source A was a forgery? Or if Jane had consorted with another pirate whose name happened to start with a J? I told myself not to be ridiculous, but still, you never know. It happened that I knew someone who could possibly procure a sample of Lafitte's handwriting. I owed her a visit anyway, so just to be safe, I called her up, and we scheduled an appointment for one o'clock. Then I buzzed Chris Keating and filled him in on recent developments.

"This is astonishing," Chris enthused. "The mere possibility that Lafitte might have been in New Orleans in the mid-1820s, in disguise or not, will be new fodder for historians. You've really stumbled on to something here, Bruneau."

"It looks that way, doesn't it?" I responded. "NOPD is jumping all over the treasure map angle. Does that seem right to you?"

"It fits the narrative that's always been out there, that Lafitte buried untold treasure," Chris said. "I don't know the extent to which that's based on actual historical information or just the assumption that because he was a pirate, he must have hidden his booty somewhere."

"Either way," he continued, "treasure hunters have been all over Grand Terre and the Barataria bayous forever and still are. Galveston too. There've been Spanish and French coins that have turned up here and there, but no mother lode of the type folks like to imagine."

"What about this La Violette," I asked, "any clue what that's all about?"

"None whatsoever, but please understand Bruneau, I'm no expert on Lafitte. I know some things about him because he was a bit player in a time and place I study, but I've never done extensive research into him."

"Understood," I said. "Any thoughts about who I might consult to learn more?"

"Yeah, I can put you in touch with some academics I know, but I doubt they'll tell you more than what you'll find in their writings," Chris said.

He paused, as if turning a thought over in his head, then continued.

"I hesitate to tell you this, but there's a weird old codger who lives in a shack down on Grand Isle. He claims to be descended from Lafitte and believes that any treasure that is found rightfully belongs to him. He's crazy as a loon, but if there is a legend about Lafitte out there, he's going to know about it."

"How did you learn about this fellow?" I asked.

"I met him one time when I went down there with a grad student who was doing a dissertation on the Battle of New Orleans and trying to retrace the approach of the British navy," Chris related.

"He didn't appreciate us poking around his homestead, but once we convinced him we weren't there to steal from him, he softened up. He's quite the eccentric, but I'm told the fringe elements of the Lafitteaholic crowd treat him like an oracle."

"What's his name?" I asked.

"Prosper Fortune."

"Prosper Fortune?" I laughed. "Is that the name his mama gave him?"

"I wouldn't know, but it does kind of fit, doesn't it?"

* * *

After hanging up with Chris, Hugo and I shuffled into the store to say hello to Victoria, who'd arrived fifteen minutes earlier and had just finished opening. We exchanged greetings, and then Victoria asked me to brief her on the history of a handsome George I walnut chest that had arrived earlier in the week. I was in the process of doing so when the door chimes jangled and in walked Phillip Boyer, sporting a pink striped broadcloth shirt and bright green bow tie, holding the door for Charlotte Duval.

Charlotte entered in typical grand dame fashion, dressed in a variation of her standard weekday uniform: white slacks, aqua silk button-down shirt, blue polka dot espadrilles, a paisley silk scarf, the usual adornment of

CHAPTER SEVEN

gold bracelets and hoop earrings, and a large opal medallion necklace. She uttered a throaty "Good morning, everyone," made a sweeping gesture with her arm and surveyed the room. Boyer slinked dutifully behind her.

"What new treasures have we to discover today in Abellard's Antiques?" Charlotte asked no one in particular.

"Greetings, Charlotte, and hello, Phillip," I said cheerfully. "I'd be happy to show you some new items we've gotten in. Can we get you coffee or tea first?"

"No, thank you, dear," Charlotte said. "I've already had my two cups."

Just then, Hugo shimmied up to Charlotte, shamelessly wagging his stub of a tail in expectation of the treat she would inevitably pull from her bag.

"Well, bonjour, Hugo! And how are you this morning, my dear? Hungry, I see. Does your master not feed you, poor thing?"

Out came the Milk-Bone biscuit on cue, which Hugo stood on his hind legs to accept. He carried his prize off to consume in private, swaggering for all the world like a fierce hunter who'd just felled his own prey.

I proceeded to show Charlotte our new chest and a few other items while Victoria set about tidying the shop. Charlotte acted interested, and Phillip asked a couple halfway intelligent questions, but both seemed distracted, and the talk soon turned to other matters.

"I shared your Jean Lafitte intrigue with Phillip, Bruneau," Charlotte announced. "He has an interesting perspective to share."

"I see," I answered. "Charlotte tells me you're a Lafitte aficionado, Phillip."

"Ah, well, that might be overstating the case a tad, old chap," Phillip said. Pseudo-anglophilia is but one of the man's annoying traits.

"But it is true that I have read up on our good Captain. Quite the Casanova, that one."

"Ah, so I take it you think Jane Placide was just another pelt on Lafitte's wall, is that it?"

"Precisely Bruneau," Boyer responded. "The simple fact is, his tastes ran in a somewhat darker direction, if you catch my meaning."

"I'm afraid I don't," I said. Actually, I did, but I wanted to hear him say it, the unctuous parasite.

"Ah, yes, well, here it is then," he said. "You see, both the Lafitte brothers preferred mixed-race women. Pierre maintained a twenty-year placage relationship with a free mulatto or quadroon woman named Marie Villard, who bore him six or seven children. And Jean …"

"Took up with Marie's sister Catherine for a short time; yes, I know," I interrupted. I shot Phillip a bored look to let him know I'd been doing some reading of my own.

"I say, well done, Bruneau!" Boyer exclaimed. "I told Charlotte this was probably old hat for you. I take it then that you know that Jean and Catherine had a son together?"

"Yes, they named him Jean Pierre," I said, trying to quash this thread before it took on a life of its own. "He succumbed to yellow fever in his teens. He was laid to rest in Girod Street, in fact."

"You see, Charlotte, I told you Bruneau would be way ahead of us," Boyer gushed.

"Yes, so you did," Charlotte said.

"Please explain to me," I said, "what Jean Lafitte's relationship with the mother of his son has to do with whatever relationship he may or may not have had with Jane Placide several years later."

"Probably nothing," Charlotte interjected. "The point is that he had many women, and he preferred them black. Any illusions your Jane had about being the special apple of Lafitte's eye, well, they were just that, illusions."

"Wait, let me get this straight," I said, incredulous despite myself. "We're supposed to jump from *Jean Lafitte sired a son with a woman who was partly African American*, to *therefore we know he preferred black women?* Based on a sample size of one?"

"Hah, touché Bruneau!" Boyer broke in. "But as I'm sure you know, there was another mulatto mistress at Campeche, and before Catherine Villard, there were others at Barataria, some of them slaves."

Then he added, with a conspiratorial wink, "bit of the old Sally Hemmings set up, eh old chap."

I was speechless. Fortunately, Charlotte jumped in before things got ugly.

"There is no need for tasteless humor, Phillip," she scolded. "I would hope

CHAPTER SEVEN

we've evolved past that sort of thing in this part of the world."

"Of course, Charlotte, you are absolutely correct," Phillip sniveled. "My apologies, Bruneau. I was merely trying to make a point and got a bit carried away. I hope I haven't burned any bridges."

"No burnt bridges," I said curtly, "although your point continues to elude me."

"Dearest Bruneau," Charlotte said, "the point is simply that the idea that Lafitte would have entrusted his treasure to this actress, who he could barely have known, if he knew her at all…well, it's simply preposterous. That's the point."

"Okay then, I will take your point under advisement. But who said anything about treasure? And anyway, it doesn't really matter what you or I think, does it? What matters is that someone, or more accurately a team of someones, went to great lengths to break into Jane Placide's casket, presumably because they thought it contained something of considerable value."

"Yes, I grant you that," Charlotte said. "But the likelihood is that they didn't find what they were looking for, which was probably based on some crackpot theory they saw on that horrid Twitter thing."

"Perhaps," I said, "but last time I checked, professional burglars weren't in the habit of taking their direction from social media."

"And last time I checked, they were not known to be nice people," Charlotte retorted. "I just don't want to see you get hurt, Bruneau."

"Don't worry, Charlotte, I'm a big boy. I can take care of myself."

***

After the scene with Charlotte and Boyer, I was happy to leave the store behind and head out to meet Sallie Mae Maguire. It had been a few months since we'd seen each other in person, and my internal clock told me I was past due for a check-in.

Sallie oversees the maps and manuscripts collections of the Louisiana Historical Center in the old U.S. Mint building on Esplanade. I had called her first thing in the morning to ask whether she could put her hands on a sample of Jean Lafitte's handwriting and gave her a brief rundown of what I was up to. She said she thought she could help and told me to swing by around one.

When I arrived for our appointment, Sallie was in her glass-enclosed office staring at her computer screen, her posture prim and erect as always. She saw me approaching and waved me in with a pleasant smile but did not get up or greet me with a hug or any other gesture that would indicate this was anything other than a business meeting.

I risked a bit more familiarity. "Hello, stranger. Good to see you. How you been?"

"Fine, thanks. You?" Pleasant, but not exactly perky, with only fleeting eye contact.

"Oh, well enough, I suppose," I replied, still taking the temperature of the room. "This Lafitte thing has me pretty jazzed up."

"Bruneau Abellard, jazzed up?" Sallie snorted. "What does that look like, I wonder? A few extra laps from the recliner to the refrigerator and back?"

"That's not nice, Sallie."

"No, I suppose not. Sorry."

To suggest that Sallie and I have a complicated relationship would, I'm afraid, rather understate the case. Sometimes, we are the brother and sister neither of us had growing up. We argue and harbor petty jealousies but share intimacies unknown to others and trust each other unconditionally. To this day, if the mood is right, we can make each other laugh like nobody else. But other times? Well, then we're like a bitter divorced couple who try to maintain a forced civility for the sake of the kids but who can't help sniping if given the slightest provocation. Could we be both these things? Spiteful exes and attached-at-the-hip siblings? I am never sure, but that's the way it feels.

Sallie and I first got to know each other when we started out as assistant curators at the Cabildo fifteen years ago. Sallie was the slender, strawberry-blonde daughter of second-generation Irish immigrants. She grew up in a working-class neighborhood in Chalmette, went on to obtain a master's in

CHAPTER SEVEN

library and information science from LSU, and started at the Cabildo soon after. She presented herself as a timid bookworm in those days, complete with cat glasses, 50s-style plaid skirts, and penny loafers plucked straight from central casting. She'd avoid eye contact, speak softly and infrequently, and generally transmit a clear if unspoken message: leave me alone. But if you took the time to chip away at the veneer, as I did, it was possible to earn Sallie's trust and get her to reveal more of herself. And once she let you in, you might be surprised to find a biting sense of humor, an endless supply of opinions, and I would soon discover, a hair trigger temper.

We were the same age, Sallie and I, with similar interests, little money, and nonexistent social lives. We fell into the habit of splitting a frugal lunch at Mother's or Café Maspero, and that led to an occasional movie night, or maybe a free chamber concert or theater production out at Tulane or Loyola. I don't think either of us were strongly attracted to the other in those days, but we ended up losing our virginity to one another, more out of mutual curiosity than romantic fervor.

That's when the awkwardness crept in. We'd established enough of a friendship by then that a one-night stand would have been out of the question. But it was also painfully apparent that there was little sexual spark between us, not that either of us had much of a basis of comparison to draw upon. So, we kind of plodded along in a relational no-man's-land, spending time together but never fully committing to coupledom, until one day, I initiated a ham-handed heart-to-heart. I tried to explain, as nicely as I could, how much I valued Sallie's friendship and always would, but that I didn't think we had a future as romantic partners. This was interpreted as, "If you think I'm ugly, why don't you just come out and say so." I didn't have a lot of experience when it came to navigating affairs of the heart, and I guess it showed.

Sallie was deeply hurt, that was clear, and I was stung by her reaction to what I considered to have been my exquisitely sensitive handling of the situation. A lengthy period ensued, during which our only contact was through the perfunctory communications that necessarily arose while carrying out our professional duties. Our little cold war didn't begin to thaw until our supervisor assigned us to a project together. We were charged with supporting the guest curator of an exhibit on Edward Livingston's attempts to draft criminal and civil codes for Louisiana in the early 1820s. This was long before I harbored any interest in Edward Livingston. Sallie and I found the topic hopelessly dry and were united in our contempt for our temporary boss, a retired judge whose lethargy was surpassed only by his boundless self-regard. His idea of running the show was to utter a few bromides, instruct us to do whatever we thought was best, and then put his name to our work product. The only thing that made the situation tolerable was the giggling fits we found ourselves collapsing into whenever we considered the absurdity of it all.

The months and years to come followed a similar pattern. We'd spend time together just hanging out, sharing meals, taking in cultural experiences, or maybe packing a picnic for a day trip somewhere. Then, inevitably, one or the other of us would say or do something to offend the other, and a chill would set in. A few weeks would go by, and then, just as surely, something would remind us of why we were friends in the first place, and we'd start seeing more of each other again. With time, the perceived slights and the convulsions that followed diminished, in part because when I left the Cabildo to open my shop, it created more breathing room for both of us. But while we don't see as much of each other as we once did, the joint undercurrents of affection and resentment persist. Now, it seemed, there was more of the latter than the former.

"It's been quite some time, Bruneau," Sallie said. "Looks like you've gained some more weight."

"How kind of you to notice," I said. "We haven't seen each other for a while, and now, what, I'm fat? If you must know, I've dropped a few pounds recently."

"And why haven't we seen each other, I wonder," she said. "Is it because you haven't needed anything from me, but now that you could use a favor, you figured why not call up your old friend Sallie and kill two birds with one stone?"

"Oh please," I answered, as if that was the most ridiculous statement

CHAPTER SEVEN

imaginable despite its undeniable truth.

"Give me a break, Sallie. I was in Savannah on a buying trip, and I've been super busy ever since I got back. I've been meaning to get in touch, and this was the reminder I needed, that's all."

"So now I'm just an occasional reminder on your calendar? I feel so honored."

"I'm not going to dignify that with a response," I sniffed.

"Fine, let's get on with this I've got a meeting at two thirty, and then I'm knocking off early to grab drinks with Jerry," Sallie said.

"Jerry?"

"Just someone I've been seeing a bit of," she dropped casually.

"Anyway, it turns out we have a few documents containing Lafitte's signature, but nothing more than that. Just loans, receipts, purchase orders, those sorts of things. Follow me. I have them laid out for you."

Sallie rose from her chair and walked briskly out of her office in a determined, confident gait, leaving behind a subtle whiff of what I guessed was orange blossom perfume. Maybe it was the mention of this Jerry character, but it had been a while since I'd taken a good look at Sallie. Gone were the cat glasses and loafers, the former long since replaced by contact lenses and the latter having given way to fashionable black pumps. She wore a pleated knee-length black skirt, a simple but elegant short-sleeved white satin V-neck, and a modest pearl necklace. Her hair was cut in a stylish bob that highlighted her squared chin, high cheekbones, and blue eyes. Pale pink lipstick and a light touch of blush completed what I had to admit was a becoming package.

"Here we go," she said as we came to a table where she'd laid out a half dozen documents encased in plastic sleeves, each with the Lafitte signature plain as day. Interestingly, all but one of the signatures contained two f's and one t, while the other had one f and two t's, which is the way I was used to seeing the name.

"Looks like your man wasn't sure how to spell his own name," Sallie said, pointing to the discrepancies.

"Yeah," I nodded.

I pulled out my phone to compare the writing on the "Source A" images Bo had sent me.

"What do you think?" I asked.

"I'm no expert," Sallie cautioned, leaning in close for a good look and brushing up against me, the orange scent unmistakable now. "But they certainly look like they could be from the same hand."

"Me neither, but I agree," I said. "Do you mind if I take photos of these?"

"No, that's fine. Just no flash, please."

After I took my pictures, I followed Sallie around as she put the documents away. Then we went back to her office, where I provided a more detailed summary of the Jane Placide mystery. She knew more about Lafitte and his era than I realized, including being familiar with Livingston's Associates, the group Chris had mentioned, as well as Padre Sedella's Spanish spying ring. She'd never heard of Jane Placide or James Caldwell.

"It's an interesting case, I'll grant you that," Sallie declared, looking right at me now, as if assessing whether I was up for the job I'd taken on.

"I know you've helped your friend Bo out a few times in the past, but don't you think this one might be a little above your weight class?"

"You mean there's a weight class above mine?"

Sallie smiled weakly, acknowledging the barb.

"I just mean, you could be getting in over your head here."

"You're not the first person to suggest that," I confessed. "All I'm doing is helping with some research. It's Bo's job to hunt down the thieves."

"It's your life; do with it what you will. I can spend some time with those transcriptions if you'd like. They're basically just puzzles if you think about it."

In her spare time, Sallie is an elite competitive puzzler. Not jigsaws, but cryptograms, logic puzzles, pattern guessing games, those sorts of things. She plays online but also travels to events, and she wins a lot more than she loses.

"I was hoping you'd say that." I smiled. "I'd really appreciate it. Will you have time this weekend, or do you and Jerry have a full slate planned?"

"I'm sure I can find some time," she flushed.

CHAPTER SEVEN

"Who is Jerry, anyway?"

"Jerry is an orthopedic nurse at Ochsner," Sallie said.

"How'd you meet?"

"We met online. Not that it's any of your business."

"I didn't realize you were doing the online dating thing."

"A girl gets bored sitting at home doing nothing, Bruneau. Even if you don't."

"Sorry, I didn't mean to get into an argument."

"I'm explaining, not arguing," Sallie rejoined, in a tone that told me this was the end of our discussion.

This had long been one of Sallie's chief complaints about me. That I sit around at home, eating and reading and not taking care of my body. She'd push me to be more active and switch up my routines and…well, I don't take well to prodding.

I got up to leave and Sallie escorted me out into the hall. I thanked her again and ventured a compliment.

"I meant to tell you Sallie, you look fantastic. I love the haircut."

"Thank you," she said, with a sincere smile this time. "It's nice of you to notice. Charlotte Duvall put me in touch with her hairdresser."

"Omar?"

"One and the same."

"I didn't realize you and Charlotte had gotten so tight," I said.

"We grab coffee from time to time."

"I see. Well, one of these days, I really must meet this Omar fellow. Does he do men?"

"He might, but probably not bald ones," Sallie said.

Chapter Eight

I had just gotten out of the shower when I heard Bruneau's sputtering old car pull up 10 minutes early. I peeked through the blinds and watched as his bulky frame squeezed out of the driver's side door. His bulldog, Hugo, jumped out at his feet and started yapping excitedly. Angie had taken to inviting Hugo to join us on these evenings, which was a big hit with the kids. And the dog, being no dummy, knew he was going to be well-fed.

After trying with little success to quiet Hugo, Bru walked to the back of the car, opened the trunk, and removed a canvas tote, no doubt containing his cocktail fixings, along with a shopping bag I recognized as coming from the high-end candy store Sucre, which meant Hugo wasn't the only one who'd be in for a treat.

As I was getting dressed, I could hear the usual greeting ritual unfold.

"Uncle Bru! Hi, Uncle Bru!" It was Monique's excited, high-pitched voice. "What did you bring us?"

"Sucre! Yessss!" Sophie and Bo shouted in unison.

"Macarons, chocolates, or both?" Sophie wanted to know.

"Now, now, patience, children," Bruneau said good-humoredly. "All will be revealed once your Uncle Bru has a chance to settle in."

"Welcome, Bruneau," Angie's smiling adult voice broke through the din, no doubt coming in for a hug. "All these gifts! You are too good to us."

"Hello, love," Bru said. "Look at you! You're more beautiful than ever! The orange becomes you, Miss Angeline."

"Why, thank you!" Angie answered. "Come on in. Let's get you squared

CHAPTER EIGHT

away."

Angie was wearing a sleeveless pastel orange cotton top over tight white jeans, and she did look damn hot, but then I'm a little biased that way.

"Wait, wait!" Monique shouted just as I entered the room. "You have to make your guess first, Uncle Bru."

The kids have a tradition wherein Uncle Bru cannot set foot in the kitchen without guessing what is for dinner. He likes to brag about his highly trained nose, and the kids get a huge kick out of how often he guesses right. More than once, I've accused Angie of tipping him off in advance, but she always denies it.

"Okay, kids, let's give Uncle Bru a break," I said, announcing my presence.

"No way, Dad, you know the rules," Bo said.

"Okay, okay, okay," Bruneau hushed the room. "Allow me to warm up the old schnozzola, that legendary proboscis renowned the world over for its feats of epicurean deduction."

Bru made a show of twitching, flaring, and generally contorting his nostrils, which never fails to send the kids into fits of laughter. He tilted his head back and sniffed the air. Meanwhile Hugo, performing his own sniffing exercises, had fastened his nose to my jeans and was looking up at me like he was skeptical of my credentials for admission to this gathering. Why didn't anyone else ever get this treatment?

"Hmm, wait, wait, wait, ah yes, there it is. I believe my olfactory sensory neurons have detected the microscopic molecules released from your mother's masterpiece in the making and are now stimulating my aroma receptors, which are sending complex messages to my brain," Bruneau said, warming to his performance.

"You're totally making that up," Monique accused him.

"No, no, he's actually not," Bo corrected his sister. "We studied this in biology class. Uncle Bru is right; that's actually the way it works."

"Like I've always said, Little Bo," Bruneau said, "you are both a gentleman and a scholar, and don't let anyone try to tell you otherwise."

"Uh huh, sure he is," Angie said. "Why Bruneau, if I didn't know better, I'd say you're trying to buy some time here. What is it exactly that those highly evolved olfactory receptors of yours are picking up on?"

"Patience, dear girl, patience," Bru said. "Such an excitable bunch, you Duplessises. Extra Olfactory Perception cannot be summoned by the flick of a switch. It must be activated gradually through a series of fine-tuning exercises. Does an Olympic athlete not stretch before running her race?"

"Come on, Uncle Bru, let's go!"

Monique had burned through her 10-year-old's supply of patience.

"Very well, very well," Bruneau said, finally giving in. "There is a nutty bouquet in the air, which suggests a blonde or possibly brown roux. There's seafood stock involved, for sure, and bay leaf. The fish is mild and slightly sweet smelling, which could be shrimp or scallops, but I'm thinking crawfish. There's some citrus in the mix as well, maybe to season rice. Yes, yes, it's coming into focus now. Ah, there, there it is. I've got it now! Ladies and gentlemen, it will be our great pleasure to dine on Crawfish Étouffé this evening."

"Bravo, Bruneau, you've done it again!" Angie laughed, clapping. "You are a miracle!"

"Uncle Bru! How do you do that?" Monique stamped her foot in exasperation, looking for all the world like her mother's mini-me.

Bruneau assumed his best Cheshire Cat, but didn't feel the need to say a word, which only added fuel to Monique's fire.

"Ugh!" she stomped off, hands on hips.

"Unbelievable," Little Bo muttered.

Sophie just grinned quietly, shook her head, and resumed her cross-legged position in the corner of the couch, where she'd been reading before Bru arrived. Hugo jumped up and curled into her lap.

"Alright, let's get this party started," I said, taking charge. "Bru, I've laid out all your fixings if you'd like to do the honors."

We were in the habit of starting these evenings with cocktails, usually Sazeracs, which Bruneau insists on mixing himself. His requirements are rigid. Elijah Craig Rye, Herbsaint, Peychaud, *and* Angostura bitters, sugar cubes rather than simple syrup, and orange peel rather than lemon. I'm not much of a cocktail guy, but I have to admit, his Sazeracs are excellent.

CHAPTER EIGHT

* * *

The drinks were great, and dinner was even better. Angie is an incredible cook, even when she's just throwing things together on a busy weeknight when she's dead tired from work. But she always makes a special effort for Bruneau, because she knows he'll notice the details. He declared the crawdads "world-class" and seemed to think the German wine he brought was a perfect match, spouting some pretentious nonsense about how "the racy acidity of the Riesling cuts through the creamy richness of the dish and refreshes the palate." I mean okay, whatever. Angie acted like she knew what he was talking about. I had my doubts. I drank a glass of the wine, which was fine, and then switched over to Miller Lite. Little Bo wolfed down his plate and went back for more. Sophie took her time but ate everything, while Monique, our picky one, mostly played with her bread and nibbled at some salad. They all went to town on the rainbow coalition of macarons Bru had bought, laughing when Hugo stole one for his own dessert, having already inhaled the hamburger Angie had prepared for his entrée.

Before they were excused from the table, each of the kids had to bring Bruneau up to speed on their lives, so we heard about Bo's braces, Monique's "so annoying" fifth grade teacher, and all the books Sophie read over the summer. Sophie and Bruneau got into a long discussion about *The Count of Monte Cristo,* which the other kids and I had never read, and Angie only vaguely remembered. Before they could get started on *To Kill a Mockingbird,* Angie mercifully sent the kids off to start on the dishes. I put one of my R&B playlists on low volume and then, leading us into the living room, Angie set her sights on our guest.

"Okay mister, your turn, tell us what's new in your world."

Angie was seated on the edge of our ottoman, elbow on her knee and hand under her chin, leaning in toward Bru, who was seated in a defensive posture on the couch. His body language told me he knew exactly where this was going.

"As you know, Angie," Bru replied, "I go to great lengths to keep my world old and familiar. There is no space in it for new."

"That's your problem!" Angie blurted, jabbing her finger at our guest. "How are you going to meet someone or experience the world if you don't step out and embrace it?"

Bru rolled his eyes, shot a pleading glance toward me, and gave one of his stock answers, which set Angie's head to shaking.

"Why must I meet someone?" he asked. "Life is complicated enough without someone else to worry about. Besides, I've got Hugo."

"What about Sallie Maguire?" Angie asked. "Seen her lately?"

"I saw Sallie earlier today," Bru said. "We're still good friends."

From the day she met him, Angie has been obsessed with Bru's love life, or his lack of one at any rate. She used to grill him endlessly and tried many times to set him up, but no dice. Between Bru's obvious discomfort and my complaints, she eventually got the message and backed off the long interrogations, but she'd still give it the old college try every now and then. When Bru leaves for home, I get the 20-question treatment. Was there anybody in his life? Did I think he was gay? Was he still a virgin? To which I'd answer no, no, and I wasn't sure, but maybe, there was that Sallie Maguire …

Personally, my take was that Bruneau was more asexual than anything and had other interests in his life he cared more about than sex and romance, but that at the end of the day it really wasn't my business, or Angie's. Sometimes that ended the discussion and sometimes it didn't.

"As for stepping out in the world and finding new experiences," Bru continued, "I count on your husband to provide me with those. Has Bo told you about our latest adventure?"

That was nicely played. Bru is an expert at wiggling out of uncomfortable conversations. Admiring his clever change of subject, I felt I had to lend a helping hand.

"Oh yeah, Ange, I haven't updated you on our grave robbing case," I said. "Turns out we're on the trail of Jean Lafitte!"

"Jean Lafitte? The pirate?" she asked, aware she was being played, but curious anyway. "What does he have to do with your actress?"

And with that, Bru was off the hook. We gave Angie the full rundown,

CHAPTER EIGHT

including our attempts to transcribe the scraps of writing left behind in Jane Placide's casket. Angie's B.S. detector was on high alert as I explained about the Electrostatic Detection Apparatus, but in the end, I think she was satisfied that I had at least a general idea as to what I was talking about.

Bruneau took advantage of the occasion to supply me with some new information. First, that he'd taken images of the handwriting in Source A to his old friend Sallie, who had located some samples of Lafitte's signature, and they appeared to match. He wanted me to check with an expert to be sure, but I told him I didn't think that was necessary. Then he told us about a recently published book he'd picked up that was getting some play among Lafitte fanatics. It's by a mother-daughter team from North Carolina and it makes a startling claim.

"They're amateur historians and don't pretend to be otherwise," Bruneau said, "but they make a convincing case that Lafitte returned to the U.S. from Cuba in the mid-1820s under an assumed name, Lorenzo Ferrer. Note the initials *L.F.* This Ferrer spent a decade or so moving around Mississippi, speculating in land and slaves, and then made his way to North Carolina, where he settled down and lived into his nineties."

"That seems kind of unlikely," I said. "What makes their case so convincing?"

"A few things, I think," Bruneau said. "They've turned up a variety of suggestive primary source material and there's a fractious meeting in North Carolina between Ferrer and a well-known Bonapartist ex-pat that they document, and some other stuff like that. And then, Ferrer was French, about the same age as Lafitte, and purportedly tall and dark, also like Lafitte.

"But for me, it's the way Ferrer never stayed in one place very long during his Mississippi years, consistent with the behavior of a wanted man. He engaged in commerce Lafitte understood well, namely slave trading. And then in North Carolina he apparently never worked but always had plenty of money."

"What about his girlfriend in New Orleans?" Angie wanted to know. "If this was true love, wouldn't he have come back for her?"

"Maybe he did," Bruneau said. "If our transcription is correct, he did ask her to go away with him and she was conflicted. Maybe she declined. He certainly couldn't stay in New Orleans, where he would have been widely recognized. Maybe he came back for clandestine visits, which would have been feasible enough if he was relatively nearby, in Mississippi.

"Or maybe it wasn't true love for him at all, and he was just stringing her along, as others have suggested to me. According to the book, Lorenzo Ferrer purchased an enslaved octoroon woman named Louisa around 1830 or so, who became his maid, longtime mistress, and possibly the mother of another son. He even gave her his last name, so that she went by Louisa Ferrer. Maybe Louisa was Lafitte's true love, not Jane, or maybe he loved them both."

"Octoroon?" Angie asked. "Help me out here."

"Oh, sorry," Bruneau replied, "meaning she was one eighth African American."

"In other words, one of her grandparents was black," I chimed in.

"Yes, possibly, or maybe two were mulatto or there was some other combination involved," Bruneau said.

"Right, got it," I said. "Just like a quadroon could have two black grandparents or one mulatto parent or four mulatto grandparents, or whatever."

"Precisely," Bru said.

"I must say gentlemen," Angie cut in with an amused look on her face, "I am impressed by your active imaginations. I usually think of police investigations as being about fingerprints and paper trails and witnesses, not as a high-flying game of historical fantasy football."

"Ha! That's my girl," I said. "See Bru, I've trained her well!"

"Indeed so," he said.

"Alright. Hypotheticals and kidding aside, what is the actual evidence telling you?" Angie asked.

"The problem is that we don't have much in the way of actual evidence, at least not in the way we usually think about evidence," I answered. "Our theory of the case, based on everything we do know, is that somebody paid this team of burglars to break into the crypt and retrieve what they believed

CHAPTER EIGHT

to be a map to Lafitte's treasure."

"If you're correct about that and the actress did have a map with her," Angie said, "the map would have been in no better condition than the scraps of paper left behind, right?"

"It's a great point Angie," Bruneau said. "If the map theory is correct, the likelihood is that the thieves didn't come away with anything usable."

"You say *if* the map theory is correct," Angie said, staring intently at Bru. "Do you have another theory?"

"No, not really, not yet anyway," Bru replied. "There are multiple references in our paper scraps to La Violette, which just means The Violet. It seems like it might be significant, but I have no idea why or how or even if it fits into the treasure map concept in any way. I don't know. I'm stumped, to be honest."

Angie crossed her arms, leaned back and looked us both over.

"What are your next steps, boys?"

I gave a stock response about revisiting the crime scene evidence and checking in with Rodiger to see if he'd gotten anywhere with his Interpol research. I was happy to let Bru work the historical angles, but it seemed like if we were going to catch a break, it would be through good old fashioned police work focused on the here and now. For his part, Bruneau told us about an eccentric Lafitte expert he wanted to visit on Grand Isle. That sounded kind of sketchy to me, but I told him to submit his mileage for reimbursement when he got back. Then we had a nightcap and some laughs and called it a night.

Chapter Nine

It's only 100 or so miles from New Orleans to Grand Isle but it takes a good two and half hours to get there as Highway One meanders its way through small towns and way stations set amid the desolate delta wetlands. There's a stark beauty to the landscape in this part of the world and driving through it is a distinctly solitary experience. There were occasional automobiles, but otherwise, it was just Liesel, Hugo, and me looking out over a vast network of sinuous waterways carving their way through swaying oyster grass. Seabirds dot the horizon, and aquatic life teems unseen below the water. To think it's all disappearing at a rate of something like 30 square miles a year is almost more than the human brain can fathom.

I'd been to Grand Isle once before, years ago, when Sallie dragged me down there for a day trip because she'd just finished reading Kate Chopin's *The Awakening,* some of which is set on the island. She wanted to see how it matched her imagination. I got the feeling she was kind of disappointed, although she didn't say that. Like Grand Terre, Grand Isle is a thin barrier island at the mouth of Barataria Bay, but about three times as long. The two islands are separated by a short straight called Barataria Pass that is maybe a half mile wide. Unlike Grand Terre, Grand Isle is inhabited and can be reached by car via a toll bridge that connects it to the mainland. There are a thousand or so residents, fishing folk mostly, who seemingly must evacuate and rebuild every other year, or whenever the next hurricane hits.

I wasn't sure what to expect with this Prosper Fortune character and realized the entire trip might prove a waste of time. Still, I figured there

CHAPTER NINE

was at least a decent chance he might have information useful to our investigation, and besides, I wanted to find out if Prosper was his birth name or a conceit he adopted to accentuate his treasure seeking avocation.

Chris remembered that Prosper lived "in the woods" on the north side of the island, facing the bay. He suggested I ask one of the locals for more specific directions. "Everyone knows Prosper," he told me.

Upon arriving, I decided to orient myself by driving the three miles or so to the state park on the island's eastern extremity. Along the way, uninterrupted beachfront lay to our right, facing the gulf, and to our left were retail establishments, houses, RV camps, and uninhabited marsh. Nowhere did I see anything resembling Chris' woods.

Before turning around to ask for directions at a gas station and convenience store we'd passed a mile or so back, I continued on into the park and pulled into the lot by the long fishing pier that juts into the gulf. I put Hugo on his leash, and together, we walked out to the end of the pier. I could just make out what looked like a squall beginning to form a few miles out and tried to envision one of Lafitte's schooners racing back to beat the storm. To the east I could see the ruins of Fort Livingston on the western end of Grand Terre. Named after none other than Edward Livingston, the fort was built for coastal defense in the 1850s, but was never fully completed, though it was occupied for a brief time by Confederate forces. Looking back across the island toward Barataria Bay, the elevated view offered by the pier presented a sweeping panorama of land and sea engaged in their perpetual struggle for supremacy. The pirates must have been acutely aware of this push and pull, as the changing wind and tides continuously altered available routes inland.

Eventually, Hugo and I made our way back to the car and the gas station we had passed. I filled up for the return trip and went inside to pay. The burly cashier with a ZZ Top beard gave me a long look when I asked him if he knew where Prosper lived.

"Prosper know you?" he finally asked.

"No," I admitted. "I'm doing some research on Jean Lafitte, and I've been told Prosper might be able to answer some questions I have."

"Uh huh, the usual," he said.

"A lot of folks come looking for Prosper with Lafitte questions?"

"I wouldn't say a lot, but if somebody's looking for him, that's usually the reason. Either that or it's social services checking up on him."

I introduced myself. The man told me his name was Joe.

"What's he like, Prosper?" I asked.

"Let's just say Prosper is a few cards short of a deck and leave it at that," Joe said.

"But he is an expert on Lafitte, right?"

"I wouldn't know," Joe shrugged. "Some folks seem to think so. Never put much stock in it myself."

"Is he friendly?" I asked.

"Depends on the day. Sometimes he's friendly enough, and sometimes he doesn't talk at all."

"I guess I'll take my chances now that I've driven all the way down here," I said.

"Suit yourself," Joe shrugged. Then he drew me an admirably detailed map with directions to Prosper's place.

"He might not be there, just so you know," he said, handing me the map. "He wanders around a lot with his metal detector, and he'll spend the day on Grand Terre whenever he can get one of the fishing boats to drop him off and pick him back up later in the day."

"What's he do over there, hunt for Lafitte's treasure?"

"Yeah, I think so," Joe said, "although you're never really sure with Prosper."

Joe's map took us back toward the state park but had me hang a left after a half mile or so. We stayed on that paved lane almost all the way to the bay, passing houses on our left and looking out at the marsh to our right. As the lane neared its end, I veered off on a dirt road that took us across the marsh, and then I turned right again on another dirt road, heading back south toward the gulf. And there, sure enough, after a couple hundred yards, stood an acre or so of trees and shrubs surrounded by marsh.

Pulling up beside these woods, I could clearly see the footpath that Joe said would lead to Prosper's home. A No Trespassing sign was posted on a

CHAPTER NINE

gum tree at the path's entrance, and an animal skull that I guessed was a deer rested at the base of the tree. It had been my intention to take Hugo with me, but now I was conflicted. If I did take him, he might not be welcome. But it was too hot to leave him in the car, unless I left the keys in the ignition and the AC running, which didn't seem like a good idea either. Finally, I let Hugo out and put his leash on, and we walked side by side into the small, forested copse, like two intrepid explorers entering a forbidding jungle.

We hadn't gone 20 yards when a fusty odor began to perfume the air. It was the rotten egg smell of decaying plant life you'd expect in a salt marsh, but with a feral muskiness mixed in. The stink got stronger as we walked on, and then the attack happened before either of us could process what was happening. A gray blur in my peripheral vision, a wild demonic scream, a cyclone of fur and saliva at my feet. Hugo screeched in terror and pain. Reflexively, I kicked at the shapeless mass as sharp claws ripped my torso and left a searing pain on my cheek. Just as quickly, the beast was off me, and Hugo had it by the hind leg and wouldn't let go as it thrashed this way and that, spinning around to slash at Hugo again.

A deep voice thundered close by, "No, Caliban! No!" Heavy footsteps rushed in, and a huge, gloved hand took the creature by the neck and pried its foot from Hugo's jaws. I got my first fleeting look at the animal, which was vaguely feline but way larger than a house cat, with long, shaggy hair and claws to match. A colossal human shape strode into the woods and tossed the struggling beast a good 10 feet into the brush. Hugo lay prone at my feet, panting and whimpering, his right ear dangling at the side of his head, above a deep gash on his shoulder. As I bent down to inspect and comfort him, I realized my pants and shirt were torn, I had a long scratch on my chest, and drops of blood were falling from my cheek.

"Follow me," the man said, walking past us. "We better get you two cleaned up."

Robotically, I scooped Hugo up and followed the giant, both of us trembling from the shock of the event. Hugo was breathing but otherwise limp, and his foggy eyes were only half open. In that moment, it occurred to me that I could lose him, and I began to seethe with fury.

"That your cat?" I shouted accusingly, trailing the behemoth I assumed was Prosper Fortune by about fifteen feet. I still hadn't seen his face. All that was visible was stringy gray shoulder-length hair under a shabby Greek fisherman's cap and a frame big enough to play offensive line for the Saints. He wore filthy denim overalls over a sweaty blue t-shirt and walked with a limp.

"He comes around from time to time," he said curtly, without turning around.

"You called him by name," I said. "You train him to attack visitors?"

"Trespassers. Can you not read?"

I offered no response, stifling my anger and following at a distance as the big man walked on. We had come into a small clearing with a fire pit, a picnic table, and a couple of crude benches. Set behind them was a tin-roofed plywood shack that resembled the fishing camps you see in the bayous, set up on stilts, with steps leading to a porch. The man climbed the steps with an exaggerated limp and motioned for me to follow as he disappeared inside without bothering to hold the screen door.

The pong of sweat, mildew, and kerosene was overwhelming, as Hugo and I entered the dark one-room cabin. Our host was pouring bottled water into a small pot he'd set on a Coleman stove and motioned for me to sit on one of the two chairs he'd set at his dining table. His profile revealed a protruding lower jaw and brow, an enlarged nose, and noticeably thick lips. When he turned toward me, I was confronted by the pock-marked scars left behind by what must have been a frightful bout of teenage acne. All in all, it was not a welcoming visage.

"You're Prosper Fortune, right?"

"He get you anywhere besides your face?" the man asked calmly, ignoring my question.

I showed him my chest and smaller scratches on my thigh and shin.

"I'll be fine," I said. "I'm worried about my dog."

"What's his name?"

"Hugo."

"Ah, as in Victor. Here, let me see. And, yeah, I'm Prosper."

CHAPTER NINE

The huge man gently lifted Hugo from my arms and set him down on the makeshift cot that served as his bed. He looked him over closely and then pulled a large first aid kit from underneath his sink. He took out a bottle of iodine and poured it into Hugo's shoulder wound and all around the base of his ear, which caused Hugo to squeal meekly in what little protest he could muster. Then he offered the bottle to me, along with some gauze.

"Here, you could use some of this too," he said. "Hugo's gonna be sore for a few days, but he'll be okay. Still got some fight in him. He broke Caliban's foot clear through, you know. I'll probably have to amputate it."

As I ministered to myself, trying to decide whether to place stock in the big man's diagnosis, I took a not very guilty pleasure in the image of the wildcat hopping around on three legs. Meanwhile, Prosper Fortune took a long needle from his kit and sterilized it in the now boiling water. Then, he wrapped a large bundle of dried herbs in cheesecloth and added it to the water.

Moving back to Hugo, he began tying what looked like a thin fishing line to his needle, and it dawned on me what he was about to do.

"Whoa, do you know what you're doing there?" I asked, alarmed. "I can take him to a vet."

"Closest one is all the way up in Houma," he said. "Don't worry, I know what I'm doing. Why don't you come over here and see if you can keep Hugo calm."

As I held Hugo still, Prosper spoke gently while carefully reattaching Hugo's ear with a surprisingly professional looking set of stitches. Hugo yelped and stirred a couple times but lacked the strength to put up much resistance.

"You're lucky, you know."

"Me?"

"Yeah, you. Another second or two, and Caliban might have ripped your throat open. You got this brave little fella to thank," Prosper said, smiling kindly down at Hugo.

"I saw the whole thing. Hugo was hurt pretty good, but he jumped up off his hind legs and pulled Caliban off you and then took some more punishment for his trouble, but he wouldn't let go no matter what."

"It all happened so fast," I said, tearing up despite my determination not to.

"Here, take this," he said, offering a filthy dish towel. "That's the shock wearing off. Perfectly normal."

"How come you know so much about medicine?" I sniffed.

"Practiced it, in another life," Prosper said.

"When you were someone other than Prosper Fortune?"

He paused to grab a pair of tweezers and remove a cat claw from Hugo's lip. Then he retrieved the herb bundle from the pot and placed it atop Hugo's shoulder wound, pressing down gently.

"This may help with the healing," he said.

"Are you avoiding my question?" I asked.

He looked at me directly. "Before I answer, maybe you can explain why you're here."

I told Prosper a bit about myself and gave him an abridged version of our grave-robbing story, leaving out key details such as the burglars' footprints, a possible romantic connection between Jane Placide and Jean Lafitte, and the specifics of our transcription beyond identifying Lafitte as the author of Source A.

"Well, that's the most interesting story anybody has brought me in a while," he said. "I've never heard of your actress. Given the dates involved, I'd say it's highly unlikely that she and Lafitte ever crossed paths. Do you have a working theory?"

"Perhaps," I answered, "but before I reveal any more, I'd like a better understanding of who I'm talking to."

"I'd say the story of a New Orleans antiques dealer and his city dog mixing it up with a feral cat in the wilds of coastal Louisiana is a lot more interesting than anything I've got to tell you."

I smiled faintly but maintained my focus.

"Somehow, I doubt it," I said. "But you still haven't answered my question. Were you born Prosper Fortune?"

Another silence. Then, an answer.

CHAPTER NINE

"No, I wasn't always Prosper Fortune," he said. The inflection in his voice led me to believe he'd arrived at an internal decision to come clean with me, something I gathered he wasn't in the habit of doing.

"My birth name is Andre Coulon. I grew up in New Orleans. Went to parochial school and was even an altar boy for a while, hard as that may be to believe. Graduated from Loyola in '64 and went through med school at LSU. Then I enlisted as a medic in the Special Forces and went to Vietnam."

"You must have seen a lot of suffering," I ventured. I did some quick mental math and figured that he must be in his mid to late 70s, a good deal older than his vitality would suggest.

"You could say that," he said flatly. "I was with Fifth Group. Most of our missions had us disrupting enemy supply lines along the Ho Chi Minh Trail. Lost a lot of good men. But that was nothing compared to when we got sent to Laos without our dog tags as part of Operation Tailwind. Four straight days of non-stop incoming. It was a bloodbath. Lost my lower leg to a rocket-propelled grenade, but that was getting off easy in the scheme of things."

Prosper pulled up his left pant leg to show me the prosthetic it had concealed.

"What was it like coming home after that?"

"The things we saw. The things we did," he said, gazing out the window. "Everything we thought we knew had been turned on its head. Our friends and family wanted us to be the same people they used to know. But those people didn't exist anymore. Couldn't exist.

"For me, it just got to the point where I felt like I couldn't breathe, and I had to get away. So, I ran. And ran and ran. Out west, to Canada for a while, Texas, and eventually here."

"Why here?" I kept on. "And why Prosper Fortune?"

"I wanted to be left alone," he replied. "I'd been to the island a couple times as a kid, when my dad chartered a fishing boat for us, and it seemed like the kind of place where I could kind of disappear. I rented a room in town for a few months until I found this patch of land and eventually turned it into my home."

"Do you own the land?"

"No, it's owned by Jefferson Parish, I think, but they don't have any use for it, and no one's ever hassled me about it."

"What about money?" I asked. "How do you pay for food and supplies?"

"By collecting Andre Coulon's pension. It's more than I need."

"You know, you have a reputation for being a bit of a wingnut, if I may be so bold," I said. "But you don't strike me as the least bit crazy. Is it all an act?"

A faint smile crossed Prosper's lips. I could see him debating his answer as he stroked Hugo.

"I must be crazy to live how I do, wouldn't you say?"

"That wasn't what I meant."

"If what you're asking is, do I sometimes ham it up a bit to keep people at arm's length, well sure, yeah, I guess I do," he admitted. "Am I rational? I'd like to think so, but I may not be the best judge of that."

"Okay then. So why Prosper Fortune, and what about Jean Lafitte and his treasure? Is all that just an elaborate cover you invented to embroider your act?"

"No," he said quickly and then paused. "Or no and yes, might be a more honest way to answer. I can trace my ancestry back to Coralie Lafitte Roup, who was the daughter of Pierre Lafitte and his long-time mistress, Marie Villard. I figure Pierre's descendants have as much right to any treasure as Jean's do, right? Whether a claim like that could ever hold up in court, I have no idea. Probably not."

"So why all the time spent looking for treasure?"

"You mean when people see me out with my metal detector?" he smiled. "I do find some cool stuff from time to time, especially on Grand Terre. Take a look over here."

Prosper walked me over to a plastic tub on the other side of the room that contained an assortment of artifacts, including a few old coins that could have been left behind by the Barataria pirates, as well as a spear head and shards of pottery that Prosper thought probably belonged to the Chitimacha tribe or their ancestors, possibly thousands of years ago. There was also a

CHAPTER NINE

piece of metal with letters on it spelling ORIZO, which he believed came from the Horizon oil rig.

"So, you just like collecting found objects. Is that about the size of it?" I asked.

"More or less, although to your earlier suggestion, my wanderings don't hurt my cover as the obsessed Lafitte treasure hunter," he said with a wry grin.

"And you adopted the name Prosper Fortune because it's an apt name for a treasure hunter?"

"That and…well…these woods are my island, you know, and *misery acquaints a man with strange bedfellows,* so I thought it would fit."

"Ah, of course, *The Tempest,*" I smiled. "That explains your cat's name, *the born devil on whose nature nurture can never stick.*"

"The man quotes Shakespeare!" Prosper applauded with a wide grin. "I am not often honored with such erudition in my houseguests. Although I doubt Caliban thinks of himself as belonging to anyone, so the analogy breaks down a bit."

I asked Prosper, or Andre, how he became so knowledgeable about the Lafittes. He explained that before he came to Grand Isle, he had lived in Galveston for a stretch. He read some of the local history, knew he had some Lafitte blood in him, and became intrigued with the legends surrounding the pirates. He kept researching, and before long, he could pass himself off as an expert. Whenever he didn't have facts at his disposal, he learned to substitute imagination.

Having established some degree of trust with Prosper and relaxing a bit as Hugo's eyes cleared and his breathing normalized, I decided to press my mission.

"Here's the big question," I announced. "Based on what I've told you and what you know about the Lafittes, how big could the Lafitte treasure be, and where do you think it could be located?"

"There's really no way of knowing," Prosper replied, walking over to his kitchen area. He continued talking while busying himself with something I couldn't see.

"I think there are misconceptions about whatever treasure there could be. First off, if there is treasure to be found, I doubt it's in Barataria. The navy wiped the brothers out. If they had hidden anything, they would have come back for it, but instead, they spent the better part of a year petitioning the U.S. government for restitution."

"You think Galveston might be the better bet?"

"Maybe, but they were only there a couple years and their operation at Campeche never got as big as it had been here. And after the hurricane, they took to the seas, acting much more like desperate men in search of new riches than successful businessmen who could turn to their nest egg to fund their next enterprise."

"Okay, I follow your logic," I said. "So where, then?"

"Maybe nowhere. But if I was going to dig deeper into anything, it would be the Arkansas River expedition."

I remembered vaguely that Jean Lafitte and Arsènne Latour had embarked on a surveying expedition up the Arkansas and that in the process they'd gathered intelligence for Spain regarding the filibustering efforts of French ex-pats and others trying to establish settlements in what was nominally Spanish territory.

"How come?" I asked simply.

"Two reasons," Prosper said. "For one, there was gold and silver prospecting going on along their route, and they apparently stopped for a few weeks near Pine Bluff to try their hand. Maybe they found a large deposit and drew a map so they could come back for it with the proper equipment.

"Also, according to Latour's journals, a bit further along on their journey, they traded with some natives who told them about large ore fields near the Caddo River. They were never able to go there because they were attacked by a different party of Indians and had to retreat to where they came from. But maybe Latour made a map with the intention of coming back. I doubt it, but it's possible."

"Okay, so gold is one reason to look into the Arkansas expedition. What's the other?"

CHAPTER NINE

"There were a handful of French expat settlements trying to establish themselves in the general area they traveled through, some of which had been funded by Joseph Bonaparte. Do you know about Bonaparte and the filibusters?"

"Yes, I'm somewhat familiar."

"Then you probably know that Lafitte and Latour had gone north together a year or so earlier to D.C. and Philadelphia. It's not clear that they met with Bonaparte himself, although they could have, but they talked to people in his circle. Bonaparte, at that time, was the equivalent of the robber barons a half-century later, just filthy rich. So, one theory would be that if they performed a service of some kind for Bonaparte, perhaps to bolster the filibusters in some way, there could have been a significant reward involved."

I made a show of raising my eyebrows.

"I know it's pretty far-fetched, but you did ask," Prosper smiled. "As I said earlier, the most likely explanation is that this is just a wild goose chase, and your actress and Lafitte didn't even know each other, or if they did, there wasn't any treasure involved."

Prosper returned from the kitchen area with two plates, each with some Ritz crackers and a small bowl of what looked like a dip of some kind.

"Here, you look like you could use some nourishment," he said.

"What is this?" I asked, taking the plate he offered.

"Have a taste and see if you can figure it out."

Doing as directed, I took a cracker and scooped up a bit of the dip. A quick sniff revealed smoked fish of some kind, which is not really my thing. Cautiously, I took a taste and was greeted with a surprisingly pleasing flavor profile.

"Tastes like smoked fish," I said, "with some creole spices and horseradish, I think. There's something else in there that I can't quite place. It's delicious."

"Thank you," Prosper smiled. "I don't often cook for others, but I manage to eat pretty well out here. You're right. It's smoked snapper with a spice blend and some horseradish. I also add a little dried seaweed and the broth from caramelized onions."

"Interesting. Just the liquid, but not the onions themselves?"

"No, I have other uses for those. I find the liquid adds a depth of flavor and a bit of sweetness I can't get any other way."

"I'll have to try this myself when I get home," I said.

We spent another hour or so discussing Lafitte, which gave the herbal salve Prosper had applied to Hugo time to do its thing. I asked Prosper if the term La Violette meant anything to him, and he said it didn't. He was aware of the book written by the mother-daughter team and allowed that the Lorenzo Ferrer angle might have merit. He also knew all about Edward Livingston and The Associates and agreed that Lafitte could have come into possession of something of value through his connections to them. In the end, we both concluded this was all idle speculation.

Moving on from Lafitte, I asked Prosper if he ever thought about re-entering society.

"Sure, I've thought about it," he said, "but as odd as it may seem to others, I'm comfortable here. Life is simple, and nobody bothers me except the occasional heedless trespasser."

I smiled to let him know his friendly jab had found its mark.

"I'm sure it's not lost on you that Prospero does end up leaving his island," I said.

"I'm aware of that," Prosper said, smiling ruefully. "Just because I named myself and Caliban after a couple characters in a play doesn't mean I'm living according to some scripted plot."

"No, I guess not."

Realizing that time had gotten away from me, I asked Prosper if there was a way I could get in touch with him if questions arose that I thought he might be able to help with. He gave me a P.O. Box that he said he checked every now and again, and I gave him my contact information as well.

As I got up to go, I saw that it had darkened outside. The temperature had fallen, and a strong breeze was beginning to blow, unmistakable signs that the squall I'd seen forming earlier was almost upon us. I carried Hugo to my car, cradled in my arms, with Prosper escorting us as security against another ambush from Caliban. Prosper asked that I not blow his cover with the locals or among the Lafitte fanatic crowd and suggested that both Hugo

CHAPTER NINE

and I procure antibiotics to guard against infection. We parted in what felt like friendship.

As we closed the doors to the car, thunder exploded above us, and the skies opened. Hugo whined softly and, trembling, gingerly rolled himself into a ball on the passenger seat. Squinting through the furious torrent streaking down the driver's window, I saw a furry gray form emerge from a stand of ferns, dragging a leg behind it as it followed Prosper into his landlocked island. I could just make out the giant man opening wide his massive arms and turning his face up to the tempest. As he faded from view, I thought I heard him shout, laughing, "Our revels now are ended…"

1835

THE LAW OFFICES OF JOHN RANDOLPH GRYMES
NEW ORLEANS, LOUISIANA
MAY 1835

When his office clock chimes, the attorney John Randolph Grymes looks up from his papers to see that it is now six o'clock and realizes he has been sitting for more than three hours. Where does the time go, he wonders not for the first time? He places his pen in its well, reclines for a moment, feeling older than his 49 years, then rises stiffly from his desk. He strolls to one of the floor-length windows behind him and peers through the drapes to see that it is still light out, though the sun has begun to recede. There are a few wagons and deliverymen moving about on Royal Street below him, but otherwise the latest outbreak of the fever has kept people at home. Who could have imagined he would so miss the clamor of hoof beats, hawkers, and pedestrians he is accustomed to hearing at this hour?

Deciding finally that soft lamp light will best suit the business he must presently discharge, he closes the drapes, slips on his frock coat, and begins to pace the room, hands clasped behind his back. The task he must perform is simple enough, yet he feels strangely uncomfortable. When Livingston left for France two years prior, he briefed his partner on this and other matters he had agreed to handle in the great man's absence, but now he feels under informed, with little documentation to fall back upon.

All he knows is that the actress came to Livingston a few years ago with one simple, confidential request: that in the event of her death, the small lockbox now sitting in his office safe be placed in her coffin. It is the condition attached to the request that gives Grymes pause. Under no circumstance is the box to pass into the possession of anyone other than Livingston or his designated agent. Most particularly, that includes the man with whom Grymes is about to meet, James Henry Caldwell, the flamboyant impresario who brought English language theatre to the city, and who lately had formed the promising New Orleans Gas Light and Banking Company.

There is a soft knock on the door, which swings open to reveal Grymes' apprentice, Simon.

"Mr. Caldwell, sir," Simon announces.

A tall, clean-shaven man not much younger than Grymes enters the room with long confident strides and a somber expression. He is dressed in a charcoal coat, a lighter gray waistcoat, and a ruffled white shirt with a high stand collar brushing against his jaw. He holds a cane with an Ivory handle at his side.

"Ah, Caldwell, good of you to come," Grymes greets his guest. "Please, have a seat. May I pour you a brandy?"

"No thank you John, I have much left to do this evening," Caldwell answers, taking his seat in the red bergère chair offered to him. "What is this about?"

"Of course, the show must go on," Grymes says. "I understand. Before we begin, allow me to offer my condolences, James. Miss Placide was a sublime actress and an irreplaceable asset to our great city."

"Thank you, John. That she was."

Grymes shifts in his seat opposite Caldwell and forces himself to get down to business.

"The reason I asked you here, James," Grymes begins, "is that I thought you should know now, rather than finding out later, that Miss Placide made an arrangement with our mutual friend Mister Livingston, regarding her interment."

"I see," Caldwell replies warily. "What sort of arrangement do you mean? I am the executor of her estate and have her last will and testament in my possession."

"Yes, yes, of course, that is understood," Grymes assures him. "It is just that Miss Placide had one very specific request, you see. There is a box that she entrusted to Edward some time ago for safekeeping, and she asked that it be placed with her, inside her coffin."

"A box? What sort of box? I know of no box."

"Just a small box," Grymes says, forming a small square with his hands. "It is locked. Neither Edward nor I know the nature of its contents, nor were we given a key. Edward, and now by extension myself as his agent, was simply charged with ensuring that the box made it into Miss Placide's coffin. I can show you the papers if you'd like."

There is an awkward silence as Caldwell leans forward and takes the measure of his host.

"It's the pirate," he mutters finally.

"The pirate?"

"Yes, the pirate Jean Lafitte," Caldwell spits out. "I believe you represented him, did you not?"

"Yes, Edward and I did represent Captain Lafitte and his brother in their restitution case against the government, that is true," Grymes allows. "I also prosecuted them."

"Right, so you did," Caldwell nods. He pauses, assessing his audience.

"Jane was possessed of a romantic notion that she and her dashing corsair were star crossed lovers who would meet again in the next life. It was ridiculous of course, but I could not dissuade her."

"I see," Grymes says. "I cannot imagine how they would even know each other."

"They met once about ten years ago when the pirate was in town to conduct some clandestine business or other," Caldwell relates. "It was at the after party for the premiere of Taming of the Shrew. I remember it well. She was all starry eyed afterwards, spewing nonsense about Captain Lafitte this and Captain Lafitte that."

"But one meeting some years ago?" Grymes prods quizzically. "Surely that is no foundation upon which to plan for the afterlife."

"No, one would not think so," Caldwell says grimly. "But there were other visits. He came in disguise, I think."

Caldwell pauses again before continuing.

"As you know John, I brought Jane here as a young woman, and in keeping with her parents' wishes I watched over her as if she were my own daughter. I managed her career, made sure she was afforded all the comforts she could have asked for.

You must understand, one develops affections under circumstances such as these. To have her taunt me with this Jean Lafitte fantasy these last several years, well ... it hurt quite a lot, I don't mind admitting."

"I feel for you, my friend," Grymes offers consolingly, then adds dryly, "as one father to another."

"In any case," Caldwell moves on, "this won't be a problem, John. If you'll give me the box, I'll see to it that Jane's wishes are honored."

"I'm afraid that won't be possible, James," Grymes replies. "You see, Miss Placide specified that Edward, or in this case me as his agent, personally place the box in the coffin and stay in its presence until it is interred. Her instructions are very clear on this point."

Caldwell considers this latest piece of information.

"Suit yourself, it is of no concern to me," he says curtly, rising now from his chair. "I will see you at the service, I suppose. In the meantime, I must be going."

"Of course," Grymes answers cordially, beating Caldwell to the door and leaning into the waiting room outside. "Simon, please show Mister Caldwell out. Good night, James, and good luck to you."

No reply is offered as Caldwell strides angrily away.

The attorney pours himself a brandy and returns to his chair.

"Well, well," he muses to himself. "The irrepressible Captain Lafitte sails once more."

Chapter Ten

On the drive back from Grand Isle, I had to pull over and let it all out. I'd been okay for a while, but when I replayed Caliban's attack in my head and looked over at Hugo, all cut up and bruised, I just lost it. There I was, a grown man parked on the side of the road in the middle of nowhere, convulsed in tears of gratitude. I know dogs don't think like humans, and it's a mistake to project our feelings onto them, but we call them man's best friend for a reason. I'm sure the scientists would say it was just Hugo's fight instinct that saved my bacon, but I choose to believe it was something more. We're a pack of two, he and I, and we look out for one another.

I thought too about Prosper Fortune. I wondered why he had opened up to me the way he had when he was so guarded with others. Did he feel guilty because of what happened to us? Did Hugo's underdog valor trigger some vestige of foxhole fellowship from his Vietnam past? Was it something about our Lafitte story that reeled him in? Our Shakespeare connection? I had no way of knowing but came away with the feeling that there would be more to our story than had yet been written.

I phoned my doctor, who agreed to call in the antibiotics Prosper had recommended, but Hugo's vet insisted on seeing him in person. She conducted a thorough examination, complimented Prosper's needlework, and expressed confidence that Hugo would retain his ear. She prescribed some meds, re-bandaged Hugo's shoulder, and gave us an Elizabethan collar for Hugo to wear for a few days. It was an indignity to which he did not take kindly.

CHAPTER TEN

When we finally got home, it was past dinner time, and we were both spent. I fed Hugo and scrambled myself some eggs and then went to bed, though not before taking some time to inventory my wounds. I guessed the three-inch scar on my face was going to last a few months at least, but everything else seemed manageable.

We slept a bit later than normal, by mutual consent. After rising, I took Hugo out to do his business. We had just returned and were getting ready for breakfast when the doorbell rang. I peered out my upstairs window and could see Sallie Maguire waiting on the stoop below, dressed in a tan linen pantsuit and light blue mock turtleneck, holding a folder. When I opened the door to let her in, she looked up at me and let out a startled gasp.

"Oh my god!" she shrieked, covering her mouth with her hands. "What happened to your face? Are you okay?"

I did my best to assure her that I was fine and may have had her halfway persuaded when Hugo appeared on the landing above us. All it took was one glimpse of him in his collar and bandages for Sallie to break into full-scale hysteria.

"Oh no, Hugo! Poor baby, what did he drag you into?"

She vaulted the steps to the landing and crouched down to hug Hugo, but his collar confounded all her attempts. Then she turned to me.

"What happened?"

"It was nothing, really," I said unconvincingly. "We got jumped by a wildcat down on Grand Isle, that's all."

"Oh, is that all?" she said. I could feel the snark coming on strong.

"Just a wildcat? Thank goodness. I thought it might have been something serious. And where on Grand Isle does one encounter a wildcat?"

"In the small wood where Prosper Fortune lives," I said, heat rising in my cheeks.

"And Prosper Fortune would be?"

"An expert on the Lafitte brothers, who we went to see."

Sallie stared at me dumbfounded.

"This is you playing at detective again, isn't it?" she snapped accusingly, rubbing Hugo's back as if to protect him from me. "If you insist on involving yourself in situations you are ill-equipped to handle, the least you can do is not drag your innocent dog into harm's way with you."

"Hugo acquitted himself most honorably," I assured her. Hugo barked once, as if in affirmation.

"Ugh, men!" Sallie muttered in exasperation.

Standing up, Sallie waved the papers she'd brought with her.

"Against my better judgment, I think I've solved your transcription gaps," she announced. "But before we get into that I want the full story of what happened at Grand Isle. And I'll take a croissant with my coffee, thank you very much."

With that, she huffed upstairs, leaving Hugo and me to exchange bewildered shrugs.

I had just gotten to the top of the stairs and was heading into the kitchen to get Sallie her coffee when the doorbell rang again. I went back down and opened the door. It was Bo.

"What the hell?"

"Yeah, yeah, I know," I sighed. "Just a little nick or two."

"Bru, what did you do?" Bo asked, concerned but also suppressing a smile.

"Why don't you come upstairs, and I'll tell you all about it," I said. "You're not my only guest this morning."

Bo followed me up the stairs, where Hugo awaited us.

"Not the dog, too! Damn it, Bru!"

Hugo emitted the low growl with which he habitually greets Bo, although the collar frustrated his attempts to carry out his usual sniffing ritual. We entered the salon, where Sallie sat on one side of my settee, her shoes kicked off and her legs tucked beneath her. I'm not sure Bo recognized her at first.

"Bo, you remember my friend Sallie Maguire?" I prompted him.

"Yes, of course," he recovered. "Hello, Sallie, it's good to see you again. It's been a while."

"Sallie, you remember Bo?"

"Detective," she nodded coolly.

"Bo, I was about to get Sallie some coffee and a croissant. Would you like something?" I offered.

CHAPTER TEN

"No thanks," Bo said. "It took my stomach a week to recover from that rocket fuel you served me the last time I was here."

As I disappeared into the kitchen and busied myself with preparing Sallie's croissant, I could hear a low murmur of conversation in the salon. I couldn't make out the words, but I could tell that Sallie was doing most of the talking. Sallie and Bo had met a few times but did not know each other well, though Angie had engineered a double date at Rock'n'Bowl some years back. As I remember it, Sallie and Angie bonded, and Bo and I ended up hanging out by ourselves most of the night.

The room went quiet when I re-entered, but the look of consternation on Sallie's face and Bo's averted gaze made it clear they had not been making friendly small talk. Bo spoke up sheepishly.

"Bruneau, Sallie just let me have it for allowing you to put yourself in danger, and she's right," he said. "Going forward we're going to have to have some ground rules about what you can and can't do when you're helping me. You are not a trained police officer. I am. I appreciate what you do, but you need to respect the difference."

"I'm not a child, despite what you two might think," I said. "It's not like we went charging into a den of thieves. Just had a little bad luck, that's all."

A stony silence from both of them.

"Okay, okay," I relented. "No more free-lancing adventures. There. Satisfied?"

Receiving no answer, I proceeded to recount our Grand Isle adventure, stressing Prosper's sanity and downplaying his unsavory physical appearance and living conditions. Sallie was having none of it.

"This 'house' in the middle of the woods, how many rooms does it have?"

"Um, one, I guess, technically."

"You guess? Technically?"

"Yes, it's a one-room house," I said.

"I see, so maybe not really a house at all?" she persisted. "More of a shack, would you say?"

"Some people might call it that."

"Some people. But not you. And does this house have running water or electricity?"

"Um, no, it's kind of rustic," I said, looking to Bo for help, but he just grinned at me, clearly enjoying his front-row seat to the interrogation.

"Ah, rustic, of course, I can see that. And what does this rustic house smell like, I wonder?"

At this point, Bo shook in silent laughter, and I knew I had to give up the goose.

"A bit earthy," I said, smiling. "Yes, I'd say it has a complex earthy bouquet."

Sallie rolled her eyes and shook her head in mock disgust, but I could tell she was relishing her power trip.

"And this Prosper Fortune," she pressed on, "you say he's a large, well-educated man, a former Vietnam medic and Shakespeare nut, who lives alone in his quaint house in the woods with his feral cat Caliban, is that right?"

"Yes, that's correct," I said.

"But his real name is Andre Coulon, and he moved around from place to place before setting up house on public land in Grand Isle?"

"Yes."

"I see," Sallie paused, weighing where to go next. "And now you think of him as a friend."

"Of sorts."

"What do the island's residents have to say about your friend Prosper?"

"I only talked to one of them, but he indicated they view him as kind of a harmless curiosity," I said.

"Uh-huh. And how would you describe this harmless curiosity's physical appearance, other than his being a rather large man?"

"He has enlarged facial features and a pock-marked complexion," I said. "I think he probably had acne as a kid."

"Is he well groomed?"

"Um, no, not exactly. Look, where are you going with this, Sallie?" I demanded, hoping to change the subject.

"Where I'm going," she said in her most annoyingly condescending voice, "is that your new pal sounds like a grotesquery straight out of a Flannery

CHAPTER TEN

O'Connor novel, is probably a fugitive from justice, and a very dangerous man at that."

"Oh, come on," I objected strongly, "you're being ridiculous."

Sallie turned to Bo. "Detective, what do you think?"

"Um," Bo hemmed, clearly not wanting to enter the fray. "To be honest, Sallie, I'd say you're getting ahead of yourself a bit. There's no evidence Prosper Fortune is dangerous."

"No evidence?" Sallie mused. I could tell her mind was racing.

"Okay, I guess I can see that," she said. "May I submit Bruneau's testimony as evidence, your honor?"

"Certainly," Bo said, shifting uneasily.

"Alright then," Sallie began. "Allow me to reframe Bruneau's characterization of his visit to Prosper Fortune, using the evidence gathered to date."

Bo and I exchanged sideways glances, neither of us comfortable with where this was headed.

"To summarize, an overweight, out of shape, unarmed antiques dealer and his small dog, neither of whom are trained in self-defense, travel to a remote island to do the work the police department is too lazy to carry out for itself."

Bo started to object, but Sallie silenced him with an outstretched hand and a look of warning. She continued.

"Upon arriving, they ignore a no trespassing sign and wander into the forest, where they are attacked and seriously wounded by the illegal tenant's trained assassin, his large predator cat. Only the quick-thinking bravery of the dog prevents a potentially catastrophic outcome."

As if on cue, Hugo lifted his head briefly, and I thought I saw his chest swell underneath his collar. A glance at Bo's face revealed rising discomfort.

"The injured pair are then escorted to the squatter's shithole of a shelter, where amid unsanitary conditions, he patches them up while ingratiating himself to the wannabe investigator so as to stave off potential police involvement. He spins a colorful life story that may or may not be a cover for a life of crime or mental health crises. How am I doing?"

Bo and I just looked at each other blankly.

"Good. So, to complete our sordid tale, our oh-so-discerning gumshoe in training and our possibly deranged, possibly felonious squatter, who may or may not be Andre Coulon, part the best of friends. As he leaves, our bumbling Inspector Bruneau hears his new bestie Prosper laughing and quoting Shakespeare, although he may really have said, 'Our devils now are befriended.'"

I clapped my hands slowly to acknowledge Sallie's bravura performance, acting more than feeling chastened.

"Well done," I said. "You have presented one possible, though in my view, unlikely version of reality."

Sallie glared at me, then rested her chin on her palm and stared out the window, ignoring us all. I sensed an opportunity to shift the subject.

"Bo, on the subject of evidence," I said, "the reason for Sallie's visit before we got sidetracked is she thinks she's cracked the remaining pieces of our transcription puzzle."

"Is that right? That's great news, Sallie!" Bo said, clearly grateful for the change of topic. "Can we see?"

"That's kind of the point," Sallie said flatly, still looking out the window. She held out her folder for Bo to take.

Bo and I sat down at the card table to review her work.

Source A

1. I can stay no longer, Cher Jane. The devil is at my heels. To the sea! I shall
2. Grand Terre, the Temple, Campeche, Pierre, tous sont morts. [Trans: all are dead.]
3. our treasure. You must keep her always even in the next world
4. JLF
5. not trust Caldwell with this. Talk to Livingston and tell him
6. JLF
7. Barataria
8. Cher Jane, Je t'aime pour l'eternite [Trans: Dear Jane, I love you for

CHAPTER TEN

eternity.]

Source B

1. Never have I seen such a man. C [Caldwell] says he is a disgraced pirate, but I see how others regard him with respect and wonder and fear. Even Livingston and Grymes make way for him.
2. J [Jean] kissed me last night and told me he loved me. He asked me to go away with him but where would we go? To be free? Free to love.
3. J [Jean] calls her La Violette. He says she is "magique!" If I keep her always, we will find each other. Even in the next world.
4. never wear it in public. I hold her at night, and I see J [Jean] as if he is here by me. She is us and we are she.
5. J [Jean] came again last night, in a different disguise this time. I told him he must not come again. The risk is too great. He said he must go away, perhaps for a long time, but that he shall return for me some day. He shall find me, no matter where I shall be.
6. I wrote Caroline and told her about J [Jean] and where to find our treasure
7. C [Caldwell] is pathetic with his complaining and his whimpering, and his tirades followed by groveling apologies. I must see Livingston about
8. must not let C [Caldwell] find our treasure. It is the map to
9. Today I met with Livingston about La Violette. He will safeguard our treasure.
10. Where is J [Jean]? Does he know I shall soon die? Does he still live? I shall keep LV [La Violette] by my side for eternity. He shall find me. We shall be together at last.

Bo and I let out a few "hmms" and "huhs" as we read. I glanced up a couple times to see that Sallie was acting indifferent, still stewing and gazing out the window, but I could tell she was covertly gauging our reactions.

"This is great work, Sallie. Thank you so much," Bo broke the silence.

"How confident are you in its accuracy?"

"Pretty confident," Sallie said, turning toward us now. "It's possible that I've gotten a word or two wrong, but overall, I think I've captured it. Your lab had already done most of the hard work."

"Are there particular words or entries you're less confident in than others?"

Sallie got up, walked over, and stood behind us so she could see the papers laid out before us.

"Well, on A7 I only had one letter to go on, which was a capital B," Sallie said. "Given the number of letters and the author's presumed identity, Barataria seems like a pretty safe guess, but it's possible it could be something else."

"Okay. Anything else?"

"Yes, I've inferred a bit in B4," she said. "It's clear Jane is talking about an object of some kind that she holds at night that makes her think of J, presumably her lover Jean Lafitte. It could be anything, some sort of gift from him maybe, but her previous reference to 'never' and what I take to be 'public,' with three words in between, makes me think it's something she might wear or in this case, not wear in public. Perhaps a piece of clothing or jewelry."

"Yes!" Bo exclaimed. "This is excellent, Sallie."

"It really is, Sallie," I agreed, "but I do have a couple of observations."

"Let's hear 'em, Bru," Bo said.

"Well, the first is that the treasure Lafitte mentions in A3 might be what he doesn't trust Caldwell with in A5, and also what Jane writes about in B6, B8, and B9. And if that's the case, despite Jane's reference to the map in B8, the treasure might be an object rather than something that a map would lead someone to. And that object is probably La Violette, whatever that turns out to be. She kept it with her, and then she turned to Edward Livingston to keep it safe."

"Yes, I had the same interpretation," Sallie said.

"That could be, for sure," Bo said, "although I'm not convinced that we should drop the map theory just yet. What else, Bru?"

"We've got some points to research," I said. "What is the Temple in A2?

CHAPTER TEN

Who the hell is Caroline in B6? And what does Jane mean by their treasure being a map to something?"

"And who do you propose should conduct this research?" Sallie asked.

"Really, Sallie," I snorted, "I think I'll be safe within the confines of a library."

"Let's make sure that's all this is, Bru," Bo said, clearly intending to mollify Sallie. "Book research only, okay? Anything else, and you come to me."

"But of course," I said.

Chapter Eleven

I got a lot more than I bargained for when I dropped by Bruneau's place. The sight of his scarred face and Hugo all bandaged up hit me hard. I'm ashamed to admit it, but for a brief second there, I was more amused than scared. The sight of my chunky friend and his lapdog looking like a dynamic duo after a scuffle with the bad guys was kind of funny. But then the reality of their actual pain, and the danger they'd put themselves in, and my part in allowing it to happen…well, it all began to sink in. I felt terrible. It's not like I told Bru to go to Grand Isle, but he did tell me what he was planning to do, and I didn't lift a finger to stop him. If Mac and the brass got a load of this one there was going to be hell to pay. That would probably be fine with Sallie Maguire, whose tongue-lashing was a bit much, even though I was sure it would be nothing compared to Angie's reaction once she found out what happened.

I'd met Sallie once or twice in the past, and she was not who I remembered. The Sallie I thought I recalled was meek and kind of homely, and I remembered Angie feeling bad for her and taking her shopping a couple times. But the woman I met at Bru's was no shrinking violet, that's for sure. She wasn't beautiful exactly, but she was certainly attractive in her fitted pantsuit and stylish haircut. And as she tore Bru and me to shreds, she struck me as damned sexy, kind of like Angie when she's pissed. I wondered whether Sallie had really changed that much, or if my memory was bad. Or was it just Bru's brush with danger that brought out the mother tiger in her?

Probably, it was all of the above, but if one thing was clear, it was that Sallie's feelings toward Bruneau were intense. Normally, I defer to Angie

CHAPTER ELEVEN

when it comes to affairs of the heart, but what I witnessed was thinly disguised, red-hot passion. And Bru, the big dummy, seemed clueless. We are going to have to have a bro talk, he and I.

In the meantime, I had business to attend to. Sallie's work on our transcription seemed solid, but to be safe I took photos and sent them to Minh to get her opinion. If it checked out, then I agreed with Bru that we needed to shift our focus to figuring out what this La Violette was, and to finding the identity of Jane Placide's confidant, Caroline. The problem was, we could find the answers to both those questions and still not be any closer to learning what, if anything, was taken from Jane's casket. My gut told me our best bet was still to find the burglars. If we could do that, maybe everything else would fall into place.

* * *

"Rodiger, what we got?" I bellowed as I entered the busy squad room and approached the rookie's desk.

"Oh, hi, detective," he said, swiveling from his computer to face me and lowering his voice. "We've got a name, sir."

"We do? Well, that's something."

"Yes, sir," Rodiger said, rising and following me into my office. He sat down and looked at me like he was waiting for something.

"You going to tell me the suspect's name, Rodiger, or are we observing a moment of silence?"

"Yes, sir. I mean, no, sir. Sorry sir. The suspect is a Moroccan by the name of Mahdi Toledano, and he's got a story."

"Don't they all?"

"Yes, sir."

"Okay, let's hear it," I said.

"Well, sir, Toledano was born into a wealthy household in Marrakesh in 1962, and his mother died shortly after giving birth to him under mysterious circumstances."

"Mysterious? In what way?"

"Officially, she fell down a staircase."

"Unofficially?"

"According to a retired police officer who worked the case, there was bruising all over her body, consistent with a beating. He told Interpol he was discouraged at the time from pursuing a full investigation. The husband was a powerful man, apparently, and this was the early sixties."

"Okay, got it. What happened to the kid?"

"He was raised in his father's harem by the other women of the household."

"A harem? In the 1960s?"

"I know; that was my reaction, too," Rodiger said. "Turns out there's more to the harem concept than our Western stereotype of a sex den of voluptuous concubines, guarded by eunuchs, serving their master's every whim."

"Educate me."

"It's really just about seclusion and keeping one's women concealed from other men," Rodiger explained. "Not just the wife, but daughters, mothers, domestic workers, what have you. In modern times, that might mean the women mostly stay at home, but it doesn't mean they're sex slaves or have no say in their households. The hijab stems from the same basic idea. Staying hidden."

I was dubious. A harem? It sounded like something out of a bad 1950s Hollywood movie, and I told Rodiger so.

"I understand, sir," he said. "I had the same reaction, especially considering that Morocco is supposed to be one of the more progressive Arab countries. For our purposes, my advice is not to think about the word 'harem' but just to focus on the fact that Toledano was raised almost exclusively by women in a conservative, patriarchal environment. It is key to what we can glean from his motivations later in life."

"Alright, noted. Let's get back to his life story."

"Right. So, the point is, his mother died, possibly violently, and he was raised by women. And, get this, he's a dwarf."

"Let me guess, four foot five?"

"Yep, thereabouts."

CHAPTER ELEVEN

"How come he wears women's shoes?"

"Probably because they don't make men's shoes that small, just boys' and women's," Rodiger said.

"Okay. Back to the bio."

"Sure," Rodiger said. "His father didn't have much use for Mahdi apparently, but he did pay to send him off to university in Rabat. From what Interpol has been able to dig up, he was a gifted student but also a very angry young man. He joined a left-wing secular student group that got pretty militant in its protest tactics, and he ended up spending most of the '80s in prison. He was released in '88 and worked for a while selling rugs to tourists, but there's no record of him in the country after 2004, when the mosque robbery occurred."

"What did they book him on?"

"Political dissent, basically. Advocating for the rights of women and other marginalized groups. Making threats, associating with undesirables, vandalism, that kind of thing. King Hassan didn't mess around in those days."

"How did Interpol get on to him, and why do they like him for our guy?" I asked.

"Well, sir," Rodiger said, fidgeting, "it turns out I may have had a hand in that. I'd been on the phone with an agent in Lyon and I mentioned that the Delacroix painting seemed personal somehow, like I shared with you. Turns out he passed that insight along to the police in Fez, and after some digging, they came up with Toledano."

I let Rodiger simmer in the limbo of a brief silence.

"My, my Rodiger, aren't you all that," I said eventually. "Less than a year on the job, and you're already cracking international crime rings."

"Hardly, sir," Rodiger said, looking embarrassed.

"Relax, Rodiger, I'm busting your balls, is all," I said.

"Yes, sir."

"Go on. Tell me more about Toledano. I get that he disappears after the mosque job in Fez, but other than that, I'm not really seeing the connection."

"The first thing is his size," Rodiger said. "He's small enough to have fit through that Mosque window, and of course, his footprints would pretty much match what was found in Marseilles and what we have here. As far as accomplices, there were plenty of hardened criminals he could have befriended while in prison."

"That it?"

"No sir," Rodiger went on. "There was a small North African man living in Marseilles in the early 2000s who went by the name Abid Bensaid. Interpol now believes that Bensaid was Toledano, living under an assumed name. He worked at one of the luxury beach resorts, first as a spa attendant and later as a concierge. He disappeared in 2007, basically right after the villa heist. Interpol can trace him to Montreal after that, but then they lose him."

"And you like him for the painting in Amsterdam because it was of a harem girl?"

"Not just for that, sir, although the psychology does fit," Rodiger said. "According to the police in Morocco, going back a few generations, the women in Toledano's mother's family actually were harem girls, or odalisques if you will, and in those days, harem girls *were* concubines. Even his grandmother, who he was close to, was an odalisque as a young woman.

"Toledano would have known all this and may have resented it. A professor the police spoke with remembered that he wrote several combative essays condemning the king and the ruling elites as corrupt and misogynistic and arguing for not just more liberal laws governing women, but also reparations for generations of subjugation. Really angry, idealistic stuff."

"So, the painting…"

"Maybe he sees an idolized image of his mother or grandmother in the Delacroix, or maybe he sees a symbol of female oppression that fuels his anger. Either way, he grabs it for himself, not his client."

"Why else do you like him?"

"The M.O. mostly, dropping down from a skylight, and the guard, saying one of the crew was shorter than five feet."

"Do we have a photo?" I asked.

"Just his student ID from forty years ago," Rodiger said, handing me a printout of the mug shot. It could have been anybody, other than his being

CHAPTER ELEVEN

a dwarf. Longish black hair, dark eyes, Roman nose. No smile.

"He'd be sixty or so today, right?" I ventured. "You think he's still scaling buildings?"

"Sure, why not? Low center of gravity would help."

"Right. I don't know; seems unlikely to me. Does Interpol have any leads as to where this guy could be now?"

"None whatsoever," Rodiger said. "The trail goes nowhere. The family hasn't had any contact with him since he left Morocco. No known friends or associates. Kind of reminds me of The Jackal."

"The Jackal?"

"You know, from the Forsyth book and the Bruce Willis movie."

"No, I don't know. Around here, we deal in facts, Rodiger, not Hollywood fantasies."

"Yes, sir. There was an actual Jackal, though, sir. Carlos the Jackal they called him. Caught up to him eventually."

"Yeah, yeah, I remember Carlos. Look Rodiger, you think maybe Toledano's been living here? Blending in, scoping things out."

"You mean here in New Orleans, sir?"

"No, I mean here in Los Angeles," I said, laying the rookie treatment on thick. "Of course, I mean here in New Orleans. We've got Toledano Street, right? And it's not an uncommon last name here. Maybe he's got family in the area."

"Maybe, I guess," Rodiger allowed without much conviction. "The name is Spanish in origin, I think. I'll look into it."

***

If I'd been a little tough on Rodiger, it might have been my way of steeling myself for what I knew would come next. On the drive home, I played a little Irma Thomas to soothe my nerves. I had expected I'd at least have the opportunity to break the news to Angie myself, but as I pulled into our driveway that evening, she was standing outside the front door with her arms crossed.

"Hi, babe!" I greeted her cheerfully.

There was silence. Then, "Are you fucking kidding me?"

"What?" I said, walking slowly toward her, knowing full well where this was going.

"You know what! First, it's 'Oh, Bruneau's just going to help me with some research on a case.' *One case.* Then it's 'gee, Bruneau seems to really like this. I think I'll use him some more.' Now it's 'maybe Bruneau can take a bullet for me.'"

"Oh, come on, you know that's not fair."

"Not fair? Not fair is sending someone with no training into an extremely dangerous situation. That's not fair at all. In fact, it's a fucking disgrace, Bo! You should be ashamed of yourself."

"Okay, okay, not my finest moment, alright? I agree. I messed up. But you were here when Bru told us he was going down to Grand Isle. All he said was he was going to meet with some eccentric dude who might know some history. It didn't sound dangerous, did it?"

"Whose case is this, Bo?"

"It's my case, obviously."

"*Obviously*? If you were in charge of the case, wouldn't it *obviously* be your responsibility to know what all your subordinates are doing at all times? Especially those who *obviously* aren't even employed by N.O. fucking P.D.?"

"Yes, yes, you're right," I said. "Mea culpa. I messed up and I feel terrible about it, okay? Is that what you wanted to hear?"

Angie began rubbing her brow and silently shaking. I wasn't sure what to do, so I took a couple cautious steps toward her and began to lightly pull her toward me. She pushed me away, but not hard, so I tugged again, and she buried her head on my chest, sobbing quietly, while I stroked her back.

It's a funny thing how his women friends all feel protective of Bruneau. Not just Angie and Sallie, but both our moms back in the day, and even all his granddames from the Garden District, from what he tells me. I guess I'm a fine one to talk, seeing as I've been watching out for the guy since we were little. But here's the thing about Bru, not many people get. In his own way, he's a tough mother. He went off to England by himself way back

CHAPTER ELEVEN

when. Had the guts to start his business and the gumption to make a success of it. He's never quit on an intellectual challenge that I can remember. He may not look the part, but he's a fighter.

"I'm so sorry," I said softly, still stroking Angie. "I was hoping to break the news to you myself. I went to see Bru this morning, and he's doing fine, he really is. Hugo, too."

"That cut on his face is awful," Angie said, her voice muffled. "And poor Hugo with that collar and the stitches."

"Yeah, I know," I said.

After a long stretch of silence, Angie gently pulled out of our embrace and looked up at me.

"I'm sorry," she said. "I know you didn't mean for anything to happen and Bruneau did kind of go rogue."

"No, like you said, I'm in charge, and he's my responsibility," I said. "I've already told him that going forward, we're going to have tightly drawn boundaries."

"Good," she sniffed.

"Can I ask you one thing?"

"Sure."

"How did you find out what happened at Grand Isle?"

"From Sallie Maguire. She called to cancel lunch because she was too upset to focus on anything other than what happened to Bruneau. She sent me a photo."

"I didn't realize you and Sallie were so tight."

"We get together once a month or so," Angie said. "She's got a lot to offer, you know, and she's goo-goo for Bruneau if he'd only see it."

"Goo-goo?"

"Head over heels, whatever you want to call it. But he makes her crazy with all his little quirks. When everything has to be just so, according to his specifications, there's no room for her to breathe or spread her wings."

"You mean like the food obsessions and his weekly routines?"

"Yeah, all that stuff," Angie said. "If he could just let go a little and give her some space, they could be a great team."

I thought about that and could see Angie's point.

"She didn't need to be given space this morning," I said. "She was red hot. Damn near tore our heads off."

"Good for her!" Angie exclaimed. "Somebody had to knock some sense into you idiots."

Chapter Twelve

Getting scuffed up on Grand Isle did wonders for my popularity. I don't know who was responsible for spreading the word, but it got out quickly. In just two days, I'd fielded calls from Grace Simmons, Pamela Roseberry, and a host of others, and customers who saw me in the store already seemed to know how I got my wound. Never one to miss out on breaking news, Charlotte Duval dropped by to express her sympathy and concern, but with a barely concealed air of "I told you so." She let me know that Philip Boyer had asked her to express his condolences as well.

"Condolences?" I snarled. "Nobody died, Charlotte. We don't need condolences."

Later, I had just returned from treating myself to a shrimp po-boy at Domilise's, and was instructing Henry and his crew on where to place a large Louis XVIII armoire they'd transported from Natchez, when Angie Duplessis walked in.

"Why, what a pleasant surprise!" I exclaimed. "What brings you to this part of town, Mrs. Duplessis?"

"There are some things a girl just needs to see for herself," Angie said, smiling radiantly and coming in for our usual warm hug. "Now turn around, you big lug, and let me see."

I did as I was told and Angie made a close inspection of my much-celebrated new facial feature, intoning a couple "mmm, hmm's" in mock admiration. She was dressed in professional work attire, leading me to believe she'd taken time off to make this visit.

Facing me now, Angie's expression turned serious.

"I hope all this excitement is going to discourage you from detective work for a while, Bruneau. What on earth were you thinking?"

"I've been told I wasn't thinking."

"Uh huh, that makes two of you," Angie said. "You and my husband. I'm not sure which of you I'm more upset with."

"Oh, come on, Angie, Bo didn't have anything to do with this," I protested. "I'm perfectly capable of producing my own stupidity."

"Don't expect me to argue that point," she said dryly.

There was a pause.

"You know, he feels terrible," Angie said.

"Who, Bo?"

"Yes. He blames himself for not going to Grand Isle himself, or at least for not going with you."

"That's ridiculous. He had no way of knowing there'd be any kind of danger involved, much less from a feral cat," I said.

"Be that as it may, I wanted you to know how he feels. You men are such idiots when it comes to sharing your emotions with each other."

I smiled to let her know I got the message and in hopes of changing the subject. It worked.

Angie made a show of examining all my wounds and instructing me in the various healing arts I was sworn to practice. Then she insisted on visiting Hugo in the office, where he was curled up on his bed, having been liberated from his Elizabethan collar that morning. He got up when he saw her and performed his usual butt-wiggling act, which resulted in the desired hugging and stroking from Angie, along with a stealth bag of chopped-up hot dogs.

"I do hope the two of you got some sense knocked into you," Angie declared, rising from her love session with Hugo.

"Don't worry, we consider ourselves duly chastened," I assured her.

"Well, that's something anyway," she said, digging into her bag. "Here, the kids made this for you."

I took the card Angie held out and smiled at the caricature sketch of me with Frankenstein stitches, holding an ice bag to my head and a thermometer

CHAPTER TWELVE

in my mouth, drawn by Sophie, I guessed. It opened to a "Get Well Uncle Bru" message in large block letters, with handwritten notes from each child.

"I want to see the other guy, Uncle Bru," Little Bo wrote. "I hear he's a crazy cat!"

Sophie said that despite the *Tempest* connection, Prosper reminded her more of Little John, who started out as Robin Hood's adversary in Sherwood Forest but became his most loyal friend and defender. What an old soul our little Sophie is, I thought to myself.

"Sorry to hear about your injuries, Uncle Bru," Monique chimed in. "At least your proboscis wasn't harmed! Tell Hugo we love him and to get well soon!"

"That's sweet of them," I said to Angie, tearing up a bit. "Please tell them thanks and let Monique know the schnozz remains in fine working order."

"She'll be relieved, I'm sure," Angie said. "Here, I brought you something else."

She reached down into her bottomless bag and pulled out a quart Tupperware container of soup and a small baggie of crumbled bacon.

"It's corn chowder," she let me know. "The traditional homeopathic cure for stupidity."

* * *

Food was on Sallie's mind, too. She'd emailed to let me know she was coming over after work to cook me dinner and share some thoughts about the Jane Placide mystery. This was not welcome news. Sallie is hopelessly inept in the kitchen, and I'd been looking forward to some alone time, but I didn't feel I could decline the offer. Another of Sallie's beefs with me is that I'm controlling. Not of people, necessarily, but of my environment. My insistence on doing all the cooking and ordering for her in restaurants is Exhibit A in her argument.

Victoria was on floor duty, and I was tired, so I knocked off work early and let her close. I'd just put on some Oscar Peterson and sat down with a Negroni and the new issue of *Architectural Digest,* when the doorbell rang.

It was Bo. He had looked for me at the store and was surprised to find that I had headed out early. He was dressed in his usual plain clothes uniform of a short-sleeved beige oxford shirt, tight fitting black pants, and black cotton knit tie. If it weren't for a small middle-aged belly bulge and a few gray hairs, he could have passed for the athlete he once was.

"What gives, Bru? You never leave the store early."

"I'm wiped out," I told him. "Plus, Sallie is coming over to cook me dinner, so I thought I should tidy up a bit. It's the last thing I'm in the mood for, but it's nice of her."

"Seems to me you shouldn't take that girl for granted," Bo said. "She's a hot little number, and anybody can see she's got a thing for you."

"Oh, come on," I said, "don't be ridiculous. We're just old friends. We tried the couple thing once before, remember?"

"Times change, Bru, and so do people. I'd keep an open mind if I were you."

"Whatever you say, detective. To what do I owe this visit?"

Bo informed me that the police had a suspect for the Hope Mausoleum break-in and the other burglaries. A Moroccan dwarf of all things, named Mahdi Toledano, who'd been radicalized at university back in the 1980s. Radicalized not in the Jihad sense, but as a left-wing secular revolutionary rebelling against the oppressive regime at the time. He had a particular thing about women's rights, apparently.

"Why women's rights?"

"I don't really know," Bo said. "His mother died when he was young, possibly from a beating her husband gave her. Growing up, his father didn't have time for him, so he was raised by his grandmother and aunts. We're trying to find out more."

"You're thinking there's a political aspect to this?" I asked.

"No, not likely," Bo said. "But he was in prison for a few years and may have made some contacts there among the professional criminal class that he's possibly used in these crimes. Guys with skills."

"I see. What's his motive then?"

"We don't know for sure," Bo said, "but if the other jobs are a guide, I'd

CHAPTER TWELVE

say it's probably the usual. Greed."

"And you don't have any leads as to his whereabouts?"

"Nope, none."

"Sounds like we're back to where we started."

"More or less," Bo sighed. "I've got Rodiger looking into possible connections to Toledano family members living in New Orleans, but other than that, we're kind of at a standstill until Interpol or the Moroccan police come up with something."

I saw Bo out and sat back down, contemplating what he'd said about Sallie. I took his meaning and could appreciate the glimmer of truth in his words, but it was painfully complicated to think about, so I swapped out Oscar for Chopin, took a sip of my drink, and returned to my magazine, seeing no reason to face today what I could just as easily put off until tomorrow. A few minutes later, the doorbell rang again, setting Hugo off once more. It was only 5:30.

When I greeted her, Sallie handed me an insulated cooler bag that felt like it had enough food in it for five dinners. She carried a salad bowl and a large paper bag full of more food and some utensils.

"Hungry?" she asked, smiling.

"Always," I said, returning the smile. "This is awfully nice of you. What are we featuring this evening?"

"Coq au vin with mashed potatoes, a salad, and a surprise for dessert. The chicken and the potatoes just need to be reheated, and everything else is prepped, so hopefully, I won't need to spend too much time in the kitchen."

"Goodness, that's a rather ambitious menu for a weeknight," I said, trying to hide my skepticism. There's nothing more tedious than dried-out chicken, which is inevitably what happens to coq au vin in the hands of an inexperienced chef.

"I've got a nice Pommard I'll open and get breathing for us. Would you like a drink, or a glass of white wine? I've just made myself a Negroni."

Sallie's not much of a drinker, but she surprised me by opting for the cocktail, and then she busied herself with unloading her various containers and utensils. She wore a simple beige sundress with tan leather platform wedges and a teardrop turquoise pendant on a silver chain with matching earrings. I didn't think Bo's "hot little number" comment got it quite right, but there was no doubt that Sallie looked beautiful in a natural, effortless kind of way. I couldn't stop myself from staring at her.

Sallie looked up a little too early as I delivered her drink, as if maybe she'd been conscious of my gaze, but hadn't wanted to let me know.

"So, how's the Jerry thing going," I asked awkwardly.

"Jerry? Oh, him. We haven't seen each other since that last time," she said flatly. "It didn't work out. I'll just leave it at that."

"Sorry," I said, "I didn't mean to pry. I guess it's for the best if it feels that way to you."

Sallie didn't say anything but nodded slightly.

"There's nothing I love better than a good coq au vin," I said cheerfully, changing the subject and lifting the lid of the Dutch oven that contained the chicken. It revealed what looked like crispy thighs and drumsticks bathing in a thick mahogany broth with mushrooms, pearl onions, and carrots. It smelled exactly as the dish should, with savory and tangy notes in delicate balance.

"Mmm, smells wonderful," I said. "I'm impressed. The carrots are a nice touch. I like the color they add. What kind of wine did you use, out of curiosity?"

"An Oregon pinot noir that I like," Sallie said. "Does that pass muster with your standards of culinary orthodoxy?"

"Absolutely it does," I replied, though in truth, mine is an Old World palate, and I would have gone with a lower-end Burgundy. "I'm not as stodgy a traditionalist as you make me out to be."

"Oh good, then you won't mind the soy milk I used in the potatoes," Sallie said.

I wasn't sure if she was serious, so I let her comment hang in the air while I fought back my gag reflex.

I must have paled, because Sallie broke into a full-throated laugh.

"Got ya!"

"I must admit, Miss Maguire, you did indeed have me there," I allowed,

CHAPTER TWELVE

smiling in relief.

"You're an easy mark when it comes to food."

Sallie and I spent an hour that felt like 10 minutes in easy small talk and playful banter. She moved confidently and efficiently around the kitchen, tasting and adjusting the seasonings in the chicken, setting the table so that I sat at the end with her next to me in a corner seat, tossing and plating the salad, and finally serving the featured attraction.

The chicken and the potatoes were swoon worthy and the zippy vinaigrette over peppery arugula was a perfect complement to the richness of the main plate. To round things out, my Pommard more than rose to the occasion.

"My God, Sallie, this is heavenly," I said in earnest. "It's been a while since I've tasted your cooking. Have you been practicing?"

"Is that your way of saying my cooking used to suck?" she answered with another "got ya" look.

"Not suck," I said, striving in vain for a witty response. "Let's just say it appears you've taken things to a new level."

"That's fair," she said, smiling. "I'm glad you like it. Can you guess the mystery ingredient in the potatoes?"

I had been contemplating that very question and was stumped. There was an extra lusciousness to the dish that I couldn't put my finger on.

"There's garlic for sure," I said, "but there's definitely something besides the milk and butter that's contributing to the velvety texture. I can't place it. I give up."

"Cream cheese!" she announced triumphantly.

"Brilliant! I never would have guessed it, but it makes perfect sense," I said. "The next time I make mashed potatoes, I shall steal from you shamelessly."

Sallie smiled approvingly and then shifted the conversation.

"Speaking of stealing, I think I've worked out a few things from the transcription in your Jane Placide mystery."

"Excellent news," I said. "Do share."

"Well, the easy one is the Temple," Sallie said. "That was what the Lafittes called their slave market. They situated it on a bluff on the western shore of Lake Salvador. The Indians built it up a long time ago, supposedly for religious ceremonies, hence the name. It served the Lafittes' purposes perfectly because it was close enough to New Orleans for their customers to get there easily, and it commanded a 360-degree view of any approaching trouble."

"Now that you mention it, I think I remember reading about the Temple, but I failed to make the connection," I said. "Well done."

"Thanks. Unfortunately, it doesn't really help us. Item A2 is just Lafitte mourning people and places that were lost. Grand Terre, Campeche, his brother, the Temple."

"You never know what might or might not help," I said. "What else?"

"Jane had a sister named Caroline."

"No way! Damn, Sallie, why didn't I think to look into her family?"

"I couldn't say, but Caroline was fifteen or sixteen years older than Jane, and she was an actress also. She lived in Charleston and then later in New York City and New Jersey. She married twice and had one daughter. She lived to be eighty-three."

"If she was that much older, do you think they could have been close?"

"I don't see why not," Sallie said. "If Jane corresponded with her and told her about Lafitte, there must have been some level of intimacy. Sometimes older sisters can be like second mothers."

"Yes, I can see how that might be the case," I said. "In terms of our investigation, what is the significance of sister Caroline, do you think?"

"I really have no idea, and maybe she won't be significant at all," Sallie answered. "But I was thinking if we could locate her modern-day descendants, maybe there is some lore that passed down through the generations that could provide some tea leaves."

"Seems like a longshot, but yes, maybe," I said.

We cleared the plates together and then Sallie kicked me out of the kitchen so she could prepare her surprise, and what a surprise it turned out to be. Two sublime Grand Marnier soufflés in eight-ounce ramekins, airy and perfectly textured, and topped with a smooth, custardy crème anglaise with just the right amount of sweetness.

CHAPTER TWELVE

"You have outdone yourself, Miss Maguire," I said. "I truly don't possess enough superlatives to do this meal justice. Expertly planned and deftly executed, with the whole rising above the sum of its parts."

"Well, thank you," Sallie said. "I'm glad you like it. I may not be at your level yet, but I think I've come a long way."

"I could not have prepared a better meal," I said. "I mean that, truly."

We smiled at each other. Then Sallie assumed a pensive expression.

"What about you, Bruneau?"

"What do you mean? What about me?"

"It's not like you to go dashing off to Grand Isle like some intrepid adventurer. Or to let me cook your dinner without managing my every move."

I smiled and shrugged.

"Even an old tiger can try to change his stripes," I said. "Just because I don't like it when you nag at me doesn't mean I can't acknowledge that you've got some legitimate gripes."

"Well, I appreciate the effort," Sallie said.

There was that pensive look again, sizing me up.

"Am I wrong, or have you lost weight?"

"A couple days ago, you called me fat."

"Maybe I wasn't looking very closely. How much?"

I shrugged.

"How much? Come on, out with it."

"Maybe ten to twelve pounds."

"I'm impressed, Bruneau," Sallie said. "How'd you do it?"

"Running from cats, mostly."

"Very funny. Come on, I want to know."

"Portion control has been the biggest thing," I said. "I've also cut back on hard alcohol, and I've been walking more."

"Do you have a goal?"

I chuckled.

"You know me, Sallie. I'm not exactly a goal-setter. I just want to feel better and not be called fat by sexy women."

"Touché," Sallie said, smiling and flushing just a bit.

"And you?" I asked.

"Me?"

"Yes, you. One doesn't just become an accomplished chef overnight."

"No, I suppose not. Let's just say I've been working on it, and there's been a lot of trial and error. Especially error, truth be told."

"Why?"

"What do you mean?"

"I mean, why, as in what was your motivation? You never seemed all that interested in food, or fashion, and now suddenly you cook like you spent 20 years at Cordon Bleu, and you look like a supermodel. That doesn't just happen."

Sallie blushed, looked down, and then spoke quietly.

"Maybe I'm an old tiger, too," she said, looking up at me and holding her gaze.

"Go on," I said.

"I don't know Bruneau; I guess for the last few years, I felt like I was in a rut. I was living this very narrow, very cloistered life. I was frustrated. I felt like I had something inside me to offer the world, but I didn't know how to raise my hand and get noticed. Does that make sense?"

I nodded gravely, having struck more of a nerve than I intended.

Sallie stopped to collect herself and proceeded slowly, choosing her words carefully, I could tell.

"This is embarrassing and maybe more information than you were bargaining for, so just chalk it up to the wine talking, okay?"

"Okay, sure."

"Remember a couple years ago when we went out with your friend Bo and his wife, Angie?"

"Yeah, sure, bowling, right?"

"Right. I don't know if you noticed, but Angie and I bonded. I kind of opened my heart to her about how I was feeling and how I didn't know how to go about rebooting my life and creating a new me.

"Well, Angie could see I needed some help, so she took me out to lunch

CHAPTER TWELVE

the following week, and one thing led to another. We went shopping, she gave me some fashion tips and a few cooking lessons and has just been there as a sounding board for me ever since. She's become a dear friend."

"I had no idea," I said truthfully.

"We call it Sallie two-point-oh, Angie and me. It's all about helping me see myself the way I've always wanted others to see me. Especially you."

I pointed at myself with a quizzical expression on my face.

"Yes, you, you big dummy. You're a pretty important person in my life, you know. You're still the only man I've ever slept with, as embarrassing as that may be."

The conversation had gone in a direction I hadn't seen coming, and I felt the heat rising in my cheeks.

"Thanks, Sallie," I said. "You're an important person in my life, too."

I paused.

"You know, I've been thinking. No pressure, mind you, but I'd like to try spending more time together again. They say the 20th time is the charm."

"I think I'd like that too, Bruneau," she said. "But let's not rush things, okay?"

"Okay."

Sallie smiled, took my arms by the elbows, rose to her tip-toes, and pecked me on the lips.

"Come on, let's deal with the dishes."

"Wait, I thought I'm supposed to be Mister Hands Off? I'm happy to rein in my worst instincts and let you handle the dishes by yourself, just to show you how evolved I've become."

"Not a chance! Come on, mister, into the kitchen with you," Sallie said, grinning widely and tugging on my arm.

We exchanged easy banter and small talk as we took on the mess. I scrubbed, and Sallie dried.

"Did I tell you Bo came by earlier to update me on the case?"

"No, you didn't. What did he have to say?"

I hadn't told Sallie much about the actual burglary, so I started at the beginning with the footprint and video evidence and then the intelligence

Bo's whiz kid had picked up from Interpol about similar heists around the world.

"So NOPD actually believes a gang of international criminals was responsible for looting Jane Placide's coffin?" she asked. "Don't you think that's a bit of a stretch? I mean, why would they?"

"I know, that is the question nobody can answer," I said. "But now they have an actual suspect with a name."

I told Sallie about Mahdi Toledano, and she perked up.

"How tall is this dwarf, do you know?"

"I'm not sure," I said, "I don't think Bo ever said. I meant to ask him how short you have to be to be considered a dwarf, but I forgot. We can look it up easily enough."

"Sure," Sallie said, her body language tense. "But you said he's Moroccan and about sixty or so, right?"

"Yes, that's what I just said."

"I know. I just want to make sure I have this right. And the heist in Amsterdam, the painting that was stolen that didn't fit the M.O., that was of an odalisque?"

"Yes, by Delacroix."

"Can you tell me anything more about it?"

"I haven't seen a photo, but I think Bo said it's a watercolor and the odalisque is half-clothed and reclining on some pillows."

Sallie put her hand to her forehead and looked down in deep concentration.

"Oh my God," she blurted.

"You're never going to believe this, but I think I know who this is!"

1826

THE CAMP STREET THEATRE
NEW ORLEANS, LOUISIANA
FEBRUARY 1826

J*ane Placide sits quietly in front of her dressing room mirror as her attendant, Abigail, loosens her costume and begins undoing her hair. The dress rehearsal went well enough, she thinks, even if her Rosalind is not yet perfected. Actually, it is Rosalind as Ganymede who eludes her, but she is not unduly concerned. Trouser roles always take longer to master, and her shepherd boy is good enough to suffice for now.*

As Abigail hums a soft tune and the oil lamp on her table flickers, the actress' thoughts turn to the man who is not there but is always there. Would she see him again? Perhaps not in this life, she muses, as a knocking on the door interrupts her melancholy.

"May I come in, Jane?"

It is a male voice she knows well, deep and measured, yet intimate, with an underlying trace of urgency.

"Yes, James," *she says.* "I am clothed. You may enter."

The door opens to reveal a tall, well-dressed man of middle age, gripping the ivory handled cane that is his constant prop.

"That will be all for now, Abigail," *James Caldwell says upon entering. The servant bows in assent and steals noiselessly from the room.*

"May I sit?" *Caldwell asks, pointing to the small armchair in the corner of the room and tapping the door shut with his cane.*

"Of course," the actress replies. "What did you think?"

"It is good but not our best, I fear," Caldwell says. "You are brilliant as always, Jane. Felix is a wonderful Touchstone, and Sara does well enough as Celia and Aliena, but I'm not sure I believe Albert as Orlando. The audience is bound to wonder how one so beautiful as you could see anything in him."

The actress, having long grown weary of her benefactor's blandishments, sighs and looks away.

"He came again last night, did he not?" Caldwell asks after a momentary silence. More silence.

"Answer me, please."

"Yes, he came. For the last time. He cannot be safe here."

"Nor should he be," Caldwell says. "The man is a scoundrel. Why can you not see that?"

"I see what I see, and I feel what I feel," the actress says flatly.

Another silence follows as Caldwell shifts in his seat.

"Have I not forbidden you to entertain this villain?" he asks. "How do you think this makes me feel? I, who have tended to your every need, tutored you, protected you. I, who love you as no other?"

"I am grateful for all that you have done for me, James, you know that. But I cannot ignore my heart, nor my destiny. We are as one, Captain Lafitte and I, and we shall always be together, whether in this world or the next."

"Oh, stop with this nonsense!" Caldwell erupts. "You are an impressionable young girl with little experience of the world. And your Captain Lafitte is nothing but a well-traveled debaucher who uses women and discards them as is his whim. This cannot end well for you, Jane!"

"How little you know of me James, or of Captain Lafitte," the actress fires back. "I have experienced more of the world than you know, despite your efforts that it not be so! And Jean loves me more than you can possibly understand."

"How you torment me! Please, stop this torture!"

"It is you who torture yourself," the actress says calmly. "Anyway, you have nothing more to concern you. Captain Lafitte has gone to sea, never to return again."

"But if he remains in your thoughts, and in your heart, he has not departed at *all, and I can know no peace."*

"I cannot help what is in my heart, nor in my thoughts, any more than you can," the actress says calmly. "I wish you no ill will and can only hope that peace will come to you with time."

The actresses' words hang in the air as Caldwell buries his head in his hands. When he sits up, his eyes are red and he speaks slowly, in a resigned tone.

"I must acknowledge that what you say is so Jane, much as it saddens me," Caldwell says. "We will go on as before, you and I, working and traveling together, and I will bear my burden silently. I ask only that you not speak this man's name in my presence."

"I shall honor your wishes James, though you shan't be alone in your silent suffering."

Chapter Thirteen

Rodiger and I sat in my office turning over the facts in our case. It was a fact, we agreed, that a crime had occurred, although not necessarily a theft, since we couldn't yet prove that anything was removed from Jane Placide's coffin or Crypt 1083-A. As Mac kept reminding me with impatient jabs about our "whacky theories," at this point we had breaking and entering and criminal trespassing, and maybe burglary if we could prove intent to steal, and that was it, although the near certainty that the break-in was performed by a team of professionals suggested that theft was the motive. It was a fact that we had evidence of three footprints at the crime scene, one a women's size four and a half, and video of three individuals appearing to leave the mausoleum. And it was a fact that we had recovered evidence enough to strongly suggest that the well-known actress Jane Placide had an affair with the famous pirate Jean Lafitte some two hundred years ago, and that he may have given her something to take to her grave.

"I mean, that's it, Rodiger, isn't it?" I said. "Everything else is a guess to one degree or another."

"Yes, I see your point, sir," Rodiger said, "but we do have a suspect who's wanted for other crimes involving objects of great value, so I think it's reasonable to assume we have a high-value theft on our hands."

"Reasonable, yes," I said. "And it's reasonable to think that because the guard in Amsterdam thought the small burglar was probably a man, that Toledano is one of the perpetrators of that crime and this one. But isn't it also possible that our wearer of women's four-and-a-half shoes is, in

CHAPTER THIRTEEN

fact...oh, I don't know...a woman?"

"Yes sir, when you put it like that, I guess it's possible," Rodiger allowed.

"And Bruneau and his friend Sallie have us thinking that the thieves were after an object of some kind that Jane Placide and Jean Lafitte referred to as La Violette. But isn't it also possible that our original theory was correct, and the thieves were looking for a map?"

"Yes, sir, it is."

"And if that's the case, isn't it also possible, if not likely, that whatever they found, if they found anything, was unreadable and therefore of little to no monetary value?"

"Yes, sir, I guess that's right."

"Finally, Rodiger, we have assumed that our would-be thieves were looking for something in Jane Placide's coffin, since that was the only one that had been disturbed. But isn't it also possible that her coffin was opened either by chance or mistake, and what they were looking for was elsewhere in the crypt, if it was in the crypt at all?"

"Yes, sir, I guess so."

"My point is simply that we've made certain assumptions and headed down certain paths, but we are not at the point in our investigation where we should be closing off other angles. Do you follow me?"

"Yes, sir, I do. Is there something you'd like me to look into that you think we may have overlooked?"

I thought that over for a second.

"Not yet," I said. "Keep working the Toledano family angle for now, but if we don't turn up anything in the next couple of days, we should probably start looking for females who might fit our M.O. and also learn more about any treasure maps Lafitte is believed to have made. If we don't come up with something soon, the captain's going to shut us down."

"Very well, sir," Rodiger replied. "Nothing yet on the New Orleans Toledanos, but I've got a bunch more calls to make."

Rodiger started to leave but stopped and turned.

"One thing, sir," he said.

"Yes."

"Regarding the map theory and the object of value theory. It doesn't have to be one or the other, does it?"

"Go on," I said. "Tell me more."

"Well, I'm just thinking, for example, that La Violette could be a map drawn on violet-colored paper, or maybe the map is to a treasure or an object that's buried in a field of violets or has something to do with violets. Those are stupid hypotheticals, but do you see my point, sir?"

"Yes, Rodiger, I do," I said. "That's exactly the kind of thinking I'm looking for. We need to stay open to as wide a range of possibilities as we can."

As Rodiger got up to leave, a text came in from Minh.

"Wait up," I said as I read through the message.

"Doctor No says Sallie Maguire's transcription looks good," I relayed. "She cautions that 'Barataria' is a logical guess to A7, but only that, a guess, which, if you'll remember, Sallie herself pointed out. From an investigation standpoint, Doctor No agrees that La Violette should be our primary focus, but she warns against closing off the treasure map theory."

"Interesting, sir," Rodiger said. "I'll plan on looking into the map angle as soon as I've worked through this list of Toledanos. And I'll look again at the forensic evidence from the crypt to see if the intruders may have been looking for someone or something other than Jane."

Just then, my phone buzzed, and I nodded to Rodiger and waved him out of the room. It was Bruneau calling to tell me that Sallie Maguire thought she knew who Mahdi Toledano was. I almost fell out of my chair, as much from amusement as surprise.

After he let me know the identity of Sallie's suspect, Bru said he realized it sounded ridiculous, which is why he slept on the information before calling me. But then he provided some details, and I asked that he and Sallie come to the station so we could interview her in person. When we hung up, I sat back in my chair to digest what I'd heard. After a half minute or so I got up, walked to my door, and opened it.

"Rodiger!" I bellowed.

The poor kid was walking from the pantry area to his desk, having just poured himself some coffee. He spilled a splash on himself as he whirled

CHAPTER THIRTEEN

around to look at me.

"Yes sir, what is it, sir?" he asked, shaking hot liquid off his hand.

"Better come back in here, please."

I was in my chair again by the time Rodiger re-entered my office and closed the door.

"We've had a development," I said.

Rodiger remained standing, waiting for me to deliver the news.

"It seems Bruneau and Sallie think they know who our Moroccan dwarf is."

Rodiger gaped at me in confused silence.

"Really, sir? Who is it?"

"A hairdresser."

* * *

"A fucking hairdresser?"

That was Mac's response when I let him know what was going on and asked him if he wanted to sit in with us.

"No, I don't want to sit in with you," he said. "Jesus, T-Bo! Pardon me if I don't want to be found guilty by association when you get run off the force for going non compos mentis."

This was vintage Mac. I couldn't help smiling.

"Who's your source again? Some bimbo who's pleasuring that fat antiques dealer friend of yours? I'm supposed to be impressed. How, exactly?"

"She's not a bimbo, Mac," I said. "Bruneau's been helping me sort through the historical aspects of the case, and his friend Sallie has been in on some of those conversations. When Bruneau mentioned our Moroccan dwarf to her, her ears perked up. She thinks her hairdresser might be our guy."

"Oy vey."

"Oy vey? You reading the Talmud these days, Mac? Here I thought you Irish were strictly New Testament folks."

"Very funny," Mac said, turning to walk off. "Let me know what your bimbo has to say."

"Her last name's Maguire, Mac," I said over his shoulder.

"Aye, an Irish bimbo then. A cut above the rest of the herd."

* * *

"His name is Omar. I don't know his last name," Sallie Maguire told Rodiger, Bruneau, and myself after we had gathered in my office.

"I've only been to him twice, but I can tell you he's so short that he has to use a stepping stool to get to certain angles when he's cutting your hair."

"And why do you suspect him of being our grave robber?" I asked.

"When Bruneau described the Delacroix odalisque that was stolen in Amsterdam, it hit me that Omar's got a painting hanging in his living room that looks just like it. And, of course, he's really short, and he could be Moroccan, although he told me his ancestry is Turkish."

"His living room?" Rodiger interjected. "You've been to his home, Miss Maguire?"

"He works out of his house," Sallie said. "It's a small, one-story shotgun on Carondolet, a few blocks up from Jackson Avenue. You have to walk through the living room to get to his salon."

"What's Omar like?" I asked. "Other than the painting, is there anything about him that struck you as off or suspicious in any way?"

"No, not at all. He was very friendly, very courteous. Quite charming, in fact. He asked me a lot of questions about myself."

"Did he talk about himself at all?"

"Just in response to formalities," Sallie said. "I asked him where he was from and how he ended up in New Orleans. He said he was born in Turkey but grew up in France and then later moved to Montreal. His English is quite good, but he does have a bit of an accent that sounded French to me, so that seemed to fit."

"And what did he say about how he came to be in New Orleans."

"He said he visited on vacation and fell in love with the city and decided to set up shop here."

"A common enough story," I said. "What's the name of his business?"

CHAPTER THIRTEEN

"The Hidden Gem Salon."

I nodded at Rodiger, who excused himself to research this Omar character and his place of business.

Bruneau leaned forward in his chair.

"What do you make of this, Bo? Does Omar sound like a suspect to you?"

"Possibly," I answered. "His height and the painting in his living room certainly fit. Rodiger is looking to see if his story checks out. Let's see what he comes back with."

Bru and Sallie looked at each other as if they weren't sure whether they were supposed to leave or stick around.

"You guys can hang out for a while if you want," I said. "It won't take Rodiger long to come back with some preliminary information. He's just looking at business and real estate records and probably Omar's passport if he can find one."

Bru had never been to my office before, and both he and Sallie seemed interested in how things worked, so we spent a few minutes chatting about the various databases we have access to, and I explained the set-up of the squad room and who did what. I was telling them about AFIS, the Automated Fingerprint Identification System, when Rodiger popped back in. He looked at Bru and Sallie and then at me, not sure whether he should share his information with two civilians.

"It's okay, Rodiger," I said. "What'd you find?"

"Well, sir, the business listing shows the owner of the Hidden Gem as an Omar Pasha, but I can't find any personal records associated with that name that fit our guy."

"Hmm, that's a red flag for sure," I said. "What about the house?"

"He must rent it," Rodiger said. "It's owned by the C. Duval Family Trust."

"Oh wow," Bru piped in. "That's my friend Charlotte Duval. She's been getting her hair done by Omar for a couple years now, so if he rents from her, that explains the connection. Charlotte raves about the guy, and if I'm not mistaken, she's the one who referred Sallie to Omar."

"Yes, that's correct," Sallie said.

"I take it then that you also are acquainted with Ms. Duval?" Rodiger asked Sallie.

"Yes, we're casual acquaintances," Sallie said. "We met through Bruneau and occasionally get together for coffee."

There was a brief silence as Rodiger and I took in this information. I decided it was time for the police to take care of police business. I thanked Sallie and Bru for their help and assured them I'd be in touch if there were new developments. After they left, and Rodiger had closed the door behind them, we discussed next steps.

"What do you think?" I asked.

"There seem to be quite a few coincidences, sir. That our emerging suspect should be acquainted with Miss Maguire and her friend Charlotte Duval is rather, well, serendipitous, sir."

"Serendipitous? Jesus Rodiger, really? If you want to get somewhere around here, son, you're going to have to learn to talk like a cop," I said.

"Yes, sir," Rodiger nodded.

"But yes, I take your point," I said. "This city can feel like a small town sometimes."

I paused for a moment and then continued.

"Putting aside coincidences, the absence of personal records for Omar Pasha is a definite red flag. If the name is an alias, it would fit the Mahdi Toledano profile."

"Do you think we have enough for a warrant, sir?"

"Maybe, but I'm leaning more toward just stopping by the Hidden Gem for a friendly chat with our man Omar," I said.

"You know Rodiger," I added, "you look like you could use a trim."

* * *

We weren't sure what we were dealing with, so I'd called ahead for back-up, and when we arrived at the Hidden Gem a pair of patrol cars were parked at either end of the block. It's rare in Property Crimes to have to draw your gun, unless you're dealing with an auto theft ring or something along those lines, but this situation was a bit of a wild card. There wasn't anything in

CHAPTER THIRTEEN

Mahdi Toledano's profile to suggest he was violent, but if he was who we thought he might be, he was a high-stakes international criminal, and he and an accomplice had disarmed and tied up a guard in Amsterdam. Better safe than sorry was my thinking, so I told Rodiger to unfasten his holster just in case. At my direction, one uniform went to cover the back of the house while the other three hung behind us on the other side of the street.

As we approached the salon, light refracted through the tendrils of a large live oak, its roots pushing up through the sidewalk. The house itself was exactly as Sallie Maguire had described. It was a shotgun cottage with a small stoop on the left-hand side of the building leading to a single front door next to a full-length window. It was painted tan, with red trim, and potted hibiscus plants stood on either side of the stoop. There was no sign out front, which seemed a little strange for a retail business like a hair salon.

I rapped the doorknocker while Rodiger stood off to the side. There was no answer at first, so I knocked again, and this time we could hear footsteps approaching. In a few seconds the deadbolt turned, the door opened just a crack, and an older woman peered out at us from inside.

"May I help you?" she asked tentatively.

"We're with the New Orleans Police Department, ma'am," I said politely. "We're looking for Omar Pasha. Is he at home?"

"Well, that makes two of us, officer," the lady said, opening the door wider now. "I don't know where Omar is. It's the most astonishing thing. He seems to have vanished into thin air."

As quickly became obvious, this was Bruneau's friend Charlotte Duval, the owner of the building and presumably Omar's landlord. She looked to be in her mid-70s, well-dressed, and clearly confused.

"Vanished, ma'am?"

"Yes, it seems as though he's pulled up stakes," she said. "There's not a trace of him left behind from what I can see."

"You are his landlord, I take it? Ms. Duval?" I probed.

"Why yes. How do you know my name, detective?"

"A trust in your name is listed as the owner of the building, ma'am," I said. "And your friend Bruneau Abellard mentioned that you were a client of Mr.

Pasha's."

"Yes, that's right. What did you say your name was, detective?"

"Duplessis, ma'am, detective Bo Duplessis."

"Ah, yes, of course, you must be Bruneau's childhood friend, the one who's always getting him into trouble."

"I'm afraid that may be true, ma'am," I said with a smile, "although I think Bruneau deserves credit for stirring up some of his own trouble from time to time."

"You're probably right about that. What is your interest in Omar, detective?"

"We'd just like to ask him a few questions," I said. "May I ask, Ms. Duval, when did you realize Mr. Pasha had vanished, as you put it?"

Charlotte explained that the day prior she had found an unstamped envelope in her mailbox. When she opened it there was a typewritten note from her tenant along with a check covering the rent for the last four months of his lease.

"Do you still have the note, ma'am?"

"Yes, I do. It's right here in my bag."

She dug into her pocketbook and pulled out an envelope with "Charlotte" written in block letters and underlined. I slipped on a pair of latex gloves, and Charlotte handed me the envelope, which contained a typewritten notecard.

> *Dear Charlotte,*
>
> *I regret that urgent circumstances take me from this wonderful city. I am sorry that I was not able to say a proper goodbye, but please know that making your acquaintance was one of the highlights of my time here.*
>
> *Enclosed please find a check covering the balance of the rent still owed to you. Please cash it today, as I need to close the account. I think you'll find the house well-cleaned and in good condition. I wasn't able to take the styling chair with me, so please consider it yours. Perhaps your next tenant could use it as a bar stool? If not, it's a vintage piece*

CHAPTER THIRTEEN

and may have some value should you choose to sell it. I'm sorry to burden you with that.

I've never told you this, Charlotte, but you remind me of my dear grandmother, who was a very special person in my life. It was she who taught me to cut hair. I shall think of you often, and always fondly.

Affectionately yours,
Omar

The letter immediately struck me as unusual. Why would a hardened career criminal like Pasha or Toledano pay up the balance of his lease before skipping town? And leave behind such a considerate note? Was he genuinely fond of his landlord? Did he have a sense of personal responsibility not often found among the criminals we're used to dealing with? It was another data point to add to our list.

"Did you cash the check, Ms. Duval?" I asked.

"Yes, I did. It went through without a problem."

"Pardon me, ma'am," Rodiger piped in, "has anyone touched the card or the envelope other than yourself?"

Charlotte looked at Rodiger with a startled expression, as if she hadn't realized he was there.

"Please excuse him, ma'am, this is Officer Rodiger," I said. "He seems to have forgotten his manners."

"Oh, I see, that's quite alright, Detective," Charlotte said, a bit flustered. "To answer your question, Officer Rodiger, no I don't believe anyone other than myself and Detective Duplessis has touched the card or the envelope."

"Apologies, ma'am," Rodiger said, casting a sidelong glance in my direction. "I should have identified myself. Would you mind if we took an impression of your fingerprints? That way, we can rule out your prints should there be a second set on the stationary."

"Of course, you may, officer," Charlotte said, confused, "but why in the world are you looking for Omar's fingerprints? What is it that you think he's done?"

"We believe the name Omar Pasha is an alias, ma'am," I said. "He is a suspect in a series of crimes. That's all I can tell you at this time."

Charlotte stared at me in disbelief.

"I don't know what to say, detective. There must be a mistake. The Omar I know is a sweetheart. A model tenant and a true gentleman in every way. Are you sure about this?"

"No, we're not, which is why we wanted to talk to him, rather than showing up with a warrant for his arrest. His sudden disappearance raises our level of suspicion, however. Do you have any idea where he may have gone?"

"No, none whatsoever," Charlotte said. "Back to Canada, maybe, or France?"

"Is that where he told you he was from?" Rodiger asked.

"Yes," Charlotte replied. "He was born in Turkey, grew up in France, and moved to Montreal as a young man. He arrived in New Orleans three years ago with the idea of setting up a hair salon."

"Did he say anything about citizenship or having a Green Card?" Rodiger asked.

"No, I just assumed he had everything in order."

Rodiger started to ask another question, but I cut him off.

"That'll be all for now, Rodiger," I said. "You've been most helpful, Ms. Duval. If we have any follow-up questions for you, we'll be in touch. In the meantime, would you mind if we look around?"

"No, not at all," Charlotte said. "Make yourself at home."

I signaled to the uniforms that they were no longer needed as Charlotte stood aside to let us through the doorway. The floor plan was typical of small shotguns, with a narrow hallway running almost the length of the house to a kitchen in the back, with a succession of rooms off to the right. As Sallie had indicated, a cozy living room came first, followed by the space Omar had used for his salon and then a full bathroom, a bedroom, and a dining area. The entire house was spotless and neatly arranged.

"Can we assume you rented the house fully furnished?" I asked Charlotte.

"Yes. The salon chair was Omar's, as he said in his note, and he had a few wall hangings and a rug or two of his own. Otherwise, everything you see

CHAPTER THIRTEEN

here is mine."

"Am I correct that there was a painting of a harem girl hanging in the living room?"

"Why yes, I believe that's correct," Charlotte said. "He must have taken it with him. It was a watercolor, I think. Quite well done."

Rodiger and I spent some time poking around, opening drawers, and looking behind and underneath pieces of furniture, but just as Charlotte had said, there was no trace of Omar or Mahdi Toledano to be found. To be thorough, I radioed a Crime Scenes team to sweep the place in case we'd missed anything and to get Charlotte's prints while Rodiger put out an alert at the airport and other possible points of departure. I doubted we'd turn up anything, though. This wasn't the first time Mahdi Toledano had been in the wind.

Chapter Fourteen

Sallie and I had returned to my apartment and were sipping tea and nibbling on scones, reviewing our visit to the police station.

"There's a lot more that goes into police work than meets the eye," Sallie said. "Databases, processes, procedures. People coming in and out. Constant activity. It's kind of overwhelming."

"I know," I said, "and impressive too. I'd never seen Bo in that environment. He seemed very much in his element. Confident, comfortable, in charge."

"Would you have expected anything different?"

"No, not necessarily," I said. "I guess there's a part of me that still thinks of him as this happy-go-lucky kid, schmoozing his way through life, making it up as he goes along."

"But that's not who he is anymore, is it?"

"No, I guess not."

"Think Angie has something to do with that?"

"Sure," I said. "Being a father to three kids. Growing older, more experienced. All those things. We all grow up eventually, right?"

"Do we now?" Sallie asked.

I looked over at her. "Right. Point taken."

Just then the phone rang. It was Bo calling to tell me about Omar Pasha's disappearance and encountering Charlotte at the Hidden Gem. He read me the note Omar left behind for Charlotte, and when I asked, gave me the go-ahead to pay Charlotte a visit.

"She's pretty rattled, which you'd expect," Bo said. "So go be a good friend, but remember that she's a material witness, so no sharing details of the

CHAPTER FOURTEEN

investigation."

After assuring Bo I would be a model of discretion, I asked Sallie if she'd like to tag along as I checked on Charlotte. She seemed pleased to be included. When we stepped outside, and I started walking toward my car, she stopped me.

"Where are you going?"

"To my car. Where else?"

"Doesn't Charlotte live like seven or eight blocks from here, ten at the most?"

"Yeah, that sounds about right."

"Come on then," she said, turning toward Camp Street, "you could use the exercise. You're supposed to be a walker these days, remember?"

Unable to summon a credible objection, I followed in Sallie's wake.

"If I knew we were going to walk, I would have worn a different pair of shoes," I said.

"Stop complaining, and let's go." A hint of a smile crossed her lips.

It was, in fact, eleven blocks to Charlotte's house, a calculation I'd worked out in my head by the time we turned right on Coliseum. When I shared this piece of information with Sallie, it elicited nothing more than an eye roll. She walked more briskly than my normal pace, but I managed to keep up lest I lose more face. When we arrived at Charlotte's, I was breathing heavily and had to wipe sweat from my brow.

"There, didn't that beat driving?" Sallie asked, smiling wickedly.

I grunted, moved past her, and knocked on Charlotte's front door. As we waited, we stood back to admire the two-story front porch supported by Corinthian columns and embellished by intricate iron railings.

"Not too shabby, eh?"

"No, not at all," Sallie said.

Soon, we could hear footsteps approaching, and the door was opened by Isabella, Charlotte's longtime live-in helper.

"Hola, Senor Abellard," she said with a big smile. Isabella and I have always hit it off.

"Hola, Isabella. This is Miss Maguire," I said, gesturing toward Sallie.

Isabella smiled and nodded at Sallie in such a way as to suggest they were already acquainted. "Is Ms. Duval in? We've come to pay her a visit."

"Yes, I think so. Please come in. It's so hot out there."

Isabella showed us into the front parlor area where Charlotte entertains visitors and left us to locate the lady of the house. The window AC unit in the room was running full bore, over the trace smell of stale cigarette smoke, and in seconds, I went from overheated to freezing cold as the sweat running down my chest and back turned frigid.

Sallie looked at me. "Are you okay?"

"Yes, fine," I said. "It's just that when I'm sweating, and I walk into an air-conditioned room, my sweat turns cold. That's one of the reasons I prefer to drive."

"Maybe next time you can bring a towel."

It was more comfortable to stand than sit and let my sweat gather, so I shuffled around the spacious room, with its sixteen-foot ceiling and heart-of-pine floors, taking inventory of Charlotte's ever-changing decorative arrangements. The English Regency sofa and chaise lounge I'd sold her long ago were constants, as was the gorgeous 18th-century Italian Savonarola chair on which Sallie sat, which had been passed down through generations of Duvals. Everything else was in a continual state of flux as Charlotte bought and sold according to her whims. As it turned out, the room was much as it had been the last time I'd visited, although I noted approvingly that her most recent purchase from my store, a French miniature carriage clock, was displayed prominently on her mantle. I was expounding to Sallie about the clock's Limoges enamel panels when muffled voices and footsteps down the hall signaled that Charlotte was on her way.

"What a nice surprise," she said, entering the room. "I'd ask 'to what do I owe this unexpected visit,' but I think I can guess. You've come to commiserate over this wretched business with dear Omar, haven't you?"

I smiled and nodded as Charlotte sank into the sofa. She looked haggard and uncharacteristically disheveled, with the tail of her shirt hanging out, several strands of hair out of place, and a trace of smudged eye shadow on her cheeks.

CHAPTER FOURTEEN

"What a frightful shock this has been," she said. "First, to get a note from Omar telling me he's leaving, with no explanation given, and then to find out the police are looking for him. None of this seems real."

"We're so sorry you've had to deal with this," I said. "At least Omar paid his rent and left you a note."

"That's what's so strange," she said. "Does that sound like the behavior of a criminal to you? If he was in trouble and had to leave, he could have just taken off, right? Instead, he leaves me a check for his final four months of rent and a note saying I remind him of his dear grandmother. And that's exactly the Omar I knew. Kind, thoughtful, responsible. Isn't that how he seemed to you, Sallie?"

"Yes Charlotte, very much so," Sallie said, "and that's what I told the police. But then again, I'd only been to Omar twice."

"He was a sweetheart and a proper gentleman through and through," Charlotte said. "The Omar I knew was as honest as the day is long and didn't have a mean bone in his body."

"It doesn't seem to fit," I said. "What else can you tell us about him?"

"What do you want to know, dear?"

"Well, I'm curious how you met him in the first place and how he came to be your tenant," I said. "I didn't even know you owned a rental property."

"There's a lot you don't know about me, Bruneau."

"I suppose that must be true," I said.

"I just mean, we all have our private affairs, don't we? Some of us manage rental properties, and some of us hunt for hermits and savage beasts."

"Ouch!"

"Bravo, Charlotte!" Sallie guffawed. "Way to hit him where it hurts!"

"I guess I deserved that," I said. "But seriously, Charlotte, maybe you can take us through your history with Omar. There might be some innocuous detail that could lead us somewhere."

"Oh dear, are we playing detective again, Bruneau? I thought you would have gotten that out of your system after your unfortunate dust-up on Grand Isle. Anyway, I've already covered this ground with the police."

"I'm sure you have," I said, "but sometimes it helps to share a story with a different set of ears."

Charlotte looked at us with a weary expression.

"Very well, if you insist," she said. "Before I begin, would either of you like something to drink? A glass of iced tea, perhaps?"

"That would be lovely," Sallie said.

"Sure," I added.

Charlotte rang a bell for Isabella and asked her to bring three iced teas. Then she fixed her gaze on me and began recounting her time with Omar.

"I've owned that house on Carondelet ever since Daddy died," she began, "but I'd only had one tenant until a few years ago when his family moved him into an assisted living place out in Metarie. A dear old man, Mr. Raymond. Anyway, I didn't want to pay a property management company to rent the place out for me, so I took out an ad in the classifieds. I had a few nibbles but nothing serious, and then I got a call from Omar, asking if I'd be open to him operating a one-man hair salon at the house if he also lived there.

"I wasn't wild about the idea, but I said I'd be open to discussing it. We met at the house, and of course, I was surprised at how small he was. But I liked him immediately, and I think the feeling was mutual. So, we hit it off. I said yes, and the rest is history."

Isabella entered the room carrying a tray with three tall glasses of tea and a small plate of lemon slices. I realized too late that the absence of sugar on the tray meant the tea was sweetened. I've never understood the appeal of sweet tea, which to me is like drinking corn syrup, but I'd made my bed, so I took a slug.

"Mmm, that's good, Isabella," I said, barely concealing my disgust. Sallie added her polite agreement, and Isabella thanked us and left the room.

"How well did you get to know Omar?" I asked Charlotte.

"Pretty well, I'd say. We didn't share our deepest secrets or anything, but we always had nice chats whenever he did my hair, or when he'd deliver the rent, which he always did on time and in person. Omar was a model tenant."

"What did he tell you about his childhood?"

"Just that he grew up in France, outside of Marseilles somewhere, and

CHAPTER FOURTEEN

was raised mainly by his aunts and his grandmother," Charlotte said. "His mother died when he was young, and his father didn't have much time for him, apparently. He seemed to have some unresolved anger toward his father and identified more with the women in his life."

"How so?"

"Just a feeling I got. There were a couple times his father came up in conversation, and it was almost like his whole personality would change, like a shadow would cross his face and his speech would become clipped. But when he talked about his aunts and his grandmother, it was always with affection. I remember one time we got into a political discussion, and he commented that the world would be a better place if it was run by women. Naturally, I couldn't disagree with that."

"What about as an adult?" I asked. "What became of Omar when he grew up and left home?"

"I don't know all the details," Charlotte said. "Only that he ended up in Montreal, cutting hair. He said he got bored with his life up there and New Orleans sounded like an exciting place to be, so he pulled up stakes and moved here and set up shop all over again."

"Did he have a lot of customers?"

"He seemed to, but I don't really know. Enough to cover the rent, anyway."

"Charlotte, did Omar ever mention anything about Jane Placide or Jean Lafitte?" Sallie asked. I had forgotten to pass along Bo's missive about not sharing details of the investigation into Mahdi Toledano.

"Jane Placide? Heavens no," Charlotte said. "Why on earth … Wait a minute, don't tell me Omar's a suspect in your grave robbing."

"No, of course not," I lied. "Sallie's just thinking outside the box and trying to connect some dots, that's all."

Charlotte didn't look convinced, so I laid it on a little thicker.

"It's true that whoever broke into the crypt had to have been small, so it's natural for Sallie to connect Omar to the break-in, but we have no reason to believe Omar was involved. There are lots of women who are small enough to fit into the crypt, and a woman's footprints were found at the scene, so I think it's safe to say we're looking for a female grave robber."

Charlotte eyed me skeptically while Sallie had enough sense not to keep pressing the Jane Placide angle.

I changed the line of inquiry, and we talked for a few more minutes. Charlotte was clearly exhausted, and her answers grew shorter and less helpful. Sallie hadn't said a word since I shut down her Jane Placide question.

"Charlotte, I can tell you're tired and we need to be going," I said, rising from my seat. "Thank you for humoring us. I know this has been a terrible shock for you. If you need anything, please let us know."

"Certainly, detective Abellard," Charlotte said dryly. "You really do have the investigation bug, don't you? Please don't worry about me, I'll be fine. And, of course, if I think of anything, I'll let the police know.

"I do appreciate the two of you checking in on me. It was kind of you. Now run along. You've got better things to do with your afternoon than to spend it holding an old lady's hand."

***

Sometime during the half hour or so we were at Charlotte's, it had begun raining outside, even though the sun was still shining. Not hard, just a steady drizzle. Sallie set a more relaxed pace this time, and the canopy of live oaks on Coliseum Street kept us mostly dry. The moisture rising off the hot pavement smelled like cedar bark mixed with petrol and steaming earth, and the patter of raindrops on wet leaves made for calming background music. Sallie cast me an apologetic look.

"I take it I wasn't supposed to ask about Jane Placide?"

"Oh, don't worry about that," I said. "It's my fault. Bo asked me not to share any details of the investigation since Charlotte could end up being a witness. There's no way you could have known."

"I didn't share any details, did I? All I did was ask a question."

"Yes, but the fact that we'd ask a question about Jane Placide at all would suggest that we think Omar might be involved in the grave robbery, which in itself is an important detail unknown to anybody not involved in the investigation."

CHAPTER FOURTEEN

"I'm sorry. I didn't know."

"Like I said, don't worry about it. It's my fault entirely, and it's not a big deal in any case."

"Bo doesn't think Charlotte is somehow mixed up in any of this, does he?"

"No, of course not. He just has procedure to follow, that's all."

There was a brief silence before Sallie spoke again.

"I'd say this has taken quite a toll on Charlotte. She looks like she's aged ten years."

"I know, I had the same thought," I said. "She'll be alright, though. She's a tough old broad, and she'll bounce back in time."

Sallie smiled and nodded in agreement. We walked side by side, brushing lightly against each other. I wrapped my arm around Sallie's shoulder and gathered her toward me. She rested her head against my chest, and we walked slowly on in silence. Sallie turned her face up toward me a couple times, and we exchanged contented smiles.

We continued on like that, not saying a word until we arrived at my doorstep. When we stopped, I turned Sallie toward me, ran my fingers through her hair, and was gently pulling her close when her face contorted, and she let out a terror-stricken scream. A long shadow moved behind me, where Sallie was looking, and a deep but anxious voice rang out.

"It's okay, miss. I'm a friend."

I spun around, and the recognition hit me.

"Prosper!" I shouted. "What in the world!"

Chapter Fifteen

In the weeks following the disappearance of Omar Pasha, leads came in from all over the world, but there were no confirmed sightings. Bo gave us periodic updates, but less frequently as time went on. His attention to the investigation seemed to wane, and I could understand why. The case had been downgraded to a breaking and entering since it couldn't be proven that anything was taken. He had other matters to investigate. And once Mahdi Toledano became the primary suspect in the Crypt 1083-A break-in, NOPD was reduced to a bit player in a sweeping international effort led by the likes of Interpol and the FBI.

I was swamped and distracted, too. The fall and winter seasons are busy times at the store, and my social calendar fills up during the holidays and the protracted countdown to Mardi Gras. Complicating matters, Sallie and I are a couple again. Eventually, people got the message, but for a long while, I had to respond to every invitation with a request to include Sallie. I don't know what became of the wallflower of old, but Sallie has charmed every audience she's been introduced to, and her inclusion is now de rigueur in any social occasion to which I am invited and some to which I am not.

Sallie and I don't officially live together, and we haven't made a long-term commitment to one another, but we spend most weeknights and pretty much every weekend in each other's company. Despite the occasional flare-up, we've been getting along great. The sex has gone well, too. In fact, sometimes, we can barely keep our hands off each other.

But for two people used to living alone, it is constant work, moderating our eccentricities and accommodating each other's entrenched behaviors

CHAPTER FIFTEEN

as best we can. Sallie has me on a low-grade exercise regimen and paying more attention to what I eat, and I've managed to drop a few more pounds. For her part, Sallie allows me my routines and has even joined me for red beans and rice on Monday evenings. She has gained my full confidence as a chef, so she is welcome to do the cooking whenever she is so inclined.

My other big project is Prosper Fortune. The night he scared poor Sallie out of her mind, it took Sallie a few minutes to compose herself. Then she excused herself and headed home while Prosper and I went upstairs to my apartment.

His appearance took some getting used to. He'd cut his hair, gave the impression of having recently bathed, and wore a flannel shirt tucked inside a baggy pair of chinos. Even Hugo seemed taken aback, administering a lengthy sniff test before signaling his approval and curling up in a ball at the big man's feet.

Prosper apologized for showing up out of the blue.

"I don't have any friends left in town," he explained. "Despite the unfortunate incident with Caliban, I enjoyed your visit, which, to be honest, is what got me thinking about coming home again. I just wanted you to know I'm around if you feel like getting together sometime."

Prosper told me that when he first arrived back in town, he spent a few nights at the Salvation Army shelter on South Claiborne. Then he summoned the courage to show up on the doorstep of his younger half-sister and only sibling, Irene, with whom he'd had no contact for almost 50 years. He tracked her down in Gentilly, in the middle-class neighborhood surrounding Holy Cross High School. Expecting an icy reception, Prosper was instead greeted with hugs and tears of joy from Irene and warm welcomes from the brother-in-law and two nephews he hadn't known he had. He choked up when he told me that Irene and her husband, Chuck, insisted he move into the furnished studio apartment they keep above their detached garage.

"Tell me about Irene and her family," I said.

"Irene is a bookkeeper and receptionist for a doctor's office," Prosper said. "Chuck manages the Winn Dixie on Veteran's Boulevard."

"And their boys?"

"Charlie graduated from UNO last year. Lives at home and waits tables. He's thinking about training to be a firefighter. His younger brother Andre is a sophomore at UNO."

"Andre? Named after you?"

"Yeah, if you can believe it," Prosper said, dabbing an eye. "When my parents divorced, my dad eventually married a younger woman and had Irene when he was in his fifties. She's almost twenty years my junior, so we weren't close growing up. I remember her as a sweet young kid, but then I went to Vietnam and only returned briefly before skipping town for good.

"But to hear Irene and Chuck tell it, she held on to this idealized notion of me as some kind of damaged war hero and truth seeker. She named Andre after me and kept her maiden name solely in the hope that one day when I was ready, I'd be able to find her."

"Damn Prosper, you trying to make me tear up? What a beautiful story."

"I know," he said. "I don't deserve their kindness."

"Why not? You're being way too hard on yourself. You never did anything to hurt anybody. You just had your own demons to deal with, that's all."

"Yeah, I guess, but I never really thought about how my actions might affect others. All this time, I've been wrapped up in my own issues. But I have so many regrets, Bruneau, and so much lost time to make up for. I don't know where to begin or how."

"One day at a time, Prosper, one day at a time," I said. "I know it's a cliché, but it's true."

We sat silently for a few moments. I locked eyes with him.

"Why did you decide to come back after all these years?"

Prosper took a second and then answered carefully.

"Well, as you reminded me, Prospero does eventually leave his island," he said with a self-effacing smile.

"And honestly, I'd been thinking about it even before your visit. I don't have too many years left before my 'insubstantial pageant' fades, and I've been thinking about what I'll leave behind. Is it just a shack on an island soon to be swallowed by the sea? Will that be the only evidence of me, or

CHAPTER FIFTEEN

can there be something more? I know it's late in the game to be having thoughts like these…"

"You're hardly alone," I said. "As the Bard says, 'our little life is rounded with sleep.' It's the human condition. We all know that at some point our tiny imprint on this earth will disappear, but we flatter ourselves that some little piece of us can live on. It's a delusion, of course, but the nobility is in the struggle. The struggle to matter."

"Yeah, so there's your answer, I guess," Prosper said. "I want to matter."

* * *

I made a point of letting Prosper know his companionship was welcome, inviting him to lunch a couple times and having him over for dinner. A few weeks after he showed up on my doorstep, I drove him back to Grand Isle. He'd made his way to New Orleans by hitching a ride with a fishing captain he knew who had business in the city, and all he'd taken with him were the clothes on his back and a few necessities. He wanted to collect the rest of his possessions and close up his shack for good.

"How do you think Caliban has been making out?" I asked him as we turned into the final approach to his plot of woods.

"He's a survivor," Prosper said. "I'm not too concerned on that front. He may be wistful for the free meals I gave him, but other than that I doubt he misses me. We were never on cuddling terms."

"You don't think his leg affects his ability to hunt for food?"

"Nah. Caliban is all about the element of surprise, not running down prey. His victims never see him coming."

"I can relate to that," I said.

As we parked and began making our way toward Prosper's shack, my head was on a swivel. Not wanting to re-traumatize him, or provide inducement for another sneak attack from Caliban, I'd left Hugo at home with Sallie. But I wasn't taking any chances.

"There's no need to be spooked," Prosper said. "I can assure you we're perfectly safe. It was Hugo the cat was after, not you."

"Right," I said. "Then again, those who fail to learn from history are doomed to repeat it."

"Suit yourself."

When we reached the shack, signs of Caliban were everywhere. Bird and rodent bones were strewn around the porch, the noxious reek of decomposition was pervasive, and clumps of fur festooned the bed he'd adopted as his own.

"Looks like your feline friend has been making himself at home," I said.

"Like I said, he's a survivor."

"Where do you think he is right now?"

"Watching us, I imagine."

I stepped back out to the porch and surveyed the perimeter of the clearing that surrounded the shack. The big cat could have been anywhere. I imagined him lying on his belly, peeking through the giant ferns that carpeted the floor of Prosper's forest. I wondered aloud if he'd recognize either of us. Prosper responded with an indifferent shrug.

While Prosper stuffed laundry bags full of tools, cooking utensils, and the historical artifacts he'd collected from Grand Terre, I boxed up his library.

"Are there any Lafitte books you haven't read?" I asked.

"There may be a few."

"I may have to borrow a couple of these."

"Have at it. What's mine is yours."

It took us a couple trips to and from the car to get everything loaded up. When it was fully packed, I began to pull away, but stopped so Prosper could take one last look. I strained for a glimpse of Caliban but saw nothing.

"Do you miss it at all?" I asked.

"Not really," Prosper said. "The simplicity, maybe, but not the isolation. It's only taken me 76 years to reach the conclusion that human beings are meant to be social animals. Imagine that."

* * *

That was about five months ago. Since then, I've done what I could to help

CHAPTER FIFTEEN

Prosper establish a new life for himself. It hasn't been easy. The changes to the city and in technology are overwhelming to him. Prosper had been at least vaguely aware of many of them, as Grand Isle is not immune to the march of progress, but there's a difference between knowing that computers, cell phones, and ATMs exist and learning how to use them. His nephews have helped as best they can. Meanwhile, Chuck got Prosper a job stocking groceries three days a week, and recently, Prosper has started cooking at a soup kitchen on Sundays.

The hardest part, he tells me, is the social stimulation. After a day at work, or the soup kitchen, or even after a meal with Irene and Chuck and the kids, all he wants to do is retreat to his apartment, curl up in a ball, and shut out the world. He keeps his place clean and tidy out of respect for Irene, but he confessed to me that the smells of cleaning solutions and the soaps and fragrances we use to mask our body odors leave him in a state of perpetual nausea.

I pick Prosper up once a week, usually on Saturdays, and we grab a bite somewhere and discuss the mysteries of the universe, or perhaps the competing virtues of ketchup and mayonnaise. Sometimes, Sallie will tag along, but usually not. Her view of Prosper has softened, but I think she senses that we become a bit inhibited in her presence and that the bond we share doesn't easily accommodate a third wheel.

Irene and Chuck were kind enough to invite Sallie and me to dinner one night, and we reciprocated, but that's probably as far as that relationship will go. They are wonderful, well-meaning people, and it's warming to watch Irene fawn over "Andre," who she clearly adores, but we don't share much in the way of common interests.

From time to time, Prosper and I discuss the Jane Placide case and, more particularly, Jean Lafitte.

"Who was Lafitte, really?" I asked Prosper recently, over an oyster loaf lunch at Casamento's. "What do you think he was like?"

"I'd say it's anybody's guess," Prosper said. "That's the thing about Lafitte. He's kind of a blank canvas. You can make him anybody you want him to be, and there'll be evidence to support your position."

"But what's your guess?"

Prosper thought for a second.

"I guess I see him as an honorable scoundrel," he finally said. "There's no doubt that Lafitte was a ruthless mercenary and an unrepentant thief, and there's only so much good you can say about anyone who trafficked in human chattel, no matter the mores of the time. But even though he was a spy, there's very little evidence of personal duplicity with Lafitte. He seems to have been a man of his word who treated his men well and dealt with them fairly. His prisoners, too. And he seems to have been capable of love and empathy, certainly for his brother anyway, and perhaps for Jane Placide as well."

"Sort of a walking contradiction?"

"No, I wouldn't say that," Prosper said. "We're too quick to place people in binary categories, I think. Good or bad, right or wrong, honest or dishonest. Human beings are complicated creatures, you know, and we can be two or more things at once depending on context and circumstance. Lafitte was no different."

Prosper made his point in reference to Jean Lafitte, but it prompted me to consider the case of Mahdi Toledano. How to square the hardened career criminal with the writer of a considerate note to an old lady? Was he an honorable scoundrel, too?

* * *

Not long after that lunch with Prosper, Sallie and I were eating breakfast, and I was flipping through a newspaper filled with Mardi Gras stories and parade route graphics. It was a week before Fat Tuesday and already six krewes had rolled through Magazine Street, with two more still to come.

"I am so sick of this crap," I said. "Two full months of parades and detours and hosting every out-of-control binge drinker in the country. Not to mention all the goddamn parties and mindless krewe gossip."

Sallie feels the same way about Mardi Gras, but on this particular morning, she was in the mood to yank my chain, as Bo likes to say.

CHAPTER FIFTEEN

"Oh, my poor, poor darling Bruneau," she mewed. "Here, I thought you were enjoying carnival season. You seemed to have such a good time the other night at Annie and Bert's, and you made such a fetching Nero."

Sallie and I had attended a lavish costume party at Annie Russell's house, and despite my having bitched about it for weeks, I ended up having a rollicking good time and making a bit of an ass of myself. Dressed as Nero no less, complete with under tunic, toga drape, head wreath, and fiddle. Sallie was determined not to let me forget.

"Very funny," I said. "One fun evening does not a season of enjoyment make."

"A fun evening, but not such a fun morning?"

"No, not such a fun morning."

"And why was that?" Sallie asked.

"I think you know why."

"Which was worse, the hangover or having to call Annie and apologize for your behavior?"

"Are you ever going to drop this? Don't you think it's getting a bit old?"

"Oh, I'm sure I will drop it one day," Sallie said, moving toward me with a mischievous grin. "But it's a long way from getting old."

With that, Sallie pushed my newspaper out of the way, slid onto my lap, and kicked her legs over the side of the armchair. She brought her face close to mine.

"Does your head still hurt, poor baby, or is it just your ego that's smarting."

"I can assure you my ego is in fine shape," I said.

Sallie leaned into my ear and purred.

"And what about your other parts? Are they in fine working order, too?"

I had to laugh at that. Sallie smiled, pleased with herself, and came in for a long, sexy kiss. When it was over, she started to get up, but I pulled her back.

"Oh no, you don't," I said.

She giggled but extricated herself more forcefully this time.

"Sorry, but the shower beckons. I've got a busy day today. I'm presenting my budget requests to the director."

"Right, I forgot," I said. "I have full confidence in your ability to win him over with your impeccable math and airtight business case. Or, failing that, your wily female charms."

Sallie smiled, bent over to kiss the top of my head, and disappeared into the bedroom. I moved to the couch, beckoned for Hugo to join me, and picked up the newspaper again. It wasn't long before an AP story caught my attention.

Gem Found Hidden
Near Bonaparte Estate Sells for $63M

HONG KONG (AP) — A blue diamond thought to have once belonged to the crown jewel collection of the French Bourbon kings and found immediately adjacent to the former New Jersey estate of Joseph Bonaparte, sold yesterday at auction to an undisclosed buyer for $63 million.

The 68-carat diamond was discovered by a maintenance worker at Point Breeze, the New Jersey estate of Joseph Bonaparte, the older brother of French Emperor Napoleon Bonaparte.

Point Breeze is today owned and maintained by the City of Bordentown, N.J., in partnership with a private land trust and the New Jersey Department of Environmental Protection.

The worker, who has not been named, is said to have found the diamond hidden on public property near the site of a recently completed archaeological excavation at the estate.

Joseph Bonaparte emigrated from France to the United States in 1815, following Napoleon's final defeat at the Battle of Waterloo. He took with him many jewels and works of art from the royal collections of not only France but also Naples and Spain, where his brother had installed him as king.

The 68-carat blue diamond has divided jewelry historians into two camps, said Julian Fields of the American Society of Jewelry Historians.

CHAPTER FIFTEEN

"We all recognize the extraordinary quality and historical significance of this gem," Fielder said, adding that the diamond is of "perfect clarity."

"Some of us believe this is the famous 'French Blue' or 'Tavernier Blue' diamond stolen from the French Crown during the revolution, as it matches historical descriptions almost perfectly.

"Others think that is impossible because the famous Hope Diamond has been shown to have been cut from the French Blue."

The 45.52 carat Hope Diamond has had several owners and is now on permanent display at the Smithsonian National Museum of Natural History.

The Tavernier Blue Diamond was named after Jean-Baptiste Tavernier, a 17th-century gem merchant who traveled extensively to Persia and India and sold most of the jewels he brought back to the Bourbon "Sun King," Louis XIV.

The diamond was originally 116 carats, but Louis XIV's court jeweler cut it to 68 carats in order to set it as a hatpin.

The record for the most ever paid for a diamond at auction belongs to the 59.60 carat CTF Pink Star Diamond, which sold for $71.2 million in Hong Kong in 2017.

I read the article a second time. The diamond captured my imagination and, of course, brought to mind our Jane Placide case, but I couldn't work out a plausible connection between the two things. True, we believed we were in search of an object of great value, and we knew that Jean Lafitte hovered in Joseph Bonaparte's orbit for a short time, but I couldn't think of an explanation for how an item stolen from a crypt in New Orleans could turn up at an archaeological dig in New Jersey. I chalked it up to coincidence but made a mental note to let Bo know about the article. Then, I pulled myself out of my chair and began preparing for the day that lay ahead.

1818

CAMPECHE
GALVESTON ISLAND, TEXAS
SEPTEMBER 1818

General Charles Lallemand wasn't sure what to make of the pirate Jean Lafitte, but he knew he needed his help.

Bonaparte and his coterie had informed the general that Lafitte ran a small trading outpost on the island he called Campeche, from which the pirate had agreed to offer assistance to Lallemand and his men as they made their way inland. But instead of the primitive settlement Lallemand had expected, he found a bustling small city populated by slave laborers, gruff merchants, a handful of working women, and a rotating cast of weather-beaten sailors. No system of laws governed what might otherwise have been a combustible assemblage, yet somehow order was maintained, apparently out of respect for, or fear of, the pirate.

Set apart from the other buildings stood a large two-story frame house, painted red, with a grand center hall that led to an open-air piazza. The locals called it La Maison Rouge. The first time he'd met with the occupant there, the pirate's welcome had been cordial, and he had readily agreed to honor the arrangement he'd made with Bonaparte. He and a band of his men escorted Lallemand and his soldiers up the Trinity River, helped them locate the high ground on which to construct their fort, and left them with enough provisions to last for a month.

In the beginning, Lafitte sent emissaries to check on Champ d'Asile, as Lallemand called his command post, but as hunger, sickness, infighting, and attacks by bands of natives increasingly took their toll on the Frenchmen, help was nowhere to be found. When a messenger alerted the general that Spanish troops were on their way to remove him and his fellow filibusters from the land they claimed as Spanish, he was left with no choice but to abandon the project and return to Campeche.

He'd been back on the island for more than a week, effectively marooned, his men treated roughly and his pleas for help ignored. Only now had he been granted an audience with the man he suspected of having tipped off the Spanish to his designs. He was desperate for food, money, medicine, and most critically, a convoy back to New Orleans. Lacking leverage and knowing he could not count upon the pirate's good will; he slipped his lone remaining asset into the pocket of his waistcoat. He was loath to play the card Bonaparte instructed him to use only as a last resort, but it was no exaggeration, he felt, to characterize his present circumstance as existential.

The general was greeted at the door of the red house by the pirate's mulatto servant and presumed mistress, who wordlessly escorted him to the piazza, leaving him alone without offering a refreshment. A long 10 minutes elapsed before the pirate finally appeared.

"Ah, hello general, what is it I can do for you today," asked Lafitte, striding up to the general and standing before him. He offered neither handshake nor chair.

"Please be brief. I have much to attend to."

"Very well, captain," Lallemand said. "I'll get right to the point. I am stranded here, as you know, and my men are in poor condition. We are in desperate need of transport to New Orleans, and I have come to ask for your assistance. I am sure Monsieur Bonaparte would expect this of you."

"I see. What happened General, if I may ask, to your fine army and your plans for a nouvelle France led by Emperor Bonaparte? It would seem your ambitions are somewhat diminished."

"I think you know what has become of our plans, sir. Somehow, it seems, the Spanish learned of our intentions before we could muster our full strength."

"Ah yes, your strength."

"We need your help, Captain, so that we may reconstitute ourselves."

"My agreement with Monsieur Bonaparte was to provide you with passage inland and to help you establish your community. This I have done."

"I gratefully acknowledge as much, captain. And now, sir, I ask you in the spirit of that agreement, to help us once again."

A grim smile crossed the pirate's lips as he turned his back to Lallemand and paced, head down, his hands clasped behind his back. When he spun back around, he looked directly at the Frenchman and addressed him sternly.

"You have observed Campeche, general. The operation we have built here succeeds only through the preservation of a delicate balance of men, provisions, and commerce. This requires my constant vigilance. I have neither the time nor the resources to help you reconstitute yourself, as you say. Perhaps you can obtain the passage you seek on one of the ships dropping its cargo here. Until then, I must insist that you and your men leave our city and set up camp elsewhere on the island. Good day, general."

As the pirate strode away, Lallemand called after him.

"Wait sir! I have something to offer you."

Lafitte stopped and turned back.

"And what might that be, general?"

Lallemand reached into his pocket and pulled out a pouch.

"This," he said.

Chapter Sixteen

As summer turned to fall and fall to winter, the Jane Placide grave robbery remained an open case, even though Mac had reclassified it as breaking and entering. But with Interpol and the FBI taking the lead in the Mahdi Toledano manhunt, and with Mike Rodiger having moved on to his next rotation assignment in Homicide, it was no longer a priority. I had other investigations on my plate, and I was happy to let Jane Placide hang out in my back files. Every now and then, Bruneau would ask me for an update, and I'd make a call or two, but that was about it.

Recently, Bru tried to interest me in the sale of a precious diamond in Hong Kong. It had supposedly been found on the New Jersey property once owned by Joseph Bonaparte, Napoleon's brother, and he wondered if it could be connected to Jean Lafitte in some way. I told him *wondering* isn't part of my job description, but I did place a call to the FBI Art Crime Team. An agent said they were aware of the sale and were "looking into it," but he didn't know anything about Mahdi Toledano, so I let it go.

Mike Rodiger was more persistent. He knocked on my door a few days after I'd gotten off the phone with the FBI.

"Hello, detective," he said, cracking my door open. "Do you have a minute?"

"Of course, Mike, come on in. Good to see you. What can I do for you?"

"Well, sir, it's about the Jane Placide case. I've been doing some research."

"The Jane Placide case? The boys in Homicide not keeping you busy?"

Rodiger smiled. "I'm plenty busy, sir. It's just that I saw an article in the newspaper that interested me, so I decided to look into it. Are you aware that a diamond sold recently at auction in Hong Kong for $63 million?"

"Yes, Bruneau Abellard told me about it," I said. "One of the French crown jewels that turned up at the estate Napoleon's brother used to own in New Jersey?"

"That's the one," Rodiger said.

"And you think this could be connected to our Jane Placide case?"

"I don't know sir, but it did cross my mind that Jean Lafitte traveled to Philadelphia and may have met with Joseph Bonaparte. Other than a treasure map, we couldn't figure out what item of value Jane Placide could have taken to her grave that would motivate someone to break into the mausoleum. What if it was a diamond worth $63 million?"

"And you think this diamond could be our La Violette?"

"It's just a theory at this point, sir, but it fits pretty well with our transcription."

"Go on," I said.

Rodiger pulled out a piece of paper for reference.

"In her journal, Jane says, 'J calls *her* La Violette. He says *she* is magique.' It doesn't seem to me that Jane would use female pronouns to describe a map. But a diamond? Maybe."

"And then there's the passage that begins with 'never wear it in public' and 'I hold her at night.' Again, you wouldn't wear a map or hold it at night, would you? But you might a special diamond, right?"

"Okay, Mike," I said, "so you have a theory. Now what?"

"Well, sir, I did a little digging."

"And?"

"Well, first off, this auction house in Hong Kong has a reputation as the place to go if the provenance of the item you're looking to sell is a little sketchy, or if, as a buyer or seller, you want to keep your name out of the papers."

"In other words, if you want to unload stolen goods."

"I don't know if I'd go that far," Rodiger said. "Most of their business seems legit. Let's just say their due diligence is known to be a bit laxer than what one might expect from a Sotheby's or a Christie's. The Art Crime folks

CHAPTER SIXTEEN

keep an eye on the place."

"Alright, I'm following you," I said. "Mysterious object, shady auction house. Who's the buyer?"

"A Chinese billionaire by the name of Lingyun Gao."

"The seller?"

"Unidentified so far, but the FBI has been able to follow the money up to a point. They know that the payment from the sale was wired to an account in the Caymans registered to a shell company called Ttaba, LLC, and then those funds were split up into smaller chunks and sent all over the place to other fictitious company accounts. Banks in Luxembourg, Macau, Bolivia, the UAE...the list goes on."

"Sounds like a sophisticated layering scheme," I said. "Scatter the money around the globe to disguise its origin. Not something your average maintenance worker could pull off, that's for sure. It may be above our pay grade, but it's nothing the feds haven't seen before."

"No, but this one's more complex than most, apparently. It's going to take a long time to peel back the onion, and when they do, there might not be any footprints left to follow."

One thing in Rodiger's account bugged me.

"But wait a second," I said. "If this worker found the diamond on the estate, wouldn't it belong to the estate, and in that scenario, wouldn't the estate be the seller?"

"Yes sir," he said, "except that it was found just off the property on public land that used to belong to the estate. In most jurisdictions, including New Jersey, lost or abandoned property goes to the finder unless the discovery is made at an owner-occupied residence."

"Just off the property? Really? How convenient."

"Yes, sir."

"Can we not find the name of the guy who found the diamond?"

"Not yet, sir. I'm working on it. The Point Breeze folks seem to be stonewalling a bit."

"Not surprising," I said. "They have a $63 million problem to solve."

Rodiger nodded.

"Where does all this leave us with Jane Placide?" I asked.

"I'm not sure, sir, other than it may help answer the 'what?' and the 'why?' a bit better. But there's one more thing."

"What's that?"

"In Moroccan mythology, Ttaba is a female jinni who preys on men. She symbolizes the avenging female force bent on the destruction of the patriarchal social order."

"I bet you were that kid who always did your homework, right? Sat in the front of the class? Took tons of notes?"

"Sir?"

"Never mind. What does this she-devil have to do with our case?"

"Well, sir, if you'll recall, one of our hypotheses was that the reason Toledano may have taken the Delacroix odalisque for himself is that to him, it may represent a symbol of the female subjugation that has fueled his anger since childhood. If that's the case, he might feel an affinity for Ttaba, and have named the company after her."

I paused to consider that.

"I don't know if I buy this idea that Toledano has a thing about liberating women," I said. "I mean, sure, maybe he hated his father and identified with his mother and loved his grandmother and aunts, but you really think that anger is what's fueling him? Isn't it more likely that he's just another greedy bastard?"

"Entirely possible, sir," Rodiger said. "It's just a theory. But childhood scars can leave an indelible mark."

"Right. Let me ask you this, Mike. If you're correct that this diamond is La Violette, how does the diamond get from Jane Placide's casket to an excavation site at Joe Bonaparte's pad?"

"I have absolutely no idea, sir, but it would probably require collusion between multiple parties. Someone to steal it, someone to place it, someone to find it and sell it, and then someone to launder the money."

"Right. So, if you've got any more spare time ..."

"I'll do what I can, sir."

I don't know what it is about this kid that brings out the bully in me, but

CHAPTER SIXTEEN

if Angie was a fly on the wall, she'd tell me it wasn't a good look. As he was leaving my office, I called out to him.

"Hey Mike!"

"Yes, sir?"

"Thank you. I don't say those words often enough, but I want you to know how much I appreciate your going the extra mile like this. In case you haven't noticed, I enjoy busting your balls a bit, but that doesn't mean I don't respect the hell out of your work, because I do."

"Thank you, sir, that means a lot coming from you. Have a good day, sir."

* * *

A couple days after Rodiger shared his info with me, Angie had invited Bruneau and Sallie to dinner, and she texted me a list of items to pick up at the supermarket. Normally, I'd stop at the Rouse's on Williams Boulevard, but I'd just finished working out at my gym in Metarie, and the Argus parade was going to disrupt my normal route home, so I took a small detour and pulled into the Winn Dixie on Veterans. There was someone I wanted to meet, and I was hoping to kill two birds with one stone.

When I asked at the customer service desk if Prosper Fortune was working, I got a blank stare from the assistant manager on duty.

"Big guy, gray hair, mid-seventies, maybe?"

"Oh, you must mean Andre," she said.

"Yeah, sorry, I should have said Andre."

"Yes, he's working today. Should be over in Aisle three or four. You want me to page him for you?"

"No, that's okay, I'll find him. Thanks for your help."

Sure enough, as I turned into Aisle 3 there was a very large man bent over on one knee, arranging cereal boxes on the bottom shelf.

"Excuse me, are you Prosper?" I asked as I approached him. He turned his head and shot me a quizzical glance. "My name is Bo Duplessis. I'm a friend of Bruneau Abellard's."

At the mention of Bruneau, the man nodded in recognition, stood up stiffly, and, clutching his lower back, extended a hand. He was as big as advertised, I'd say 6-7, 310 or so, a prototypical right tackle. He was clean-shaven with a pock-marked complexion, a full head of gray hair, neatly trimmed, and he wore a short sleeve, light green Oxford tucked inside loose-fitting chinos.

"Sorry, you caught me off guard. I go by Andre these days," he said. "Yes, Bruneau has mentioned you several times. It's *Detective* Duplessis, isn't it?"

"Yes, that's right. Sorry to show up unannounced like this, but I was in the neighborhood and had to get some groceries, so I thought I'd see if you were working today and introduce myself. I don't suppose you have a break coming up. There's been a possible new development in this Jean Lafitte business, and I was hoping to bounce a couple things off you."

"Yeah, sure, I'm due a break. Can you give me a couple minutes?"

"No problem," I said. "I'll meet you outside."

I paid for the items Angie wanted, and waited for Prosper by my car, checking my texts and letting Angie know I hadn't forgotten her errand. I looked up to see Prosper exiting the store and making his way toward me, walking with a limp, but otherwise moving quickly for a man his age.

"Old war wound?" I asked as he approached.

"Yeah, it gets better once I'm up and moving for a while," he said. "What can I do for you, detective?"

"Do you have time for some coffee? There's a PJ's a couple blocks from here, or we could walk over to that Subway," I said, pointing across the shopping center.

"No thanks, I'd rather enjoy the fresh air if it's all the same to you."

"Works for me," I said. "Should I call you Prosper or Andre?"

"Either is fine," he said.

"I'm curious. Did you play ball?"

"You mean football?"

"Yes. I played at Grambling for a couple years, and we could've used a tackle built like you. Just curious."

Prosper smiled faintly.

"I played a bit at De La Salle, but other than being big, I wasn't very

CHAPTER SIXTEEN

good. Too slow and not much of a killer instinct, I'm afraid. I was better at basketball."

"Yeah? You play center?"

"Yep. I could rebound and score some in the low post, but again, too slow and not aggressive enough for the next level. Sorry to be rude, but what did you want to ask me about? I've only got a few minutes."

I gave him the rundown on the Hong Kong diamond and shared the broad outline of Rodiger's theory.

"What do you make of it?" I asked.

He shrugged. "Anything's possible when it comes to Lafitte."

"How could Lafitte have gotten the diamond? Any plausible scenario you can think of?"

"Well, the most obvious is the one your colleague mentions," Prosper said. "It's possible, though in my view unlikely, that Lafitte met with Joseph Bonaparte when he went north seeking restitution for the Barataria property that was seized before the Battle of New Orleans."

"Why unlikely?"

"The dates don't quite line up. Bonaparte arrived in Philly in September of 1815, right after Lafitte and Arsènne Latour headed home. The dates commonly cited by historians could be off a bit in either direction, so it's possible they met, but most accounts suggest they just missed each other."

"For the sake of argument, let's say they did meet. Why would Bonaparte have given Lafitte something so valuable?"

Prosper thought that over.

"Possibly as a down payment for services to be rendered."

"What kind of services?"

"Well, remember, this was late in the summer. Napoleon had just fallen for the second and final time, and Joseph and his fellow ex-pats were busy scheming to rescue him from Saint Helena and bring him to North America. Lafitte was central to a few of those plans because of his ability to command a fleet."

"Fascinating. Clearly, I should have paid more attention in European History class. I have only the vaguest sense of Napoleon and his era. He ends up dying on the island, right?"

"Right, in 1821. They never got a rescue attempt off the ground, although they were still scheming right up until his death."

"You said this was the most obvious scenario," I said. "Are there others?"

"The only other possibility I can think of is that Joseph could have given the diamond to one of the so-called 'filibusters' he sponsored, perhaps as surety to establish a French refugee colony in Texas. Lafitte, at that point, had re-established his smuggling operation at Galveston, so he was uniquely positioned to help, not only through navigation and transportation but also by providing sustenance and dealing with hostile natives and the even more hostile Spanish, for whom, ironically enough, he was spying at the time."

"The filibusters were the French exiles who tried to claim land?"

"Yes, basically."

"Christ," I said. "This guy was a piece of work. If he were alive during the Cold War, he'd have been a triple agent."

"No doubt," Prosper said. "He was nothing if not an opportunist."

"When you say the diamond could have been used as surety, what do you mean by that?"

"Just that if the filibuster got in a jam, some dire life or death situation, he could have used the diamond to essentially buy himself out of the predicament."

"Let me make sure I understand," I said. "You're saying that, in that scenario, this filibuster is in trouble and goes to Lafitte for help, but Lafitte demands payment in return for his assistance."

"Yes, something along those lines."

"Is there a particular filibuster you have in mind?"

"As I said, there were a few of these attempts to establish colonies," Prosper said, "but the best known was led by Charles Lallemand, one of Napoleon's generals who left France around the same time as Joseph Bonaparte. It's well known that Lafitte helped Lallemand and his men sail up the Trinity River and establish his Champ d'Asile settlement, which literally translated means Field of Asylum. The colony failed within a few months, and by the time the Frenchmen made their way back to Galveston, they were starving

CHAPTER SIXTEEN

and penniless."

"And did Lafitte help them?" I asked.

"He did," Prosper said. "He fed them and eventually provided transport back to New Orleans. But the flip side of the story is that he may have secretly been the one undermining Lallemand all along by reporting on him to the Spanish."

"Huh. So, it's possible that Lafitte could have extorted the diamond in exchange for his help, isn't it? He was profiting off everybody."

"Yes, it's possible," Prosper said, "but just to be absolutely clear, there is zero historical evidence I'm aware of that any of this went down this way."

"Yeah, I get that," I said, "but you've given me a lot to think about. I really appreciate it."

"My pleasure," Prosper said. "I really need to get back to work now, but I do have a question for you."

"Sure, shoot."

"What do you make of Bruneau and Sallie Maguire? I take it this is new territory for him."

I let out a hoot.

"Yeah, you could say that," I said. "I never thought I'd see the day, to be honest. But my wife and I are thrilled. We think Sallie's good for him, and they seem happy together."

"It's good to hear you say that," Prosper said. "That's my impression, too."

We said our goodbyes and Prosper turned and limped his way back to the store, nodding to a friendly young mother pushing her tot in a cart and waving to a co-worker who was changing out bags in the garbage receptacles. If stocking grocery shelves seemed below the station of a learned medical man, you wouldn't have known it by watching Prosper. He seemed perfectly at ease in his surroundings.

I got into my car and smiled to myself as I considered our brief conversation about Bruneau. There was no doubt that having Bru in a relationship took some getting used to, but anyone could see he and Sallie were happy together. Angie was ecstatic, and not just because she thought of herself as the matchmaker. Being with Bru brought out an "inner glow" in Sallie,

Angie said, and Sallie was good for Bru in all kinds of ways. She'd helped him slim down a bit, and that added a new spring to his step. But more than anything she brought out a tenderness in Bru that his close friends have known was always there, but now it was closer to the surface. He'd still try to pull off the grumpy old man act, out of habit, I guess, but it wasn't as convincing. And that in itself was funny, even if he didn't always get the joke.

A couple days ago, Angie told me, "They just fit, like peanut butter and jelly."

I said, "Yeah, or sweet and sour."

Chapter Seventeen

When Sallie, Hugo, and I pulled up to Bo and Angie's, Little Bo was shooting baskets over the garage, Monique was chalking up a Hopscotch court on the driveway, and Bo was watering his vegetable garden, clutching a Miller Lite in his free hand. It could have been a Norman Rockwell painting were it not for the beer.

"Hello you two!" Bo shouted over the clamor of what sounded like Zydeco on his boom box. "Angie's expecting you inside, I just need a couple minutes to finish up out here. Bo, help them with their stuff, will you?"

The children welcomed Sallie before they said hi to me, which by now was par for the course. The first couple times Sallie joined our dinners there was some awkwardness with the kids, but no longer. Now Monique seeks Sallie out for help with her art projects, Sallie has usurped my role as Sophie's chief literary sounding board, and she's even showed up at a couple of Little Bo's games. Basically, she has ensconced herself as a member in good standing of our extended family.

While Monique spirited Sallie away for a game of Hopscotch, Hugo and I followed Little Bo inside, where I was greeted by Angie coming from the kitchen, drying her hands on a dish towel.

"Hello, baby!" she purred as we exchanged hugs and pecks on each cheek. Sophie rose from her usual reading spot on the couch and added her own greeting. Then she knelt down to stroke Hugo.

"And what are we into now?" I asked, pointing to her open book.

"*Tess of the d'Urbervilles*," Sophie said. "Do you know it?"

"Of course. Are you enjoying it?"

"It just makes me mad."

"At Alec d'Urberville?"

"At men in general."

"Yeah, I can understand that."

I was about to elaborate when Angie interrupted.

"Bruneau, let's get you to work. I'm dying for a Sazerac."

One byproduct of Sallie having joined our gatherings is that the ritual of me identifying the evening's featured dish sight unseen has fallen by the wayside. It might have something to do with the fact that the first couple times Sallie came, I failed spectacularly. Or maybe not. Maybe the kids just outgrew the game. Either way, I kind of miss it.

Fortunately, one thing the Duplessis kids have not outgrown is their sweet tooth. I'd brought some cannoli from Angelo Brocato's, so I walked into the kitchen and placed them in the fridge. Then I sidled over to the stovetop, where Angie had a Maque Choux simmering in a large skillet. I opened the oven door for a quick peek and was hit with a blast of hot vapor and the sound of sizzling fat. When the cloud of steam cleared, two ducks sat snugly nestled in a roasting pan, surrounded by citrus, potatoes, and shallots.

"What are you doing!" Angie shrieked. "You know better than to let cold air in the oven."

"Sorry, madam chef, I forget myself," I said. "But inquiring minds…"

"Inquiring minds want to know where their cocktails are. That's what they want to know." Angie picked up a wooden spoon and scooted me toward the bar with a rap to my backside.

Bo came inside just as I finished mixing the first batch of drinks. He asked Little Bo to take Sallie's outside to her and then clasped my shoulder.

"How you been, my man?"

"Oh, not too bad, I guess. You?"

"I'm good. You'll never guess who I met today."

"Who's that?"

"Prosper Fortune, or maybe I should call him Andre."

"Really? How did that happen?"

"I stopped at the Winn Dixie on Veteran's on my way home and figured

CHAPTER SEVENTEEN

I'd see if he was working."

"What did you make of him?" I asked.

"I liked him," Bo said. "I liked him a lot. He's just like you said, but better groomed."

"Yeah, that's a fairly recent development," I said. "All credit to his sister."

"He's a big boy," Bo said. "Must take a lot to feed him."

"Probably so."

"Anyway, he was quite helpful," Bo said. "Remind me to relay a couple theories he has about the Hong Kong diamond."

That got my attention, but before I could learn more, the dinner table banter had begun. Having come inside, Monique extolled Sallie's Hopscotch skills, and the kids updated us on their various pursuits. Bo described the dormer he and Angie were thinking about adding to the house, and Sallie fielded questions about the annual meeting of the American Cryptogram Association she was planning to attend in San Antonio. Little Bo was studying World War II and had apparently developed an interest in ciphers.

"Is it true you won the ACA's cipher contest?" he asked Sallie.

"Yes, I did," she said. "I haven't competed the last couple years, but I did win two out of the previous five tournaments."

"That is *so* cool! How do you do it, Sallie? How do you even get started on solving a cipher?"

"There's no one answer to that question, Bo," Sallie said. "There are different types of ciphers, for starters. You've got substitution ciphers, Caesar ciphers, Vingenere ciphers, and so on, and your solving strategy differs depending on the type. But most of the time, you start by looking for relationships between characters, like characters that appear most frequently, or in combination with other characters. Usually, there's a key, and if you can identify the key, then it's just a matter of methodically working with the key to decode the message."

"You make it sound so easy," Sophie said.

"I wouldn't call it easy, Sophie," Sallie said, "but it's also not as hard as most people think, if you know a few tricks and have the right temperament."

"Sallie, have you heard of Bletchley Park?" Little Bo asked. He was becoming something of a military history buff.

"Of course. The home of the British code breakers."

"I bet if you were alive back then, you would have been on the team that helped decode the Nazis' Enigma machine."

"Well, thank you, Bo!" Sallie said. "Both for the kind thought and also for recognizing that I *wasn't* around back then."

"Bo, has your dad told you about the grave robbing case he's been working on for the last several months?" I asked.

"Yeah, a little bit. Is that the one that has to do with the pirate?"

"Yes, Jean Lafitte," I said. "There were some old, mostly illegible pieces of writing found in the crypt that nobody could figure out until Sallie helped decipher them. They weren't part of a cipher, but basically, Sallie used some of the same principles to figure it all out. Do I have that right, Sallie?"

"More or less," she said, "but just so you know, Bo, your Dad and his team played a big role in giving me a head start." I could tell Sallie was at once apprecive of the shout-out and pained by my oversimplification.

"That is so cool!" Little Bo said.

"Your dad could have paid big bucks to bring in some expert from New York," I said, "but instead, he had one of the best in the business right under his nose. And the price was right."

Sallie rolled her eyes but smiled all the same.

"Okay, gang, that's enough Sherlock Holmes for one night," Angie called from the kitchen. "Dinner is ready. Monique, can you help me serve, please."

Angie's duck turned out to be a little on the tough side, but it was rescued by a delicious gastrique she'd made from local satsumas. The Maque Choux was excellent, sweet and hot and creamy, but still crunchy, with the corn, onion, and peppers commingling in perfect equilibrium. The citrus and spices somewhat overwhelmed the Sonoma pinot noir I'd served, and I found myself wishing I'd brought something more substantial, something from the Rhone perhaps, or a Nebbiolo.

Normally, discussion of Bo's cases is reserved for our "grown-ups only" time after dinner, but the kids are getting older and had some familiarity with the Jane Placide mystery, so I guess Bo felt comfortable raising the

CHAPTER SEVENTEEN

topic.

"So, Mike Rodiger did some digging," Bo announced.

"Wait, Mike Rodiger? Didn't he rotate out of Property Crimes?" Angie asked.

"He did, yes. This was on his own time. The kid takes initiative. He's going to be a good one."

"Maybe back with you?"

"Maybe. We'll see."

"What did he dig into, and what did he find?" I asked.

"Well, he started with a theory," Bo said, "and the theory is that this diamond that sold in Hong Kong is our La Violette."

"I suggested as much to you," I reminded him.

"Yes. Like you, Rodiger pointed out that Jean Lafitte traveled to Philadelphia and may have met Joseph Bonaparte, Napoleon's brother. But then he went back to Sallie's transcription of Jane Placide's diary."

Bo pulled out a note card.

"He pointed out that Jane uses female pronouns to describe La Violette. She talks about never wearing *her* in public and holding *her* at night, remember? Those references don't make sense in relation to a treasure map, but if we're talking about a precious diamond…well, maybe they kind of fit."

"You said he started with a theory," I said. "Did he find evidence to back it up?"

"Circumstantial evidence, yes. Turns out the proceeds from the sale of the diamond were wired to an account in the Cayman Islands and then smaller amounts were sent around the globe to the accounts of various shell companies. The feds see this all the time in white-collar crime. It's called layering, the idea being to scatter money all over the place to disguise where it came from and send investigators down one rat hole after another."

"Are you assuming that the maintenance worker who found the diamond is behind all this?" I asked. "Wouldn't the diamond belong to the owner of the property on which it was found?"

"I asked about that, too," Bo said. "The answer is normally, yes, that's exactly what would happen. But conveniently, the diamond was found just off the Bonaparte property on public land, which means finders keepers."

"Do you know who the finder was?" Angie asked.

"Nope, not yet. We're working on it," Bo said.

"But here's where it gets interesting. The account in the Caymans where the money was wired is registered to a company called Ttaba, LLC. Rodiger did some research, and it turns out Ttaba is a female spirit in Moroccan folklore who preys on men in order to disrupt the male-dominated social order."

"That fits, doesn't it," Sallie said. "Officer Rodiger thought that maybe Omar Pasha identifies with oppressed or exploited women, which might have been why he kept the Delacroix odalisque for himself."

"Correct," Bo said. "That's exactly the point Mike tried to make. Maybe Toledano thinks he's an avenging spirit, like Ttaba, out to free women from the chains of subjugation."

"I can relate to that!" Angie said. "This is turning out to be the case of cases, isn't it?"

"Could be," Bo said. "I'm not sold on the liberator of women angle quite yet."

"What about Prosper?" I asked. "You said he had some theories about the diamond?"

"Yes. I told him about the sale in Hong Kong and Rodiger's hypothesis.

"He doubts that Lafitte met with Joseph Bonaparte, but he admitted it was possible. He floated the idea that if they did meet, Bonaparte could have given Lafitte the diamond as a down payment for services yet to be performed."

"What kind of services?" Sallie asked.

"Possibly to command a fleet to rescue Napoleon from his island and bring him to America."

"Oh, come on, Dad, give me a break," Little Bo snorted, tossing his napkin on his plate and leaning back in his chair. "Your pirate was going to rescue Napoleon? No way!"

"It's true, Bo," I said. "There were a bunch of plots to rescue Napoleon,

CHAPTER SEVENTEEN

and Lafitte was smack dab in the middle of a few of them."

Little Bo crossed his arms and shot me a skeptical look but allowed his father to continue.

"Anyway, based on his understanding of the timing of Lafitte's northern trip, Prosper thinks it unlikely that Lafitte met Bonaparte. He said that the way the dates line up, they probably just missed each other."

"Well, that shoots that theory," Angie said.

"Maybe, maybe not," Bo said. "Prosper didn't say it was impossible, but he offered an alternative scenario, which is that Bonaparte might have given the diamond to one of the ex-pat Frenchmen he sponsored, hoping they could successfully settle in Texas."

"The filibusters?" I asked.

"Right. There was one in particular," Bo said, pausing to glance at his note card. "Charles Lallemand. He was one of Napoleon's generals, apparently. Lafitte was based in Galveston at that point, and he helped Lallemand get his little refugee colony up and running."

Bo looked at his card again. "It was called Champ d'Asile."

"Field of Asylum," I said, dusting off my lapsed French.

"Yes, exactly. Anyway, the colony failed, and by the time Lallemand and his men made it back to Galveston, they were in bad shape. Prosper thought that if Lallemand was desperate for help, maybe he paid Lafitte off with the diamond in exchange for food and transit back to New Orleans."

"Pretty compelling stuff," I said, "but it's still just supposition. We've still got the problem of how the hell does a diamond get from Crypt 1083-A to New Jersey."

"That and the fact that all of this is still circumstantial," Bo said.

The energy that just a few seconds ago had animated the table seemed to dissipate all at once. Hugo let out a loud sigh from underneath the table. Then Sallie spoke up.

"I've got another piece of circumstantial evidence for you," she said.

We all looked at her.

"If you'll remember, in my transcription there was a nine-letter word that began with a B that I guessed must have been *Barataria*?"

Bo and I nodded.

"You know what else starts with a B and has nine letters?" Sallie asked.

Blank stares all around. "What?" I finally asked.

"*Bonaparte,*" she said, attempting to suppress a triumphant smile.

"Wow!" Bo exclaimed.

"You're amazing," I said.

Sallie smiled but said, "If I was truly amazing, I would have gotten it right the first time."

"I'm with Bruneau," Angie said. "You're definitely pretty amazing, Sallie. Bo, the evidence seems to be piling up. Where do you go from here?"

Bo started to answer but was interrupted by Sophie.

"Excuse me," she said, looking around nervously. "Before you move on, there's one more thing. It's kind of obvious, so like, maybe you've already noted it."

"What's that, Soph?" Bo asked.

"I mean, like, you do realize that Omar's salon was called *The Hidden Gem*, right?"

Sophie was greeted by silence as we digested her bombshell. Her eyes darted around the table in search of validation.

"Oh…my…god," Sallie finally said. "I think we can all agree that if anyone's amazing at this table, it's not me."

"Well done, Sophie!" I said. "Your powers of observation and deduction continue to amaze. May I propose a toast to Sophie, our young detective-in-waiting?"

"You may!" said Angie, raising her glass. "Here's to Sophie!"

Bo just sat there, transfixed. I couldn't tell if he was in a state of shock, or deep in thought. Finally, he spoke.

"Soph, sweetie, you're incredible," he said. "Thank you, thank you. You've just added an entirely new wrinkle to the case."

That seemed a bit hyperbolic, but I was happy to ride the congratulatory wave.

"I can see the headline now: eighth-grade sleuth solves two-hundred-year-old mystery."

CHAPTER SEVENTEEN

"You realize what this means, Bru?" Bo asked, casting me a serious look.

"I think so," I said. "It means we've likely met the preponderance of evidence standard, whether circumstantial or not."

"Yes, there's that, good enough for a warrant if we need one," Bo said. "But that's not what I was thinking of. The thing is, the Hidden Gem Salon was incorporated more than three years ago."

"Which means…that if the name was intentional…Omar, or Mahdi Toledano, had been planning this heist for at least that long," Sallie said.

"And may even have moved to New Orleans for the express purpose of disturbing Jane Placide's eternal resting place," I added, catching on late.

"Exactly," Bo said. "Which means we have a whole new set of questions to answer. The first of which is, if Toledano was in Canada, how the heck did he find out about La Violette and Crypt 1083-A?"

"Anyone for more wine?" I asked.

Chapter Eighteen

I am not alone in regarding jeweler Rene Fanchon "Fancy" Rigard as, among other things, a pompous pain in the ass. If Uriah Heep coupled with Becky Sharp, a friend once said to me, he might have been their issue. Nonetheless, when it comes to jewelry, and more particularly the history of jewelry, there is no denying that "Fancy," as he prefers to be called, is as knowledgeable as they come. He is an adjunct professor in UNO's fine arts department, consults regularly with law enforcement, and commands top dollar as an appraiser. Our social circles and professional interests overlap from time to time, so I've gotten to know Fancy a bit, though we are in no way close. We maintain a professional decorum, albeit with a passive-aggressive edge.

It was, therefore, not without apprehension or swallowed pride that I visited his "by-appointment-only" Royal Street shop in search of assistance. I had called ahead, yet when I arrived, I was escorted to the sitting room outside his large second-floor office, with its sixteen-foot floor-to-ceiling windows and cobalt silk curtains and made to wait fifteen minutes past our appointed time. When finally, I was called to enter, I found Fancy leaning back in his chair, his feet resting on an enormous mahogany desk with brass adornments and tortoiseshell marquetry. His head was freshly shaven, and he was dressed in a burgundy smoking jacket with matching velvet pants and a ruffled green shirt open at the collar, revealing a conspicuously hairy chest. Green suede Milano loafers and purple paisley socks completed the garish ensemble. Fancy was puffing on a long cigarette holder and smiled between clenched teeth as I entered.

CHAPTER EIGHTEEN

"Well, well, if it isn't Bruneau Abellard," he said with a bemused smirk, pointing to a straight-back wooden chair in front of his desk. As soon as I sat down, I realized the chair was cut low, ensuring that I'd be looking up at Fancy throughout the course of our conversation.

"How nice to see you, Bruneau. What brings you to my humble place of business? Looking for something special for that tasty little mouse from the Cabildo? I hear you've been spending time together."

I wanted to slug the unctuous bastard then and there, but I knew from experience that if I pissed him off, I wasn't going to get anything out of him. My defense of Sallie's honor would have to wait for another day.

"Nothing so prosaic, I'm afraid," I said.

"Ah, what a shame. Even the most self-effacing specimens of the fairer sex appreciate a little bauble every now and then."

"I'll take that under advisement, but today, I come in hopes of a history lesson."

"I see," Fancy said. "And what confounding piece of historical esoterica may I demystify for you today?"

"I assume you're aware of the diamond that sold in Hong Kong recently for $63 million?"

"Of course! The supposed French Blue."

"Right. I take it from your use of the word 'supposed' that you don't think the diamond in question is, in fact, the French Blue?"

Fancy shrugged, slid his feet off the desk, and sat back, regarding me suspiciously, his belly folding heedlessly over his waistline.

"Who's to say? It seems unlikely, I'll say that much. Why do you want to know?"

"I've been helping a detective friend of mine with a rather strange case that may be tangentially related to this diamond, although admittedly, probably not."

"Would the investigator in question be our mutual acquaintance, the distinguished Detective Bo-*dacious* Duplessis of NOPD's Property Crimes unit?"

"Yes," I said with a pained smile. "As a matter of fact, it would. How did you know?"

"I'm aware that T-Bo was your childhood babysitter, Bruneau," Fancy said. "Like you, Detective Duplessis seeks my counsel from time to time. I always enjoy our tête-à-têtes."

"I see," I said. "I guess it makes sense that if expensive jewelry goes missing, Bo would come to you."

"Oh yes, I am in much demand among our protectors in blue," he said. "I am not, however, aware of any recent jewelry thefts in town. What is it that you're trying to track down?"

"Maybe nothing. That's what makes this case so strange. It involves a disturbance at a grave site, but we don't know for sure if a robbery occurred."

"A grave site? Are you investigating the unholy disturbance of the Girod Street remains some months ago? There was just a brief snippet about it in the *Times-Picayune,* but it did catch my attention."

"It seems you know everything," I said.

"Not everything, I'm afraid, but I do like to keep abreast of the activities of our fair city's criminal elements. Those with a modicum of taste anyway."

Fancy stubbed his cigarette, clasped his hands over his belly, and cast me a self-satisfied grin.

"Now tell me," he said, "what could the French Blue diamond possibly have to do with the ghoulish breach of eternal repose out at Hope Mausoleum? I'm *dying* to know."

Fancy emitted a self-congratulatory chuckle at his pun. I knew I needed to offer up an answer to his question, but Bo would kill me if I let him know we were on the trail of Jean Lafitte.

"Like I said, probably nothing. But clearly, the burglars were after something they thought to be valuable, and there were some Bonapartist ex-pats interred in that crypt. Just trying to be thorough."

"Your theory then is that one of these Bonapartists stole the French Blue, crossed the Atlantic with it, and took it to his grave?"

"Something like that," I said. "I wouldn't call it a theory so much as one of a few imaginative leaps we're exploring."

"I see," Fancy said, eyeing me warily. "I'd say your imaginative leap is more

CHAPTER EIGHTEEN

like a quantum shot in the dark. Even if that's what happened, how would your thieves have found out where the diamond was hidden, presumably for posterity?"

"Point taken, and you're right, we have no idea. Still, I'm curious, why are you skeptical that this Hong Kong diamond is the French Blue?"

"Dear Bruneau," Fancy sighed, "if you've read about the sale of this diamond and spent any time on the internet, you know that most experts believe the Hope Diamond was cut out of the French Blue, right?"

"Yes."

"Well, I was part of the team of experts that helped make that determination. The evidence is quite convincing, and I believe in our work."

"Ah, understood," I said. "How fortunate I am that you're even more knowledgeable about this subject than I had hoped. I've never really seen a full explanation as to why this team of yours believes the Hope is the French Blue. What is your evidence, exactly?"

"My, you really are interested in this, aren't you?" Fancy said. "Is there more to this 'imaginative leap' of yours than you're letting on, Bruneau?"

"No, not really," I lied. "The little I've learned about the diamond has piqued my curiosity, that's all."

Fancy fixed his stare on me, as if trying to decide if he was buying what I was selling. Then he shrugged.

"The theory has been out there for two hundred years at least," he said. "It wasn't until 2005 that a couple of computer scientists were able to build us models to make the case. But for you to appreciate the power of the evidence, I need to take you back in time."

"Excellent. That's exactly why I came to you."

"Right," Fancy said as he assembled and lit another cigarette. "So, it's the mid-17th century, and a Frenchman by the name of Jean-Baptiste Tavernier takes his sixth trip to what was then known as the Orient. That word, Orient, is a bit of a faux pas these days, did you know that?"

"Yes, I am aware."

"People put too much stock in words, if you ask me. I mean, it's just another word, as harmless as any other."

I waited.

"But you didn't ask me, did you?" Fancy allowed. "Very well then, back to our history lesson. One way or another, Tavernier makes his way to the Kollur mines in the Guntur district of southeast India, where he procures several very large stones, the largest and most beautiful of which was a 115-carat blue diamond that came to be known as the Tavernier Blue.

"Tavernier was an experienced trader who sold his gems to royalty throughout Europe, but his biggest client by far was Louis XIV, to whom he sold his magnificent blue diamond."

Fancy went on to explain that the Sun King's royal jeweler cut the stone into a triangular 68-carat gem and set it in a seven-faceted gold backing, so that when the light was right it appeared as though the sun shone through the blue diamond. This is the point at which the Tavernier Blue became the French Blue. Almost a century later, Louis' great-grandson, Louis XV, had the diamond reset as a pendant and incorporated into the French insignia of the Royal Order of the Golden Fleece. The diamond passed down to the ill-fated Louis XVI, and then in 1792, during the upheaval of the revolution, it disappeared along with the rest of the royal collection. Most of the jewels were recovered during Napoleon's reign, including parts of the fleece, but the whereabouts of the French Blue remained a mystery.

It wasn't until 1812 that a large blue diamond, this one, 45 carats, made its appearance in London without any documentation as to its provenance. This was just days after the twenty-year statute of limitations on the theft of the French jewels had run out. Unsurprisingly, there was speculation from the outset that this was the French Blue, recut to disguise its origin, but it couldn't be proven. The diamond changed hands several times but was eventually acquired by its future namesake, Thomas Hope, a wealthy English banker, sometime in the 1830s. The stone remained with the Hope family until the turn of the next century, when it was sold to a London jeweler. The Hope then endured various owners, and settings, during the first half of the 20th century, until American jeweler Harry Winston donated it to the Smithsonian in 1958.

"Thanks Fancy, that helps," I said, "but most of that I've seen on the internet.

CHAPTER EIGHTEEN

How were you able to prove the Hope is the French?"

Fancy rose from his chair, strode to the wet bar he'd cut out of his wall-length bookcase, and pulled a Diet Coke from his refrigerator.

"May I offer you something to drink, Bruneau?"

"No thanks, I'm good."

"How about to nibble on?" he asked. He grabbed a glass jar of jellybeans in one hand and a bowl of peanuts in the other, showing them to me.

"No, really, I'm fine," I said.

"Very well," he said.

"Can we get back to how you proved the Hope and the French are one and the same?"

"My, my, aren't we antsy," Fancy said. He left me hanging for a few more seconds as he slowly walked back to his desk and sat down.

"The Smithsonian sponsored the research," he said. "They assembled a team that included jewelry historians such as me, gem-cutting experts, and computer engineers. We started with detailed drawings of the French Blue from pre-revolutionary France and of the Tavernier by Tavernier himself. From those, the engineers were able to build detailed models of the French Blue using CAD software. Then they essentially placed the dimensions of the Hope inside the French, and it was a perfect fit."

"You must have had a lot of confidence in those sketches," I said.

"There's no reason to believe they weren't accurate. If the Hope wasn't a perfect fit, we might have said that it was because the drawings were off. But what are the odds that the drawings were bad, and the Hope still fit?"

"Yes, I see your logic," I said. I wondered to myself if the team felt incented to produce the fit but didn't see the point in raising Fancy's dander.

"Have I spoiled your conspiracy theory, Bruneau?" Fancy asked. "Are there other 'imaginative leaps' you'd like me to entertain?"

"You've been most helpful," I said.

Fancy flashed a patronizing smile and rose from his chair, preparing to usher me out.

"You know," he said, pausing, "there's an elaborate occult mythology that surrounds the French Blue diamond."

"How so?"

"There's an alternative origin story that says that rather than buying the gem from the Kollur mines, Tavernier stole it from the eye of a sculpture of Sita, the Hindu goddess. Ever since, the legend goes, all who have possessed the stone have encountered misfortune."

"It's cursed, is that the idea?"

"Yes, or so the story goes," Fancy said. "And it is true that there have been a smattering of verifiable murders and suicides and such among those who've come in contact with the diamond, but a lot of what was alleged has been debunked or remains unconfirmed."

"How interesting," I said. "I'm trying to remember who Sita is in Hindu theology. She was the consort of Rama, wasn't she?"

"That's right. In shorthand, she's usually referred to as the goddess of beauty and devotion."

"Would she be vengeful if somebody stole her eye?"

"Wouldn't you?"

I laughed. "Yeah, I guess so. Touché."

Fancy smiled and walked me to the door of his office, opening it and ushering me through.

"You know, the human capacity for making what we want out of the little mysteries we encounter in life is nearly endless," he said. "There's an entirely different school that believes the French Blue is capable of forging spiritual connections."

"In what way?"

"It goes back to the seven facets of the sun Louis XIV had his jeweler create for the Blue's backing. As you probably know, the number seven is laden with cosmological meaning in the Bible. Usually, it connotes the sacred or the mystical."

"In other words, if two people are connected to the diamond, they may also be spiritually connected to each other?"

"Beats me, but yeah, maybe."

We walked back to the lobby and stood at the top of the staircase, about to say our goodbyes. I decided to press Fancy on one more point.

CHAPTER EIGHTEEN

"Can I ask a final question?"

"Sure," Fancy said, making a show of checking his watch.

"Given the well-publicized work this team of yours did, how was the seller of the Hong Kong diamond able to pawn it off as possibly being the French Blue?"

"It's a good question," Fancy said. "A combination of factors, I imagine. It's clearly an extraordinary diamond in its own right. In size and clarity, it's in the same ballpark as the French Blue. And the oh-so-convenient location of the stone's discovery doesn't hurt its case. All that plus our human capacity to believe in the wondrous."

"Too convenient a location, you think?"

"It's not for me to say, but I mean of all the gin joints in all the towns, you know?"

"Yeah, that had occurred to me too," I said.

"Plus, I don't even know that Joseph Bonaparte would have been a plausible possessor of the diamond," Fancy said. "If I'm remembering my history correctly, the theft of the French Blue occurred before Napoleon assumed power. And then, while Napoleon was busy trying to recover as many of the stolen crown jewels as he could, Joseph was off plundering Naples and Spain."

"What about after?"

"After what?"

"After Joseph returned to France during The Hundred Days, mightn't he have had access to the French Blue then? Perhaps on the black market?"

"Yeah, I guess so," Fancy said, sounding dubious. "So would anyone else, in that scenario."

"Okay, how about if I turn the question around," I said.

"I thought you said one final question."

"That was One-A. This is One-B."

Fancy smiled and shook his head.

"Fine. Fire away."

"Let's say someone brought you the Hong Kong diamond, and you could see that in size and clarity, it looked like it could be the French Blue. Short of going back to your engineers, how would you go about disproving its identity?"

"First thing I'd check is its phosphorescence," Fancy said.

"Phosphorescence?"

"Yes. If you shine an ultraviolet light on the French Blue or the Hope, it will glow a brilliant orange or red."

"What? Really?"

"Oh yes. All blue diamonds are phosphorescent, but most give off bluish light, as you'd expect. The French isn't unique in glowing red, but it is unusual. It has to do with the mix of boron and nitrogen in the stone."

"That's fascinating."

"Yes," Fancy said. "Tavernier didn't have the benefit of ultraviolet light back in his day, but even he noted that in certain conditions, the Blue would change to what he called a 'beautiful violet.' In fact, his pet name for the diamond was La Violette."

1830

THE LAW OFFICES OF U.S. SENATOR EDWARD LIVINGSTON
NEW ORLEANS, LOUISIANA
JUNE 1830

It has been less than two weeks since the senator returned from Washington, the states' rights quarrels of Webster and Hayne still rattling in his ears. He is tired. Tired of the thundering pomposity of Washington politics. Beaten down by the arduous travel home, over land and river. Drained from his decade-long struggle to secure the adoption of his Louisiana codes. He longs for the return of a not-so-distant yesteryear, when he attracted interesting cases, and could safely pursue auspicious business opportunities with trusted associates.

Edward Livingston has grown weary of the rote practice of law. Nor does he much care for the constituent service expected of him in his elected role as the junior senator from Louisiana. He is not, by breeding or temperament, a man of the people. But every so often an appointment appears on his calendar that stirs him to ardent anticipation. The imminent visit of the actress Jane Placide is one such occasion. He knows the actress only casually but has long admired her beauty and her talent. He could think of no obvious reason for her to seek his counsel but is flattered that she would.

The actress appears in his doorway escorted by his secretary, Mr. Timmons. She wears a long, lightweight peach dress with puffed sleeves, a tightly cinched waistline, and a white lace chemisette. She moves with the lissome strides and composed carriage of a ballerina, as the senator takes her hand and guides her to one of the Empire armchairs that faces his desk.

"Your visit, Miss Placide, is a most welcome distraction from the drudgery of an old lawyer's day. Please, how may I be of service to you?"

"You are most kind, Mr. Livingston," the actress says. "The truth is, I have a matter of some delicacy that I would like to discuss with you."

"You may count on my absolute discretion, Miss Placide."

"Thank you, sir. What I have to tell you must be held in the strictest confidence."

"I understand, miss. As an attorney, it is my sworn duty to guard my clients' secrets as if they were my own."

"Very well then, sir. The crux of the matter is this: I am in possession of an object that is very dear to me, and I should like to arrange for it to accompany me when I depart this world for the next."

"I see," Livingston says. "I hope you aren't planning on leaving us anytime soon, Miss Placide."

The actress smiles demurely.

"No Mr. Livingston, I have made no such plans. But with the fever taking so many of our friends, year upon year, one can never know when one's time may come."

"Alas, this much is true, Miss Placide. What can you tell me of this object of yours?"

"It is a jewel, sir, given to me by our mutual friend, Captain Lafitte."

"Captain Lafitte? I did not know you were acquainted with the good captain. He was a most singular and, I'm afraid, misunderstood man."

"Yes, I am afraid so. It has been my good fortune to befriend the captain and learn that the things they say of him are not true."

"Indeed," Livingston says. "I knew Jean Lafitte to be a brilliant leader of men, and a man of his word. As your attorney, miss, may I ask, was he a romantic as well?"

The actress flushes and looks down at her hands, folded on her lap. She brings her head up slowly and fixes her eyes on the senator.

"You say 'was,' sir, as if Jean were no longer with us. Have you received intelligence to this effect?"

Livingston considers the question.

"Pardon my presumption, Miss Placide. As you must know, it is widely believed that our friend perished at sea many years ago now. Do you know differently?"

"I last saw Captain Lafitte four years ago, Mr. Livingston, and have received correspondence from him as recently as three months past."

"Why this is a most remarkable piece of news, Miss Placide!" Livingston says. "Please accept my apologies for having believed an apparent falsehood. Where did you encounter Captain Lafitte, if I may ask?"

"He visited me often in this city for a period of several months, sir. He would come in disguise, but eventually even that became too dangerous. He writes to me now, when he can, through a mutual friend, who acts as an emissary. I do not know his exact whereabouts."

"Why does he write to an emissary and not to you directly, miss?"

"Because sir, my benefactor, Mr. Caldwell, cannot be trusted, and this is why I have come to you now."

"I see," Livingston says. "You ask that I ensure that your jewel goes with you to your grave because you cannot rely on James Caldwell to carry out your wishes?"

"That is correct, sir. He is a jealous man, you see. A good man, in his way, but a passionate one who cannot think clearly on the subject of Jean Lafitte."

"I understand, miss," Livingston says. "I can prepare a document to supersede or append to your last will and testament, expressing your intentions."

"I would be most grateful, Mr. Livingston," the actress says.

"In the meantime, I have one more question for you, sir. In the unhappy event that you precede me in death or that your travels have situated you elsewhere at the time of my demise, can you assure me that my instructions will be carried out?"

"Yes Miss Placide, of course. Our firm has strict protocols to ensure that in the absence of the drafting attorney, all agreements shall be enforced and followed to the most exacting degree."

"It does my heart good to know this, Mr. Livingston," the actress says. "And now, a final request: May I leave the jewel with you for safekeeping? Jean said I may trust you with it."

"You do not wish to keep it until the time comes?"

"It is more important that it is with me then, than now. If I die suddenly, or should I become so ill that I cannot express my wishes, how could I be sure that it *would find its way to you? It is too much to risk."*

"Very well, miss. We can keep it in our safe if you wish."

"That would be good of you, Mr. Livingston."

The actress unties her reticule and withdraws a small white opaline lock box with gold filigree borders. She passes it to the senator.

"I ask that you not view the contents of this box, Mr. Livingston," she says. "It contains a secret known only to Captain Lafitte and myself. It represents our spiritual connection, you see, and the medium through which we shall find each other in the hereafter. We cannot have its powers diluted through contact with others. I hope you understand, sir."

"Of course, Miss Placide. I shall respect your wishes unconditionally."

"Thank you, Mr. Livingston. You have lifted a great weight from my shoulders."

Their business concluded, the actress and the senator exchange further pleasantries as he escorts her from his office.

Returning, Livingston opens the wall safe behind his prized Luny seascape and picks up the actress' box. He holds it to his face for a brief moment, as if considering a decision. Then, shaking his head, he places the box in the safe, unopened.

Chapter Nineteen

When Fancy Rigard let it slip that Jean-Baptiste Tavernier's pet name for his blue diamond was La Violette, it was all I could do to maintain my poker face. Sallie or Bo would have picked up on a tell, I'm sure, but Fancy is too self-involved to have noticed anything. I played it cool just in case, lingering for another twenty minutes while he presented the showpieces of his current inventory and name-dropped from his celebrity client list. We parted with an empty promise to meet for drinks.

Once outside Fancy's store I was so excited I couldn't decide who to call first. I was heading home to Sallie, so I opted for Bo.

"Nice timing, Bru," he answered. "I was just getting ready to call you."

"Oh yeah?"

"Yeah. Jersey State Police located the worker who found the Hong Kong diamond."

"That's excellent news. Who is he?"

"Name is Ronald Walker. He was employed by Point Breeze for a little over three months and then quit a couple days after finding the diamond."

"Why did it take so long to run him down?" I asked.

"Companies can be squirrely about sharing information on employees, and for the Point Breeze Land Trust this is a sensitive situation for obvious reasons. They were just lawyered up and being careful, I guess."

"What does this Ronald Walker have to say for himself?"

"Don't know yet," Bo said. "He's coming in tomorrow, with his attorney, of course. We'll see what the Jersey cops can get out of him."

"Do you know anything about his background?"

"Still working on that, too. He's in his mid-thirties. Heavy-set black guy. Wears an eye patch, not sure why. His employment history is a long series of short-term menial jobs in New York and New Jersey. He does have a record, mostly misdemeanors and low-level street crime. Did a couple years for grand theft auto."

"Doesn't sound like a mastermind," I said.

"No, he's most likely someone's pawn."

"Well, hopefully, the Jersey cops can get him to sing," I said.

"Sing? Listen to you, talking the talk!" Bo laughed. "You been watching *Law and Order* or what?"

"That's right, detective. Been working my sources, too."

"Oh, it's *your* sources now, is it?" Bo chuckled. "And what have your sources offered up, Officer Abellard?"

"That'll be Detective Abellard to you," I said. "And just so you know, I now have it on good authority that Jean-Baptiste Tavernier, namesake of the Tavernier Blue Diamond, referred to his gem as … can you guess?"

"I'm afraid I'm at a loss, detective," Bo said.

"He called it La Violette," I said.

There was a brief pause.

"Get outta town, Bru! Seriously?"

"Cross my heart and hope to die."

"Damn! How the hell did you get this?"

"From our mutual acquaintance, Fancy Pants Rigard, master jeweler and perpetual pain in the ass. He asked me to pass along his regards to Detective Bo-*dacious* Duplessis."

"Fancy? I didn't know you knew Fancy," Bo said, laughing. "I'm trying to imagine the chemistry between you two. How does that work?"

"Not very well, most of the time, but I sucked it up and sought him out for a history lesson. He knows a ton about the Hope Diamond and the Tavernier Blue, which he believes are one and the same. In the course of our conversation, he told me that the Hope is known for its phosphorescence and that under ultraviolet light, it glows a reddish color. Tavernier didn't

CHAPTER NINETEEN

have the benefit of 21st-century technology, but he did detect purple hues in his blue diamond, and so he took to calling it La Violette."

"Holy shit. Nice work, Bru."

"Thought you'd be impressed."

"That I am."

"Now, where do we go from here?" I asked.

"We? I don't know that *we* go anywhere," Bo said. "Rodiger and I are going to video conference into the Walker interview. See what he knows, if anything. We'll dig into his background, try to help Jersey secure a warrant so we can see his finances. That kind of thing."

"What about La Violette?"

"What about it?"

"What are our next steps now that we know for sure what it is?"

The line went quiet, and I could hear muffled conversation in the background.

"Sorry, Bru, the captain wants a word with me. I need to run. As far as La Violette, that's really more your department. I get that the history is cool and all, but it doesn't really have much to do with our investigation at this point."

"What do you mean? In what way does it not have to do with the investigation?"

"Look," Bo said, "whether the Hong Kong diamond is or isn't La Violette is an interesting question. I get that. But at this stage, it doesn't alter the fact that, either way, a very valuable diamond was obtained under suspicious circumstances and then sold at auction. For now, our focus needs to be on that. We've got to determine whether this Walker fella really just found the diamond, or if he stole it from Jane Placide's coffin? And if he stole it, who was he working with, and where did the money from the sale of the diamond go?"

I didn't say anything.

"We cool?"

"Sure, we're cool," I said flatly.

After Bo hung up, I felt deflated, and a little bit pissed. But the more I thought about what he'd said, the more sense it made. After all, his job is to solve a crime. A priceless diamond may have been stolen. To Bo, the history behind that diamond is of interest only insofar as it may help to illuminate the present-day whodunit or lead to arrests. My interest in what transpired between a famous actress and a notorious pirate more than 200 years ago might seem to him a flight of romantic or intellectual whimsy. Sure, I wanted to know who stole the diamond, and how he, or *they*, found out about Crypt-1083A. But I was even more interested in the unlikely romance between Jane Placide and Jean Lafitte and in the backstory of the jewel they hoped would bind them for eternity. I couldn't shake the feeling that our star-crossed lovers were trying to speak to us, if only we could hear them.

* * *

Sallie and I were both heading out of town for the weekend. She was going to San Antonio for her puzzlers' convention, and I was expected in New York for the annual Winter Show on Park Avenue, where I'd been asked to join a panel discussion on regionalism in Beaux Arts furniture and design. Because we would miss the weekend before Fat Tuesday in New Orleans, Sallie had taken it upon herself to bake a King Cake and invite Prosper over for a quiet weeknight dinner. When I got home from my visit with Fancy, she was prepping a salad to accompany the Moussaka I'd assembled the day before.

"Well, hello!" she sang out as I crested the stairs. "That took longer than expected."

"Yeah, sorry about that," I said. "Fancy was a font of information."

I recounted my visit to Royal Street. When I got to the part about Tavernier calling his blue diamond La Violette, Sallie nearly knocked the dressing she was making off the counter.

"You've got to be kidding me!" she squealed. "This is amazing! Do you think it really was the Tavernier that Lafitte gave to Jane?"

"I don't know. Fancy was adamant that the Hope was cut from the Blue,

CHAPTER NINETEEN

in which case it couldn't have been, but I think we have to treat it as a possibility."

"I should say so," Sallie said. "This case gets more fascinating all the time."

"I know," I said, "it makes you wonder what's next."

"Well, now that you mention it, it's a long shot, but I do have a next step for you."

"Oh?"

"Remember Jane Placide's older sister?"

"Yes, Caroline, the actress."

"Correct, good memory," Sallie said. "If you recall, she had a daughter from her first marriage to the comedian. I tried tracing her lineage to see if I could locate any living relatives, but with all the births and marriages and name changes through the generations, it just got too complicated, so I gave up."

"Understandable," I said.

"But then I decided to call in a favor with an old friend from LSU."

"Ah, that's my girl, always resourceful."

Sallie ignored the compliment.

"My friend, Maura, works at the Family History Library in Salt Lake City, which, as I'm sure you know, is the largest genealogical repository in the world."

I nodded.

"Anyway, she has access to data and tools the average researcher can only dream about, so I called her up, explained our interest in descendants of Caroline Placide, and turned her loose."

"Bravo. Did she find anything?"

"Yes, she did. She was able to identify several living relations of Caroline Placide, but only one direct matrilineal descendant, and it turns out she lives in Hoboken, New Jersey, just across the Hudson from Manhattan. I thought you could look her up this weekend."

Sallie was pleased with herself, so I smiled and thanked her for her persistence, but the thought of paying a visit to a total stranger made me more than a little uncomfortable.

"You want me to cold call her? Under what premise? That she might know something about her great aunt from a couple hundred years ago?"

"Sure, why not?" Sallie said. "See if there's any family lore that might prove useful. Maybe she has a scrapbook or something along those lines."

"I don't know, Sallie," I said, "this sounds like a lot of trouble for a total shot in the dark. I've got a busy schedule up there this weekend, and it would be just my luck for this woman to call the cops on me for stalking or harassment."

"A lot of trouble? Really? You think I didn't go through a lot of trouble to get this name for you?"

I could see where this was going and it wasn't likely to end well, so I tried to shift gears.

"Oh no, I know you did, and I really appreciate it. I promise I'll do my best to get over to Hoboken, but if I can't, maybe we can get her email or her phone number and we can contact her that way."

"In person is always better," Sallie said, avoiding eye contact.

Mercifully, the doorbell rang.

"That must be Prosper," I said. "I'll let him in."

Our guest had dressed for the occasion, though not altogether stylishly. He wore a white Oxford shirt buttoned to the collar. Red suspenders hoisted his brown corduroy pants, revealing white athletic socks cresting the tops of leather chukka boots. A black trench coat and a rain hat were folded across Prosper's left arm, and he held a bottle of wine in his right hand.

"Good evening," I said as Hugo pawed excitedly at the big man's leg.

"Evening, Bruneau," he answered back, bending down to engage Hugo. "It's nice of you to have me over in the middle of the week like this."

"Sallie's idea," I said. "As you know, since you're dog-sitting, we're going to be out of town this weekend. She thought it would be nice to do something in advance of Fat Tuesday. Come on upstairs."

"I should have offered to come pick you up. How did you get here?"

"Bus, then trolley, and then a short walk from St. Charles. It was no trouble at all."

"Hello, Prosper, how good of you to join us," Sallie called out as we climbed

CHAPTER NINETEEN

the stairs.

"The pleasure is all mine," Prosper said, "this is quite a treat."

He handed me the bottle he'd brought, a Chilean Cab that I'd probably cook with but would be unlikely to drink.

"Thank you, this looks great," I said.

"I don't know much about wine, but the guy at Martin's said it's pretty good," Prosper said.

Fortunately, I'd already opened a couple bottles of Gattinara to have with dinner, so I poured each of us a glass and refilled Sallie's Orvieto. Sallie asked Prosper how his Mardi Gras was going.

"Truth be told, I do my best to avoid it," he said. "Too much stimulation for this old hermit."

"I agree completely," I said. "Every year, I feel like we're under a weeks-long siege from an invading army of inebriants."

Prosper smiled.

"While we're on the subject of Mardi Gras," he said, "I have a question for you. What happened to the Krewe of Comus? My dad belonged to Comus and always made a big deal of it growing up. I was looking at the parade schedule and didn't see it listed."

"It still exists, but they don't parade anymore," Sallie said. "Back in the Nineties, the city passed an ordinance requiring all the parading krewes to certify that they don't discriminate on the basis of race, gender, religion, or what have you. Comus refused to do so and withdrew its parade application. My understanding is that it still operates as a social organization but without the parade."

"It saddens me to hear that," Prosper said. "As a kid, it all seemed perfectly normal, but Comus was probably racist through and through. Dad never behaved in an overtly racist way that I can remember, but I guess he wasn't immune to the mores of the time."

"Few of us were," I said.

"But you and Bo were tight from the time you were little, weren't you?" he said. "How did you manage that, Bruneau? I knew some African American kids growing up, or *coloreds* as we called them back then, but I never had any close friends who were black until Vietnam. It embarrasses me now to look back on those days."

"Well, I'm almost thirty years younger than you, and I'm sure a lot changed over the course of three decades," I said. "Plus, Bo and I were neighbors, our dads worked around each other, and our moms were friendly, so it was all very natural. It wasn't something either of us gave a lot of thought to, at least not the way I remember it. By the time we got to high school, there was a fair amount of self-selecting segregation going on, single-race cliques, and such. But I was mostly a loner, and Bo hung out with the jocks, which was more of a mixed-race fraternity, so it didn't really affect us."

"Did you ever talk about it?" Sallie asked.

"Talk about what? Race?"

"Yeah. Race, civil rights, what was going on in the world."

"Seems like we must have," I said, "but I can't really recall any specific conversations."

"Mm-hmm," Sallie muttered.

"What's that supposed to mean?"

"It means mm-hmm, as in yet another example of male avoidance behavior."

There was a break in the conversation as I strained for a witty response, and Sallie fixed me with an imperious, arched eyebrow look. Prosper chuckled quietly but then intervened.

"Dinner smells great," he said. "What can I do to help?"

Thanks to Prosper, the transition to dining went off without any fireworks, and as we sat at table the discussion turned to the Tavernier Blue. I relayed my conversations with Fancy and Bo, and characteristically Prosper jumped right in.

"I understand Bo's point of view," he said. "But it is interesting to contemplate which diamond might be which. As I see it, there are four possibilities."

"Which are what?" I asked.

"Well, the first and most likely is the one your friend puts forth," Prosper said. "The Hope was cut from the French Blue and the diamond that sold

CHAPTER NINETEEN

in Hong Kong is a different stone."

"And the second?"

"The Hope was cut to fit the drawings of the French Blue."

It took me a second to grasp Prosper's meaning.

"You mean a London gemstone cutter was in possession of a large blue diamond and sought to increase its value by cutting it to fit the specs of Tavernier's stone?"

"Correct," he said.

"In that scenario, the Hope is not the French Blue, but Jane Placide's diamond could be," Sallie chimed in.

"Yes, and the fact that Jane's diamond is roughly the same size as the French Blue strengthens the case," Prosper said.

I whistled. "The third possibility?"

"The drawings are forged or are of another diamond."

"I'm not following you," I said.

"Let me try," Sallie said, raising her hand and looking at Prosper. "You're saying that this same London gem cutter or an associate could have made a drawing derived from Tavernier's sketches and then passed it off as the French Blue, and then they used that drawing to create the future Hope Diamond."

"That's right," Prosper said. "Or there could have been an honest mistake. Maybe the drawings were actually of another diamond in the royal collection, and amidst the chaos of the revolution, they got misidentified as being of the French Blue."

"In either case, the diamond we call the Hope today would not have been cut from the French Blue, but Jane's stone could have been," Sallie said.

"Exactly," Prosper said.

I was having trouble keeping up with the conversation but asked Prosper about his final possibility.

"The team changed the drawing to fit the Hope."

"Wait, what team? The Smithsonian team?"

"Yep."

I frowned and shook my head.

"I don't think so," I said. "I wouldn't put a little sleight of hand past Fancy Rigard, but that would require collusion among a number of presumed experts. And what would their motive be? I'm not feeling this one."

"You're probably right," Prosper said. "It's the least likely of the scenarios, but logistically, it would have been possible to do, so I thought I should mention it."

This was the longest stretch of time Prosper and Sallie had spent together in a relaxed setting, and I could see them growing more comfortable in each other's company. Prosper's gentle bearing tugged at Sallie, I could see, and it was obvious that he appreciated her quick-witted smarts. The food and wine went down easily, helping the conversation along, and even the King Cake was palatable. Sallie had used a spice cake recipe and decorated it with the trademark purple, green, and gold sprinkles, so we were spared the stale brioche atrocity one normally encounters at carnival season dinners.

I was leaning back in my chair, enjoying my friends enjoying each other, when my phone buzzed on the kitchen counter. I needed to use the bathroom anyway, so I collected some plates and dropped them in the sink before picking up the phone. It was a text from Bo with a photo of Ronald Walker. Other than the eye patch, he had no obvious distinguishing characteristics. He was heavyset, with a receding hairline, but otherwise, he was just a guy, more or less like any other.

"Huh," I said, raising my phone and showing it to Sallie and Prosper. "Bo sent a pic of the Walker fella up in New Jersey, if you're interested."

I placed the phone back on the counter and headed for the bathroom. When I returned, Sallie was rinsing some dishes, and Prosper was leaning over my phone. As I approached, he turned to me.

"I could be wrong, Bruneau, but I swear I think I've seen this guy before."

"Really?"

"Yeah, I think so."

"Are you sure? Do you remember when?"

"I had forgotten about this, but a couple years ago, two guys visited me on Grand Isle," Prosper said. "They had a bunch of questions about Jean Lafitte. I think this was one of the guys. The only reason I remember him is

CHAPTER NINETEEN

because of the eye patch. He was the quiet one. His friend did all the talking. A skinny white guy, maybe mid to late fifties. Friendly enough. Seemed halfway sane, which is more than I can say for a lot of my visitors. I can't remember the names they gave me."

"How sure are you?" Sallie asked, picking up my phone and studying Walker's pic. She had turned the water off and was leaning into the conversation.

"Pretty sure," Prosper said. "Now that I think about it, everything about that visit was unusual."

"How so?" I asked.

"They were an odd match, for one thing. Usually, when these Lafitte freaks come in pairs or in groups, they're all enthusiasts, and they try to outdo each other with their esoteric knowledge. The white guy was kind of like that, but this other guy seemed indifferent."

"What else?"

"Most of the time, folks are hunting treasure, and they have a theory they want to bounce off me. But the white guy didn't seem interested in any of that. He kept asking me about Lafitte's love life and when and how I thought he had died."

Sallie piped up at that.

"Do you think he was trying to figure out if Lafitte could have visited New Orleans in the mid-1820s?"

"He didn't ask me that directly, as far as I can recall, but I guess it's possible. I can't believe I'd forgotten about this. I should have mentioned it before now."

The three of us stared at each other in silence.

"I think we better talk to Bo," I said.

Chapter Twenty

The interview with Ronald Walker started out the way we expected. He kept his story simple, and his lawyer, a woman named Harris, made sure he didn't take any foolish detours. According to Walker, the day after a heavy thunderstorm he was part of a crew clearing limbs and brush from the side of state Rte. 662, just off the Point Breeze property line, when a sparkle of light a few feet away caught his eye. Thinking it was the sunlight reflecting off a piece of tin foil someone had tossed from a car, he went to pick it up, and that's when he came upon the diamond.

The officer leading the interview, Larry Moretti of the New Jersey State Police, interrupted Walker.

"It was just sitting there? In the broad daylight?"

"Yes, sir, in the grass. I figured maybe it got dislodged from somewhere during the storm."

"Dislodged from where?"

"I don't know, a tree maybe."

"Oh, a tree, of course. Why didn't I think of that?" Moretti said. "Let me ask you, Mr. Walker, were you in the habit of cleaning up the area outside the property?"

"Yes, sir," Walker answered. "It's the entrance corridor to the estate, and they like to keep it tidy."

"They, being management?"

"Yes, sir."

"What did you do when you found the diamond?"

Walker said it didn't occur to him at first that the gem might be real, but

CHAPTER TWENTY

he thought it was pretty, so he put it in his pocket with the idea that he'd clean it up and maybe give it to his girlfriend. But when he went home and began polishing the stone, he started to wonder if it might be genuine.

"I thought maybe it was a sapphire," he said.

"How'd you figure out it was a diamond?" Moretti asked.

"I took it to a jeweler."

"This jeweler have a name?"

"The Ice House, in South Philly."

Moretti jotted down a note.

"So now you knew you had a blue diamond on your hands?"

"That's what the guy said he thought it was, but he wanted to keep it overnight and do some research," Walker said. "But at that point, I'm starting to realize it might be worth something, and I didn't trust the guy with it."

"So, what did you do?"

"I took it home. Next day, my girlfriend and I look up this guy who does appraisals for rich folks out on the Main Line, and we took it to him."

"Name?"

"Alan Henderson. He's in Bryn Mawr."

"And he identifies it as a blue diamond?"

"Yes, sir. Says it's an incredible specimen with what he called perfect clarity. Says it's probably worth a few million, easy. I'm like, holy shit, I won the damn lottery. Couldn't believe it."

"He tell you anything else?"

"Yeah, he gets real interested when I tell him it came from Point Breeze. He took a bunch of pictures and measurements and said he'd do some research and get back to me. Told me I should put the rock in a safe deposit box, which I did right away."

"And did he? Get back to you?"

"Yeah, a couple days later. Said the stone might be historically significant. Explained about Mr. Bonaparte and the crown jewels and all that."

"Okay, so then what'd you do?"

"Started researching the best way to sell it," Walker said. "It didn't take long to figure out an auction was the way to go."

"Why Hong Kong rather than one of the big U.S. houses?"

"Mr. Henderson said that demand at the top end of the jewelry market is driven by Chinese buyers, so Hong Kong seemed like the right place."

"You pay this Henderson for his counsel?"

"Yeah, a couple hundred dollars up front and then ten thousand out of the sale. Seems like he did me straight, so no complaints. I wouldn't have known what to do otherwise."

"He the one who came up with the French Blue theory?"

"I think so. He talked to the auction people in Hong Kong, and they decided to market it that way. I don't know if it is, or it isn't."

"Did you expect the diamond to sell for $63 million?"

"Lord, no. I was thinking a few million, maybe. Still can't believe it."

"Point Breeze give you any trouble?"

"You mean in terms of saying the diamond is theirs?"

"Yeah."

"They made some noises, yeah. That's when I retained Ms. Harris here," Walker said, nodding toward his attorney.

"There were two other gentlemen on the cleanup crew," the Harris woman said. "They said they saw Mr. Walker pick up the diamond on public land. Once we got their statements, Point Breeze had no cause to pursue."

"What about the auction house in Hong Kong?" Moretti asked. "They give you any hassle?"

"Just asked a bunch of routine questions, is all," Walker said. "Seemed satisfied with my answers."

"And why wouldn't they have been?" Harris asked. "My client's been on the up and up about everything."

Moretti ignored the attorney and spoke to Walker.

"What are you going to do with all that money?"

Walker's face tightened, and he looked at Harris.

"I've advised my client not to discuss financial matters," she said. "What Mr. Walker chooses to do with the proceeds from the sale of the diamond is his business and immaterial to whatever you think you're investigating, Officer Moretti. Can you remind us what it is you think you're investigating?"

CHAPTER TWENTY

Moretti again ignored her and turned to Walker.

"Does the name Ttaba mean anything to you?"

"No," Walker said.

Moretti wrote something on his pad, probably for effect. Then he looked up and popped another question.

"You ever been to New Orleans, Mr. Walker?"

"New Orleans?" Walker paused, looking surprised and suspicious. "Yeah, I've been there a few times, as a kid mostly. I grew up in Houston and my mother had a brother who lived there who we visited a few times."

"When were you last there?" Moretti asked.

Harris interrupted him.

"Excuse me, Officer Moretti, does this line of questioning have a point?"

"Yes, Counselor, I can assure you it does."

"Then I suggest you get to it. My client is here of his own volition because you said you needed his help. This is starting to feel a lot like an interrogation."

"Apologies, Counselor," Moretti said. "We do appreciate Mr. Walker coming in to help us out like this. I was just getting ready to introduce an old friend of Mr. Walker's and was simply setting the stage."

Walker and Harris looked at each other in confusion.

"If I may turn your attention to the video screen, you may recall that earlier, I briefly introduced you to officers Duplessis and Rodiger, who have been patiently waiting for us to get to this portion of our program."

Rodiger and I waved and said hello.

"I should have mentioned at the outset that officers Duplessis and Rodiger are with the Property Crimes section of the New Orleans Police Department," Moretti continued. "They've got a case they've been working on down there that they're hoping Mr. Walker can help them with. Officers?"

Before I could get started, Walker interrupted.

"I don't know nothing about no robbery in New Orleans," he said, casting a pleading glance at his lawyer. She was about to say something, but I jumped in.

"No, of course not, Mr. Walker," I said. "Although I am curious. How did you know it's a robbery we're investigating?"

There was a pause.

"You did say you were with Property Crimes, detective," Harris said. "You investigate anything else?"

"Well, yes, but I take your point, Ms. Harris," I said.

"Mr. Walker, we're hoping to jog your memory about a visit you made to Grand Isle, Louisiana, three years ago, because while there you may have come into contact with a person of interest to our investigation. We'd like to ask you some questions about him."

"Grand what?" Walker said. "I have no idea what you're even talking about."

"You did visit New Orleans about this time three years ago, did you not? I suppose it's possible the airline records we found are for another Ronald Walker from East Camden, New Jersey."

"No, that's right," he said, hesitating. "I was there for a few days of vacation."

"Ah, I see. While you were here, did you drive down to Grand Isle one day? It's one of the islands that sits between the Mississippi Delta and the Gulf of Mexico. It's about a two-hour drive."

"If I did, I don't remember."

"What is the meaning of this, officers?" Harris objected. She was about to launch into what I feared might be a long-winded protest, so I pulled Prosper in front of the camera before she could get started.

"Do you remember this man, Mr. Walker? I believe you and an acquaintance of yours visited him on Grand Isle. He went by the name Prosper Fortune in those days."

"Hello Mr. Walker," Prosper said, "my hair was a bit longer when we met back then and I'm afraid my hygiene at the time left something to be desired, but I do remember you and your friend. I can't remember his name. What was it again?"

Walker looked flustered, as we'd hoped. When Bruneau called to tell me about Prosper recognizing Walker from his photo, it was only two hours

CHAPTER TWENTY

before the interview was scheduled to start. I talked to Prosper on the phone long enough to convince myself that his memory might be legit. Then I asked Bru to bring him down to the station and got on the horn to Moretti. We would have liked more time to plot our approach, but we agreed it was worth a shot to haul Prosper out in front of the camera.

"I...um, sorry, but I don't think I know you," Walker stuttered.

"This is outrageous!" Harris jumped in. "Don't say another word, Ronald. We did not come here to get ambushed by a two-bit stunt, Moretti. I'll be speaking to the commissioner about this. You can rest assured. Let's go, Ronald, we've been here long enough."

As Harris and Walker got up to leave, Prosper spoke up.

"If it helps to jog your memory, Mr. Walker, your friend asked a bunch of questions about the pirate Jean Lafitte. He was an associate of Joseph Bonaparte's."

Walker turned his head but did not respond, and Harris nudged him out of the interview room. Moretti stood up, poked his head into the hall to make sure they were out of hearing distance, and then shut the door.

"Thank you, Mr. Coulon, that was well done," he said.

"I hope I didn't lay it on too thick," Prosper said. "Calling Lafitte an associate of Bonaparte's is a bit of a stretch."

"Not at all," Moretti said. "You produced the desired effect. He was rattled for sure."

"Do you think we have enough for a warrant, Officer Moretti?" Rodiger asked.

"Not sure," Moretti said. "We don't have much in the way of evidence, but the amount of money involved and Walker's overall sketchiness may help our case. I'll see what I can do."

"If you've got the manpower, it might be a good idea to keep him under surveillance for a few days," I said. "If he's rattled like you say, he might try to get in touch with his buddy."

"Yeah, see if he leads us anywhere."

"Thanks, Larry," I said. "We'll keep poking around down here."

***

I had allowed Bruneau to sit in on our interview, off camera, in the corner of the room. As soon as we ended our video session, he spoke up.

"Is that the guy you remember, Prosper?"

"Yes, no doubt about it."

"Nice job finding that airline record, Bo," Bru said.

"What airline record?"

"The record you found of Walker visiting New Orleans."

"Oh, that. Roll of the dice."

"You made it up?" Bru looked at me with wide eyes, like I was crazy.

"Who says cops can't get creative when they need to?"

Bru took that in with a chuckle and a shake of his head.

"Walker looks guilty as hell to me," Bru said. "How come you didn't press him on the grave robbery?"

"Because we don't have anything to press him with," I said. "We accomplished what we set out to do, which was to spook him. Criminals get spooked, they make mistakes."

"So that's it? All we do now is sit around and wait for him to slip up?"

"No," I said. "Moretti's going to follow up with the girlfriend and the jewelers, make sure those parts of his story check out, which I expect they will. But the warrant is key. If we can get into Walker's bank accounts, we can follow the money."

"Meanwhile, we've got a lot of time to account for," Rodiger said.

"How do you mean?" Bru asked.

"If our theory of the case is accurate, Mahdi Toledano somehow finds out about Jane Placide and her diamond while living in Montreal more than three years ago," Rodiger said. "He moves to New Orleans and opens a hair salon called the Hidden Gem. Around that time, Walker and another man seek out Mr. Coulon here on Grand Isle and ask him a bunch of questions about Jean Lafitte and his love life. Yet almost three years go by before our grave robbery occurs. What were Toledano and Walker and their presumed third accomplice doing all that time, and why did they wait so long before

CHAPTER TWENTY

putting their plan into action?"

"My guess is they were trying to validate their theory," Prosper said. "Somehow, we don't know how exactly, but presumably from a source they viewed as credible, they got the idea that this diamond, maybe the French Blue, went to the grave with Jane Placide. But they didn't want to go through the trouble, not to mention the risk, of breaking into the mausoleum, without convincing themselves that their theory was credible."

"And when they start doing their due diligence, they run into some of the same obstacles we've encountered," Bru said.

"Right," Rodiger said. "Such as the fact that there's no evidence that Jane Placide and Jean Lafitte knew each other, or that Lafitte even stepped foot in New Orleans during the time Placide lived here. Or the fact that Placide couldn't have possessed the French Blue if the Hope was cut from it."

"Which explains the questions they asked me about Lafitte," Prosper said.

"Yeah, that all makes sense," I said. "But we've still got more questions than answers. Such as, how the hell does Toledano learn about Jane Placide while living in Montreal? How could Toledano and Walker have known each other? And who is the third accomplice? Is he the link between them? And is he maybe the one who found out about the diamond first? We've been assuming that Toledano is the mastermind, but maybe it's this other guy."

"Good point, but somehow I doubt it," Bru said. "If there's one thing we know about Toledano, it's that he's smart as a whip and wants everyone to know it."

"Tell me more," I said.

"Well, he's got to be smart to have stayed ahead of law enforcement all these years, right? I mean, how many Moroccan ex-pat dwarfs can there be out there? But somehow, he eludes detection. And then there's his word games. The Hidden Gem, Ttaba. That's him showing off. Look at me, right? I'm so clever. And finally, all the bank accounts and the money laundering. That's a whole lot of complexity to manage. Bottom line? We're talking about a first-rate mind. I don't see him suffering fools or carrying out someone else's scheme."

"And the letter to Ms. Duval, that's interesting too," Rodiger said. "It's not just that he wants people to know he's smart. He cares about how people see him."

"Yes, exactly," Bru said.

"I think I agree with you, Bruneau," Rodiger said. "Odds are Toledano is the alpha of this crew."

There was a brief silence before Prosper spoke up softly.

"I don't want to speak out of turn," he said, "but there are a couple more questions I haven't heard asked."

"By all means, let's hear 'em," I said.

"Well, if I understand the chronology correctly, Mahdi Toledano did not leave town immediately after the robbery, right? Shouldn't we ask ourselves why?"

"That's true," Rodiger said. "It wasn't until our investigation was well under way and we had his name that he suddenly vanishes."

"Are you suggesting someone tipped him off?" I asked.

"I'm not suggesting anything," Prosper said. "Just pointing out a fact that seems like it may be of consequence."

"Okay, that's a fair point, consider it noted," I said. "You said you had a couple questions."

"Yes, and my second question may be related to the first," Prosper said.

"Fire away."

"We've been assuming it was a coincidence that Toledano rented his salon from Bruneau's friend, Charlotte Duval. What if it wasn't?"

Chapter Twenty-One

I try to keep my fear of flying close to the vest. It's exactly the kind of thing Bo would go to town with, so I don't bring it up around him. But it's no coincidence that I limit most of my buying trips to drivable locations. My aversion is not so extreme that I'd call it a phobia, but when I do fly, I take precautions. And so it was that I'd popped a couple Valiums before boarding my flight to LaGuardia. By the time my seatmate jostled me awake, we'd already landed, and half the plane had disembarked.

I was still wobbly when I exited the jetway, so rather than rush to grab a cab, I sat down at the gate to let my head clear, and my legs return. Then I called Sallie.

"Hey there," she answered. "You make it okay?"

"I did. How about you?"

"Yep, everything went as smoothly as could be."

The night before, I'd conveyed to Sallie the highlights of the Ronald Walker interview and our subsequent group discussion. She agreed with Prosper that the most likely explanation for the three-year lag between Toledano learning about the diamond and the break-in at the mausoleum, was the difficulty he would have had in ascertaining that the diamond would actually be there. And she agreed it was suspicious that Toledano disappeared right after the police named him as a suspect. But she wasn't biting on Prosper's suggestion that it might not have been a coincidence that Toledano chose to rent from Charlotte. In fact, I think it pissed her off.

"Did you think about our conversation anymore?" I asked her.

"That was pretty much all I thought about during my flight," Sallie said.

"I turned it around every which way, and I just don't get where Prosper's coming from. Charlotte doesn't have anything to do with Jane Placide or Jean Lafitte or Girod Street. It doesn't make any sense."

"I know. I think maybe his point is just that Toledano seems to be purposeful in everything he does. He's extremely careful and detailed in his planning, and he doesn't seem to leave anything to chance. If that's all Prosper meant, it's a fair point."

"Well, sure," Sallie said. "If you put it in that context, yeah, renting from a trusting old lady makes sense. And so does setting up his salon a bit off the beaten path. If he wanted to keep a low profile, he was able to do so."

"I bet that's all he meant," I said, less from conviction than in hopes of mollifying Sallie.

I wished Sallie luck in her puzzling competition. We said our goodbyes, and I headed off to find my cab.

* * *

If there's one thing that unsettles me more than flying, it's an underwater tunnel, something I don't have to worry about in New Orleans. When I gave my Uber driver the address in Hoboken, it didn't occur to me until it was too late that he might take the Holland Tunnel. As we descended into the westbound tube, cars were moving slowly in heavy traffic. Exhaust filled the air, and it felt as though the soot-coated tile walls were closing in. I was short of breath, my palms went cold and clammy, and I sensed a bout of nausea coming on. The night before, I'd joined a group of friends at an Indian restaurant, and now the taste of the curry I'd eaten was returning, and not in a good way. I closed my eyes, leaned my head back, and tried to let my mind go blank.

The tunnel seemed to go on forever, but eventually, we made it to the New Jersey side, and my symptoms began to fade. I made a mental note to insist upon the George Washington Bridge for the return trip, even though I knew it would cost more.

The Caroline Placide descendant Sallie's friend had located was named

CHAPTER TWENTY-ONE

Shirley Hoffman. She lived in a modest brownstone a few blocks from the Hudson. When I climbed the steep steps to her front door, I stopped to gather my courage before ringing the doorbell. A thickset sixty-something man in gray flannel pants and a white t-shirt answered, opening the door partway.

"Hi there," I said. "I'm looking for Shirley Hoffman. Is she at home?"

"Who wants to know?" the man asked, eyeing me warily.

"My name is Bruneau Abellard. I'm working on a genealogical research project that I'm hoping Ms. Hoffman might be able to help me with. I live in New Orleans and I'm in New York on business, so I thought I'd try to kill two birds with one stone."

The man paused to process my tangled introduction.

"Shirley!" he called over his shoulder. "There's a man here to see you about some research."

"Just a minute," came a woman's voice from what sounded like a few rooms away.

"You can come inside if you like," the man said. "I'm Ralph Hoffman, Shirley's husband."

Ralph and I exchanged handshakes and brief pleasantries as he ushered me into a small sitting room and motioned me to an armchair. No sooner had I seated myself than Shirley appeared, and I rose to introduce myself all over again. She was a nondescript woman of 70 or so with short white hair and a kind, somewhat vacant face. She wore a pale blue sweat suit and was untying an apron as she sat down next to her husband on the couch that faced me.

"Please excuse my appearance, Mr. Abellard," she said. "You caught me in the middle of cleaning the oven."

"No need to apologize, ma'am," I said. "It was rude of me to show up unannounced."

"That's quite alright," she said. "Now that you're here, what can I do for you? Can I get you some tea or coffee? I'm afraid I'm not much on genealogy."

Declining the offer of a hot beverage, I fabricated a long story about how

I was helping a historian of the American theatre trace the lineage of the Placide family into the present day.

"I'm afraid I don't recognize the name Placide, Mr. Abellard," Shirley said. "Are you sure I'm related to these people?"

"Oh yes, quite sure," I said. "But it's not surprising that you wouldn't know the name Placide. The ancestor we're interested in was married twice, once to a man named Waring and then again to a man named Blake. And then her daughter, who was also an actress, was named Anne Duff Waring Sefton Wallack. Do any of those names ring a bell?"

"I'm afraid not," Shirley said. "My grandmother was the family historian, but she passed away a number of years ago. I do have a vague recollection of her telling us about a famous actress in our family, but I'm afraid I didn't pay much attention at the time."

"That's alright," I said. "What was your grandmother's name?"

"Gladys Hunter. She was my father's mother. She lived in Milwaukee."

"Your maiden name is Hunter?"

"Yes, Shirley Hunter."

"Did your grandmother keep written records or a scrapbook of any kind? Or do you have a sibling or perhaps a cousin who shared your grandmother's interest in your ancestry?"

"I'm an only child, so no siblings and no first cousins either," Shirley said. "My grandmother had boxes and boxes of files that she left to me. I never really had much interest in them, but I remember that there were a bunch of old handwritten letters and things that she made typed copies of because she was worried about the writing fading over time, and it was important to her that future generations be able to read them."

"Do you still have these boxes?"

"No, I'm afraid not. Ralph was always on me about how much room they took up, so I emailed a bunch of relatives, most of whom I'd never even met, to see if anyone was interested in them."

"Who are these relatives?" I asked.

"All Hunter family descendants of one kind or another," Shirley said. "I'm on an extended family email list, and I get occasional messages about this

CHAPTER TWENTY-ONE

and that. There must be a hundred or more names on that list. One day, I hit reply to all, explained what I had, and asked if anyone was interested."

"And did anyone respond?"

"Yes, a very nice woman," Shirley said. "I can't remember her name, or how we are related, but we spoke on the phone. She paid to have everything shipped to her."

"How long ago was this?" I asked.

"Oh goodness, I don't know. Ralph, do you remember?"

"If I had to guess, I'd say ten years," Ralph said. "Must've been 20 boxes or more."

"Do you remember where this woman lived?"

"Somewhere down south, I think," Shirley said.

Ralph closed his eyes and tilted his head back, as if trying to summon a memory. Then he leaned forward.

"You know, I could be wrong, but I think it might have been New Orleans."

"Really?"

"Like I said, I could be wrong, but for some reason, New Orleans sticks in my head."

"I think you may be right, Ralph," Shirley said. "If I'm not mistaken, she had a French-sounding last name. I wish I could remember."

"Do you have a way of checking?" I asked. "It would mean a great deal to me to have that name."

Shirley said she thought she could find the name by sifting through the addresses on the latest Hunter family email, but it might take some time, and she had someplace she needed to be. She said she'd look for it later that afternoon and would let me know if she found anything. I didn't feel that I could press her any harder, so I gave her my contact info, thanked her and Ralph for their time, and said my goodbyes.

* * *

My mind was racing as my Uber driver navigated the frenetic lower level of the GW. He referred to it as "Martha" and winked to make sure I understood that George was on top of his wife. I smiled conspiratorially. Then, as we entered the off-ramp to the Henry Hudson, my phone rang. It was Bo.

"Hey, Bo."

"How's the Big Apple?" he asked.

"As big as ever. And loud and filthy and full of itself, like always."

As I spoke, it occurred to me that Bo may never have been to New York. He didn't have opportunities to travel far as a kid, and when he and Angie took the family on vacation, it was usually to Pensacola or some other place they could get to by driving. I remembered that he'd taken Angie to a couple of law enforcement conferences he'd attended, one in Denver and the other in Tampa, but for the most part, he's never shown much curiosity about seeing the world.

"You doing anything fun?" he asked.

"Like what?"

"I don't know. Seeing a show. Catching a Knicks game."

"Um, no," I said, "nothing like that. Just checking out the exhibitions, sitting in on some lectures, catching up with old friends, that sort of thing. You know, *real* fun."

"Damn, Bru, you're pathetic, you know that?"

"Is that why you called me? To tell me I'm pathetic?"

"No," he said, "but seriously, get a life, will ya?"

I waited.

"I'm calling to let you know that we got the warrant," he said. "I thought you'd want to know."

"For Walker?"

"Yep. We're limited to his financial records for now, but if we find anything suspicious, the judge is open to widening our scope."

"Nice," I said. "Does New Jersey have to do the searching?"

"Officially, yes," Bo said. "But Rodiger is providing what you might call *unofficial* assistance."

"Excellent," I said.

I thought about telling Bo about my visit to Hoboken, but a voice in the back of my head told me to hold off for now. No point in raising expectations

CHAPTER TWENTY-ONE

before I had something concrete to report. We talked for a while longer, and by the time I hung up, the driver was pulling up to my hotel. I had just enough time to freshen up before meeting the rest of my group for a light lunch in advance of our panel discussion.

* * *

The session went well. Attendance was on the light side, maybe seventy people, but the moderator did a good job moving the discussion along, and I was able to contribute some helpful insights. Afterward, I took in the Frick Collection a few blocks from the Park Avenue Armory, where the Winter Show was held, and then went for a walk in Central Park. It was a clear, brisk day, the fresh air was invigorating, and it was an easy way to get my steps in, so I could pass Sallie's Fitbit inspection when I got home. I stopped at a bench near the boathouse to soak in some sun and take in the scene. Dog walkers were everywhere, along with rollerbladers, skateboarders, and parents walking with young children on tricycles. It was a wholesome scene, at odds with the popular me-first image of the big city.

I checked in with Sallie, who reported that she lost in the semifinal round of her competition, but she sounded in good spirits, nonetheless. She'd never been to San Antonio. She was predictably underwhelmed by the Alamo, but said she enjoyed exploring the River Walk area. I was due to arrive back in New Orleans an hour before her that evening, so we made plans to meet at her gate.

After hanging up with Sallie, I gave Prosper a call. He was still an unreliable operator of the cell phone Irene had given him, but he managed to answer on the fourth ring. A fumbling noise preceded his answer.

"Hello?"

"Hi Prosper, it's Bruneau."

"Bruneau, hi," he said. "How's New York?"

"It's good. Hugo giving you any trouble?"

"Nah, not at all. We're buds. Having ourselves a great time."

"That's what I was afraid of. You're not encouraging bad habits, are you?"

"Perish the thought."

"Uh-huh." I chuckled knowingly.

"Hey, listen, assuming everything runs on schedule, I'll see you tonight. But something's been eating at me, so I thought I'd give you a quick call. This a good time?"

"Sure. What's up?"

"You made a comment when we were talking after the Ronald Walker interview. You said that we shouldn't assume it was a coincidence that Toledano rented his salon from my friend Charlotte."

"Yes, I remember."

"We let it go at the time, but it's been bothering me ever since. What did you mean by that?"

"Just what I said. I mean, what are the odds, right? There's what, 400,000 people in this city? And he rents from your friend?"

"I'm not really following your logic," I said. "Charlotte doesn't have anything to do with Girod Street, and Toledano would have had no way of knowing I would become involved in the investigation."

"No, I guess not," Prosper said. "It just seems like such a fluke coincidence. Everything we know about this guy suggests that everything he does, he does for a reason."

"I get that part," I said. "I just wanted to make sure that there wasn't more to your point that I was missing."

"No, that's all it is, really," he said.

Prosper and I said our goodbyes, and I started making my way back to the hotel. I hadn't gotten far when my phone rang. I didn't recognize the number, but the 201 area code offered a clue, so I answered.

"Hello, Mr. Abellard, this is Shirley Hoffman," the caller said. "We met earlier."

"Yes, of course, Shirley," I said. "Thanks for getting back to me."

"I wanted to let you know that I was able to find the name of the woman who took all my grandmother's boxes."

"That's wonderful news," I said. "Hang on just a minute while I find something to write with."

CHAPTER TWENTY-ONE

I grabbed the pen I had clipped to my shirt pocket, and for something to write on, I pulled the Winter Show program from my overcoat. Then I cocked the phone to my ear.

"Okay," I said, "go ahead."

"Her name is Charlotte Duval."

Chapter Twenty-Two

I didn't bother with Valium on the return trip. My mind was so preoccupied with Shirley Hoffman's bombshell that I barely noticed we were in the air. It hardly seemed possible that Charlotte was related to Shirley, or that it was she who had responded to Shirley's plea to take her grandmother's files off her hands. And yet, Shirley said she was certain that it was, and Ralph corroborated her account.

As soon as I met Sallie at her gate, I let her know what I had learned, that it was Charlotte who had taken possession of the Hunter family records kept by Shirley's grandmother. I told her we were past the point of plausible coincidence, and she agreed.

"Do you think this is what Prosper had in mind?" she asked. "Did he know something the rest of us didn't?"

"I can't imagine how he could have," I said.

Sallie took that in.

"What are you going to do?" she asked, looking at me solemnly.

"I was hoping you could tell me," I said.

During the drive home, we turned the matter over, and debated next steps. To tell Bo, or not to tell Bo? To confront Charlotte, or not? Do we follow up with Prosper? What do we know about the Hunter family and Charlotte's place in it? We were all over the place, each of us changing our positions by the minute. The only thing we could agree on was that we both needed a good night's sleep to clear our heads.

When we got home, Prosper and Hugo were waiting for us. It quickly became apparent that Hugo had treated himself to a grand old time in our

CHAPTER TWENTY-TWO

absence. After greeting us at the door, he dashed back upstairs and jumped on my recliner, where he assumed an entitled pose. As he well knew, the recliner is one of the few pieces of furniture he is not allowed on. I couldn't blame Prosper for this breach of etiquette since I had failed to brief him on the house rules. Hugo eyed me warily from his ill-begotten new throne. I was too tired to argue with him, so I let it go for the time being, but I shot him a warning glance to let him know there'd be a reckoning.

When we told Prosper about Charlotte, he was as taken aback as we were, but denied having had any foreknowledge or a premonition. Characteristically, he was quicker than us to put things in perspective.

"Let's back up a couple steps," he said. "Obviously, this doesn't look good for your friend, but we don't know that those boxes contain correspondence between Jane Placide and her sister. And even if they do, we don't know that Charlotte did anything with them."

"Now *you're* the one who believes in coincidences?" I asked.

"No," he smiled, "not me. I'm just trying to put my detective's hat on. Even with this latest bombshell, we've got a bunch of facts that seem suspiciously related, but we're missing causal links. Until we can establish those, we probably shouldn't jump to conclusions."

"Speaking of detectives, shouldn't we alert Bo?" Sallie asked.

"No, not yet," I said. "I think if you and I approach Charlotte first, we've got a better chance of getting her to open up. If the police interrogate her, she might just shut down. Plus, she'll be traumatized."

"I know that," Sallie said, "but aren't there issues with admissibility of evidence if the police decide to place charges?"

"I don't know. Probably. I'm prepared to take the heat. But *charges*? Jesus, Sallie. Let's not get too far ahead of ourselves, okay?"

Sallie looked at Prosper to solicit his opinion.

"Don't look at me," he said, throwing his hands up. "Charlotte's not my friend, and I don't have a dog in this fight."

* * *

When I drove Prosper home that night, he sided with Sallie.

"I understand that Charlotte is your friend, and you want to give her a chance to explain herself," he said. "But I think Sallie's right that you'd be infringing on police business. And Bo's your friend, too, right? Is your relationship with Charlotte worth the risk of messing up Bo's case?"

If I'd stuck to my guns, it wouldn't have been the first time my stubbornness had clouded my judgment. But as I thought it over on the way home, I couldn't help but admit to myself that Sallie and Prosper were right. They had logic on their side and ethics too. I made up my mind to concede as much to Sallie, but when I got home, she was already asleep, so I let it go until morning.

Before going to bed myself, I took Hugo out, and when we got back, I placed an upside-down dining room chair on the recliner. He stared at me in disbelief before retreating to his bed, ruefully resigned to the restoration of our former world order.

When I rose at seven the next morning, Sallie was already out of bed, and I could smell coffee. I donned my robe and found her in her nightgown with her face in her laptop at the dining room table. Hugo was curled up in a ball at her feet.

"What are you doing up so early?" I asked.

"Top of the morning to you, too," she said, barely turning. "Grab some coffee. I'm digging up some intel on the Hunters."

I did as commanded and took a seat beside her. Hugo ignored me.

"Not that we need any more convincing, but Charlotte's mother Adelle's maiden name was Hunter, and Adelle's father, Charlotte's grandfather, was George Waring Hunter," Sallie said. "I'd have to get my friend Maura to map a line back to Caroline Placide, but the middle name Waring certainly suggests there's a familial connection there."

"It certainly does," I said. "Nice work."

Sallie smiled faintly but kept her eyes on her screen as she worked her mouse.

"Listen, I've thought about it, and I realize you're right about it being Bo's job to speak with Charlotte," I said. "I'll give him a call in a little bit."

CHAPTER TWENTY-TWO

Sallie pushed her chair away from the table and turned toward me, a sly smile on her face.

"That's interesting," she said, "because I thought it over, too, and realized *you* were right. There's no reason we can't approach Charlotte first, so long as we're careful not to wade into police business. We're not going there to force a confession or ask gotcha questions, just to feel out what she knows."

This was an unexpected turn of events.

"You make it sound like a fait accompli," I said. "Shouldn't we talk this over?"

"No time for that," Sallie said. "I texted Charlotte last night to say it had been a while and asked if we could stop by to catch up. Her reply was waiting for me when I got up. She's expecting us at nine."

* * *

Sallie's announcement that we'd be leaving for Charlotte's in a short while knocked me out of kilter, and I let my agitation show. First, I made an exasperated show of calling Victoria to ask her to open the store, which she kindly agreed to do. Then I told Sallie to go ahead and take her shower first and leave me some hot water before adding, "I need to write up instructions for Victoria and make some notes for our interview." Then, I took a conspicuous glance at my watch.

"Calm down, will you?" Sallie said. "We've got plenty of time."

"I wish you'd given me some advance notice," I said. "I like to be prepared."

"Don't be ridiculous. You're as prepared as you'll ever be. You're like a little child sometimes."

Rather than dignify that comment with a response, I buried my head in my notepad as Sallie traipsed off to her shower.

A while later, when we arrived at Charlotte's a couple minutes early, Isabella was waiting for us.

"Buenos dias!" she said, smiling as always. "Senora Duval is waiting for you in the dining room."

"Thank you, Isabella," I said. "Why the dining room? Is Senora Duval planning to feed us?"

"She has made some arrangements, yes, Senor Abellard."

Isabella led us through the foyer to the dining room, a long Victorian-accented expanse organized around an exquisite walnut table that sat 12 comfortably, 14 in a pinch. Charlotte was stationed at the near end, smoking over an ashtray, white lace placemats on either side of her. A silver tea and coffee service and a platter of pastries completed a study in elegant informality.

"Hello, dear hearts," Charlotte said, "it's so good of you to come. It's been too long. Please, have a seat."

"We weren't expecting such an elaborate reception," I said. "La Boulangerie? I recognize those croissants."

"And those cheddar chive biscuits!" Sallie drooled.

"Yes, I sent Isabella out at seven when they opened, so we'd have the pick of the litter," Charlotte said.

She patted Sallie on the hand. "It was such a nice surprise to get your text last night, dear. It gave Isabella and me time to pull a little something together."

Charlotte was dressed smartly in khaki slacks and a pink paisley shoulder drop shirt, her voice as stately and her bearing as regal as ever. The Omar Pasha incident had thrown her off her stride for a bit, but she was back in form now.

"Tell me what my favorite young couple has been up to. It really has been a while. And please, have something to eat and drink."

"It's nice of you to call us young, Charlotte, but a bit of a stretch, don't you think?" Sallie smiled.

"Of course not, dear. You are mere babes, the two of you."

"If you say so," Sallie said, still smiling. I snatched an almond croissant and poured myself a coffee I did not need.

"We were both out of town for the weekend," Sallie proceeded. "Bruneau was in New York for the big Winter Show, where he was an invited speaker. And I was in San Antonio for a puzzler's convention."

"Ah yes, the puzzling, I'd forgotten about your hobby," Charlotte said. "I

CHAPTER TWENTY-TWO

was in San Antonio once. Must have been the sixties, because my husband was alive, and he had business there. Ghastly place, as I remember."

"It wouldn't be my first choice, but it has its charms," Sallie said. She poured tea to go with the biscuit she'd plated.

Charlotte ignored Sallie's assessment and turned to me.

"And tell me about New York, dear. Did you make a splash?"

"I don't know about that," I said, sensing my opening, "but you'll never guess what the highlight of my weekend was."

"What was that, dear? Do tell."

"Making the acquaintance of one of your relatives."

"What? In New York? Who in the world could that be? I'm not aware of any Duvals in New York."

"Not a Duval. A Hunter. Shirley Hunter. She goes by Shirley Hoffman now, her married name."

Charlotte looked genuinely stumped.

"Shirley Hunter? Or Hoffman, you said? I don't think I know anyone by that name. Does she live in New York, or was she visiting?"

"She lives in New Jersey," I said. "Hoboken. She said that she spoke with you over the phone some years ago and you paid for her to send you boxes of Hunter family ancestral files that her grandmother had kept."

A dawning recognition crossed Charlotte's face, whether real or affected, I could not discern.

"Oh yes, of course, I do know who you mean now," Charlotte said, finally. "Seemed like a nice gal. A bit simple, maybe. Shirley, you said. Yes, that sounds right. She had all these boxes she didn't know what to do with, poor thing.

"That was a long time ago, Bruneau, so long I'd completely forgotten about it. How in the world did you meet this person? And how did my name come up?"

"It's a long story," I said. "But before I explain, tell us what prompted you to take these boxes off Shirley's hands? Have you gone through them? Do you still have them?"

Charlotte looked taken aback, at once offended and suspicious.

"Why am I the one answering questions when you're the one who met this person? Am I being interrogated again?"

I waited.

"Oh, very well. Yes, I still have the boxes, and yes, I've looked through them, but not closely or thoroughly. Why are you so interested, Bruneau?"

"Just curious. What can you tell us about the Hunters, Charlotte?"

Charlotte narrowed her eyes, letting us know she knew there was a game afoot, even if she wasn't sure what it was.

"I don't actually know that much, which is why I thought I'd take those boxes if nobody else wanted them. As you obviously know, mother was a Hunter, but growing up we didn't have much contact with her family. They were in North Carolina mostly, where mother grew up, and we were down here."

"How did your mother and father meet, Charlotte?" Sallie asked.

"In North Carolina, dear. Daddy went to Duke and he and mother met at a dance, or 'social' as they called them back then. She was just finishing up high school. He swept her off her feet and whisked her down here. The rest is history, I guess you could say."

"You said you didn't have much contact, but did your mother stay in touch with her family?" Sallie asked.

"Yes, some, but being Mrs. Duval was a big deal in those days, and I think she just got swept up in all that," Charlotte said. "After my grandparents died when I was just a toddler, mother stayed in touch with her brother Johnny, but I only remember him visiting once, with his family."

"If you were more or less estranged from the Hunter family, how did you end up in the loop regarding these family papers," I asked.

"We weren't estranged, dear," Charlotte said. "There was no animosity. We just didn't have much contact. But, to answer your question, many years ago now I was contacted by this woman who said she was a distant cousin on the Hunter side. She'd found me while building out a family tree. Her plan back then was to put together an annual Hunter family newsletter, and she asked if I'd like to be on the distribution list. I said sure, why not. The newsletter lasted two or three years, but the email list has stayed active all

CHAPTER TWENTY-TWO

this time. People post messages every now and then. Sometimes to share some piece of family information they've come upon, or sometimes to ask a genealogical question."

"And that's how you saw Shirley Hoffman's message about her grandmother's records," Sallie surmised.

"Yes, dear, exactly. When nobody else took the bait, I thought, why not? Maybe I'll learn something interesting about Mother's family."

"And did you?" I asked.

"No, sadly. I spent some time flipping through what she had, but it was overwhelming. I didn't recognize any of the names except those of my immediate family. There were a lot of property records, birth and death certificates, that kind of thing, and quite a bit of correspondence. I didn't have the patience or the energy to really dig in and try to make sense of it all."

"They've just been sitting in your attic or wherever you keep them, gathering dust?" I asked.

"For a long time, yes," Charlotte said. "But then I asked Phillip if he'd be interested in organizing everything and writing up a summary for me. I told him I'd pay him."

"Phillip, as in Phillip Boyer?"

"Yes, dear."

"And did he?"

"Did he what, dear?"

"Organize the materials and produce the summary?"

"He started to," Charlotte said. "He went at it for a few weeks, gave it the old college try, but eventually, he gave up. He said it was just too much."

"How long ago was this, Charlotte?" I asked.

"Oh golly, I don't know, maybe three or four years."

"Speaking of Phillip, I haven't seen him or heard you mention him for quite a while," I said. "What's he up to these days?"

"Phillip has been up north the last several months. Some kind of business up there. New Jersey, I think, or Pennsylvania. He thought he'd be back in town by summer."

"When was the last time you spoke with him?"

"September, maybe? I haven't talked to him since he left town. Why all the questions, Bruneau? You haven't told me what this is about."

"I'll tell you in a second," I said, "but just to confirm, you haven't spoken with Phillip in six months? Did I hear that correctly?"

"Yes, dear, that's what I said."

"Isn't that a long period of time, given how close you've become?"

"I suppose so, but Phillip and I aren't as close as you seem to think," Charlotte said. "We're friendly, and Phillip is entertaining company, but we don't share intimate secrets."

"It seemed like you spent a lot of time together."

"Do I detect a hint of jealousy, Bruneau? I can assure you you've nothing to worry about from Phillip Boyer."

Charlotte winked at Sallie and patted her hand.

"Now, dear, I believe you've used up your twenty questions," Charlotte said. "Are you going to tell me what this is all about?"

"It's about your relative, Jane Placide," I said.

"What? The actress? You can't be serious, Bruneau? This is preposterous. What do you imagine my relation to Miss Placide to be?"

"She is Shirley Hoffman's great aunt, five or six generations back."

Charlotte looked to Sallie for confirmation of my having taken leave of my senses.

"It's true, Charlotte," Sallie said in her most earnest voice. "Jane Placide had an older sister named Caroline, who was also an actress, in New York. She married a man named Leigh Waring, and they had a daughter, and the family tree branches out from there. We don't yet know your precise relation to the Placide sisters, but if you're related to Shirley Hunter, then you must be related to the Placides in some way. And your father's middle name was Waring, right? That would also indicate a connection."

Charlotte stared at Sallie, glanced at me, and turned back to Sallie.

"Yes, Daddy's mother's maiden name was Waring. This is really quite remarkable. You've given me a bit of a shock, I must say."

"You've no memory of your father mentioning a famous actress in the family?" Sallie asked.

"No, dear, never."

There was a lull in the conversation as Charlotte considered what she'd just learned.

"You said you still have Shirley Hoffman's boxes?" I asked as gently as I could.

"Huh? Yes," Charlotte said. "They're stacked up in one of the guest bedrooms. What is it you're looking for, exactly?"

"We know that Jane and Caroline corresponded," Sallie said. "It's a long shot, but we're wondering if Caroline kept any of Jane's letters and if she did, whether some of them survived and made their way into Shirley's grandmother's collection."

"Don't tell me you're playing detective now, too, dear," Charlotte said to Sallie. "I should have thought one in the family would be quite enough."

Sallie reddened a bit but smiled politely.

"I'm an archivist, Charlotte, and we archivists enjoy nothing so much as the thrill of the hunt."

"Oh lord, it's the thrill of the hunt now, is it?" Charlotte said. "Do me a favor, dear, and promise me you'll confine your hunting to the world of letters, will you? We've had quite enough misadventures from self-styled detectives with overactive imaginations."

"Ouch!" I said. "You cut me to the quick, Charlotte."

"I should hope so," she said.

Chapter Twenty-Three

April 17, 1825

Dearest Sister,

I hope this letter finds you well. Thank you for sharing the splendid review of your *Saw Mill* with me. You must have been in fine voice that evening! I wish Mother was alive to see you follow in her operatic footsteps. She must be so proud, Caroline, watching you from above!

Does the young man Mr. Blake still court you? Have you introduced him to your darling Anne? Please write soon with as much news as you can gather. I so enjoy learning of your triumphs and even sharing in your misfortunes. I want always to be close to you Caroline, even as circumstances place us far apart.

I must tell you about the most extraordinary man whom I met last night. He is a Frenchman named Jean Lafitte. Have you heard of him? He is "très notorious" down here. People call him a pirate or a smuggler, or worse. My good friend Officer Shields tells me that no one thought to call him such names when he kept the city stocked with foreign necessities during the time of the embargoes, or when he made possible General Jackson's glorious defeat of our English invaders. Back then Captain Lafitte was a dashing hero, admired by all. Now that his services are no longer so valued and the government seeks his arrest, it would seem that memories are short-lived.

It is well known that Captain Lafitte has not appeared in New Orleans for many years, for he is a wanted man here, and many presume him deceased. Yet, who should show up at the after-party for the premiere of our latest

CHAPTER TWENTY-THREE

Taming of the Shrew? None other than the man himself! He is the most magnificent creature I have set eyes upon, Caroline! Tall and dark and dashingly dressed, with deep set eyes that puncture a woman's defenses. And so charming, Caroline! A perfect gentleman.

At my request, Officer Shields introduced me to Captain Lafitte. We conversed at length, just the two of us, and it was plain that we shared an attraction. When I expressed surprise that he would risk apprehension by appearing in public, he confided that powerful interests had assured him of his protection in the evening's company. By powerful interests, I imagine he meant our distinguished Mr. Livingston, whom he counts as a trusted friend. Before James beckoned me away to parade in front of another group of admirers, Captain Lafitte asked if we could arrange to meet again, perhaps in a public garden or in my rooms ("avec une chaperone," naturally). I expressed concern that he would risk capture, but he said he is adept at disguising himself and has, from time to time, slipped in and out of the city in this way.

I know you would counsel me not to court danger, Caroline, and that nothing good can come of an association with such a man, but I feel drawn to him, and he to me, I believe. I have determined that I shall meet him at least this once. Have I taken leave of my senses? I think not, dear sister. Rather, it feels as though I have awoken from a long slumber. I shall report to you as soon as events transpire. Until then, I am...

Your naughty but devoted sister,

Jane

* * *

June 4, 1825

Dearest Caroline,

I received your letter of May 10 only yesterday. I am happy to learn that Anne does so well with her schoolwork that she may take on small roles with you. And it is a great credit to you that you should insist on satisfactory marks before she is allowed to take the stage. As you know, Mother and Father were less exacting of us, and I suffer a deficit even today. How brave you are, Caroline, to raise Anne so well while deprived of your dear Mr. Waring, may God rest his soul. I wish I were as strong as you. I fear I depend on James far too much. Much as he vexes me, I perish to think of where I should be without him.

It seems that you and your Mr. Blake enjoy each other's company splendidly, and it cheers me to learn that he is so attentive to Anne. Have you discussed matrimony? I should think you are well-suited to one another. Could you live in New York, or would you follow him back to Canada? I have heard it is dreadfully chilly up there in the winter, but love travels where it must, does it not?

While you receive the affections of a younger man, dear sister, I find myself in the opposite circumstance. Yes, it is true, I have fallen in love with a man almost 20 years my senior! I speak, of course, of my dear Captain Lafitte. Where he resides, I know not, but he visits as often as he is able, usually two or three times a week, in a different disguise each time. A distinguished scholar one day, a common fur trader the next. His ingenuity knows no bounds.

Though we have known each other for only a short while, Jean and I find ourselves deeply in love, Caroline. He is the most gracious and charming gentleman. And so handsome. When he looks at me, it is as though his being inhabits mine, and he feels what I feel, as if we are two halves of one whole. We have already decided that we wish to spend what is left of our lives together. But where, sister? That is the question. Jean cannot dwell here, nor can I live as a sailor on the seas. We have discussed Cuba, or perhaps Mexico, but each solution brings a new set of problems. Am I fated to play Dido to my captain's Aeneas? It is a role I have no wish to inhabit, yet these are the thoughts that torment me.

The hour is getting late, and I must transform to my Beatrice for this evening's *Much Ado*. Please write back soon with more happy news, dear sister, and I shall do the same. Until then, I bid you adieu.

Your loving sister,

CHAPTER TWENTY-THREE

Jane

* * *

June 10, 1825

Dear Caroline,

I write to report that my captain and I have engaged in our first quarrel! The episode has shaken me, and I've no one here I may safely confide in, so I turn now to my dear sister for a warm shoulder and a sympathetic ear.

I have not disclosed this to you previously, but Jean's business sometimes involves the sale of Negroes at auction. I cannot help but find this abhorrent, Caroline! I avow that negro labor is a necessary nutriment to our planting economy. This is what Jean argues. He says there are winners and losers in life, and for the duration of humanity, the former have risen upon the backs of the latter. And that if the planters were not supplied with the means to produce their abundance at a profit, there would be no fine shops or refined society to grace our fair city. No theatre even, Jean reminds me!

I know what he says to be true, sister, but this trading in the misery of slaves is a dirty business, one I think beneath the dignity of Captain Jean Lafitte. The forced separations of husbands from wives and children from mothers. The feculent living conditions. The brutal discipline of the masters. I see now that Mother and Father tried to shelter us from these repugnant details, as James does for me now, but I do not live in a cocoon. I know what transpires in the world.

My captain did not raise his voice with me, nor I with him, but an early frost blanketed our intercourse and did not fully thaw even upon our parting. Jean said we could continue on the topic when next we meet, but it is not likely that either of us shall change our sentiment. And so, we go on, still in love, but more cognizant of our differences.

What do you think, sister? Am I wrong to make my feelings on this subject known to my captain, who in all other respects is the most admirable of men? Have I overstepped my station? I look forward to your counsel. Until

then, I remain ...
   Your loving sister,
   Jane

***

September 3, 1825

Dear Sister,

It has taken me too long to respond to the three letters I have received from you since I last took up my pen. You must accept my deepest apologies. Alas, much has conspired to confound my best intentions. I was taken terribly ill not long after I last wrote to you, and then, just as I began to regain my strength, we performed with our traveling revue in Natchez, Huntsville, and Mobile. All summer, the heat has cruelly oppressed us. One may scarcely concentrate on anything, Caroline, save cooling oneself as best one can. I hope you can see fit to forgive my negligence.

Jean, too, was away for most of the summer. I knew not of his whereabouts or when, or even if, he would come again, which caused me terrible distress. Thankfully, my fears have abated, at least for the present. Captain Lafitte presented himself unannounced two weeks ago, disguised as a free negro this time, if you can believe it. My heart melted at the sight of him, Caroline. He held me tight and stroked my hair as I sobbed into his bosom. My tears were born of relief and happiness but also from the anguish of knowing we must soon part again. We have seen each other six times since then and will meet again tomorrow, but it won't be long until my love must sail once more.

We talk of our future often, Jean and I. He says he thinks Cartagena will take us in, but I don't know if he really believes this. He talks of assuming a new identity and starting over in business. Buying and selling land in Mississippi, perhaps, with no more trafficking in human currency. But he needs capital to begin anew, so there is always one more voyage he must embark upon. He doesn't say this to me, but the sea calls to him. Even as he

CHAPTER TWENTY-THREE

loves me and is faithful, the sea is his favored mistress. When he speaks of beginning a new life on terra firma, I know he means what he says, but there will always be that bewitching temptress, "la mer." She is a most fearsome rival, Caroline.

The nights begin to cool, sister, and soon, the days will follow suit. I look forward to writing more frequently in the comfort of autumn. Until then, I am your...

Devoted sister,

Jane

* * *

October 5, 1825

Dear Caroline,

Congratulations, dear sister! What splendid news! I should think that your Mr. Blake is a most fortunate young man. A February wedding, you say? I've half a mind to attend. What would you say to that, Caroline? Truly, I shall find the right time to approach James on the subject. (He is cross with me just now.) In the meantime, please tell me all there is to know. What shall you wear? Is Anne beside herself with excitement? Will you remain in New York?

Alas, Captain Lafitte has set sail once more. I don't know when I may see him next. He says he will return by the Yule at the latest, but with a turn of good fortune, it will be sooner. Every day he is at sea I am in anguish. There are so many dangers! A deadly storm. A naval battle. Capture and imprisonment by a foreign government, or worse, our own! Oh, woe is me, Caroline! I worry so. What am I to do?

James has learned of Jean's visits and is beside himself with temper. He regards my captain as a "base outlaw" who deceives me with women in every port. And how could he know this? It is only his jealousy talking. He has forbidden me to accept more visitations, Caroline! Does he think he can stop me? Foolish man!

Our run of *Much Ado* is almost complete, and we are deep into rehearsals for Garrick's *The Clandestine Marriage.* Do you know it? The title is delicious, don't you think? I play the naughty Fanny, who has secretly married below her station while her father tries to arrange her betrothal to a stuffy old lord. It all seems rather hysterically apropos. I do hope Jean returns in time to see it. Afterward, we shall laugh together.

Do write again soon, dear sister. I shall try to prevail upon James to grant me leave to travel to your celebration. Normally, he is loath to let me roam unattended, but perhaps he will welcome the opportunity to send me far from the clutches of the notorious brigand, Captain Jean Lafitte! Until then, I wish you nothing but joy.

Your loving sister,

Jane

* * *

December 17, 1825

Dearest Caroline,

It is almost Christmas, and still, there is no word of Captain Lafitte! I am beside myself with worry and longing. Only your letters offer respite from my torment. I am delighted that Anne has accepted Mr. Blake as her new father, and you shall soon enter a new and happy chapter in your lives. You deserve all that you are given, dear sister.

Oh, Caroline, I am wretched! No matter how I try, I cannot force myself to partake in the gaiety of the season nor warm in the acclaim bestowed upon our new comedy. Jean weighs on my mind always. Romeo says of his love that it is "a madness most discreet; a choking gall and a preserving sweet." Must it always be so, sister? I fear that, like Romeo and his beloved Capulet, we shall never find peace on this earth, Jean and I.

James has been provoked with me of late, for he sees me pining for Captain Lafitte and it stirs his anger, but when I asked him for leave to join your celebration, his response was judicious. He said he would not stop me but

CHAPTER TWENTY-THREE

reminded me that February and March are the company's high season. He offered that perhaps I could wait until summer and plan a longer visit then. Would you be cross with me if I accepted his compromise? The prospect of escaping our summer heat is not unwelcome. And if I could stay for a few weeks, it would afford Ann and me the opportunity to become well acquainted, as a doting aunt and her precious niece surely should be. Would this be agreeable to you?

I endeavor to smile at the world, sister, but the darkness closes in on all sides. Only my Jean can release me from this turmoil. Until then there can be no light on this earth.

Do be a good sister, Caroline, and offer your prayers for Jean's safe return. Only then shall my heart know peace.

Your devoted sister,

Jane

* * *

February 5, 1826

Dear Caroline,

He has come! At long last, my beloved Jean has returned to me. I have neither the time nor the clarity of thought to write to you at length, for we are to meet again this evening, perhaps for the last time. I simply wanted you to know that all is not lost. Jean is in great danger and cannot stay long, but our love shall endure. I will write soon, explaining all. Until then, I remain...

Your faithful sister,

Jane

* * *

February 12, 1826

Dear Caroline,

    It is with a heavy heart but a peaceful soul that I write to inform you that my Captain and I have bade our final farewells in this world. A hundred Cerberuses pursue my beloved Jean, and he fears he cannot elude them for long. As I write, he is off to sea with the intent of reaching Cuba. Should he achieve safe passage, he will attempt to re-establish himself on the island under a new identity, eventually, to return to America, though not to here, where he is well known. He vows to send for me when it is safe, but we both know the prospect of a reunion is mere fantasy.

    Why, then, is my soul at peace? Because our time on this earth is short, Caroline, and soon I shall reunite with my beloved for eternity. Jean has bestowed upon me the most remarkable gift, you see. It is a prodigious diamond, the biggest by far that I have seen. It is blue like the ocean, and Jean calls it La Violette. Besides being large, Jean says this exquisite gem is "magique." Many years ago, a French jewel trader removed the diamond from the eye of a sculpture of a Hindu goddess. As the goddess' eye, its vision is said to extend into the spirit world. If we are fated not to meet again on earth, Jean has instructed me to take La Violette to my grave, so that it may pass with me to the hereafter. With this enchanted eye, I shall find Jean in the afterlife, and in this way, we shall be joined forever in kingdom come. Jean says we shall be Iwa, "Si bondye vie," by which he means that if God wills it, we shall live on together as angels.

    So, you see, dear Caroline, all is not lost. Though I may not again encounter Jean here on earth, I do hope to hear from him. If he attains landfall in Cuba, he will write to me through his good friend, Mssr. Latour. By employing that most discreet gentleman as our emissary, we may communicate freely without arousing James' suspicions.

    And so, there you have it, dear sister. I am melancholy but possessed of an inner serenity. I shall carry on with James as before, though my heart and my thoughts lie elsewhere. It accords me endless joy to know that by the time this letter reaches you, you shall be Mrs. Blake. I do so look forward to seeing you finally this summer and making the acquaintance of my precious niece and your dear Mr. Blake. Until then, I remain your…

CHAPTER TWENTY-THREE

Devoted sister
Jane

* * *

April 3, 1826

Dear Caroline,

I write to express my displeasure with your most recent correspondence, which has distressed me greatly. From your aspect, so far removed from your sister in time and distance, it is easy to regard as a deluded fantasy my talk of a magical diamond and a love that transcends mortality. But you do not know Jean, and you have not beheld our lustrous treasure. Alas, I fear you know not your own sister.

I am happy that you have found a father for your Anne and a husband who is agreeable to you, but if you loved as Jean and I do, perhaps then you could appreciate the sacred joining of souls that is possible when a man and a woman find in each other the one for whom they are predestined. Such a love is a rare and precious thing and is not confined by the boundaries of time or space. It is a disappointment to me that you cannot find it in your heart to acknowledge, much less celebrate, this wondrous gift the Good Lord has bestowed upon us. Still, I remain...

Your loving sister,
Jane

* * *

June 29, 1830

Dear Caroline,

It has been too long since we last corresponded. Despite our differences, we are sisters, after all. And so, I write to you, both to share a confidence and to request a favor.

The confidence is that yesterday, I met with the jurist Edward Livingston, our distinguished senator and my captain's trusted friend. He agreed to draft a document ensuring that our diamond, La Violette, shall be interred with me, no matter what James should try to do. Likewise, I have entrusted our treasure to Mr. Livingston's safekeeping.

The favor I ask is this: If you should learn of my release from mortal strife, will you please correspond with Mr. Livingston or his office to ensure that my wishes were carried out? If for some reason they were not, then I consent by way of this letter to you that my remains may be exhumed so that La Violette may be returned to me. I know you think my preparations for the afterlife delusional, but I ask you this as my sister and most intimate confidant.

It has been three months since I last heard from my captain. Jean has reinvented himself as Captain Hillare and runs a small fleet of merchant vessels that travel from island to island. He thinks that in time he shall have saved enough money to return to our country and start a modest new life. This is the dream we share.

Thank you, Caroline. I trust that this letter finds you and Mr. Blake well. Your Anne turns fifteen next month. Give her a kiss from me.

Your only sister,

Jane

**

May 11, 1835

Dearest Caroline,

I am resigned that this shall be my last letter to you. The fever has taken me at last, and I grow weaker by the hour. I am at peace, dear sister. My thoughts are with my beloved captain. It has been two years since his last letter informing me that he expected to return soon to these shores. Does he still live? Does he know I shall perish? Alas, these are but mortal concerns. Soon, we shall be joined for eternity.

CHAPTER TWENTY-THREE

I will watch over you from above, Caroline, you, and your darling Anne. Please remember the favor I have asked of you. I grow tired and must sleep now. Know that I shall always be...

Your loving and devoted sister,

Jane

Chapter Twenty-Four

Not for the first time, I wasn't sure whether to be pissed off at Bruneau or thankful. Initially, I was furious. Once again, he had waded into police business and mucked up the works. When he told me over the phone that he discovered that Charlotte Duval was a descendant of Jane Placide and had letters written by the actress to her sister that establish that Jean Lafitte gave her the blue diamond, I exploded. I couldn't believe he'd take it upon himself to interview Charlotte Duval, who had become a key player in our investigation. Or that he and his friends would handle the letters, which could become important pieces of evidence.

"Do you have any idea the position you've put me in?" I yelled at him.

"I'm sorry, Bo," he said. "We didn't know what we'd find in the letters or if they even existed. You have them now, right?"

"That's not the point. You've given a key witness a chance to prepare her story before we talk to her, and you've gotten your prints all over our evidence. Mac is going to kill me."

We went at it for a while until I was satisfied that Bru understood how serious this was.

After we hung up, and I was able to take a few deep breaths and stare out the window for a bit, I was able to gain some perspective. The simple truth was that if it wasn't for Bru and Sallie, we wouldn't know about Jane Placide's letters or Phillip Boyer. And together with their buddy Andre Coulon, aka Prosper Fortune, they'd saved Rodiger and me hours of sifting through Charlotte Duval's family scrapbooks to find the letters in the first place. So, on balance, the more I thought about it, I was more grateful than

CHAPTER TWENTY-FOUR

not. But I caught an earful from the captain.

"What the hell, T-Bo!" Mac barked at me after calling me into his office. "You running this investigation or subbing it out to your civilian friends?"

"I can explain, Mac," I said.

"Explain what?" he yelled. "Jesus Christ! They took a perfectly harmless B and E and turned it into an international shit show. They left their prints all over the fucking evidence and compromised a key witness. Don't even try to explain that away. And don't call me Mac! It's Captain MacLaren from now on. Is that clear?"

"Crystal, captain," I said. "You're right that I should have reined them in, but I didn't know what they were up to."

I paused for a second.

"You do realize, captain, if it weren't for them, we wouldn't have these letters as evidence, and we wouldn't have Phillip Boyer as a suspect. I get that it looks like amateur hour, but they've given us a big break here."

"Is that right? Maybe from now on, I should give your friends all the cases you can't solve on your own. How would you feel about that?"

I knew I needed to let Mac have the last word, so I let that one go. Having made his point, his tone shifted.

"How you gonna get this thing on track, T-Bo? Talk to me about next steps."

"Yes, sir, captain. Well, let's see, Bruneau Abellard, Sallie Maguire, and Andre Coulon have given their fingerprints to the lab, so hopefully, we can isolate Boyer's prints if he left any. We haven't been able to find any photos of Phillip Boyer, so Abellard and Coulon are sitting with a sketch artist to come up with a likeness of him, as is our witness, Charlotte Duval. Rodiger is working with the feds and Interpol in his spare time to try to find out what we can about Boyer. Any chance I could get him back on loan for a week or two?"

"I'll see what I can do," Mac said. "Now that I know what everyone else is up to, mind telling me what you're doing, T-Bo?"

"Getting my arms around the evidence and putting the pieces together, captain, so I can run a clean investigation from here on out. That and sizing up a space on your wall for the commendation we're gonna get when we crack this thing."

"Go on, get the fuck out of here."

"Yes, sir, captain."

* * *

After leaving Mac's office, I opted for a walk in the fresh air to clear my head. I headed uptown on Gravier, toward Xavier, with the idea of surprising Angie at work and taking her to lunch around the corner at Five Happiness. We used to go there when we were dating, and it's still our go-to for a Chinese fix.

I didn't like hearing it, but Mac was right to bust my chops for letting Bruneau and his friends get too close to the investigation. I knew I had to cut that cord, but I was conflicted. The truth was that for all my talk of investigating the Crypt 1083-A break-in like any other robbery, it had been Bru's curiosity about Jane Placide and Jean Lafitte that led to most of our breakthroughs. And, after all, I was the one who asked for his help in the first place.

"You can't just shut them out completely," Angie said after we were seated.

"I know. But I can't have them handling evidence or hanging out at the station. How do I manage this?"

"You said you've been investigating this robbery more or less the same way you would any other present-day crime, right?"

"Yeah, more or less."

"So, running down footprints, fingerprints, video surveillance, financial records, that kind of stuff?"

"Yes."

"But the breaks in the case have come from Bruneau and Sallie and now Prosper leaning into Jean Lafitte and Jane Placide?"

"Most of them, yes."

"So maybe, then," Angie said, smiling, "you should be thinking in terms of if you can't beat 'em, join 'em."

CHAPTER TWENTY-FOUR

"I'm not sure I follow," I said.

"I'm saying maybe you should wade into the archives with them. Maybe you'll learn something, and as a bonus, you can keep an eye on what they're doing, so they don't get into more trouble."

As Angie was talking, our egg rolls arrived. She dipped hers in mustard and I went for the sweet and sour sauce.

"You mean read through the letters and follow whatever lines of inquiry Bru and company come up with?"

"Yeah, something like that."

I nodded and took a bite of egg roll, nice and crispy like I like them.

"You know what bugs me about all this Lafitte business?" I asked.

"No, what's that?"

"They're all hung up on the secret romance between the pirate and his actress, and I get that. I mean, it's a new piece of history nobody knew about. So, fine. But meanwhile, this dude was a slave trader, Ange. He sold people who looked like us for profit. Our ancestors, maybe."

"Uh-huh. Yep. There is that."

"I mean, it's not like Bru hasn't said as much, but I feel like this story they're painting treats Lafitte like some kind of tragic hero."

"They're romanticizing him, you mean?"

"Yeah, I guess that's what I mean."

"I can see that," Angie said. "Maybe you should bring it up with Bruneau. Clear the air. If you're stewing, it doesn't do any good to keep it inside."

***

It may not have been a working lunch, but Angie had given me two solid pieces of advice, so I felt it was time well spent.

When I got back to the office, I had three emails waiting for me. The first was from Minh, letting me know that after accounting for Bru, Sallie, and Prosper, there was another set of prints all over the letters. She was going to run them through AFIS and get back to me. The second was from Mac, telling me that Rodiger was all mine for the next two weeks. And the third was from Larry Moretti, the New Jersey state cop who'd been executing the warrant to look into Ronald Walker's finances. I was reading it when Rodiger appeared at my door.

"Excuse me, detective," he said, "I understand I have you to thank for getting me kicked out of Homicide."

"That a problem, Mike? It's only for a couple weeks."

"No sir, it's not a problem at all," Rodiger said, closing the door behind him and seating himself in front of my desk. "In fact, I was wondering if maybe we could make it permanent. That is, if you would be okay with that, sir."

"Above my pay grade," I said. "You'd have to talk to Captain MacLaren. Are you saying you want to make Property Crimes your permanent home?"

"Yes, sir. Homicide hasn't been my cup of tea and Property Crimes was my favorite rotation stop by far. I enjoy the research aspect of it, and of course, working with you has been an honor, sir."

"Uh huh, I bet you say that to all your lead detectives."

"True, but I don't always mean it," Rodiger smiled.

Rodiger told me he'd been freed up to start his two-week stint immediately, so I brought him up to speed on the Placide investigation and then read him Moretti's email. According to Moretti, Jersey police had been able to identify more than $600,000 wired into three different accounts in Walker's name, each with a different bank, and they were still looking for more. I asked Rodiger to cross-reference the accounts of origin with those associated with Ttaba.

As Rodiger was getting up to leave, there was another knock on the door. It was Rosie Batiste, who works in accounting but doubles as our sketch artist.

"Hi, Rosie, come on in," I said. "You know Mike Rodiger?"

"Yes, I think so," she said, looking at Rodiger. "Homicide, right?"

"That's right," Rodiger said, extending his hand. "For the time being, anyway."

"Mike's helping us with this case," I said. "What've you got for us?"

Rosie goes to the same church we do, so we're friends. She's a big woman

CHAPTER TWENTY-FOUR

with pudgy hands and fingers, but somehow, she manages a delicate touch with a pencil. As she shuffled into my office, she held a small sheaf of papers in her left hand while her right pinned her sketch pad against her ample chest. She flipped the pad around to show the face of a thin, sixty-something white man with sharp features, narrow eyes, and a cleft chin. He wore a bow tie.

"Your friends and your witness all said this is your man, Boyer," Rosie said, handing each of us some papers. "Here, I made copies for you."

"Great work as always, Rosie," I said. "Thanks for this."

"My pleasure, Detective. See you on Sunday."

As Rosie turned to leave, I asked Rodiger to put the sketch out on the wires. Then I took a long look at Boyer's face. There wasn't much that I could read in it. He wore a breezy smile, but his eyes were cold. I decided to call Bruneau.

"Hey Bo, what's up?" he answered. "Still mad at me?"

"No, I've calmed down some. Just calling to thank you for working with Rosie. You satisfied with the finished product?"

"Yeah, very. That's Boyer, alright."

"Tell me about him," I said. "How well did you know him, and what was he like?"

"I did not care for the man, let's put it that way. I didn't know him all that well, but he was always following Charlotte around, so we had a fair number of interactions."

"What didn't you like about him?"

Bruneau exhaled loudly before answering.

"He's a bullshit artist, for starters. Tries hard to give the impression he's an expert on almost any subject that comes up, but if you press him, he can't go deep. To me, he was a parasite, and not just with Charlotte, but with some other society women I know, too."

"Did he prey on them?" I asked.

"I don't know. I guess it depends on your definition of prey. I'm not aware that he stole money or was running some kind of con game or anything like that, but he went out of his way to ingratiate himself with a certain type of woman. Lonely. Aging. Well off."

"We're going to need the names of those other women," I said. "Did he have any guy friends?"

"Not that I'm aware of. I see his type in the store from time to time, Bo. They offer their company to these women, who are happy to have someone to lunch with or to escort them to a social occasion. We call them walkers. In theory, it's a win-win. The woman gets an agreeable companion for public appearances, and the walker gets free meals and nice gifts, maybe a trip to the Riviera. Most of the time, it's harmless. Just kind of gross."

"Okay, got it. Thanks, Bru, this is helpful. If you think of anything else about Boyer, let me know. And remember to email me that list of his female acquaintances with whatever contact info you have."

"Sure," Bru said in a sarcastic tone. "Anything else I can do for you, detective? Polish your badge? Shine your shoes?"

I laughed. "Sorry if that came off as bossy. I appreciate all you do, Bru. Especially the stuff you clear with me first."

As our conversation was ending, I thought about what Angie had said.

"Hey, Bru, actually, I do have one more favor to ask."

Bru sighed loudly.

"When did you become such a needy person? What is it this time?"

I thought about a snarky response but decided to play it straight.

"I've been thinking that maybe I haven't been as tuned in to the historical aspects of this case as I should be."

"You mean the Jane Placide, Jean Lafitte story?"

"Yes, exactly," I said. "I was wondering if you could set up some time for us with Sallie and Prosper to talk it through. Especially Jane's letters and what we can learn from them."

"Sure, I can do that. You want us to come down to the station?"

"No, I'd rather we did it at your place if that's okay. The captain's been riding my ass about leaning too much on you all. I'd like to keep this quiet for now."

"No problem, I'll round up the troops and get back to you."

"Great. I'll bring Rodiger with me, and maybe Angie too."

CHAPTER TWENTY-FOUR

"Should we turn it into a meal?" Bru asked.

"Your call," I said. "I don't want to put you out. Totally up to you."

"Okay, I'll talk to Sallie."

I started to say goodbye, but Bru interrupted me.

"Hey Bo, before you hang up, anything new with the case?"

I told him we'd lifted another set of prints from the Jane Placide letters, and we knew that Walker had received some wire transfers, but I kept the information intentionally vague.

After hanging up with Bru, I picked up the sketch of Phillip Boyer again and tried to imagine him as Charlotte Duval's walker. Bru said he was a bullshit artist, but it seemed to me that he'd have to be fairly slick to pull off that act. And charming. Your classic grifter.

As I mulled these thoughts, my phone rang again. It was Doctor No.

"Hello, Minh," I answered.

"Hello, detective. I ran your fingerprints."

"And?"

"They belong to a man named Peter Burns, though he uses various aliases. He's got a record, and he's in AFIS."

So, Phillip Boyer was Peter Burns, and he had a record. Now we were getting somewhere.

* * *

Once we had the name Peter Burns, things moved quickly.

Peter Burns in AFIS was originally from Illinois. According to the information Rodiger pulled together for me, Burns got in trouble as a young man for running some small-time cons but didn't do any time. Somewhere along the line, he learned how to crack safes, which is what he got busted for in a failed jewelry heist in Spain in 2001. He did three years in a Spanish prison and then spent some time on the French Riviera, living under the alias Paul Banks. He was suspected but never arrested in a string of home burglaries. The next time Burns surfaced was as Parker Babcock in New Jersey. He was convicted of elder fraud and spent 18 months in the state pen. He served out his parole eight years ago, and that is the last record of him in the database.

It didn't take long for Rodiger to connect the dots. Paul Banks was briefly employed at the same resort in Marseilles as Abid Bensaid, the suspected alias of Mahdi Toledano at the time. They were both there in 2007 when the $10 million jewel heist occurred.

"What about Walker," I asked. "Any connection there?"

"Yep," Rodiger said. "Burns and Walker did time in the same New Jersey prison. Their sentences overlapped by four months, so they could have known each other."

To complete the circle, Rodiger was able to establish that the accounts of origin for the wire transfers to Ronald Walker were associated with the Ttaba, LLC layering scheme.

That gave us plausible connections among all three of our suspects. Toledano and Burns may have known each other in Marseilles, where they may have collaborated in a jewel heist. Burns and Walker could have met in a New Jersey prison. And Walker received at least three six-figure wire transfers from accounts probably controlled by Toledano.

Our theory was that Toledano, Burns, and Walker conspired to rob Jane Placide's grave, sell the blue diamond, and launder the proceeds. Now, all we had to do was prove it. And to do that, we needed Burns and Toledano in custody.

Chapter Twenty-Five

When I agreed to host Bo's meeting, I initially figured I'd just brew us a pot of coffee and maybe put out some store-bought pastries. But Sallie and I were feeling guilty about getting Bo in trouble with his boss, so when he suggested a 1 p.m. start time, we decided to do something a bit more involved. Sallie whipped up a Caesar salad, I made a batch of Vichyssoise, and together, we assembled a platter of ham biscuits. We offered iced tea and seltzer as beverage options.

While Sallie straightened up the kitchen, I picked up Prosper at his sister's place. He seemed a little off, like something was bothering him.

"You okay?" I asked.

"Yeah, I'm alright," he said. "There's something I need to get off my chest, but not now. Maybe later, after we're done?"

"Yeah, sure. No problem."

When we got back to my place, Angie had already arrived. She and Sallie were chatting in the kitchen, and Hugo was scavenging for crumbs at their feet. I introduced Prosper, who Angie had yet to meet, and then Bo and Rodiger showed up and let themselves in.

"Looks like the gang's all here," Bo trumpeted from the doorway over Hugo's shrill yapping. When he got to the top of the stairs, he turned toward Angie with his hand on Rodiger's shoulder.

"Angie, this is Mike Rodiger, who I've told you about."

"Yes, of course," Angie said. "It's nice to finally meet you, Officer Rodiger."

"The pleasure's all mine, ma'am," Rodiger said, bowing slightly.

"Leave it to Bruneau to turn a simple meeting into a gourmet event," Bo said, gesturing at the spread Sallie had laid out on the counter.

"Nothing too fancy," I said. "Just a little something to keep our energy up. Consider it an offering of atonement for getting you in hot water with the brass. Sallie deserves most of the credit."

"Water under the bridge, and thank you, Sallie," Bo said. "I'm looking forward to hearing what great minds have to say about these letters. We're getting really close to cracking this thing, and your all's help is a big reason why."

"How do you want to do this, Bo?" Sallie asked. "We can sit at the table or take our food into the parlor if you prefer."

"Either way," Bo said, with a side glance toward Angie. "Maybe the table, if that's okay with everybody."

"Sure thing, the table it is," Sallie said. "Grab some food, everyone. We made hard copies of the letters, so I'll lay those out for us."

"How thoughtful of you, Sallie," Angie said. "I haven't seen the letters, so it'll give me a chance to catch up with everybody else."

As our guests worked their way through the food line, Sallie and I exchanged nervous smiles. The atmosphere was collegial, but not yet comfortable. Mike Rodiger looked as though he felt out of place and Prosper was subdued. Something was bothering him, and I was dying to know what, but now was not the time.

It seemed like the group needed an icebreaker, so I asked Bo to update us on the case.

"Yeah, sure, thanks for asking. As a matter of fact, we do have a couple important developments to report," Bo announced.

He paused to make sure he had our attention.

"The first is that Phillip Boyer's prints were all over the letters, except that his real name isn't Phillip Boyer, which surprises exactly no one. The man some of you knew as Boyer is Peter Burns, and he's gone by various aliases over the years, all of which have the initials P.B. Burns has been a small-time con man for most of his career, but he's also a safe cracker. And he's done some prison time, both here and in Europe."

"You think he was working a grift on Charlotte?" I asked.

CHAPTER TWENTY-FIVE

"Probably, but our guess is that when he found the Placide letters, his plans changed. He started thinking bigger."

"Can you connect him to Omar, or Ronald Walker?"

"Not yet, but the facts we have so far do line up. We think Burns and Mahdi Toledano were in southern France at the same time, when there was a jewel heist that we suspect Toledano of masterminding. And Burns and Walker were in the same New Jersey prison for a few months."

"Wow!" I said. "That may not be conclusive, but it's darn close. You think Boyer told the other two about the letters, and then the three of them got together and planned the whole thing?"

"Something like that," Bo said. "It's too early to say. Walker doesn't strike us as the planning type, but you never know."

We were letting the news sink in, and digging into our food, when Angie piped up.

"What's the second, Bo?"

"The second what?"

"Development. You said you had two developments to report."

"Oh yeah, right, of course. Mike, would you like to share the news we got this morning? I'd like to have a bite or two of my lunch."

"Um, sure, Detective," Rodiger said, gathering himself.

"You all may recall that when the blue diamond sold at auction in Hong Kong, the purchaser was a Chinese billionaire by the name of Lingyun Gao. Well, according to Interpol, Gao's penthouse apartment in Shanghai was robbed last week. We don't have any more information than that."

"You're kidding," I said. "Did he keep the diamond in the apartment?"

"We don't know. The Chinese aren't exactly big on sharing information. The robbery could be completely unrelated to the diamond."

I chewed on that.

"Have they arrested anyone?"

"No sir, not that we know of."

"If it's a billionaire's place, it's probably got state-of-the-art security, wouldn't you think?"

"Yes, I would think so," Rodiger said.

"So to break into a place like that, steal something, and make a clean getaway, you'd have to a) be fearless and b) know what you're doing, right?"

"That's a logical assumption, yes," Rodiger said.

"A guy spends sixty-three million dollars on a diamond we think was stolen by a team of professional burglars, and then he's robbed, probably also by pros," I said. "What the heck? Doesn't sound like a coincidence to me. Was the M.O. similar? Did the burglars drop in through a skylight or window?"

"As I said, we don't have much in the way of details, so we can't say," Rodiger said.

Nobody ventured an opinion. Bo broke the silence.

"Okay, so as I think you all know, the reason we're all here today is to talk about the letters Jane Placide wrote to her sister. Obviously, the headline is that Jane confirms that Lafitte gave her the diamond, which they called La Violette, and that she made arrangements to have it interred with her. That's as much as Burns needed to learn to set the wheels of this plot in motion. But we're interested in hearing other takeaways you have from the letters, even if they don't seem related to our case."

"Why?" Angie asked.

"Why, what?"

"Why do you care about insights from the letters that aren't related to the case?" she pressed Bo, knowing the answer but forcing him to say it.

"Because I have realized that if I had paid more attention to this group's take on what Jean Lafitte and Jane Placide were up to way back when we might be a little further along than we are. I don't want to keep making the same mistake."

"Why, Detective Duplessis, is this your attempt at a mea culpa?" I asked, grinning.

"Should I get down on my knees and beg forgiveness?"

"That won't be necessary, but I do think we should get this on tape."

"Absolutely not. You've yanked my chain as far as it's going to go."

There were some low chuckles throughout our exchange, but Sallie brought the room back around.

CHAPTER TWENTY-FIVE

"Well, I appreciate your forthrightness, Bo," she said. "Should we begin sharing our observations?"

"Yes, that sounds like a great idea," Bo said. "Will you start us off?"

"Sure," Sallie said. "I guess the thing that struck me the most was Jane's ironclad belief in the afterlife and the magical powers of the diamond. I kept wondering if Lafitte believed it, too, or whether he was selling her a bill of goods."

We took a moment to consider Sallie's question.

"Why would he?" Prosper spoke for the first time.

"Why would he what?"

"Sell her a bill of goods."

"I don't know," Sallie answered. "Maybe as a way of ensuring that she remained his. If she believed there was this supernal connection between them, and they'd be reunited in eternity, maybe she'd be less bothered by his long absences and less likely to look for comfort elsewhere."

"Or maybe it was out of kindness," I ventured. "Lafitte seemed to know he wasn't coming back, at least not for a very long time, so maybe this was his way of softening the blow."

"What do *you* think, Prosper?" Bo asked.

Prosper shrugged his shoulders.

"I think he was probably a believer. He had a romantic streak, Lafitte did. This was a guy who dreamed of crossing the Atlantic to free Napoleon. And remember, it would have been easy for him to accept the offer the British made prior to the Battle of New Orleans, but instead, he lent his services to Jackson, who was the decided underdog. Was there a calculation involved? Yeah, sure, almost certainly, he was angling for a pardon. But he seems also to have felt a patriotic duty to defend a country he believed had treated him badly.

"And then, think about his brother, Pierre, who in the eyes of everyone but the law, lived as man and wife and raised children with the same Creole woman for the almost three decades leading up to his death. In their own way, the Lafittes were men of honor, as apt to follow their hearts as to do the expedient thing."

As he often does, Prosper had grabbed our attention. I could see Angie sizing him up in a new light.

"For what it's worth," I said, "the story Lafitte told Jane about the diamond coming from the goddess' eyes, he didn't just make that up. Fancy Rigard told me that legend has been around since Tavernier's time. Lafitte could have heard it from Joseph Bonaparte or Charles Lallemand, or whoever gave him the diamond."

"I was wondering about that," Sallie said, looking down at one of the letters. "What do Jane's references to 'lwa' and 'si bondye vie' have to do with the Hindu spirit world?"

"Absolutely nothing," Prosper said. "Bondye is the supreme god of Haitian Vodou, and Iwa are divine spirits, kind of the rough equivalent of Christian angels. Lafitte was conflating elements of two religions to fit his narrative, in the same way that Vodou itself is a mash-up of Roman Catholicism and traditional West African belief systems."

"Lafitte was a Vodouist?" Sallie asked.

"I don't know about that," Prosper said. "But remember, he and Pierre came to New Orleans and Barataria from Haiti, or Saint Domingue as it was called in those days. He would certainly have been exposed to Vodou, and I imagine a good number of his Baratarians practiced it. Whether he was a full-on practitioner himself, I have no idea."

"He would have been raised a Catholic, right?" I asked.

"Yes, almost certainly. My guess is he just cherry-picked bits he knew from different religions to construct the story he was spinning for Jane. Which doesn't mean he didn't believe it."

There was a brief pause. Then Angie spoke up.

"How do you know so much about Vodou, Prosper?"

"I don't really," he said. "I served with a guy in Vietnam who grew up in the tradition, and I picked up some basic knowledge from him. I know only enough to tell you that Vodou is much misunderstood."

"How is it misunderstood?" Angie wanted to know.

"It's not black magic, which is the way it's portrayed in the movies and popular culture," Prosper said. "You know, sticking pins in dolls and

CHAPTER TWENTY-FIVE

summoning demonic spirits, that kind of thing. It's not that. It's a religion like any other, with its own rituals and theology."

Again, there was a break in the conversation, until Bo re-inserted himself to take us in a new direction.

"Right. I guess this is as good a time as any to get something off my chest that's been bothering me for a long time now," he said, shooting a quick glance at Angie.

"Prosper, the picture you paint of Lafitte is consistent with most of what I've learned from you all. Lafitte was a pirate, but he was a man of honor. He was a spy and a smuggler, but he had good qualities. He was a crook, but he's our crook, so to speak. That sound about right?"

"More or less," Prosper said. "A little simplistic, maybe."

"Hey, I'm a simple guy, just ask my wife," Bo said, turning toward Angie. "My issue is this: can a guy who sells human beings for a living be a good guy?"

The room went quiet.

"I had a feeling that's where you were going," Prosper said slowly. "It's kind of the eternal question when it comes to the Lafittes, and you're right to raise it. There's a letter in this collection that indicates Jane had some of the same misgivings."

"That letter was revealing," I said. "For Lafitte, selling slaves was just business, pure and simple. There's winners and losers in life, I think he said, and business is about the winners getting rich on the backs of the losers. Jane claimed to be repulsed by the slave trade, yet she acknowledges Lafitte's crude logic. After what seemed like a small spat, they pick up as if it was no big deal."

"That was the context of the times," Prosper said. "Lafitte's views were in no way remarkable, sad to say. Jane's aesthetic sensibility was offended by Lafitte trafficking in human beings, but only in the way you or I might say we're appalled by the crude brutality of a slaughterhouse and then go home and grill a steak for dinner."

"That's quite an analogy, Prosper," Angie said. "Are you equating African Americans with cattle?"

"Of course not. But slave traders and plantation owners certainly did."

"And yet," Angie pressed on, "the Lafittes both shacked up with brown-skinned women and in Pierre's case, maybe he even loved his woman as something like an equal?"

"Yep. It's hard for us to square, looking back from the 21st Century," Prosper said. "But it was a different time. And New Orleans was distinctive in that a large free black population lived alongside the enslaved. They mingled freely and conducted business with whites, and in many cases owned slaves themselves."

"Right," Rodiger interjected. "In one of the letters, there is a reference to Lafitte disguising himself as a free black, which suggests he wasn't concerned that his movement or access would be restricted in any way if he was perceived as a negro."

"Would it be a stretch," I asked, "to say that the value system of early 19th-century New Orleans placed less value on the color of your skin than on your lot in life?"

"Probably a stretch for the population as a whole," Prosper said, "but that may describe Lafitte's outlook. More Darwinian than racist, perhaps. Survival of the fittest and all that."

"Except that Darwin's theories didn't appear for a few more decades," Sallie said.

"Well, yes, but you take my point," Prosper said.

"So, I shouldn't be bothered by Lafitte's trafficking in slaves because it was just the times," Bo said. "Is that what I'm hearing?"

"I don't think that's what Prosper was saying, Bo," Angie said.

"Right," I added. "He was explaining, not condoning."

Prosper nodded, and before Bo could say anything, Angie popped in again.

"Aren't we getting off track here, Bo? I've been reading these letters, and I have a couple questions if nobody else does."

He did his best to hide it, but I could see that Bo was less than satisfied with our slavery discussion and wanted to press the issue. Angie was attempting to diffuse the situation before his temper flared.

"Alright, fire away," Bo said. He was frustrated, but he hid it well enough

CHAPTER TWENTY-FIVE

that only Angie and I were aware.

"Does Jane ever make it to New York to see her sister?"

"I don't think we can say for sure," Sallie said. "The fact that it isn't mentioned leads me to believe she didn't go, but who knows."

"Do you think James Caldwell wouldn't let her?" Angie asked.

"Maybe, or maybe she decided not to go because she was upset that Caroline scolded her about buying into Lafitte's afterlife spiel," Sallie said. "The trip she was planning would have been only a couple months after she sent that letter telling Caroline off."

"Right, and then she doesn't write again for four years," I said. "So yeah, probably she was pissed and didn't go."

"Just to clarify, we don't know that Jane stopped writing," Rodiger said. "The letters we have are the ones that were saved and passed down through generations of descendants. There could have been others."

"Good point," I acknowledged. Prosper and Sallie both nodded.

"Which leads to my second question," Angie said. "Was Jane's niece Anne the only child Caroline had?"

"Yes," Sallie said. "Caroline and William Blake were married for almost 40 years until his death in the 1860s, but they never had any children. Anne became a successful actress in her own right, was married twice, and had children with both husbands."

"So, Anne must have kept her mother's correspondence and passed it down to her children," Angie said.

"Correct."

"Amazing that you tracked these letters down, Sallie," Angie said.

"Thanks. We got lucky. Bruneau deserves credit for charming Shirley Hoffman and uncovering the connection to Charlotte."

I smiled, modestly I hoped.

"And your friend Charlotte is an innocent in all this?" Angie asked.

"Yes," I said.

"Not so fast, Bru," Bo said. "We still need to interview her down at the station."

"Forgive me, detective," I snapped, annoyed at his tone. "There I go, forgetting my place again. Going forward, I'll be sure to leave all interrogations of fragile old ladies to New Orleans' finest."

Bo sat there, stone-faced.

Now, it was Sallie's turn to change the subject before the temperature rose.

"Prosper, I have a question for you," she said. "Does Jane's report that Lafitte was living in Cuba under an alias lend credence to the theory of that mother-daughter team that he came back to the States and lived to an old age? That letter was written in 1830, long after any of the accounts of his death."

"Yes, I think so," Prosper said. "Captain Hillare was a known alias of Lafitte's. Jane mentions in an earlier letter that Lafitte intended to return to America and send for her. So yes, I think it quite likely that they've cracked the mystery of Jean Lafitte's earthly demise."

While Sallie and Prosper were talking, Rodiger stepped out of the room to receive a phone call. When he re-entered, he pulled Bo aside, and they spoke in low tones.

"Excuse us, everyone," Bo said. "Mike and I need to go. They've found Peter Burns."

2008

MONTREAL, CANADA
FEBRUARY 2008

The big man turns up the collar of his fraying wool overcoat and blows warm air into his hands as a bitter wind careens off the river and funnels up Saint Denis Street, lashing his face. The thermometer outside the bank reads -17° Celsius, which he converts in his head to 2° Fahrenheit, but he decides it has to be even colder than that.

It has been years since he's eaten in a fine restaurant, or any restaurant at all really, save the occasional greasy spoon. He doesn't have much use for fancy food, stuffy waiters, or genteel manners, but he'd checked out the menu of the French bistro to which he'd been invited, and it looked straightforward enough. If he is being honest with himself, nothing would go down so well right now as a bowl of piping hot onion soup.

He'd met Aram only the week before, when he happened upon him struggling to carry boxes up the stairs of the townhouse apartment he was moving into. He stopped to help the little man with his belongings, and afterward, they chatted for a bit. They were both new to the city and exiles, each in their way, from other lives. They found they shared interests in history, philosophy, and literature. Aram's claim that Voltaire was Shakespeare's equal spurred the big man to a rousing rebuttal, and they laughed together at the lines they could remember from Swift's *A Modest Proposal* and Dunne's bawdy poetry. They parted as friends, Aram inviting the big man to dinner in an expression of gratitude.

Aram is already seated when Andre enters the comfortable eatery, a blast of *sizzling garlic fusing with the sweet, yeasty aroma of freshly baked baguettes. He sits at a corner table by the window, his feet resting on a stepping stool the waiter had found in the kitchen. He is dressed simply in a crisp white shirt and black blazer, black pants held up by matching suspenders. His dark, wavy hair is parted in the middle, accenting his deep brown eyes and distinctive Roman nose.*

"Hello, Andre," he says. "Cold enough out there?"

"I should say so," the big man says, taking off his coat and seating himself, rubbing his hands together to purge the icy chill.

"Thanks for the invite, Aram. I don't often treat myself to nice meals."

"Nonsense, Andre. No good deed should go unrewarded, as my grandmother used to say. Your help the other day was most appreciated.

"Do you drink wine? I took the liberty of ordering us a bottle of Chablis."

Andre knows little about wine, but gladly accepts his glass.

"I've eaten here and can confidently recommend the steak frites," Aram says.

"I kind of have my heart set on the onion soup," Andre replies.

"Good idea. That to start, and then the steak. A big man like you should be able to handle three courses at least."

The meal lasts more than two hours, and Andre enjoys his diminutive companion's musings and friendly humor. They are an odd sight, the dwarf and the giant, but neither particularly cares. They talk of their childhoods, Andre's in Louisiana, and Aram's in Armenia, where he says he was raised by his grandmother and his aunts. They speak of war and peace, of hopes and regrets, of home and faraway lands. But it is the subject of home that most animates them.

"What is a home, Andre?" Aram asks. "Is it a house? Is it the place where we live or were born? Or is it something less tangible?"

Andre considers the question.

"It is something we return to, I think. A place perhaps, or the womb, as Freud thought. Or maybe the simple feeling of being at home, in our surroundings, with our people."

"Yes, it could be that" Aram says. "Augustine thought there was no home on earth. Home is heaven, he said, the place from which we come and to which we hope to return. He and Freud are not so far apart on this."

"It's a cliché, but home is where the heart is," Andre says. "In different ways, *that is what we are all trying to say, I think."*

"Yes, I think you are right. Have you found your home, Andre?"

"No, not yet. You?"

"The same."

* * *

Spring comes late to Montreal, but when it does, it erupts, showering the senses. People emerge invigorated from their hibernations. Children frolic on green fields warmed by the midday sun, and elderly couples and young lovers stroll arm in arm, lured outside by shimmering apple blossoms, the heady scent of blooming lilacs, and the merry trills and whistles of birdsong. Andre and Arum, too, take long walks amid the city's gardens and parks. Aram says the glistening tulip gardens remind him of Amsterdam, a place he had lately resided. And Andre contrasts the delicate hexagonal blossoms of the city's mountain laurel with the huge magnolia flowers and conspicuous azalea clusters of his native Louisiana.

It is near the end of one such outing when Andre informs his friend that he will be leaving Montreal soon. There is no particular reason, he says, just the restless feeling that comes over him when it is time to move on.

"It saddens me to hear this, though I understand all too well," Aram says. "Where will you go?"

"To Texas, I think."

"Closer to home?"

"Yes. I don't know if I can ever truly go home again, but maybe proximity will bring me closer."

When it is time to part, the two men stop to shake hands.

"I wish you nothing but the best, my friend," Aram says. "May you find all that you seek, and may your fortunes prosper."

Chapter Twenty-Six

Peter Burns was a lot easier to find than Mahdi Toledano. His big mistake was using the same initials for all his aliases. The federal agents charged with monitoring payments from the bank accounts associated with Ttaba, LLC, simply cross-referenced payments from those accounts to holders of the receiving accounts who bore the initials P.B. They found Burns in Naples, Florida, where he'd been living under the name Patrick Brennan. When they arrested him, he was sitting poolside at the Ritz-Carlton, chatting up a gaggle of blue-haired ladies. Old habits die hard, I guess.

Burns would face charges in multiple jurisdictions, including the three counts of bank fraud the feds picked him up on, but as had been previously agreed to, we got first dibs. We convinced a judge to add a couple of state fraud charges of our own so we could have him extradited to Louisiana. When Rodiger and I began interviewing him, with Mac watching from behind the one-way glass, I asked Burns if he would like to have a lawyer present, and he declined, claiming not to understand why he'd been brought to New Orleans. I reminded him of the fraud charges he'd been Mirandized on and assured him he'd know more soon enough.

"Does the name Charlotte Duval mean anything to you, Mr. Burns? Or Bruneau Abellard?" I asked.

"Of course," he said readily. "Charlotte and I are great friends. And yes, I know Bruneau, though I'm not sure how friendly we are."

"But they know you as Phillip Boyer, not Peter Burns, is that right?"

"Is it against the law to change one's name, detective?"

CHAPTER TWENTY-SIX

"It can be if you use your alias for fraudulent purposes, or to commit a crime."

"Ah, I see. Is that why I'm here, detective? Because you think I changed my name to commit fraud?"

"Let's just say it's one of the topics we'd like to explore with you."

His Oxford shirt and bow tie had been replaced by an orange jumpsuit, but in every other respect, this guy could have walked right out of Rosie's sketch. We'd taken his cuffs off, and he was leaning back in his chair, smiling as if he were amused by a children's game. His squinty blue eyes made him hard to read, but from time to time, a coldness flashed across his face. I saw it in a slight tic at the mention of Charlotte's name and again when I referenced Phillip Boyer.

Before sitting down with Burns, Rodiger and I interviewed Charlotte Duval. She didn't tell us much we hadn't already learned from Bruneau. She swore that she didn't know about her family's connection to Jane Placide until Bru and Sallie told her about it and that she was as shocked as everyone else. She'd asked Phillip Boyer to organize the family records she'd received from her distant cousin in New Jersey but hadn't been surprised when he gave up on the project owing to the sheer volume of material. Yes, she was friends with Boyer and enjoyed his company, but she didn't know very much about him. When he left town, she thought he was going to New Jersey for a few months and expected him to return after that. She wasn't aware that Boyer and Omar Pasha may have known each other, but she had probably mentioned each to the other. She hadn't spoken to either man since they left town.

It wasn't much to go on, but we used what we had.

"Did you work on a project for Ms. Duval that involved sorting through boxes of family records?" I asked Burns.

"Yes, I did help Charlotte with that," he said. "I tried to organize some of the records and correspondence for her and hoped to summarize the information I'd found, but I must confess, detective, I rather underestimated the time commitment involved. It was a bit of a mess, I'm afraid. Are you going to charge me with failing to finish the project?"

I ignored the taunt.

"When you were going through those records, do you remember coming across some letters from an actress named Jane Placide, written to her sister in New York more than two hundred years ago?"

There was that tic again, ever so slight.

"I don't believe so. I don't recognize the name, at any rate. There were so many names."

I didn't expect to get anywhere with this line of questioning, but I wanted Burns to see that we knew more than he might have thought. It's always a good idea to fatten the hog during the lead-up to the slaughter.

"Ms. Duval thought you were going to New Jersey when you left New Orleans and that you'd be returning after a few months," I said.

Burns shrugged. "Plans change, detective."

"Why Florida?"

"Why not? Great weather, beautiful scenery, interesting people. What's not to like?"

"By interesting people, you must mean rich old ladies," I said. "It seems you have a weakness for women of a certain age and net worth. Such as Ms. Duval, for example."

"Yes, I suppose I do," Burns said, trying but failing to hide a smirk. "I find there's so much to learn from people with a broad swath of life experiences to draw from."

I switched the topic again.

"Do you remember Ms. Duval and Mr. Abellard discussing a grave robbery?"

"A grave robbery? Goodness, detective, that's not a question one gets every day. Let me think about that one."

Burns put his finger to his temple, like he was searching his memory banks.

"Yes, now that you mention it, I do remember talk of a grave robbery," he said as though it had just come to him. "It involved some actress who Bruneau was convinced had had a love affair with the infamous pirate, Jean Lafitte."

CHAPTER TWENTY-SIX

"Her name was Jane Placide," I said.

"Ah yes, of course, I remember her now. You believe there are letters from Jane Placide in Charlotte's collection? There may have been, I don't remember. I wouldn't have recognized the name, at any rate, because the grave robbery occurred a good many months after I tried to tackle Charlotte's family records."

Rodiger and I exchanged glances. I nodded, and he began jotting down a note. It's an old trick we use in interrogations to make the subject nervous. It must have worked with Burns, because he kept right on talking. When people get nervous, they talk.

"I remember that Charlotte was concerned that Bruneau was getting himself involved in some dirty business with a detective friend of his who she didn't trust. She enlisted me to pour some cold water on his theories. Any idea who that detective might have been? I got the impression he was either lazy or in over his head. A colleague, perhaps?"

I smiled faintly to acknowledge the dis.

"Did you think Mr. Abellard's theories had merit?" I asked.

"None whatsoever," Burns answered. "I did some research at Charlotte's behest, and it turned out that Lafitte wasn't even alive during the period when Bruneau thought he was consorting with the actress. And if he had been, it wouldn't have been the pirate's style to distract himself with a love affair. He had plenty of women, and unlike Bruneau, he was no starry-eyed romantic."

It wasn't hard to see why Bru didn't like this guy. I was itching to bring the hammer down but knew I couldn't rush it.

"Let me run another name by you, Mr. Burns," I said. "Omar Pasha. Ring a bell?"

"No, I'm afraid not."

"He was Ms. Duval's hairdresser."

"Okay, yes, I remember now. She did mention an Omar who was her hairdresser, but I didn't know his last name. She seemed quite fond of him. He was a tenant of hers, I believe."

"And an old acquaintance of yours from France, if I'm not mistaken."

Burns stiffened.

"I'm sure you must be, detective. Mistaken, that is. I'm quite certain I didn't know any Omar's during my brief time in France. Not that I can remember, anyway. That was a long time ago."

"He wasn't Omar back then," I said. "He went by the name Abid Bensaid in those days. When you were Paul Banks."

"The name doesn't sound familiar," Burns said a little too quickly.

Cracks were beginning to appear in his cool façade.

"What about Ronald Walker?" I pressed him. "Does that name mean anything to you?"

"I'm afraid not."

"That's surprising, because he remembers you quite well," I lied. "You see, Mr. Walker was recently taken into custody in New Jersey. He told the police up there that he met you in prison some years ago."

Burns took that in.

"As you undoubtedly know, detective, I did spend a short spell behind bars in New Jersey. It is possible I met someone named Ronald Walker, but I don't remember him if I did. What is this all about, detective? What is it you think I've done?"

I was turning up the heat, and Burns was starting to lose his cool. It was just a matter of time before he shut down and asked for a lawyer, so I went in hard.

"The thing is, Mr. Burns, we have a witness who puts you and Ronald Walker on Grand Isle three years ago, questioning a resident there about Jean Lafitte. And we have your fingerprints all over Jane Placide's letters, in which she tells her sister about her affair with Jean Lafitte and a very valuable diamond he gave her, which she arranged to have interred with her."

I paused to let the weight of what I'd just told Burns sink in. Then I continued.

"We also know that Omar Pasha, or Abid Bensaid, whose real name, by the way, is Mahdi Toledano, is the leading suspect in a series of international jewelry thefts involving an M.O. similar to the one used at Hope Mausoleum

CHAPTER TWENTY-SIX

here in New Orleans, including one you probably helped him with in Marseilles. And we know that Ronald Walker miraculously 'discovered' a diamond identical to the one Jane Placide described, just outside the former property of Joseph Bonaparte, which he then sold at auction for $63 million. And that the money from that sale was laundered through a network of bank accounts controlled by Mahdi Toledano, from which at least $2 million was wired into accounts held by Patrick Brennan. That would be you, Mr. Burns."

I paused again. Burns was stone-faced but ashen.

"So, you see, Mr. Burns, we know quite a lot. Enough, in fact, to lock you up for a very long time."

"That's quite an imaginative tale you've spun, detective," Burns said quietly. "Given the weight of the allegations you have made, I suppose this is the point at which it would be prudent of me to request the assistance of counsel."

"That is certainly your right, Mr. Burns," I said. "Please let your attorney know that you have one chance, and one chance only, to buy yourself a bit of a break. To Interpol and the FBI, you are a relatively small fish. Mahdi Toledano is the big game they're after. If you cooperate fully and give us information that helps lead to Toledano's arrest, they are prepared to show you some leniency."

* * *

While we waited for Burns to line up a lawyer, Rodiger and I compared notes with Mac, who'd been watching through the one-way window into the toaster. We were pretty sure we had Burns where we wanted him, which was scared and ready to deal. But Mac was worried I'd played too loose with the facts, particularly when it came to Ronald Walker.

"Christ, T-Bo! Just for once, can you go by the book," he complained.

"Relax, Captain," I said, "we got this."

After Mac walked off shaking his head and muttering, we called Larry Moretti, our counterpart with the New Jersey State Police, and explained the situation. He agreed to pull Walker in and tell him that Burns had given him up. If we could get them both singing about the other, there wouldn't be any problem later with having to explain the use of false or misleading information to trap our suspect into implicating himself.

Burns retained Gino Randazzo as his counsel. Gino and I go way back. He started out as a criminal defense lawyer about the same time I became a cop, and our paths have crossed many times. Everybody thinks Gino has ties to the mob, mainly because he grew up in a Sicilian American neighborhood on the west bank, where back in the day various Mafiosi were known to live. Whether that is true or not, I'd never had a problem with the guy. Like a lot of defense lawyers, he is full of bravado, but when push comes to shove, he's going to do the right thing by his client. Usually, that means cutting a deal.

When Rodiger and I re-entered the toaster, Gino was seated next to Burns, his large forearms folded across his massive chest. He was dressed in a navy pin-stripe suit, a blue spread collar shirt hung over his belt, and a loosened gold and blue paisley tie was splayed over his gut. The top button of his shirt lay open, revealing graying chest hairs and beads of sweat were visible on his mostly bald head.

"Well, if it isn't my old friend, Detective Thibodaux Duplessis," he said, rising to offer his hand. "How are you, Bo?"

"I'm fine, Gino; it's good to see you," I said. "This is Officer Mike Rodiger."

Gino and Rodiger nodded at each other, and then Gino got down to business.

"My client tells me you've got some grandiose notions about the extent of his alleged criminal activity. I must say, I'm disappointed, Bo. It's not like you to spin wild tales in an effort to implicate an innocent man. Grave robbing? Jean Effing Lafitte? Really, Bo? Mac put you up to this?"

"I can assure you, your client is no innocent, counselor," I said.

I proceeded to lay out our case against Burns, point by point. Gino listened patiently while Burns looked down at his lap, expressionless but fidgety. When I was done, Gino leaned forward, his elbows on the steel interrogation table.

"I appreciate all the detail, detective, and I'd almost believe your story if it

CHAPTER TWENTY-SIX

weren't for the rather glaring absence of hard evidence. Everything you've put forward is circumstantial. You haven't placed my client at the crime scene or in the chain of custody of this diamond."

This was the obvious tact for Gino to take, and I was prepared for it. I played up Walker's confession, which I hoped he was in the process of giving, knowing that Gino would quickly grasp that if we got what we needed from Walker, his client would lose what little leverage he had.

"From what you described of this Walker fellow, he was pretty much just a flunky, Bo," Gino said. "Doesn't seem like he'd know a whole lot about what his supposed co-conspirators were up to."

"Walker might not have been calling the shots, but he was way more than a flunky," I shot back. "We have a witness who can testify that Walker accompanied your client to Grand Isle to dig up info on Lafitte. He's admitted to participating in the break-in with your client and Mahdi Toledano. And he was the front man for getting the diamond found and sold. Trust me, Walker knows a lot."

"He said, he said," Gino spat dismissively.

"There's one more piece of circumstantial evidence I haven't mentioned, Gino."

"What might that be, detective?"

"We recovered three sets of footprints from the break-in at the mausoleum. One was a women's four and a half, which is consistent with someone Toledano's size. Another was a men's twelve, which fits Walker. And the third was a men's ten and half. That would be your client's shoe size."

Gino sat back in his chair, fixed me in a long stare, and exhaled.

"Christ, Bo, half the men in the world are a ten and a half, including me. But humor me. Suppose, just for kicks, that I buy what you're selling, and I'm not saying I do. What's your offer?"

"If your client plays us straight and we get Toledano as a result, Interpol has said they won't charge him in the Marseilles job, or with any other criminal activity he may have abetted, other than the theft of Jane Placide's diamond."

"Marseilles?" Gino looked at Burns.

Burns nodded gravely.

"What else?" Gino wanted to know.

"Nothing specific," I said. "Just my assurance that we'll put in a good word with whatever judge he ends up in front of."

From there, things moved quickly. Gino and Burns talked quietly for maybe a minute. It looked like Gino was trying to get Burns to hold out a bit longer, but Burns seemed done. He could see we had our dots connected and that it was just a matter of time before the evidence fell into place. Finally, he shook Gino off. They spoke a few more words, then Gino turned toward Rodiger and me.

"Alright, gentlemen," he said. "My client agrees to tell you what he can. However, he wishes to be clear at the outset that he has no idea where your man Toledano is. And given that individual's history of avoiding capture, it is not reasonable that your offer of clemency be contingent upon Toledano's arrest. Mr. Burns' good faith cooperation should be enough."

"We can agree to that," I said.

"Very well," Gino said. "He's all yours."

"Thank you," I said, turning toward Burns. "Take us back to the beginning, Mr. Burns. Tell us how your plan took shape and who did what."

Burns looked to Gino, who nodded his approval.

"As you surmised, detective, I came across the Jane Placide letters at Charlotte Duval's house, and they sparked my curiosity. I did some basic Internet research into Jane Placide, which led me to the Girod Street Cemetery and then the crypt out at the mausoleum.

"That's when I got in touch with Abid, who you call Toledano. Both because I wanted a second opinion as to whether this was a legit opportunity and because if it was, I was going to need help."

"How did you communicate with him?"

"Abid had set up encrypted email addresses for us," Burns said, "so that the two of us can communicate without anyone else having access."

"When did he set this up?"

"About ten years ago, I guess, after the last time we worked together."

"That would have been in Amsterdam?" Rodiger asked.

CHAPTER TWENTY-SIX

"Yes."

"When you worked together, you were his safe cracker?" I probed.

"Among other things."

"Okay, back to how you communicated about the Jane Placide letters."

"I emailed him that I had something that might be big, but didn't provide any details, knowing that he wouldn't want me to do that over email, even if it was encrypted."

"We both bought burner cell phones. I texted him photos I'd taken of the letters and then we talked over the phone. We did that a few times with different phones until he was convinced this might be real, and he came down here and set up shop in Charlotte's rental."

"Where did he come from?"

"I don't know, it could have been anywhere in the world," Burns said. "If there's one thing you should know about Abid, it's that he doesn't share anything about himself that he doesn't have to, especially not his location."

"Why was it important for him to set himself up as Ms. Duval's tenant?"

"Again, I don't really know. I guess maybe he thought she might have some information that could prove useful if he could get it out of her without raising suspicion."

"Because she was a descendant of Jane Placide's?"

"Yes."

"That would suggest Ms. Duval was not involved in your scheme," Rodiger interjected. "Am I reading that correctly?"

"Yes, that's correct. Charlotte had no idea what we were up to or even that Phillip Boyer and Omar Pasha knew each other."

So far, it seemed that Burns was telling the truth. He probably didn't think he'd coughed up anything useful, but he'd given me an idea.

"We're going to need those email addresses," I said.

Burns looked to Gino, who nodded.

"When you were both in New Orleans, how did you communicate?" I asked.

"We'd meet every so often, usually out by the lake, or sometimes at City Park. Places where we wouldn't attract notice or run into Charlotte."

"Tell me about your relationship with Abid."

"It was strictly professional," Burns said. "I don't know a thing about him other than he's smart as hell and knows a lot about technology."

"But you go back a long way. You must have some observations you can share."

"When he has a use for me, he gets in touch. It's all very matter of fact. He runs the show, and it's all business. If he has an opportunity, he'll explain it and offer terms, which he always honors, although this last one kind of pissed me off."

"How so?"

"I mean two million dollars sounded great, more than I'd ever made by a longshot, but in relation to sixty-three million? If I had known we were talking that kind of money, I sure as hell would have demanded more."

"Did you know the diamond might have been the famous French Blue?"

"No. Or at least I didn't. I don't think Abid did either. We were both amazed at how big the thing was, but other than the Jean Lafitte angle, we didn't know about the history."

"How did Ronald Walker factor into all this?" I asked.

"As you said, I met him in prison. He seemed like a trustworthy guy. Not the sharpest tool, but steady. Not a talker. When Abid explained his plan, it was clear we needed a third member of the team, someone to help with the break in and then later to be the front man for the sale of the diamond. I told him about Walker; he vetted him a bit and then had me approach him."

"And you and Abid coached him through the supposed discovery of the diamond and then the vetting with the jewelers and the sale at auction?"

"Yes, every step of the way. Abid would give me instructions, and I would relay them to Walker. And that's how we found out about the French Blue stuff, from the jeweler we sent Walker to. Anyway, the only time Abid and Walker had any contact was on the night of the break-in. Like I said, Abid is a careful man."

"And a small one," I said. "He ever talk about his size, or what it was like growing up as the runt of the litter?"

"No, not really. When we met in France he told me he was from Morocco,

CHAPTER TWENTY-SIX

but then another time I heard him tell someone he was from Armenia. That's literally all I ever heard him say about his past. And the only time he mentions his size is in relation to it being an asset when it comes to getting into tight spaces."

"Like the crypt."

"Yeah, like the crypt."

"There's only so many dwarfs in the world, so in theory, he should be easy to find," I said. "Yet he's eluded Interpol for twenty-plus years now. How does he do it?"

"I have no idea," Burns said, "and I didn't realize he's officially a dwarf. That's pretty funny."

No one laughed.

"Anyway, like I said, Abid is careful. And maybe a bit of a chameleon, too. The guy I worked with in Amsterdam looked a lot different from the one I knew in France, and then he had a whole new look as your New Orleans hairdresser."

"Can we talk about Amsterdam for a second?" Rodiger interrupted.

That roused Gino.

"Hold on," he said, extending his arm to silence Burns. "This interview is supposed to be about the diamond that was taken from the cemetery."

"Absolutely, Gino," I said. "But Officer Rodiger has a question that may help us better understand Mahdi Toledano and how we might find him."

Gino eyed me skeptically.

"Anyway," I said, "we've already made it clear that your client will not be charged in any crime other than those that relate to our diamond."

Gino motioned Burns to answer Rodiger's question.

"Thank you, counselor," Rodiger said. "Mr. Burns, can we assume that your objective in Amsterdam was the diamond necklace?"

"Yes."

"But Jan Van de Berg also has a world-famous art collection. There were many precious paintings in his house, but you only took one, and it wasn't one of the most valuable. Why?"

"I don't know," Burns said. "I think it might have been something Abid wanted for himself. We were aware all those paintings were there, but Abid was clear we weren't going to touch them because he didn't know any fences who trafficked in art, so he thought it was too risky. But then he grabs that one painting, and I'm like, what the hell? He said don't worry, I'm not selling it."

"Any idea why that particular painting?"

"None. I couldn't even tell you who painted it or what it was."

"It was by the French artist Eugene Delacroix," Rodiger said. "And it was of a harem girl. Does that mean anything to you?"

"No, not at all."

"Okay, back to the here and now," I said. "From the time Abid arrived in New Orleans, three years went by before you broke into Hope Mausoleum. Why so long?"

"Have I mentioned that Abid is a careful man?" Burns smiled. "He wasn't convinced that the diamond was going to be there and didn't want to take the risk unless we were sure. That's why he had Walker and me go down to Grand Isle to talk to that big whack job down there, because supposedly he was some kind of expert."

"What finally convinced him?"

"I don't know. A preponderance of evidence, as you guys like to say? I do remember that Abid found a book that makes the case that Lafitte took a new name and lived to be an old man. If that was true, then it's plausible that he could have come and gone during the time Jane Placide was writing those letters. And why would she make the whole thing up, anyway?"

I paused to take that in and made eye contact with Gino. He looked like he was close to pulling the plug. Time to wrap things up.

"Okay, Mr. Burns, I'm satisfied that you've been truthful today, and we appreciate your cooperation. I do have one more question. Why did you and Abid hang around after grabbing the diamond, and why did you then leave town so suddenly?"

"That's two questions, detective."

"You know us folks down here, Mr. Burns, we like our lagniappe."

"Ah yes, a little something extra. Very well. It's always been Abid's policy

CHAPTER TWENTY-SIX

to blend into the local community during the lead-up to a job and then not to leave suddenly afterward, which could raise suspicions. When he feels the time is right, we quietly slip away.

"In this case, because Charlotte had involved me with Bruneau and his theories, I was able to learn as much as she knew about what was going on in the investigation, which was quite a bit. When I found out you had a suspect from Morocco, we couldn't get out of town fast enough."

As we paused to take that in, Burns let out a quiet snicker.

"What is it?"

"Nothing. Sorry, I've said enough."

"I'd like to hear what you have to say, Mr. Burns," I said. "As a reminder, your deal has already been cut. We expect full disclosure."

"Very well, detective, though I don't think this adds anything to your investigation. It's just that when you asked me about Abid as a person, I said our relationship is strictly professional, and that's true."

"Go on."

"Well, this may sound crazy, but I think he liked it here. The city, the way of life. And for some reason, he seemed genuinely fond of Charlotte. He was as close to happy as somebody like Abid gets, so I think maybe he was in no rush."

"Anything else?"

Burns made a show of pausing to consider.

"Well, this is just me talking, and nothing he ever said. But I think Abid may have identified with Lafitte. The enterprising mind, the picking up of stakes and the setting up of shop in new places, the aliases, even the idea that he gave up this priceless diamond for a romantic idea. Except for that last part, I might have just described Abid."

Chapter Twenty-Seven

The way Bo tells it, he played Peter Burns like a Stradivarius. When their interrogation began, Burns had been characteristically cocky, but when Bo hit him with our theory of the case and layer upon layer of the evidence we had gathered, the extent of his predicament began to dawn on him. And when Bo let him know, not altogether truthfully, that Ronald Walker was in the process of spilling all, Bo said all the blood drained from Burns' face. God, I wish I'd been there to see that.

Burns found a decent lawyer and cooperated fully, so he was going to get off lighter than he deserved, but according to Bo, he was still going away for a long time. Walker also confessed to everything and would probably receive a similar sentence.

Bo thought he'd come away from the Burns interrogation with a new arrow in his quiver. Burns and Mahdi Toledano had communicated over encrypted email, so he obtained those addresses from Burns and sent Toledano a message, impersonating Burns, to draw him out. He had Burns write it for him, so it would sound like his voice:

Abid. We need to talk. In person. Our friends in blue are getting close. Let me know when and where. P.

A few days went by before there was a response.

Nice try, Detective.

When Bo tried to reply, he got an automated response saying the email address he'd entered was no longer valid. Like Bo said, it's like the guy is wise to everything his pursuers do. He always seems to be a few steps ahead of everybody else, and it's driving Bo crazy.

CHAPTER TWENTY-SEVEN

Still, nabbing Burns and Walker was no small feather in Bo's cap, and so he is back in Captain Maclaren's good graces. The department even received a commendation that MacLaren has hanging in his office.

For our part, Sallie and I were ready to put Toledano behind us. Jean Lafitte and Jane Placide too. We'd driven to Destin for a couple days of relaxation, to clear our heads before returning to what we hoped would be restored normalcy. Prosper dog-sat for us and when we got back that Sunday evening, we were greeted by the luscious fragrance of a simmering Bolognese.

"Welcome home," Prosper's baritone resounded from the kitchen.

"Prosper, you shouldn't have!" Sallie shouted cheerily. "It smells divine."

"Cooking gives this old man pleasure, Sallie. I don't often get the opportunity at Irene's."

As we reached the top of the stairs, I saw that Hugo had reclaimed his throne atop the recliner and wasn't going to budge to welcome us.

"Did his highness behave himself?" I asked Prosper.

"Oh yes, we had a fine time, as always."

"I bet," I said. Then, I moved on to more important matters.

"I'm going to make myself a cocktail. Would either of you like to place an order?"

"No thanks, just a glass of white wine for me," Sallie said.

"I'll pass also," Prosper said. "There's something I want to talk to you about over dinner, and I want to have a clear head when I do."

I remembered that when Bo had assembled us to discuss the Jane Placide letters, it seemed that Prosper was bothered by something. I'd made a mental note to follow up with him but had neglected to do so. I was tempted to ask him about it now, but if that's what this was about, better to let him raise the subject on his own terms.

I poured Sallie her wine, mixed myself a rum and tonic, and opened a Chianti to serve with dinner. Then, I stepped out on the balcony to take in the evening. The twilight was fading to dark, and a crescent moon was rising across the river. A gentle breeze stirred the leaves of the crepe myrtle across the street, as Sallie stole silently up behind me and tapped me on the shoulder.

"What is it, do you think?" she whispered. "What does he want to tell us?"

"I don't know, but something's been bothering him for a while. We'll find out soon enough, I guess."

There is no greater comfort food than a well-made Bolognese, and Prosper's was superb, the subtle anise notes of fennel enriching the hearty meat and the sweet tang of the tomatoes. I sat in my customary spot at the head of the table, with Prosper to my right, facing the kitchen, and Sallie across from him, looking out toward the living room and to the balcony and street beyond.

"What is it you'd like to speak to us about?" I asked Prosper. "I can tell something's been troubling you."

"Yes, that's true," he said. "I feel like an idiot, but I've had a dawning realization. I don't know how to say this except to say it, but…"

A high-pitched shriek interrupted Prosper mid-sentence. It was Sallie, her eyes wide with sudden surprise. Hugo leapt from his roost and scrambled to the balcony door, growling and barking maniacally.

"What is it?" Prosper and I yelled in unison, turning from Sallie to the commotion.

"Oh god, someone's out there," Sallie gasped.

Slowly but purposely, Prosper strode to the door, Sallie and I trailing tentatively behind. He opened it just a crack, wide enough for Hugo to dart outside, then peered his head out and looked both ways.

"There's nobody out there," he said, turning back toward us with a puzzled expression. Behind him, we could see Hugo sniffing madly at the base of one of the wrought iron columns. I thought maybe it was shaking slightly.

"What is it you think you saw?" Prosper asked Sallie.

Flustered and shaking, Sallie tried to catch her breath.

"A man, I think, dressed in black."

"Could it have been a bat?" I suggested. "Or a raccoon, maybe?"

"No, it was much bigger than that. It darted by, but I got enough of a glimpse that I'm pretty sure it was a person."

Prosper walked out on the balcony and looked over the railing. Sallie and

CHAPTER TWENTY-SEVEN

I followed.

"I'm not sure what to say, Sallie," Prosper said. "There doesn't seem to be anyone down there."

I put my arm around Sallie, who was almost hyperventilating. We turned around to face the building, and it was only then that we saw the cloaked shape in the back corner of the balcony that had now drawn Hugo's attention.

"What is it?" Sallie asked.

No one spoke as we regarded the upright object, maybe two feet tall, wrapped in cloth and leaning against the wall.

Slowly, I approached the bundle and lifted it up. I drew back the cloth and grabbed the basket handle of what felt like a short sword. When I pulled it from its sheath for a closer look, we could see that it was old, with the curved blade of a cutlass.

"A pirate's sidearm of choice," Prosper said quietly.

There was a tag hanging off the handle, which Sallie bent down to read.

"Prosper, it seems that this is intended for you," she said in wonderment.

"What does it say?" he asked.

"It says, 'To Andre: If you've found your home, surely this deserves a place in it.'"

Prosper said nothing but gently took the sword from me, and handling it with care, walked inside to the light, where he could examine it in detail. As he did, I thought I heard a noise on the roof, but maybe not.

"Look here," he said, pointing to a spot near the tip of the blade, where three letters were engraved in a rough cursive. The letters were JLF.

Sallie and I looked at each other in astonishment and then toward Prosper. He smiled grimly and ran his hand through his hair.

"It's Aram," he said.

"What? Who's that? I don't understand," Sallie said.

"Oh my, this is awkward," Prosper sighed. "What I had wanted to tell you is that incredible as this may sound, I have come to realize that I know Mahdi Toledano. By a different name, from when I lived in Canada for a spell."

"Wait. What?" I coughed.

"In fact, he is, or was, a friend," Prosper continued. "It was him that Sallie saw on the balcony."

"What? Are you sure?"

"Positive. Only he could have written that note, and with his abilities, this ironwork would be easy to climb."

"Just like that?" Sallie asked. "In and out like a ghost?"

"Yes."

"I don't understand," I said. "This is too much to take in. I need to call Bo."

Bo didn't pick up, so I left him a short message asking him to call me, emphasizing that it was important. Then I turned to Prosper.

"Come, let's sit down," he said. "Our visitor is long gone, and I have much to tell you."

Embarrassed but composed, Prosper walked Sallie and I through the timeline of his brief friendship with Mahdi Toledano, who he knew as Aram Zakaryan, an itinerant Armenian. He described their chance meeting and told of their long walks and deep philosophical discussions. The topic of "home," both physical and figurative, was one that preoccupied both men, which Prosper said explained the significance of the note Toledano had left behind.

"A family heirloom for your home?" Sallie ventured.

"Something like that."

We chewed on that thought for a few long seconds. Then I started asking questions.

"What did Aram Zakaryan do for work?"

"He said he represented high net worth individuals interested in building fine arts collections."

"That's rich. Did you ever discuss Jean Lafitte with him?"

"Now that you mention it, yes, one time. I can't remember how it came up, exactly, but we were both expressing displeasure with the modern world, and he said sometimes he wished he had been alive in the 17th-century and that if he had been, he would have liked to have been one of the Barbary pirates, living a life of adventure on the high seas.

CHAPTER TWENTY-SEVEN

"I told him about my relation to Lafitte, who he'd never heard of. When I mentioned that Lafitte was a slave trader, he reminded me that the Barbary pirates were too, which is why he would have been the pirate who made his name by freeing the slaves held by other pirates."

"Did he say anything about women?" I asked.

"Yes. He said the pirates raped and pillaged, and he wouldn't have been that kind of pirate. He would have come to the rescue of fair damsels, or something along those lines."

"Do you think he sent Burns and Walker to talk to you in Grand Isle?" Sallie asked.

Prosper shrugged his shoulders.

"I don't see how. He knew me as Andre Coulon, not Prosper Fortune. We hadn't kept in touch, and I was living off the grid. Seems unlikely, but clearly, he made the connection. If anyone could, it would be Aram."

"Probably from just asking around about Lafitte," Sallie said. "No offense, Prosper, but you cut a memorable figure. My guess is either Toledano heard the description of you and figured it out or Burns and Walker described you when they got back from Grand Isle, and he put two and two together at that point."

"Yeah, maybe," Prosper said. "If he knew I was there, it makes sense that he wouldn't have come himself. He had a new identity to protect and wouldn't have wanted to compromise his planning."

Prosper didn't seem particularly interested in how Toledano found him, only that he had.

"Tell us what he was like, in your experience," Sallie asked. "Toledano, or Aram Zakaryan as you knew him."

"He was a good guy," Prosper said. "Smart, considerate, cultured, observant. I'm having a very hard time squaring the man I knew with a notorious international outlaw, but there's no doubt that's who he is."

"When did you realize Aram Zakaryan was Mahdi Toledano?" I asked.

"It wasn't like I had some great epiphany," Prosper said. "An idea had been forming in the back of my mind, but when you relayed the comment Peter Burns made to Bo about Toledano identifying with Lafitte, that's when it clicked, and I knew for sure. That stuff about picking up stakes and starting new lives over and over again, and his being a closet romantic, that describes Aram in a nutshell.

"I should have figured it out earlier. I think it was Toledano's Moroccan upbringing that threw me off. I mean, Aram was convincingly Armenian. That and the fact that, as small as he was, I never thought of him as a dwarf. Just a small man."

We sat in silence for a half minute or so, the three of us trying to process what had happened and what we had learned.

"You're going to have to take this to Bo," I said finally.

"Yes, I know," Prosper said. "But first, I think I'll take you up on that drink you offered earlier."

"You got it. Brandy?

"Sure."

"Do you think the sword was really Lafitte's?" Sallie asked.

"It's called a cutlass, to be precise," Prosper said. "Lafitte and his pirates preferred them to swords because they were more effective in cramped quarters and an easier tool to handle when cutting ropes and that sort of thing.

"But to answer your question, yes, it is certainly possible that this was Lafitte's. There are other items of his on display in various museums and historical societies. It looks like it's of the right vintage, and it was common for sailors to engrave their initials on the blade of their weapon."

"How would he have gotten his hands on it?"

"Who knows?" Prosper said, accepting the snifter I handed him. "From a museum or a private collection, maybe. A man resourceful enough to track down a missing crown jewel would certainly be capable of finding Jean Lafitte's cutlass."

Hugo kept sniffing around out on the balcony and growling periodically. It occurred to me that when Sallie caught a glimpse of Toledano, he could have gone up rather than down and that when we were looking for him out on the street, he might have been looming over us on the roof, listening. He could still be up there.

CHAPTER TWENTY-SEVEN

I was whispering my theory to Prosper and Sallie, when my phone rang loudly on the tabletop. It was Charlotte calling at an unusually late hour for her, so I picked it up.

"Charlotte?"

"Oh, thank god!" she blurted, clearly in distress. "Bruneau, I've just had the most frightful scare, and the strangest thing has happened."

"What is it? Are you okay?"

"Yes, I think so. But please, can you come right away?"

"Yes, of course. Just hang on. We'll be right there."

The three of us hurried down the stairs, packed into Liesel, and made it to Charlotte's in less than five minutes. I tried Bo again on the way, but no luck. When we arrived, the drapes at the front of the house were drawn, but there was light behind them. I led the way up the stoop and rapped loudly with the knocker. After a brief delay, Isabella peered tentatively through the sidelight, regarded me with a look of relief, and opened the door. Charlotte stood perhaps ten feet behind her in a terry cloth bathrobe and slippers, her hair undone.

"We came as quickly as we could," I said. I could see both women eyeing Prosper with a mix of awe and trepidation.

"Charlotte, Isabella, this is our friend Prosper Fortune," I said. "He was over for dinner when you called, and we thought if there was trouble there'd be strength in numbers."

"Hola, senor," Isabella said.

"Hola, miss," Prosper said.

Charlotte motioned us to come inside and led us into the parlor. Prosper brought up the rear, and as he did, Charlotte extended her hand.

"It is nice to finally make your acquaintance, Mr. Fortune," she said. "I have heard so much about you."

"That's what worries me, ma'am," Prosper said, smiling politely.

"Tell us what this is about, Charlotte," I said as we took our seats. A package sat in the middle of her centerpiece oak coffee table. It had been opened, but I couldn't see inside.

"It has been the most remarkable sequence of events," Charlotte said, holding her hand to her heart. "I hardly know where to start."

"How about at the beginning?" Sallie suggested gently.

"Yes, thank you, dear, that's a good idea."

Charlotte paused to collect herself and organize her thoughts.

"Well, Isabella and I had retired for the evening, you see. I was reading in bed, and Isabella was in her room down the hallway when there were, I think, five loud knocks on the front door. Do I have that right, Isabella? Was it five knocks?"

"Si, senora, five knocks."

"Needless to say, I am not in the habit of receiving company at such an hour, and we didn't know who or what it could be. Someone in trouble maybe, or one of those homeless people who wander through here sometimes. We had no way of knowing. We tiptoed to the top of the stairs and looked down, but we couldn't see anything. There were no more knocks, so we went back to our rooms.

"No sooner had I climbed back into bed, still very much on edge, than I heard the side door to the courtyard below my bedroom open and shut, followed by the sound of footsteps on the gravel. I was frightened to death. I picked up the phone and started to call 9-1-1, but I was so panicked that I couldn't get my fingers to work. Then, as I was fumbling with the phone, a pebble bounced off my window, and then more pebbles."

"What did you do?" I asked.

"I went to the window and looked down. I realize now that that wasn't very smart, but I wasn't thinking clearly. There was a person down there, a man, I think, dressed in black, with a mask or scarf of some kind covering his face. He was waving up to me and holding a package. He pointed to it and set it down on the glass table right below my window, then he backed away, waved again, pointed to the package again, and left, closing the door behind him."

"And this is the package?" I asked.

"Yes. Isabella and I waited for a few minutes, then crept downstairs and turned on all the outdoor lights. Isabella bravely stepped outside to retrieve the package while I stood guard with that."

CHAPTER TWENTY-SEVEN

Charlotte pointed to an ancient pearl-handled snub-nosed revolver she'd left on a side table.

"That was brave of you, Isabella," Sallie said. Isabella blushed and smiled sheepishly.

"I see that you've opened it," I said, nodding toward the package. "What was in it?"

"I wouldn't have believed it if I hadn't seen it with my own eyes," Charlotte said. "But unless someone is playing a nasty trick, I think it contains the French Blue diamond."

"What?" I exclaimed as Sallie, Prosper, and I looked at each other, dumbfounded.

"Here, have a look for yourself, dear," Charlotte said, sliding the package in my direction.

I picked it up, reached inside, and pulled out a purple velvet box, approximately four inches by four inches. The gem inside was like nothing I'd seen, in size or beauty, except maybe in a museum. It was shaped like a squat triangle, an inch wide at least, its facets arranged in perfect symmetry. Its brilliant, deep blue hues glistened seductively in the lamplight. If I didn't feel its weight in my hand, I might have thought it celestial rather than of the earth.

"Behold, La Violette," I said, holding the jewel out for all to see.

"Is it possible?" Sallie gasped.

"I wouldn't have thought so, dear, but there was a letter in the package, along with some money, that leads me to believe this is indeed the genuine article," Charlotte said.

"A letter?" I asked.

"Yes, from Omar."

"From Omar? How much money?"

"Thirty thousand dollars in cash, dear."

As we sat, gaping, Charlotte reached into the pocket of her robe and handed me two folded, handwritten pages on plain, cream-colored stationery. I opened them and began to read aloud.

Dear Charlotte,

By now, you know that I am not who I said I was. I am sorry to have deceived you in this way, but my situation requires that I take such precautions. You have doubtless received shocking reports about me. I cannot deny that I have done some bad things in my life, Charlotte. But I am not a bad man; at least, I don't think I am. Perhaps you can be the better judge of that. You and our maker.

I have a large favor to ask of you, and if you decline to grant it, I will understand and bear no ill will. Inside this package, you will find some money and the blue diamond that my accomplices and I removed from Jane Placide's casket. The diamond has served its purpose in enabling me to do some good in this world, and I should like to see it returned to its rightful owner. My request is presumptuous, I know. But I should be forever grateful if you would use this money to erect a new tomb for Miss Placide, and to place the diamond with her remains.

I have no right to ask this of you, Charlotte, and if you do what most would deem the right thing, and go to the police, I will not think the worse of you. If you do decide to do that, please consider turning over the diamond but keeping the cash. It would please me to know that it would be spent in good taste.

I have enjoyed returning to your fine city, however briefly. If things had gone differently in my life, I would have liked to have settled here. As it is, I cannot stay. Though the police persist, there is no use in looking for me. I am a leopard who knows how to change his spots. We will not meet again, Charlotte, but I remain ...

Your Admirer,
Omar

The only sound in the room was the ponderous ticking of Charlotte's Limoges clock.

"Well, that's a lot to unpack," Sallie commented finally.

"Yes, it is," Prosper spoke for the first time. "What do you suppose he meant when he said the diamond had allowed him to do some good?"

CHAPTER TWENTY-SEVEN

"I don't know, I was wondering the same thing," Sallie said. "You knew him. What do you think?"

"I'm not sure. Maybe he used the money from the sale to fund a cause of some kind. I'm just speculating."

"How on earth did he get the diamond back? That's what I'd like to know," Charlotte said. "I thought it had been sold."

"It had been," I said. "To a Chinese billionaire. A few weeks ago, that billionaire's apartment was broken into."

"I wouldn't have said this about Aram, but Mahdi Toledano is nothing if not audacious," Prosper said.

As Prosper was talking, I thought I heard something creak outside in the courtyard area where Charlotte had seen her masked visitor. Sallie heard it, too. I motioned to Prosper and the three of us got up and walked quietly to the kitchen, where a side door leads to the courtyard. We flicked on the outdoor lights and rushed outside, but there was no one there.

The gate that opens to Coliseum Street was slightly ajar, so Prosper and I walked out and looked around. It was a dark night, and the street was shrouded in the shadows of the live oaks that lined the sidewalks. More than once we thought we saw a figure lurking in the gloom, but as we approached, we realized our eyes were playing tricks on us.

I couldn't shake the feeling that someone was watching us, but eventually, we gave up and returned to the courtyard. Charlotte and Isabella had joined Sallie outside, and Charlotte was pointing a flashlight at an area where the gravel had been disturbed by what might have been a child's shoe print.

"He's like a phantom," Sallie said.

Heads nodded.

Later, as we moved back inside, we contemplated what we knew of the inscrutable dwarf. Who was this man, after all?

A charming companion, a deep thinker, a considerate friend. So say all who knew him. But also a super thief. A specter, invisible to us, yet omnipresent. And now a returner of stolen goods who speaks of doing good in the world. Is he Robin Hood, reborn to a later age? An avenging angel?

These were the thoughts that perplexed us as we tried to make sense of him. Who can possibly know? Perhaps he is all the things we have said or none of them. He may not know himself.

What I did know was that the hour was getting late, and we had practical matters to discuss. Clumsily, I changed the subject.

"Listen, folks, I'm sorry to break our mood, but in case you haven't noticed, we've got a situation here. We're sitting on a mountain of evidence that's material to a major criminal investigation. We need to call Bo."

Nobody said anything.

I waited.

"What?"

There was more silence and no eye contact in the room.

It took me a while, but I understood.

"You can't be serious. There can be no question about this, people! If we withhold evidence and Charlotte carries out Omar's instructions, we could all be looking at jail time. Lots of it!"

More silence.

"I'm sure you're right, Bruneau," Sallie said eventually, patting my leg.

"But it's late, and we're all tired. Maybe we should sleep on it."

Epilogue

A lot has happened since Mahdi Toledano paid us his nocturnal visits. As we were driving home that night, Bo returned my call. I needed time to think, so I told him Sallie thought she'd seen a figure on the balcony, but that he seemed to have run away. Bo asked if I wanted him to come over and check things out, or maybe send a patrol car. I told him no, that it could wait.

After a full day of debate among Sallie, Charlotte, and myself, I finally convinced them that it would be wrong not to inform Bo of what had transpired. Wrong legally, but also just wrong. Bo is my oldest and closest friend, and it would have been difficult to face myself in the mirror if we had kept the deception alive. Still, I was not unmoved by Sallie and Charlotte's argument that by redressing a historical wrong, the return of Jane Placide and La Violette to their rightful resting place would achieve a deeper, more enduring justice than the fleeting satisfaction of recovering a billionaire's stolen property. Therefore, I chose my time and place carefully.

I passed Little Bo, Sophie, and Monique at their bus stop that morning, and we waved to each other as I neared their home and pulled into the driveway. Moments later, I found Bo and Angie lingering over their coffee, catching them by surprise.

"Bruneau!" Angie exclaimed. "For goodness' sake, what are you doing here? Is everything alright?"

"Yes, I'm fine, and I apologize for the intrusion," I said. "I was hoping to have a quick word with you before Bo leaves for work. It's important."

"Of course, sugar," Angie said, "let me get you some coffee."

Bo hadn't said a word but was staring at me quizzically.

"You sure you're okay, Bru?"

"I'm fine, I promise."

As I related all that had transpired, Bo was incredulous, but every time he tried to interrupt, Angie told him to be quiet and let me finish. I'd been counting on that. It was important that he listened to everything I had to say, not just the headlines. When I finished, he shook his head but spoke in measured tones, conscious of Angie monitoring his temper.

"You realize what you've done? Again? Going through Charlotte Duval's family records and compromising that evidence is one thing, but at least I could defend you on the grounds that you didn't know what you might find. This is next level, Bru. You've let two outdoor crime scenes degrade for 36 hours now, and that's thirty-six hours our fugitive has had to skip town and cover his tracks."

He sounded more sad than angry, like I'd disappointed him. I would have preferred a tongue-lashing.

"I'm going to have to bring the four of you down to the station for questioning and don't be surprised if the captain takes charge of the interviews. He is not going to be happy. I'll send crime scene teams over to your place and Ms. Duval's. Maybe we can still find something of value. And obviously, we're going to need the diamond and the money."

"I understand," I said. "I was hoping you might be able to exercise some discretion, but I do appreciate your position, Bo. It's what I expected."

Bo got up, muttering, and started to gather his stuff for work.

"You better be there in two hours," he said and headed for the door.

"Hold on, Bo honey," Angie interjected. "Don't you think we should talk about this a little longer?"

"What's there to talk about? There aren't any options here, Ange. It's cut and dried."

"Are you sure? Just sit down for a couple more minutes. I want to ask you a few questions."

"Really? I'm the one who's facing questioning now?"

"That's not the way I meant it," Angie said. "Humor me. Please?"

EPILOGUE

Bo exhaled loudly, dropped his stuff on the table by the door, and collapsed back into his chair.

"Thank you, I appreciate it," Angie said. "Now, when I ask you these questions, I want you to answer as Bo Duplessis, the person, not the cop, okay?"

"There's no point in that," Bo said. "What I think as a private citizen doesn't matter. The fact is, I'm a police officer, and this is police business."

"Please?"

Bo tilted his head back and looked at the ceiling, exasperated.

"Fine. Let's get this over with."

"Thank you. My first question is this: As a person, do you particularly care if the Chinese billionaire gets his diamond back? What's his name again?"

"His name is Lingyun Gao, and no, I don't care in the least whether he gets his diamond back, but that's not the issue."

"I understand, honey. Just bear with me, please. Answering as a police officer now, do you think it likely that the diamond would even end up back in Gao's possession, given the history of the diamond and all the countries and legal complications involved?"

"I really couldn't say. That's above my pay grade and not my concern."

"Okay, fair enough. Next question: other than Lingyun Gao, would anyone be personally harmed by not reporting the recovery of the diamond?"

"You mean anyone other than me losing my job and going to jail for aiding and abetting a criminal conspiracy if word ever got out? No, I suppose not."

"Nothing to take lightly, I understand. But just suppose, hypothetically, that the return of the diamond wasn't reported. How would anyone ever find out about it? Especially if the diamond was set to rest with Jane Placide?"

"There's four other people who know about this, Angie," Bo said. "Any one of them could let something slip, even if they didn't mean to. Including you, Bru. Not to mention, Toledano could get apprehended and tell all."

Angie persisted.

"If Toledano has made it this long with the whole world looking for him and no one has even gotten close, you think they're going to find him now?"

"It's possible."

"Okay, let's say he is captured. He took a huge risk stealing the diamond a second time and coming back here to do something he didn't personally profit from, quite the opposite, in fact, presumably because he thought it was the right thing to do. Why would he confess to returning the diamond? And how would anyone even know to ask him about it?"

"I couldn't say."

"And as far as Bru and Sallie and Prosper and Charlotte Duval go, given the risks they'd be taking, you don't think they'd be careful?"

"I'm sure they would, but that doesn't mean they might not screw up by mistake. Even just sending an innocent email or text could leave a trail."

Angie thought about that.

"Bruneau, why did you come here this morning rather than calling or texting Bo?"

"Because I didn't want to leave a digital trace of this conversation having taken place," I answered truthfully, though not with the whole truth.

"That's what I thought. Bo, is this conversation being recorded?"

"No."

"So, what it boils down to then, is do you trust your friends?"

"Oh, come on, that's not fair," Bo complained. "First of all, Charlotte Duval is not my friend, and I barely know Prosper Fortune. And anyway, this is all beside the point, Angie. The fact is a crime was committed. Several crimes, and I know about them. In case you two have forgotten, it's my job to solve crimes and enforce the law. And at this point, I'm running a half hour late to that job."

With that, Bo got up, pecked Angie on the forehead, and headed for the door.

"One last question," Angie said. Bo stopped and turned.

"Suppose it was me in that crypt 200 years from now, and suppose this was with me," she said, holding up her wedding band. "And suppose you were in the next crypt over, wearing your ring, like we've talked about. And then suppose somebody 200 years from now broke in and took my ring. Would you want to see it returned?"

EPILOGUE

"Of course, I would, if I had the ability to think conscious thoughts," Bo said. "Look, I see what you're trying to do, Ange, and I appreciate the effort, but I've got a job to do. That's all there is to it. Bru, I'll see you in a couple hours."

This time, Bo grabbed his stuff and headed out the door, and Angie didn't try to stop him. She and I looked at each other, defeated.

"Thank you for that," I said. "I couldn't have asked for a better devil's advocate. It's the other reason I drove out here. It wasn't just to avoid leaving a trail. There's no one he listens to like he listens to you."

Angie waved me off and fixed her gaze.

"It would have been a huge ask, which is why I never actually framed it that way. He's a good man, you know. Nothing he said was wrong."

"Trust me, I know," I said. "On both counts."

Angie and I finished our coffee and consoled ourselves in a long embrace. Then I walked to my car, and she went to tidy up before leaving for work.

As I was driving home, I called Prosper to tell him I was on my way to pick him up. I told Charlotte to meet us at my place, and then I got ahold of Sallie at work to deliver the same message, which did not please her. I never mentioned the reason we needed to gather, but they all knew.

"No luck with Bo, I take it?" Prosper asked as we pulled out of his sister's driveway.

"No."

I told him about my talk with Bo and Angie.

"Well, you gave it the old college try. It's probably for the best."

I nodded, and we drove on in silence.

Ten minutes later, we were sitting at a stop light on South Carrollton when my phone buzzed. I looked down to see that it was a text from Bo.

"Bru, I've been thinking. No need to meet. End of discussion, okay?"

"Okay," I typed.

* * *

It's been more than a year since my friend chose cosmic justice over secular law. We've never discussed his decision. There's an understanding between us that some things are better left unsaid.

There was some awkwardness with Bo for a while, but it feels like we're almost back to normal now. He hasn't asked me to help with any new cases, but I guess I can't say I blame him. I did see he tried calling me this afternoon, but I was busy and didn't pick up. That was followed by a text that said, "Call me asap." I'll get to it in the morning. No point in seeming too eager.

Bo wasn't present for the re-interment of Jane Placide in the new mausoleum Charlotte built for her with Mahdi Toledano's money at St. Louis Cemetery #3. With the help of Sallie's research, Charlotte was able to fashion a convincing replica of Jane's original tomb, complete with the engraving of James Caldwell's epitaph on the headwall. We enclosed La Violette in a purple velvet drawstring bag and placed it in Jane's new coffin. Angie joined Prosper, Sallie, and I as pallbearers as we slid the long black lacquer box into its chamber. Charlotte and Isabella looked on. Prosper spoke a few words of commemoration, and then we watched the cemetery staff seal the chamber for eternity.

St. Louis #3 is a good deal statelier than Girod Street had been, with its stacked crypts and encroaching vegetation, but less atmospheric. It is virtually treeless, with long double rows of mausoleums separated by wide paved avenues. Nonetheless, there was an eeriness about the place, and I couldn't shake the feeling we were being watched. I kept turning around to look, but never saw anything. If Mahdi Toledano had been there and wanted to conceal himself, it wouldn't have been difficult. I don't subscribe to supernatural beliefs, but I couldn't stop my mind from wondering if the spirit of Jean Lafitte hovered nearby.

When our little ceremony had concluded, we walked to Lola's a few blocks away and shared a curbside drink. Charlotte and Sallie did most of the talking while Prosper and I stared off into the distance. Prosper had stayed out of the debate about whether to report Mahdi Toledano's last known sighting. We've never talked about it, but I think he was embarrassed about his prior connection to the man he knew as Aram and felt that, somehow, it deprived him of his right to voice an opinion. Maybe I'm projecting too

EPILOGUE

much, but I think he's pleased that we did what we did. He didn't keep Jean Lafitte's cutlass, making an anonymous donation to the Cabildo instead. A team there verified its likely authenticity.

Unsurprisingly, international law enforcement seems to have made little progress in apprehending Mahdi Toledano. Bo doesn't talk about it, but I've seen Mike Rodiger a couple times, and he says there are occasional rumors of sightings in remote outposts around the globe, but nothing has ever been verified. They're probably on the lookout for a tiny midget spending lavishly in some tropical paradise. My guess is he lives humbly, hiding in plain sight, not as a dwarf, but as a small man.

There has been an interesting development, known only to Sallie, Prosper, Charlotte, and me. A couple months ago, an article in the Sunday *New York Times* caught Sallie's eye. It concerned a network of a dozen or so girls' schools that had opened across Morocco. According to the executive director of the non-profit organization that runs the schools, the funding has come from a mysterious private source called The Fadila Trust. She was quoted as saying she has never met or talked to anyone from the trust other than receiving occasional instructions through encrypted emails and notifications of pending wire transfers. She said that the trust plans to spend the equivalent of several million more dollars opening still more schools in the years ahead. The article was accompanied by photos of schoolgirls in smart uniforms, engaged in creative learning, in modern-looking classrooms.

According to Sallie, the name Fadila means "lady of merit" in Darija, or Moroccan Arabic. It was also the name of Mahdi Toledano's grandmother.

As for Sallie and me, well, maybe the best way to put it is that we feel *comfortable* with each other. We still have our spats, but it never feels nasty or threatening, just a natural outgrowth of sharing a living space and spending so much time together. She doesn't know it, but I've started looking at properties where we might move in together. I'd like for her to have an equal hand in designing and decorating the space we decide to call home.

The weather has been beautiful lately, and we've taken to bringing Hugo, a couple of folding picnic chairs, and a thermos of daiquiris to the high ground of the Riverbend levee to watch the sunset. Sometimes, during these idylls, we muse about Jean Lafitte and Jane Placide consorting in the heavens, though not as frequently as we used to.

One night last week we stayed later than usual. It was one of those rare evenings when the sky is filled to abundance with stars, and the stars themselves seem more brilliant and effervescent than usual, like so many sparkling diamonds. As it happened, we were both looking up when a shooting star came streaking across the firmament from the west. Seconds later it was followed by another, as if in hot pursuit.

Astronomers would say we had witnessed a meteor shower.

We couldn't help but think otherwise.

A Note from the Author

The idea for *The Lafitte Affair* emerged gradually from a series of casual inquiries into topics that were only tangentially related but began to intersect in unforeseen ways. Some 20 years ago, I embarked upon an ancestral research project on behalf of my mother. While engaged in that endeavor, I happened upon the role my ancestor Thomas Shields, the purser who introduces Jane to Lafitte, played in the Battle of New Orleans. At the time, I had only the vaguest sense of the circumstances surrounding that event, so I dug into a handful of books on the topic. I was surprised and impressed to learn of the pivotal roles played by the pirates Jean and Pierre Lafitte in securing that unlikeliest of triumphs for then-General Jackson. That led to an interest in learning more about the Lafittes and, ultimately, a bit of an obsession with the remarkable life and many legends of Jean Lafitte.

It was also while researching my ancestor that I became intrigued by the macabre history of the Girod Street Cemetery, where Purser Shields was interred. I had never considered what happened to human remains removed from a deconsecrated cemetery. Morbid curiosity about the fate of my forebear's bones led me to Hope Mausoleum and Crypt 1083-A, and then to an interest in the crypt's other residents, notably the actress Jane Placide. And so, a decade or so ago, the germ of an idea began to form, and I penned a draft of what eventually became the scene in which Lafitte visits Jane's tomb. It was nothing more than a writing exercise at the time; none but the vaguest sense of plot had yet occurred to me.

In the spring of 2022, I retired from my day job. I returned to my earlier writing and began to wonder whether I might have something with which to work. New Orleans has occupied a large parcel of my imaginative real estate ever since I attended school and met my future wife there, four-plus decades ago. If I were to locate a novel anywhere, it would have to be there. And so, I began to think I had the building blocks of what might become a compelling story: an atmospheric setting, an enigmatic hero and formidable heroine from the distant past, and a mysterious grave robbery as a ghoulish hook. All I needed now was a cast of characters and a plot.

The characters came first. Bruneau Abellard was not, as some early readers suspected, modeled after his creator. Bru and I share a body type and an abiding interest in food and wine, but we differ in other ways. If there was a model who occurred to my mind's eye, it was Frank Cannon, the erudite private detective portrayed by William Conrad in the eponymous Seventies T.V. series *Cannon*. Both men are intellectually curious, skilled in the culinary arts, and portly and balding. But Cannon is a man of action who regularly gets into fistfights and shootouts, while Bru is a mostly passive observer who engages with the world from a safe remove.

I struggled with how to portray the character of Mahdi Toledano. At times I thought of him as a less sinister Professor Moriarty, at others a modern-day Robin Hood. Ultimately, I think he is more like Jean Lafitte. A pirate of sorts, morally compromised in some respects, virtuous in others. Like the Lafitte of the novel, I think of Mahdi less as a three-dimensional character than as a catalyst and an organizing idea around which plot and characters orbit.

Once I had Bruneau and Mahdi figured out, Bo fell easily into place as Bru's friend and foil, and then the rest of the cast came each in their turn. Plot was another matter entirely. It wasn't until I was two-thirds through an initial draft that I began to see how the story might end. The details fell into place only as I wrote them. In a real sense, the characters were as responsible for developing the story as its nominal author.

The romance between Jean Lafitte and Jane Placide is fiction, but in most other respects, I have aimed for historical accuracy while occasionally wielding poetic license in the service of plot. For example, while Jane Placide's remains are contained in Crypt 1083-A, so far as I know, they are mixed in with those of the other residents, not set aside in a coffin. Additionally, there are events described or implied that, while not implausible, likely never happened, such as Lafitte meeting with Joseph Bonaparte or extorting Charles Lallemand. In such cases, one of the characters, usually Prosper Fortune, flags speculation for what it is. Similarly, the meetings and dialogues involving historical figures are fanciful exercises. Finally, there is no historical evidence to suggest that the French Blue Diamond crossed the Atlantic with Joseph Bonaparte or came into the possession of Charles Lallemand or Jean Lafitte. Almost certainly, it became the Hope.

Acknowledgements

The archetypal image of the lonely writer toiling in his spartan garret is deeply embedded in our collective psyche, and for good reason. Writing, by its nature, is a solitary pursuit. But for those of us blessed to count among our network of associations an abundance of generosity, patience, and discernment, authorship can become a paradoxically social activity.

I am one such fortunate soul, and so it was for me. Each time I wrote, or re-wrote, a new chapter to this novel, I sent it out to a couple dozen family members and friends, old-school serial style. Remarkably, no one protested this imposition, though imposition it certainly was. It is no exaggeration to say that were it not for the steady encouragement and timely feedback of my kindhearted readers, and the stimulation I received from our ongoing dialogues, *The Lafitte Affair* might never have been completed. I am humbled by a reservoir of support I neither expected nor deserve.

My wife Lori and our children, Nathalie, Alexander, and Rachel, were steadfast supporters of this project and valued critics of its various iterations. My brothers, Eric, Tim, and Stephen, encouraged me throughout, as did my mothers-in-law Sue Foster and Eunie Deter, brother-in-law Wright Deter, and sisters-in-law Deneise Deter-Liss and Drake Patten. Many thanks to Wright for the beautiful map of Barataria that appears at the front of *The Lafitte Affair*. When the novel was roughly halfway to completion, my nephew Isaac Rankin, himself a published writer, said he looked forward to learning what Prosper Fortune's role would turn out to be. That offhand comment flipped a switch for me and altered for the better the trajectory of the novel's plot.

I am beholden to New Orleans natives Thierry Drapanas and Winifred Wegmann for reviewing my manuscript with an eye toward authenticity of place. Between them they caught a handful of errors and added clever local touches. Were it not for Thierry, Charlotte Duval would merely have "used" rather than "visited" the ladies room. Mercifully, Winifred rescued me from referring to the "neutral ground" as the "median," a non-native tell if ever there was one. I am both amazed by and indebted to my dear friends Barbara Kessler and Nancy Jo Krueger, who along with Thierry, consumed the entirety of *The Lafitte Affair* in a single, day-long reading. I also owe thanks to Nancy Joe and Sarah Gorman for inviting me to meet with their delightfully spirited book clubs, the "Worms" and "Low Brows" respectively. I enjoyed those evenings immensely and benefitted greatly from our discussions. Sarah deserves additional credit for helping to improve the story of Sallie Maguire's blossoming, prodding me to transform the stock Pygmalion tale it started out as into something more plausible and nuanced.

From the outset, fellow writer Proal Heartwell was a wellspring of positive reinforcement and occasional cathartic commiseration. Our shop-talk coffees with our talented co-conspirator, Claire Holman Thompson, remain a source of ongoing literary sustenance. Connie Weck, who I did not know when my wife shared early chapters of *The Lafitte Affair* with her, quickly secured her status as one of my most insightful readers and exacting critics, in the best possible sense. I so very much appreciate her taking an interest in a stranger's work. Finally, I owe a special debt of gratitude to my closest reader, and most skilled editor, Cullen "Big Red" Couch, whose gentle coaxing, thoughtful commentary, and sharp eye for detail improved *The Lafitte Affair* beyond measure.

For helpful advice relating to the business side of publishing, I am indebted to my childhood friend Gigi Priebe, author of the clever *Henry Whiskers* children's series, and to Jenny Ackerman, the best-selling science and nature writer whose ornithological tour de forces, most recently *What an Owl Knows*, are must-reads for anyone the least bit curious about the fine feathered visitors who appear at our lawn feeders. Thank you also to the talented Molly Wraight Ring for her help with my authors' website and other digital marketing matters. And to my cousin, Christopher Combemale, whose industry insights and advice were invaluable.

Finally, I am grateful beyond words to Verena Rose for taking a chance on an unpublished author. She and Shawn Reilly Simmons, Deb Well, and the talented team at Level Best Books have been wonderful to work with, and I look forward to our continuing collaboration as the Bruneau Abellard series unfolds.

I read widely in preparing to write *The Lafitte Affair,* but the source I returned to again and again was *The Pirates Lafitte: The Treacherous World of the Corsairs of the Gulf* by William C. Davis. Exhaustively researched, it is as close to a definitive treatment of the Lafitte brothers as has been written. Less comprehensive but no less compelling is *Jean Laffite Revealed: Unravelling One of America's Longest-Running Mysteries*, by Ashley Oliphant and Beth Yarbrough, the mother-daughter tandem referenced by Bruneau Abellard. The case they make for Lafitte's second act as Lorenzo Ferrer is persuasive, and the journey of discovery that fuels their narrative makes for an engaging read.

For readers interested in learning more about the Bonaparte family, and in particular, the machinations of Joseph Bonaparte and his fellow French expats in America, I recommend visiting Shannon Selin's website, "Imagining the Bounds of History" at www.shannonselin.com. The author of an alternative history novel titled *Napoleon in America,* Selin's blog includes multiple entries on the Lafittes, as well as portraits of Charles Lallemand, Nicolas Girod, the Villiard sisters and more.

The Lafitte Affair treats the Battle of New Orleans only tangentially, which is a shame, because that conflict represents a truly fascinating episode in military history. For readers who would like to learn more about the battle, and the roles played by the Lafittes and the Baratarians, I recommend Winston Groom's *Patriotic Fire: Andrew Jackson and Jean Laffite at the Battle of New Orleans.* Groom is best known for his novel *Forrest Gump,* and it occurs to me only in hindsight that it is possible to view Jean Lafitte as a sort of Forrest Gump for his time, popping up here, then there, influencing consequential people and events from the shadows of history. Run Jean, run.

In closing, I would be remiss if I did not acknowledge the selfishness inherent in my early retirement and subsequent retreat to my writer's den, and the toll this may have taken on the person closest to me. I owe the deepest possible gratitude to Lori, the great love of my life, for allowing me this indulgence.

About the Author

Norman Woolworth is a retired corporate executive, and *The Lafitte Affair* is his first novel. A graduate of Tulane University, Woolworth maintains an abiding fascination with the City of New Orleans, which he visits as frequently as he is able. Like his protagonist, Bruneau Abellard, Woolworth appreciates nothing so much as a great meal, paired with a well-chosen wine, shared with close friends. Unlike Bruneau, Woolworth enjoys hiking, active vacations, and exploring the natural world.

A journalist before embarking on a three-decade career in Corporate America, Woolworth holds a M.A. in English Literature from the University of Virginia. A father of three grown children, he resides in Charlottesville, Virginia, with his wife Lori and their blue-blooded mongrel, Nola.

SOCIAL MEDIA HANDLES:
   https://www.linkedin.com/in/norman-woolworth-7803884/
   https://www.facebook.com/norman.woolworth.2024/?viewas=100000686899395
   https://www.instagram.com/uwoolnx56/
   https://www.amazon.com/stores/Norman-Woolworth/author/B0DB1144NX?ref=ap_rdr&isDramIntegrated=true&shoppingPortalEnabled=true

https://www.goodreads.com/author/show/51115315.Norman_Woolworth

AUTHOR WEBSITE:

https://www.normanwoolworth.com

Printed in the USA
CPSIA information can be obtained
at www.ICGtesting.com
JSHW021046260824
68638JS00002B/14